THE FALL OF CHAOS

THE LOST PANTHEON BOOK ONE

C.M. ARAGON

Contents

For my Grandmother, Marian, who was always the sun on my darkest days.

CHAPTER ONE

T HE RESOUNDING CHIME OF the ancient grandfather clock rang out and dragged Rue from her concentration. Five times, the bells tolled, signaling the late hour. The librarian's work had yet to be finished, but even staying an extra hour or two wouldn't be enough time to get everything done, and she desperately missed her bed.

Defeated and exhausted, Rue shelved the last book on her cart and climbed down the ladder, steadily hooking her boot heels into each step as she descended. Tomorrow would be another day, she reminded herself as she gathered her things and arranged them in her satchel bag.

Rue moved to the far wall of the library and ran her fingers along the wall, feeling for the tell-tale seam that hid one of the many secret passage doors. "Aha," she murmured, fingers finding purchase in the practically invisible indent. With an ear pressed to the wall, Rue waited for the familiar click of the locking mechanism.

The wall slid open, revealing a barely lit winding tunnel. The opening to the passage was tall enough for her to step inside without crouching as she entered. Rue slid the wall shut behind her and headed down the dim corridor toward the main area of the duke's manor. The passageway itself was rough in appearance. Crumbling foundation exposed through haphazard patches and littered with cobwebs and the corpses of dead insects, though these were mostly an afterthought as a means to an entrance to the hidden library she spent most of her days in.

In the four years she'd worked for duke Ashworth, these labyrinthine tunnels that twisted through the inner walls of his home had become so familiar to her. Now, she could navigate them with her eyes closed. The darkness of the tunnels no longer frightened her as it once did.

A sliver of amber light glimmering through a seam no thicker than a strand of hair marked the arrival of her destination. Rue pushed on the wall once again with another click of the lock and stepped out into the unused side room before exiting into the manor's opulent main hall.

"Ah, Miss Umberwick. Heading home for the night?" Delnan, an old, balding butler who never wore anything other than a sour expression asked. Rue gave an apologetic smile and nodded. She was absconding with a mountain of work left behind, and the butler's judging expression said he could tell.

"Very well. I shall inform the duke of your departure," he replied with a curt bow.

"No need. I will see Miss Umberwick off myself," another voice cut through with confidence and authority. The click of heels against polished marble floors signaled his approach.

Ryker Ashworth. The young duke of the Isle of Penrith and her employer.

Delnan made a displeased face only Rue could see and turned to offer the duke a deep bow but ultimately continued on his way back into the manor proper.

"Duke Ashworth, I didn't expect to see you," Rue admitted, brushing a stray orange curl from her face as she attempted to hide a flustered blush. The duke's mouth pulled into a grin as he reached for her hand, taking it in his own and pressing a soft kiss to her knuckles.

"How many times must I ask of you? Please, call me Ryker. No need for formalities between two friends."

"My apologies...Ryker." His given name felt odd on her tongue. She may have worked closely with him for years, but at the end of it all, he was the duke of Penrith, and she was just his assistant and now librarian.

The small tug at the corner of his mouth told Rue he was delighted by her acquiescence to his request. A swarm of invisible moths assaulted her insides as he took a step closer. The sweet, yet spicy scent of his cologne enveloped her. A scent she had come to associate with him.

"Be safe on your way home, Rue. You and I both know what lies in wait in the dark corners of this city."

Rue opened her mouth to respond, but before she could, Ryker had already turned to leave, disappearing as fast as he'd come. Feeling flustered by the duke's unexpected appearance, she cleared away the unsaid words stuck to her throat. She smoothed out her dress, grimacing at the wrinkles that had formed there, before sliding her arms into her thick woolen coat and stepping out into the night.

Outside of the manor, bitterly cold winds nipped at her nose, making it tingle. Rue made a mental note to wear a scarf tomorrow and pulled the collar of her coat up around her chin, though it didn't quite reach her nose. Taking the few short steps from the front entrance, Rue slid open her umbrella and held it over her head in a pathetic attempt to stay dry in the city's ever-present rain.

"I should have called for a carriage," she groused under her breath and began the short journey back to her flat.

The normally bustling streets of Penrith were quiet at this time of night. Thick smoke endlessly piped from chimneys and the diffused glow of lantern light illuminated the edges of dark curtains in street facing windows.

Tall housing buildings lined the craggy and broken cobblestone roads. They stood nestled next to one another as though their neighbor was the only thing holding them up. Dense moss and ivy climbed the edges, outlining washed-out greys and dismal blacks with pops of verdant color.

Penrith was a place where the sun didn't shine often, but it was home. Rue had gone away to University on the mainland but had returned to the isle as soon as she had graduated. She told herself it was because she missed Penrith, but in truth, her inevitable return had a lot more to do with her mother's passing and how her older brother was — or rather, wasn't — coping with the loss.

When her mother passed, Rue was devastated. It was unlike any other loss she had experienced. Her grief ran as deep as fathomless the depths that surrounded the small isle and had threatened to swallow her just the same as the rising tides.

Rue had grieved and eventually recovered enough to move on with her life, but Jasper spiraled and never stopped. He'd gone from an upstanding citizen to an unscrupulous drunk who collected gambling debts as though they were precious gems. Alcohol, women, and card games were just some of the ways he would distract himself from the pain. Time and time again, it was Rue who had bailed him out, giving him money or a place to stay, only for him to disappear when he no longer needed saving.

Rue continued her trek, lost in her thoughts, nearly back to her flat that sat at the edge of the city proper. Torrential rain pelted her umbrella with so much force, she thought it may tear through. Her grip tightened on the handle, trying to hold it steady as the wind whipped it back and forth. Raindrops coated her rounded spectacles, rendering them mostly useless. Rue's vision blurred but remained clear enough to see the outline of the path before her, smoothed over by years and years of foot traffic.

Rue gathered the hem of her skirts — though they were already beyond dripping — and continued on. Her normally sunny hair had darkened and plastered to the sides of her face where it peeked out from under the hood of her coat. Another sound of bells chiming from the clock tower at the center of the isle rang through the night air, alerting citizens that the hour was very late indeed. From the edge of her vision, Rue noticed a group of men huddled together, passing a cigarette between themselves on the street corner.

She gripped her umbrella tighter, preparing to use it as a weapon if needed, knowing full well that a decent man wouldn't be standing on the street corner in a downpour. These men looked like the types of ruffians her brother constantly found himself in trouble with. The kind of men that spent their nights in the seedy gambling dens of Fool's Hope — the thieves' town on the other side of the forest. The kinds of people Ryker had warned her about on her way out of the manor.

Please don't look at me, just keep doing whatever it is that you're doing, Rue silently begged, trying her best to keep her head down and not draw attention to herself.

Before she could turn back to the pathway, an arm wrapped around her waist and tugged her off the road. Without a second thought, Rue screwed her eyes shut and began to swing her umbrella wildly, hoping to hit her attacker at least once.

"GET. OFF. OF. ME," she demanded, punctuating each word with another swing of the makeshift weapon.

A mirthful laugh cut through her frantic swings.

She knew that laugh.

Rue abruptly stopped moving, but still held the umbrella poised for another strike and furrowed her brows, "Jasper!?" she whisper-screamed her brother's name, turning to face the gangly man whose face was clearly visible now that he had fully stepped out of the shadows.

Jasper was about a head taller than Rue, sporting shaggy ginger locks and hunter-green eyes that matched her own. He had always been on the thinner side with sharp angular features, in direct contrast to Rue's generous curves and soft, rounded face.

Jasper looked at his sister, rubbing at the scruff on his chin with an overly smug grin on his lips. He looked entirely too pleased with himself and his little prank.

"I got you good, didn't I?" He crossed his arms over his chest, lifting his chin and looking down his slightly crooked nose at her. Rue shook her head with an exasperated sigh and swatted his chest as hard as she could with the umbrella. Of course she was annoyed by his antics but also grateful it had been him and not some other strange man grabbing at her.

"You're lucky I didn't have that blade you gave me; you would have found yourself stabbed, dear brother," she retorted, lifting the umbrella above her head again, though it wasn't doing much other than keeping the rain out of her eyes at this point. Jasper slung his arm around her, pulling her against his side.

"You never change, Ruby." Rue's nose crinkled at the use of her full name. He knew she hated it, just like Rue knew he only did it to annoy her.

"Gods, Jasper, you're always such a child. What do you want now? I don't have any money to give you if that's what you're about to ask me for," Rue told him, her tone clipped, clearly irritated with his antics. Jasper never came just to say hello.

He let out a long, dramatic sigh and brought his hand to his heart, "You wound me! Can't a fellow just scare the daylights out of his sister from the goodness of his heart?"

Rue rolled her eyes and attempted to pull away from his embrace, "You've never done anything from the goodness of your heart, Jasper Antoine Umberwick. Now let me go. I need to get my keys so I can get out of this dreadful rain." She elbowed him, making Jasper move back with a grunt, rubbing his rib. Rue pulled out her keys, quickly unlocking the door to her flat and pushing through the threshold, desperately wanting to be somewhere dry. Jasper followed her in without waiting for an invitation.

She shrugged out of her sopping wet coat and hung it over a chair beside the fireplace. "Well, make yourself useful and at least get the fire going if you're going to stay." Rue waved her hand dismissively toward the stone hearth, immediately heading up the short set of steps to her bedroom, not bothering to play hostess of any kind. "And take off those boots, too, before you get my floors dirty!" Rue called over her shoulder. She heard Jasper grumble something under his breath, but she didn't care what he had to say.

As soon as the door closed, the relief of finally being home after an exhausting day washed over her. Rue closed her eyes and breathed in the warm, soothing scent of lavender and bergamot from the oil diffuser that hung in the corner of her bedroom. With a heavy exhale, Rue opened her eyes, feeling calmer now. She grabbed her night clothes and quickly changed out of the sodden skirt and blouse, warmth immediately coming back to her frigid skin.

She tried not to think too hard about the multitude of reasons Jasper might have come to her. Whatever it was, it couldn't be good. Rue heaved another exhausted sigh and pulled the satin nightgown over her head.

Long apricot curls still dripped down her neck and back, but she was too tired to do much more than give it a cursory once over with the towel slung over her vanity chair. Rue sat before the mirror, taking slow, deep breaths to calm herself before going back into the main room to deal with her brother.

"Whatever this is, it better be the end of the world," she muttered to her reflection before pulling her house coat over her shoulders and leaving the room.

Jasper had made himself at home as usual, already rummaging around in her cupboards for whatever crumbs he could find. The sound of

Rue's slippered feet padding over the wooden floors caught his attention, making him turn to face her.

"Caught red-handed once again." Rue shook her head in mock disappointment but didn't reprimand him further as she moved past him to one of the many cabinets lining the walls of her small kitchen. If she was going to sit and hear what he had to say, she needed a cup of tea first. Pushing several mismatched jars out of the way, Rue located the particular blend she was looking for. Her brows knit in disappointment when she saw the bottom of the tin through what was left of the tea leaves.

"You're going to get me more tea for me after this, I hope you know," Rue told her brother, shaking the mostly empty jar at him.

"Anything for you, dear sister," Jasper conceded through a mouthful of bread and butter, crumbs spilling from his lips onto his dirty and soaked shirt.

With her cup of tea now in hand, Rue pulled out one of the creaky wooden chairs at her small kitchen table and nodded for Jasper to join her.

"Before you start talking, if you are here to ask me for money or any other kind of bailout, you can take the rest of that loaf of bread and leave. I'm not giving you anyth—"

"Hey, hey, hey!" Jasper cut her off, hands up in a pleading gesture, "Calm down. That's not at all what I'm here for. I'll have you know. I am square on all my accounts, thank you very much!" His voice was indignant, offended that his little sister would ever think him so careless. Rue leveled him with a deadpan look. Jasper cleared his throat before continuing.

"I came to you because I need your help," he paused, swallowing nervously, "and if any of what I am about to tell you is true, everyone will need your help." His eyes met hers, deadly serious in a way that was so unlike him. Rue held his gaze with a healthy suspicion, saying nothing but nodding for him to go on.

"A few nights ago, when I was in Fool's Hope — and don't give me that look — I heard a man talking about something, a kind of artifact," Jasper looked away from her as though he was trying to recall all the details from memory. Rue continued to give him 'that look' when he mentioned where exactly he'd collected this information. However, in a bit of good faith, she let him finish before outright refusing his request.

"They said it was a book or a tome of sorts," Jasper continued, "I heard them say there were passages in it that, if put in the wrong hands, could bring about the Cataclysm." Jasper picked nervously at his nails as he spoke. It was obvious he was trying so hard to say all the right things. "I know you remember the stories we were told when we were just kids, but I dunno, something about what they were saying scared me. It felt like a warning."

Rue's brows knit together in equal parts confusion and surprise. It was so unlike her brother to fear anything — except maybe a debt collector. She remembered the stories her father told them before bedtime. About the pantheon of old gods that used to rule over the land they now knew as Penrith. Long lost to time and changing ideals, the pantheon was little more than a fairytale to her.

"Those were just stories, Jas. Something Papa told us before we went to sleep at night." Rue sighed, wrapping her still cold and stiff digits around her warm teacup, "Why did you feel like it was a warning?" she asked, still regarding him with suspicion in her eyes.

Jasper chewed his lip as he spoke, "They mentioned that the book might be hidden in the duke's manor, and I know you work for him."

Rue's grip tightened on the cup, the scalding porcelain burning her palms. The idea of thieves having their eye on the duke's manor for such an artifact had her pulse quickening. She worked for the duke, yes, but what she did for him was much more than her job title let on. Beneath the manor, through the maze of hidden passages in the walls, was a vast library. A trove full of secrets, cursed items, and other ill-gotten goods. Of course she hadn't begun working in that library immediately. After a few years of service to the duke as his personal assistant and a certain level of trust being gained, Duke Ashworth had told her his secret.

The duke bought, sold and traded in the time since she'd been put in charge of the library. The amount of money exchanged was more than she liked to think about, as many of the objects stored there were worth a fortune. Objects thieves would love to get their hands on to make a fortune of their own.

"Oh? And what about the duke's manor did you hear from these mysterious folks?" Rue's voice wavered as she asked, sitting straighter in her chair. She'd never been a great liar, especially when she was nervous; she knew she would admit it if Jasper asked her to confirm it.

"Only that they heard it was there. That he has some precious things hiding behind those walls," he told her.

Rue swallowed hard, "Interesting choice of words." Clearing her throat, she began again, "And what do you want me to do about this? Why are you coming here to tell me this? And give it to me plainly because I am in no mood to solve riddles right now."

Jasper's cheeks pinked, clearly feeling the authority she'd put behind her words. "I need you to find it."

"Find it? Why? So you can steal it and take it to sell to the highest bidder?"

"No, no, no, that is *not* what I am asking you to do, Rue. If you would let me finish," He paused, giving her a pointed look before continuing, "I need you to find it...and destroy it." There were no traces of mirth in Jasper's eyes as he spoke.

"Destroy it? And that's supposed to be better than stealing it somehow?"

Jasper sighed, his shoulders slumping, "I know I have asked you to do many...unbecoming things in the past for me, Rue." His tone was hushed and sincere as he spoke, his eyes aimed somewhere far away from her face, as though he couldn't stand the idea of seeing disappointment in her eyes,

"This may sound ridiculous to you, but I am well and truly terrified at the possibility of this book ever meeting the wrong hands if what I heard them say about it is true." The atmosphere between them quickly turned dark. "The feeling I got when I heard them talking about this..." he paused for a long moment, searching for the words, "It was nothing I ever felt before. Something told me I needed to listen to this feeling, so here I am. Listening and hoping to do something before it's too late."

For a long moment, Rue stared at her brother, eyes raking over his features and searching for any signs of deception. When she found nothing, she removed her glasses and pinched the bridge of her nose, willing away the dull ache that was beginning to form behind her eyes. She uttered a silent prayer to whichever deity would listen, begging for some small morsel of wisdom to tell her how to deal with the situation her brother had just so lovingly laid in her lap.

"If what you are saying is true, and you really are as fearful as you say..." Rue hesitated, her eyes locking with Jasper's, trying as best she could to convey just how deadly serious she was. "I will help. But you have to promise me. Swear on whatever it is you find holy, and tell me that this isn't another scheme."

Jasper made a motion over his heart like an 'x' and solemnly nodded.

"Jasper, if you take me for a fool with this, I swear I will never forgive you." Mimicking her brother's motion, Rue crossed over her chest in the shape of an 'x'.

Chapter Two

J ASPER HAD FALLEN FAST asleep. Curled up on her couch, all awkward and gangly limbs, Rue threw an old quilt over his body. The pair had continued to talk about the situation until the rush of emotions and tension finally got the best of him, knocking him out cold within the hour.

Rue knelt beside Jasper's sleeping form, gently brushing a stray lock of hair off his forehead as he snored softly. A small smile curled around the edges of her mouth as she watched him. Like this, he seemed so innocent, incapable of all the unsavory things he'd done. She knew it hadn't been easy on him to lose both his parents, suddenly thrust into becoming man of the house. Without their mother's guidance, Jasper fell from grace.

At first, it had infuriated Rue, seeing him act the way he did. With so little regard for her or what she was feeling. It was his selfishness, she thought. But the more she lingered on that reasoning, the more she realized it was deeper than that.

Although she would never truly admit it, Rue envied Jasper at times. Envied his ability to throw all caution to the wind while she, his younger sister, was forced to be responsible and make something of herself, despite the sadness that tore her apart.

Rue shook her head, trying to rid herself of those unhelpful thoughts. Ruffling Jasper's hair lightly, she stood and made her way back up to her bedroom.

"Goodnight, dummy."

Rue closed the door behind her and breathed out a heavy sigh of relief. On top of her already long work day, she'd been up for far longer than she'd intended and was more than ready to sink into her soft sheets and kiss the world goodbye for a blissful few hours. She shrugged off her robe and draped it over one of the posters of her bed frame before turning off the oil lamp next to her bedside and climbing in.

"Oh, how I have missed you," Rue mumbled, turning her face into the pillow and hugging it to her chest. Not long after she had closed her eyes, she was dragged from the waking world and slipped under the deep tides of slumber.

Rue was falling.

Plummeting into the abyss below from an unknown height. Wind whipped her hair around her face and forced her to close her eyes.

Where was she?

Where had she come from?

The fall was endless, creating a constant anxiety in her chest that held her tight in its grip.

Over the sound of rushing wind, a crack echoed through the air. Loud enough to be thunder but without the flash of lightning beforehand. Her eyes shot open once more, searching in the darkness for the source of the ominous noise.

Even in the darkness, she could have sworn she saw the glint of raven wings. But not those of a normal bird, no. These were much larger. Squinting harder in an attempt to make out exactly what she was looking at, Rue saw the blurred form of a man. He seemed to be wearing leather armor with those enormous wings splaying out from behind his back.

The figure moved closer to her with hands reaching out. Without thinking about it too hard, Rue desperately grasped at his hands, praying he would stop this fall. With another sonorous crack of his beating wings, they slowed to a steady float. Rue still couldn't see his face through the shadows but remained enamored with the oil slick on black wings that shimmered behind him.

"I've got you, love," he said, voice deep and soothing. The man wrapped his arms around her, pulling Rue to his chest and cradling her gently, as though she were something precious. Something to be treasured. Rue curled into him, trusting the stranger implicitly without knowing why. His arms felt so familiar around her. Like a memory that only remained in scattered pieces. She felt safe and warm with him. The cold, biting wind no longer permeated her skin.

"Who are you?" she whispered, trying to make sense of his blurred features.

The man answered but ignored her question entirely.

"You have to wake up now."

Rue sat bolt upright in her bed with a start.

It was just a dream.

She scrubbed a hand down her face, somehow feeling more exhausted now than she had before.

A gentle, but insistent tapping on her window interrupted her thoughts. She swung her legs over the side of her bed, sliding onto the cold floor with a thud. It was too early and she was much too tired to try and be graceful. Pulling on her robe once more, Rue pulled back the curtains that hung over her window trying to see what exactly was making the noise.

It was a little difficult to discern without her glasses but it looked like...a raven. Her spine stiffened as she recalled her dream. A strange yet familiar man with raven's wings, holding her as she fell.

"Curious." Was the only thing she could really say. The raven tilted its head, looking back at her with question in its abyssal black eyes before tapping on the glass again. Rue placed her hand on the glass pane, where its beak had touched.

"Are you trying to tell me something?" she asked, more to herself than anything, knowing the glass was too thick for the raven on the other side to hear. It tapped the pane twice more before lifting its wings and soaring away into the dreary grey skies.

Downstairs, Jasper still lay curled in the awkward position he'd fallen asleep in, snoring lightly. Rue decided to allow him to sleep for a while longer while she made her morning tea and had a few moments of quiet to really ruminate on what exactly her dream meant.

The antique dented brass kettle had seen better days, but Rue refused to replace it. It was the same kettle her mother had used to make their daily cups of tea. Jasper would accuse her of being overly sentimental, but Rue told herself she didn't care what he thought of the trinkets she kept.

"Perfect. I'm going to need all the help I can get today," she muttered, looking over the scrawled handwritten label. A special blend of chamomile and a particular mushroom that was supposed to improve focus. She spooned a generous amount into her sieve and placed it into the boiling kettle. The sound of pattering footsteps behind her told her Jasper had risen from his small coma.

"Morning. I've got tea going if you plan on staying for the morning," she informed him, never one to assume any of his plans. Although she hoped that this time, he would stay for a while.

Jasper rubbed his eyes and nodded, his only answer a boisterous yawn. He pulled a chair from the small kitchen table and spun it around, sitting with his chest pressed against the back and both legs over the sides like a saddle.

"I've got to go to the manor in a bit, but you're welcome to stay if you want to." Rue offered, "But it would be helpful if you could do me a favor."

"Whassat?" Jasper yawned again and rubbed the last bits of sleep from his eyes.

"If I'm going to look for this book, I need a little more information. I need you to find someone with knowledge of magical items," she paused when the kettle whistled, "Maybe not about *this* book specifically, but maybe someone who has more knowledge about the lost pantheon beyond the stories that Papa told us."

Rue poured herself a mug, perfumed steam wrapping around her like a hug. She closed her eyes and inhaled deeply, yes, this was exactly what she needed. She poured another for Jasper, setting it in front of him before taking her own seat across the table.

"Couldn't you just find that in some books in the duke's library? He's bound to have every single thing ever written with the kind of money he's got." Jasper scoffed, taking a sip of the tea and visibly scorching his tongue before setting the cup back down.

"Yes, I could do that, but what's written in books isn't the same as stories passed down by spoken word. The only things that make it onto the pages of books are what we are *allowed* to know. Not what we need to know," she countered pointedly and stirred an overflowing spoonful of honey into her tea.

"So you're asking me to go on some kind of wild goose chase to find nothing but a bit of crumbs?"

"If that's how you want to look at it, then I suppose so."

Rue dressed and readied herself for the day. It shouldn't have felt different than any other day she'd gone into the manor, but after last night, things had definitely taken a turn. Pulling her coat up over her shoulders and tucking the thick woolen scarf around her neck, Rue pressed a kiss to the crown of Jasper's head, "Behave and please don't leave a mess when you go. You know where the spare key is, so lock the door on your way out."

Jasper just made a mocking face as she spoke but there was no malice behind it. Rue only shook her head and stepped out into the overcast light of the early morning.

It always seemed to be raining in Penrith. The dirty, crumbling cobblestone streets were slick with spilled oil on the water as Rue trudged her way through the deep puddles, boots already soaked through to her stockings underneath. The dreary sky above was full of dark clouds, making the fading black paint of the buildings on the main road swallow what little light managed to pierce through.

Wrought iron street lamps gave off a dim glow despite the daytime hour. In the distance, rising far above the rest of the city stood the old clock tower. Black, spade shaped hands ticked around an ivory face as its bells rang out loud enough to be heard through the entire isle. Rue swore under her breath as she picked up her pace. If she didn't hurry, she was going to be late.

Despite the dreariness of the day, life carried on as usual. Children ran through alleyways with their sticks and pinwheel toys, chasing one another with chastising mothers barking at their heels, without a care of how muddy their shoes got or how soaked their clothes became.

Young, able-bodied men carried crates of goods and other supplies from the shipyard's docks, a mix of sweat and rain plastering their thin white linen shirts to their well-muscled chests. Carriages drawn by horses crossed through the streets, looking for their next fare. Under an old awning, a group of old men sat huddled around an upended barrel-turned-table, smoking their pipes and slamming cards down, sending coins, jewels, and hand-rolled cigarettes flying.

The duke's manor sat on the north edge of the city, surrounded by grey brick and mortar walls and closed off by a black iron gate that read *Ashworth* in a curling script across the top. The Ashworth family had presided over Penrith for generations; the manor had been built when the first duke came to the isle and stood fast through the test of time and the more harsh elements that came with living on an isle.

Rue approached the gate and pushed it open slowly, trying to avoid the scream of the old, rusted hinges but cringed inwardly when the sound still came. She would have to ask the maintenance staff to fix them again.

When Rue first came to the manor, she had been completely enamored by the statuary in the courtyard. Although it lacked the lush greenery of a traditional garden, there was still a macabre beauty about it. Filled with stone and marble statues of various types, the courtyard seemed more like a mausoleum than a garden. Each of the statues seemed so life-like, with an array of expressions carved on their faces. However, there were some that Rue had felt more drawn to than others—the ones she'd dubbed, 'The weeping women'.

They stood still in their stone, faces turned toward the heavens with hands stretched out before them, clasped together as though begging for something. The ever constant rain had caused streaks of mold to run down their cheeks, like trails of dark tears. Although it was unsettling, something about these statues had intrigued Rue. Sometimes, when she was able, she would sit there with them. Hoping to keep their sorrows at bay just for a few moments.

Rue let herself into the main doors of the manor, her breath coming out in harsh puffs from her effort to be on time. Delnan stood at his post as he did every day when Rue arrived.

"Miss Umberwick, you've finally made it," he said, looking down his nose at her. Rue glanced at the large clock that stood at the base of the double staircase. She was a whole five minutes late. Resisting the urge to roll her eyes at the man, Rue instead gave a wry smile and an insincere apologetic bow.

"I'll be heading down now."

The duke's staff knew about the library hidden below the manor. Each one sworn to secrecy upon pain of death if they even uttered a word about it outside of the manor's walls. A drop of blood and a simple but incredibly expensive binding spell made sure of that. Learned magic never came cheap.

Rue made her way into the library, following another of the dark paths hidden within the walls before coming out on the other side. The library was enormous, taking up the entire basement level of the already vast manor that rested above. But Rue enjoyed the quiet solitude of working alone among the books and artifacts.

Her desk sat in the middle of the room, carved from a giant slab of mahogany that was far too large and much too opulent for her needs, but the duke had insisted. Behind her was a small hearth, fire already lit and roaring. Warming her frozen hands by the flames, she sent a small thanks to whoever had come down and started it before her arrival.

"Alright. I suppose I'd better start looking if I'm going to make any kind of progress today," Rue muttered to herself. The depth of her monumental task hit her all at once as she took in the endless sea of books on the shelves that lined the walls. From floor to ceiling, bookcases adorned each and every wall in the library, with only a handful of empty spaces between them. In those sparse few alcoves between the shelves hung collections of paintings ranging from priceless landscapes and portraits to much more grotesque and sinister images. In others were more shelves and display cases, housing a multitude of artifacts that were anything from inane trinkets to dangerous weapons.

The collection of items in the library spanned over centuries, most likely belonging to each generation of Ashworth men rather than to the duke alone. How they had managed to keep all of it a secret for centuries was impressive.

Rue unbuttoned and rolled up the sleeves of her cream blouse, tying her curls back with a ribbon she'd kept in her pocket. It was time to get to work. She slid the ladder she had been using the previous night over, using the polished surface of the wood to glide it along the bookcase in place of rails.

Rue grasped the edge of the ladder firmly, but before she could get her boot into the first rung, she heard one of the passageway entrances slide open with a screech. None of the other staff came down here while she worked, so it could only be one person.

"Duke Ashworth," she called out, turning toward the sound. The duke stepped out of the tunnel, sliding the wall closed behind him with a quiet click.

"Again with the formalities? I insist you call me Ryker," he reminded her. He adjusted his cuff links as he strode toward her, a tiny grin curling at the corner of his mouth. Rue opened her mouth to argue but felt the words stick in her throat as he came into view. He looked *particularly* handsome today. A heated flush doused cheeks and she silently cursed herself for tying her hair back, unable to hide behind it.

The current duke was the youngest in history to take the title. In his mid-thirties, Ryker had a much more modern sense of fashion than most of the older wealthy men who lived on the isle. Today, he'd worn nothing more than a perfectly starched white shirt with a beautifully embroidered jewel-toned waistcoat over it that popped against dark trousers. His dark hair was pushed back and perfectly coiffed where it was longer on top, the sides neatly trimmed short behind his ears and around his neck. Not a single strand out of place.

Ryker's face was flawless, save for a small silver scar over his lip — which made him all the more handsome in her opinion — but what Rue had always been so drawn to were his eyes. They were striking. An almost unnatural icy blue that seemed to glow like moonstone in the muted light of the library.

Rue cleared her throat, suddenly flustered by his surprise visit, "Yes, my apologies, Ryker."

"Much better." His grin fell, "Unfortunately, I didn't come to chat. There is to be a sale tonight and I need you to oversee it. I have another meeting I am unable to step away from at the time the buyer has asked to meet."

Rue nodded. This was not the first time she'd facilitated Ryker with a sale or trade of one of his many artifacts. "What's the item for sale?" She asked.

Ryker reached into the pocket of his waistcoat and produced an envelope, handing it over to her from between his middle and index fingers, "the information you need is here. The paperwork has already been drawn up, and all he will need to do is sign and take the item. I trust you will be able to handle this for me, won't you?" His voice dripped like honey with the request and threatened to make her knees give in.

"Of course." Rue took the envelope and held it to her chest.

"Excellent. You never let me down," he praised, reaching out and cupping her cheek against the palm of his hand. A jolt of nervous energy shot down her spine. It wasn't the first time he'd touched her like this, but it was still a gesture she would never be accustomed to. Rue tried not to read into it, as she was well aware it was completely inappropriate for a man of his station to have any kind of serious relationship with a woman he employed. That fact, of course, didn't stop her from daydreaming about it anyway.

Ryker slid his hand back, slower than necessary, dragging his digits against her freckled cheek. With a beleaguered groan, he reached back into his pocket and produced a watch he'd kept on a chain and checked the time.

"As much as I would love to stay, there is no rest for the wicked. I must be going."

"I'll have this ready when you come back."

"Very well. I do hope to see you again before you leave for the night."

Ryker dipped his head, bidding her farewell, and headed back out the way he'd come in. Rue watched him go, waiting until she heard the final click of the locking mechanism before she tore open the wax seal on the envelope.

A soft but horrified gasp left her lips once she realized what the item on the sale docket was.

Among the duke's many belongings, there was a small trove of items that were considered to be too dangerous for general display. These items were kept in a another room toward the back of the library, locked tight behind a thick slab of iron. He'd called it the heretic's closet, but Rue had always just referred to it as the black room. And the things that were stored beyond that door were, in Rue's opinion, evil.

CHAPTER THREE

THE BLACK ROOM WAS held shut with a number of different locks, each made from a different material and woven with different even more expensive spells. Rue wasn't sure if she believed that magic was what made the lock work more effectively, but she would take any reassurance that whatever was behind this door was kept secured and contained.

Each lock had its own key with a different colored jewel embedded in the top that corresponded to the matching lock. The keys themselves were hidden away deep in the library, tucked in a false book that sat unassuming next to countless others. Rue pulled the book from the shelf, turning it over in her hands and input the number code onto the lock. Easily popping it open, she took the key ring and set the book aside.

Rue took a deep, steadying breath and slowly moved toward the heavy iron door. Entering the room had always made her feel sick, but at the same time, she'd always been oddly drawn to it. She chalked the feeling up to an overactive imagination being met with her endless curiosity.

Methodically unlocking each bolt, Rue tried not to focus on the erratic, nervous beat of her heart behind her ribs. With the last lock open, she pushed the heavy door with her shoulder, its old hinges groaning with the motion.

Inside, the walls were bathed in an eerie green glow. Thick chunks of luminous crystals in lanterns being the only light source. Too many precious and flammable things to trust firelight, Ryker had told her. She took a hesitant step inside, the sound of her shoes immediately muffled by a dense rug covering the wooden flooring. The heavy silence of the room was ominous. Not even the sound of the softly crackling fire could be heard from within.

The walls were lined with various glass cases of different shapes and sizes. Some were covered with shrouds that were supposedly woven with protection sigils and runes, some with objects plainly visible through their glass panes. Rue pulled the envelope Ryker had given her out again, making sure that the object in question really was what she'd read the first time.

"Who would even want something like this?" she asked no one and tucked the paper back into her skirt pocket. Before her, locked away in its glass prison, was a skull. Though it looked vaguely humanoid, it was no ordinary skull, of course. This one boasted six eye sockets instead of the normal two. Its jaw pulled wide with unnaturally elongated bones that looked as though they'd been stretched in an endless tortured scream for all eternity. Protruding from the crown were gnarled, twisted, and curled horns of various lengths and thicknesses. One of the horns looked as though it had grown too far inward and eventually punctured through one of the many eyes of whomever—or whatever—this skull had originally belonged to.

Rue shivered and grabbed a gray cloth from one of the shelves beside her, throwing it over the case, unable to keep looking at the thing any longer. Once it was covered and out of view, Rue gently pried the case from its place on the shelf. It was thankfully much lighter than she'd thought. She carried it over the threshold and set it on an empty book cart.

Securing each lock once more, Rue tossed the keys into the false book and slid it back into the gap on the shelf. She let out a long breath, allowing the relief of being out of that room to flood over her. The sound of the fireplace and the low rumbling of pipes through the walls created a soothing white noise that was almost too loud in comparison.

Rue checked the tall grandfather clock. The client wasn't set to meet her for another few hours, so she pushed the cart into a darkened corner and left it out of sight for the time being.

"Alright, where were we?" Rue clapped her hands together and set out to find anything she could that might help her locate the tome Jasper had spoken of.

The chime of the clock echoed through the library once more, alerting Rue that it was nearly time to meet with Ryker's client. She slid the book she'd been thumbing through back into the shelf carefully and unrolled her sleeves, buttoning them at the cuff once more. She pulled the ribbon from her hair and set it in a drawer in her desk before fluffing out her curls. Her shirt sleeves had gotten wrinkled from being bunched at her elbow for most of the day, but she just shrugged to herself and hoped the client didn't take notice.

Ryker's note had informed her that the client would be waiting for her in a room on the west end of the manor, in one of the side rooms reserved for these kinds of quiet meetings. Rue opted to take the book cart with her to transport the case, lest she trip and smash the thing to pieces before the papers could be signed.

Rue opened one of the passageways nearest to the west side and carefully slid the cart into the tunnel before closing the wall behind her. The tunnel led out into a wide closet inside the room, meant to hide the passageway from whoever might be sitting on the other side of the door. Rue brushed her skirts down and adjusted her collar, trying to make herself look as presentable as possible before entering the room on the other side of the false door.

Her fingers brushed the necklace that normally hung against her sternum. A gold charm in the shape of the sun hung from the matching gold chain, a large citrine stone lodged in the center of it. It had been an heirloom from her mother and one of the last things Rue had of her. She held it in her hand for a moment, letting its calming aura wash over her.

After taking one more centering deep breath, Rue pushed the door open and cautiously pulled the cart in behind her. The room was dim, only lit by a few small oil lamps and a fire blazing in the small hearth. Ryker's client was seated on a settee before the fire with his back to her. The acrid smell of the tobacco in his pipe made her nose twitch, and she had to resist the urge to cough.

"Mister Garroway?" Rue called softly, trying to get his attention without startling him. The man lurched forward off the small settee, his massive frame causing the wood to groan as he stood. Mister Garroway dabbed his forehead with a filthy handkerchief before shoving it back into his breast pocket. It took everything in Rue not to make a face.

"Yes, yes, that's me, girl," he replied, wheezing as he spoke. It took even more not to recoil at the way he'd addressed her simply as 'girl.'

"Duke Ashworth has sent me to conduct the final part of the sale you'd previously discussed on his behalf. Unfortunately, he had a scheduling conflict he was unable to step away from," Rue explained, drawing the papers from the cart and unfolding them as she spoke.

"A pity, but at least the man's sent me a lovely little morsel in his stead," Garroway licked his lips, bloodshot eyes raking over Rue's plump but curvaceous figure. She ignored his lewd actions and cleared her throat, trying as she may to maintain the air of professionalism.

"All I need is for you to sign here and here," Rue pointed to the marked spots on the pages, "and then you are free to leave with your item."

Garroway didn't say anything for a long moment as his eyes lingered on Rue. He took a step closer, eyes slithering up and down her, but never once even bothering to spare a glance at the purchase contract.

"And do you think for the right sum he'd throw his pretty little assistant in? To sweeten this deal, eh?"

He reached out and stroked a calloused finger against her cheek. Rue wanted to vomit. She could smell the bitterness of pipe tobacco on his yellowing fingertips. She swallowed down the bile rising in her throat and took a step back.

"Mister Garroway, that is highly inappropriate, and I suggest you not touch me again. Sign the papers, give me the payment, and leave." Rue kept her face schooled into cold indifference and her chin held high, but Garroway didn't seem too keen to heed her warnings. He moved even closer, uncomfortably so, and reached out his hand again.

Rue slapped it out of the way before he could make contact and took another step back. The arm of the sofa hit the back of her legs, and immediately, panic rose in her chest. He had her cornered. Trapped between the furniture and his obese body.

"Mighty rude of you to speak to me in such a way, girl. I may not be a duke like your Mister Ashworth, but my name holds enough weight in this city."

Rue leaned back as much as she could, but Mr. Garroway had caged her in on either side with his forearms, his large stomach pressing against her abdomen.

"He doesn't need to know a thing, sweetheart." He leaned forward, coming entirely too close to her face. His breath smelled of stale coffee and rot. The horrific stench wafted from his parted lips into her nostrils and made her stomach lurch.

Rue turned her head away from him, unable to tolerate the stink of his breath any longer. Searching the room with panic building in her gut, she spotted the vent on the ceiling above, which she knew sat directly under Ryker's study on the upper floor of the house. He would hear her if she screamed, right? She took in a deep breath, and with every bit of strength she could muster, Rue bellowed out, crying for the duke to save her.

Garroway snarled and raised his hand, cocking it back as though he would strike her. Rue pulled her arm up, protecting her face, and squeezed her eyes shut, anticipating the blow.

It never came.

Not even a breath later, the door burst open, nearly flying off the hinges with the force behind it.

It was Ryker.

He'd heard her call. Shocked from the speed he'd managed to reach her, Rue's eyes opened wide as she silently pleaded with desperation to her rescuer.

Ryker grabbed Garroway's arm, yanking it hard enough that Rue heard an audible pop from the man's limb as he wrenched the offender away from her.

"You slimy bastard. You think you can prey on my staff?" Ryker was livid. A vein in the duke's temple pulsed as he slammed Garroway into the wall. The force pushed the older man into another coughing fit, spittle flying from his lips. Ryker didn't seem to care. From what Rue could tell, he was a bit more preoccupied with trying not to repeatedly shove this man's head into the wall behind him.

Garroway opened his mouth to speak, lips wordlessly opening and closing like a fish out of water. Ryker released his collar and pressed a long finger into the man's sternum, "I'd better never see your face on this isle again." He was still breathing heavily through his nose, trying as best as he could to contain the inferno of rage visibly burning inside of him. "And if I do, I will make damn sure you never see the light of day again. Do you understand me? You know plenty well what I am capable of, Simon, and you do not want to cross me."

Garroway's face paled to a ghostly white in fear. Ryker was barely two inches from his nose.

"Go home, pack your things, and take the next barge out of here. If you refuse…" Ryker didn't need to finish his sentence. It seemed his promises were enough to instill the fear of the Gods in Garroway. The older man said nothing, just grabbed his hat and made a hurried exit from the room.

Ryker turned to Rue, his face crestfallen. "I am so sorry, Rue. I didn't think he would try anything like this in my own home, or I would never have asked you to meet him alone."

Rue pushed sweat damp hair back off her face and shakily slid her rounded glasses back up the bridge of her nose.

"It's alright," she said once, trying to convince herself that it was true more than anything, "I'm alright."

Ryker moved toward her in slow, cautious steps. Rue remained standing where she was, frozen with her mind reeling and her hands shaking as she tried to process what had just happened. Her gaze was far off, looking past Ryker. She barely noticed when he wrapped his arms around her.

"I'm sorry, Rue. Please forgive me." He muttered apologies over and over, hands gently rubbing soothing circles into her back. His lips touched her hair as he spoke and immediately Rue melted into his embrace. His touch was soft and tender, sending goosebumps creeping all along her skin.

"He didn't do anything; he just—"

"He didn't need to. He touched you, and that was enough. I meant what I said. He will never show his face in this city again if he's got any sense in that thick skull of his." Pure venom was palpable in Ryker's voice. Rue said nothing but nodded against his chest, believing full well he would make good on those threats.

"Thank you for coming," Rue whispered, her fingers curling into the fabric of his shirt in a feeble attempt to keep them still.

"This will never happen again," he assured her. Ryker took a step back and slid her hand into his, pressing a soft kiss to her knuckles. Another swarm of wings flapped wildly in Rue's stomach, and her cheeks blazed with the duke's attention.

"Let me call you a carriage home tonight. I would be a monster if I allowed you to walk home alone after this mess." His tone left no room to brook disagreement, so instead of following her first instinct to politely decline, Rue simply nodded and squeezed his hand in agreement.

Ryker led her to his study, offering her a seat on one of the deep emerald green sofas. Rue sat, quietly muttering a thank you as she folded her hands in her lap, still clasping them together firmly.

Ryker tugged on a cord that hung above his desk, the chime of a bell followed. Almost instantaneously, a flustered and out of breath maid — who Rue knew to be called Beth — entered the room.

"Yes, your grace?"

"Call a carriage for Miss Umberwick's use, if you would."

"Right away." Beth nodded and swiftly exited the room.

Ryker took his own seat on a tall wingback chair beside the sofa where she sat. He reached for one of the crystal glasses that rested on the silver table next to him, pouring himself a generous amount of an unknown amber liquor from the matching decanter beside it.

"Would you like a drink, Rue?" he questioned, tentatively reaching for a second glass.

She shook her head, "No, thank you. I'm not much of a drinker."

"Very well."

Replacing the jeweled stopper into the decanter, Ryker knocked back the entire glass of liquor in a single swallow. He let out a soft hiss and clenched his teeth. At this, Rue was suddenly grateful for declining.

An easy silence fell between them. Sounds of rain pelting against the windowpanes and the occasional crackle and pop from the blazing logs in the hearth were the only sounds around them. Rue's eyes fell to her hands as she began nervously picking at her nails.

"Rue?" Ryker called her name, barely above a whisper but loud enough to pull her back to the moment.

"Yes?"

"I would love to have you for dinner." Ryker stood from his chair, setting his glass back down on the silver table, and slid onto the sofa next to her.

Rue blushed, trying not to hear the implications nestled into his choice of words. He moved his arm to rest along the back of the sofa behind her, long fingers nearly touching her. With the duke so near, the scent of his cologne invaded her senses. She barely resisted the urge to lean in and inhale the spiced fragrance deeply.

"I..." she began but was abruptly stopped by Ryker leaning into her. His other hand moved to cup her cheek, his fingers caressing her jaw.

"You are absolutely radiant, did you know that?" Rue could feel his breath on her lips. He smelled like cinnamon from fiery alcohol he'd just imbibed. The scent itself seemed to make her head feel fuzzy. Maybe she did want to have a taste of it after all. Her lips parted, and her eyes fell to his, body leaning into his magnetic pull.

"Ryker, I don't think—" Her half-hearted objections were silenced by his lips against hers.

Rue closed her eyes, submitting easily and allowing him to take the lead in this dance between them. His lips lingered over hers, whisper light at first as though waiting for her response — her permission — before continuing. A shiver ran down her spine. This was everything she'd wanted for longer than she'd like to admit. Rue tugged on his shirt just enough to encourage him to continue.

Ryker's lips parted just enough for her to taste the last bits of alcohol on his tongue. Tentatively, the tip of Rue's tongue brushed against his, pulling a breathy sigh from her chest. For a moment, she couldn't believe she was actually doing this. Every rational part of her urged her to stop, but a baser, needier part of her pushed in opposition.

Ryker's hands slid into her hair, fingernails brushing against the nape of her neck, sending another zing down her spine. Rue felt him smile into the kiss, his lips gently curving upward against hers. She leaned closer, pressing her chest against his. His fingers tugged at her hair softly, but just enough to pull another small sound of pleasure from her.

Before she could urge him to take more, a sharp and repeated tapping sound cut through the haze of lust, making her jump and frantically search for the source.

"W-what's that?" Rue asked, fists still balled into his shirt.

Ryker groaned with clear annoyance and reluctantly pulled away, moving to one of the massive floor-to-ceiling windows. "Filthy ravens, again," Ryker growled under his breath, slamming his hand against the window in an attempt to get the bird to leave. "Such pests." His face pulled into a look of utter disdain.

Her brows knit in confusion. Could it be the same raven she'd seen that morning? No, that would be impossible. Her thoughts were cut short by Beth returning to inform them that the carriage had arrived.

Ryker sighed, sounding almost disappointed, but nodded and dismissed the maid.

"You should get home. Get some rest and take the day off tomorrow," he told her, tucking a stray ginger curl behind her ear.

"I will. Thank you," Rue nodded, pulling her lower lip between her teeth nervously, unable to meet his gaze. Rue turned to leave, but before she could take a step, Ryker had pulled her back against him and pressed one last kiss to her lips. Her eyes fluttered shut for a moment as the hazy feeling in her head returned. She willed herself to commit the feel of his mouth on hers to memory.

Once Rue was in the carriage and Ryker's form was no longer in view, she sunk her head into her hands and let out a muffled scream. She hoped the pounding rain and the clopping of the horse's hooves on the pavement would drown out the sound.

She'd absolutely wanted it, but now that her judgment was less clouded by Ryker's sweet words, she knew it was incredibly inappropriate to have such a relationship with the man who employed her — and not to mention the timing of everything.

He'd asked her to dinner.

Rue slid her glasses off and pinched the bridge of her nose.

"Of course this would happen now," she grumbled into her hands before sliding them down her face in frustration. How was she supposed to have a relationship with not only her employer but also the man she was now potentially planning to steal from?

The carriage stopped abruptly, jerking her forward slightly. She slid her glasses back on and collected her things, exiting the carriage and bid the driver a good night.

Once she'd entered the apartment, she unceremoniously dropped her belongings in the entryway. Her mind was far too occupied to deal with putting everything in its place.

She began to pace in a short line back and forth across the wood floor of her sitting room. Her hand found its way to her mouth, teeth gnashing into her cuticles and fingernails. A nasty nervous habit she'd yet to break.

Perhaps she could use the dinner date to her advantage to collect some information, she thought. Ryker knew she was naturally curious, so she didn't think her reason for inquiring would seem too obvious. But that also ran the risk of her accidentally offering too much information with her chronic tendency to over-share.

Rue groaned and shook her head, "I need to go to sleep before my head implodes." These were problems for tomorrow Rue to deal with.

Chapter Four

*R*UE'S EYES OPENED WITH *a jolt as she found herself standing in an empty room. She spun around, trying to figure out where one wall started and another ended, but to no avail. Pitch-black darkness extended endlessly in every direction. Where was this? Last she remembered, she'd fallen asleep at home in her bed. How had she gotten here? Rue wrapped her arms around herself and tried to remember something, anything about how she'd gotten here. Complete silence encased her. Not even the sound of her breathing seemed to penetrate it.*

"Run."

The sudden voice broke the silence and commanded in a whisper she could almost feel against her ear. Her skin prickled with fear as she sprinted. She didn't know where she was going but knew that whatever she was running from was not far behind. Her bare feet slapped against the ground, and she pumped her arms, willing her body to move as fast as it could.

"Don't let him take you," another voice called, but this time she recognized it. The same voice she had heard in her dream before. This only urged her to run faster. Her lungs burned and her thighs ached, but she couldn't stop. The echoing thud of heavy footsteps gaining behind her sent a shock of terror through her. She couldn't get away. Rue ran for what felt like miles, the endless dark stretching out before her with no end in sight.

"Keep going!" that same voice called to her again. As much as she wanted to stop, she knew she couldn't. Something inside her told her she had to keep moving no matter what. Rue closed her eyes, putting one foot after another, but suddenly found no purchase below her. The ground had opened up, swallowing her whole.

Rue sat upright in her bed as a half-formed scream died on her lips. Early morning light filtered through the thick curtains, illuminating her bedroom around her.

"Another dream," she realized, rubbing her eyes so hard she saw stars. She reached for her glasses, sliding them on before climbing out of bed. Ryker had instructed her to take the day off, but with restlessness from the dream now buzzing uncomfortably under her skin, she knew she wouldn't be able to sit idly by.

The sun had yet to fully rise over the horizon. It sat lazily against the water's edge, painting the early morning sky in an array of soft pinks, dusty purples, and muted peachy oranges. Sunrises had always made being out of bed this early worth it. Giving Rue something different from the same shades of grey she saw day in and day out. Eventually, the clouds would come back and hide the sun once more, but Rue enjoyed these moments while she could.

After a meager breakfast of toast and too-strong tea, Rue shuffled through a stack of letters Jasper had been nice enough to gather before he left. Most of them were official-looking mass correspondence from her university that she tossed aside without opening, but wedged between them was a single brown paper envelope.

"Oh!" Rue ripped open the envelope with little grace, tugging the letter out and hastily unfolding it. It was from her former classmate at university. The person who had initially introduced her to the duke and someone she would feel forever indebted to.

Since leaving the mainland and coming back to the isle, the two of them had written back and forth, mostly simple updates and various unimportant things. It had been quite a while since she'd heard from her friend, and today, it was just what she needed.

Rue hadn't managed to make very many friends since her return, finding it easier to throw herself into her work and spend her spare time worrying about whatever trouble Jasper might be getting into.

That was what she told herself anyway.

The truth of the matter was — even if Rue wouldn't admit it to herself — she was scared. Orionna had been the kind of person to force her way into Rue's life whether she liked it or not. At first, Rue had kept her at arm's length, feeling as though the other woman had some kind of ulterior motive for getting close to her. But through the years, Rue's walls fell, allowing Orionna in little by little.

Although she wouldn't say they were the best of friends, Rue was still grateful to have someone out there who thought of her fondly enough to send a letter every once in a while. Rue quickly scanned over the letter, making sure there was nothing of dire importance before she tucked it away. She would have to find time later to send a reply.

The sun had fully risen over the horizon, its rays struggling to pierce through the clouds that had now rolled in. With a deep sigh, Rue gathered her belongings and headed out into the chilly morning air.

She arrived at the manor far earlier than her normal shift, hoping to get down to the library and start searching once again before anyone could ask anything of her. The still quiet of the library hadn't bothered her in a long time, but after the dream she'd had, her mind was on edge. Damp logs crackled and hissed in the fireplace behind her as she surveyed the rows of shelves, contemplating where she should start to make the most of her time.

Each of the library's shelves were categorized by subject, then alphabetically by name. Though it was meticulously arranged, there were still hundreds, perhaps thousands of books here.

"This is going to be impossible," she grumbled under her breath, "but I suppose the history section would be a good start." And with that, Rue began.

Hours had gone by, marked by the incessant chimes of the clock, and still, Rue had come up empty-handed. Everything she had found was either too vague to give her anything to go on or was written in languages she couldn't decipher. Rue wiped the sweat from her brow and lodged the last book back into its slot on the shelf. She hoped that wherever Jasper had gone, he was having better luck finding something than she was.

Giving up for the time being, Rue let out a sigh of defeat and trudged back to her desk, trying to convince herself that the hours she'd spent searching weren't for nothing. She stepped out from between one of the shelves, rubbing at her tired eyes when she saw someone standing at the other end of the library.

A figure stood, unmoving in the shadowy darkness across from her. Her heart thumped in her chest. She hadn't heard anyone come in as she was absolutely certain she would have heard the sound of the heavy passageway door open in the quiet.

"Hello?" Rue called out, tentatively moving toward the shadow.

The shadow remained in its place, answering only with silence.

"Who are you?" she called, slowly moving closer. The figure didn't budge, but as Rue approached, the once blurred edges began to sharpen. Unable to believe what she was seeing, Rue fervently rubbed at her eyes once more, trying to force her vision to focus on the figure before her.

"Orionna?" she asked, voice going soft with disbelief.

The shadow bolted from the place it had been standing. Rue rushed after it. There was no way it could be her, but Rue would not stop until she knew for sure.

"Wait!" she cried again, catching a glimpse of the figure darting between the shelves, coming so close but finding it just out of reach every time. Rue swung around the edge of one of the display stands, careful not to knock anything over.

The shadow slipped away once more, but this time Rue turned the other way, hoping to cut whatever — or whoever — this was off before they could get away.

It was a dead end. The shadow had disappeared, vanishing into thin air but now Rue found herself standing before the ominous iron door. Her heart hammered with fear against her ribs, breaths coming out in harsh and almost panicked pants. Did that figure lead her here?

But why?

Rue grasped her necklace once again, rubbing her thumb absently over the citrine gem like a worry stone. She took another step closer, feeling something beyond the door pull her. Without thinking, Rue reached out, pressing her palm against the cold, dark iron. Her eyes closed of their own accord and suddenly, her body was plummeting. She was sinking deep down into that endless black abyss from her nightmare – and yet, she stood still.

When she returned to herself, Rue wrenched her hand from the door. The sudden jerky movement sent her stumbling backward, tripping over the hem of her skirt. She squeezed her eyes shut and braced for the impact when a pair of strong hands broke her fall.

"Rue?"

It was Ryker's voice.

Rue opened her eyes, blinking rapidly and trying to make sense of what had just happened. She turned to face him, concern clearly visible over his features.

"Are you alright? I told you to take the day off." His hands caressed her arms as he pulled away.

"Y-yes, I just—" How could she explain when she didn't even know what had happened? She rubbed her temples as throbbing pain blossomed behind her eyes.

"I was informed you'd come for your shift and came to find you. I called your name, but you didn't answer." He paused, frowning. "You should go home and rest. You don't look well at all."

"I'm sorry, I—"

Ryker cut her off with the raise of his hand before she could give him any sort of explanation or apology.

"You don't need to explain yourself to me, Rue. I know I can't force you to go, but please, for your own sake, don't overwork yourself if you choose to stay."

Rue slowly nodded, unable to trust herself to form a coherent sentence while her mind was still reeling from what had just happened.

"Very good." He gave her a small approving nod, "And while you're here, I wanted to let you know I have arranged for a private dinner for the two of us at the end of the month."

He wasn't asking her; he was telling her. Again, Rue only nodded, wordlessly agreeing.

"I'll leave you to it." Ryker slid his hand under her chin, tilting her head up to meet his gaze. Rue found herself enraptured in his brilliant moonstone eyes, and a feeling of calm washed over her for a fleeting moment. He regarded her fondly for what felt like too long before tugging her toward him and closing the small gap that remained between them with his lips on hers.

Ryker left without another word, leaving Rue there, rooted to the spot in a flurry of conflicting emotions. But before she could even begin to process that, she turned back toward the sinister door once more, brows knitting in confusion.

How long had she been standing there, trapped in her own mind? How long had he been calling her name without any response? Maybe he was right and the lack of sleep was catching up to her. Perhaps it was nothing and she'd simply fallen asleep standing up. Neither explanation seemed to fully encompass the feeling she'd had in her chest pulling her towards that door, but for now, Rue chose to ignore it and go back home before she could think any more of it.

The short walk back to her apartment passed in a blur. Her mind singularly focused on what happened in the library, much to her dismay. She couldn't understand it and trying to come up with a logical answer seemed impossible.

Rue pulled her keys from her skirt pocket. Rain poured down from above, leaving her glasses fogged over from her breath, obscuring the keyhole.

"Damnit, come on!" Her slippery fingers fumbled the keys. She grasped at them uselessly as they fell between her fingers and clattered to the ground.

Great.

This day was just getting better and better.

She let out a loud, irritated groan as she bent to pick them up. She pressed her shoulder into the door to hold herself up but let out a screech of surprise when it swung open, sending her toppling over the threshold.

She sat frozen where she had fallen into the entryway, eyes wide and pulse thumping in her ears. There was no way she left the door unlocked. Slowly, Rue pushed herself up on the palms of her hands, her eyes darting around to try and see what might be lurking inside in the darkness.

Rue swallowed hard and pushed her keys into her fist, letting the serrated edge stick out from between her knuckles, just like Jasper had shown her. She pulled the door closed behind her, throwing the deadbolt and tugging on the handle to ensure that it was fully locked this time.

She prayed that whoever it was that may have broken into her apartment just took what they wanted and left. Rue was a simple woman of few possessions, so there wasn't anything of much value to be taken anyway. She resisted the urge to call out for her brother. As much as she hoped this was one of his stupid little pranks, her gut told her otherwise. Even Jasper wouldn't go this far. Not after everything they'd talked about.

Nothing but an ominous silence greeted her. Rue crept slowly into the sitting room, mentally taking inventory of all of the items she knew to be in there. Nothing seemed amiss. There was no sign that anyone else had been there aside from herself.

She continued through the house, peeking her head into every room. The keys were still lodged between her fingers in a vise grip. She started up the short staircase that led to the upper landing. If anyone truly was waiting for her, it would be in there. She swallowed down the bile rising in her throat, willing herself to stay calm, not allowing her fear to overtake her.

Rue squinted, waiting for her eyes to adjust to the heavy dark. She reached for the matchbox on her vanity, striking one with unsteady hands to light the lantern hanging from a sconce next to her door. When the room illuminated, it was exactly as she had left it. Rue breathed a sigh of relief and slumped into her dressing table chair.

"I must have left the door unlocked..." She tried to convince herself that it had just been a small mistake and that she would be more careful before leaving the house, but part of her still remained unconvinced. Rue leaned forward, looking over her face in the mirror for the first time. Ryker hadn't been joking when he said she'd looked unwell. Her already pale skin seemed nearly white, and the dark circles beneath her eyes stood out more than normal.

Although exhaustion ate at her, sleep felt too distant. Rue stood and removed her wet clothes, letting them fall onto the floor in a heap to be dealt with later. She slid back into her thin night dress and began toweling off her hair.

"I should really get a haircut," she muttered as she mindlessly ran the small towel over her thick tresses. Without focus, her mind began to wander, bringing her back to the library and the door. Why couldn't she remember what happened? Why had the figure in the shadows led her there? Something wasn't quite right, but she couldn't seem to put a pin in exactly what was off. Maybe she just needed a good night's rest. Her mind was most likely playing tricks on her.

With her hair sufficiently dried, Rue tossed the towel on the floor, along with the other pile of clothes that needed to be washed in the morning. She turned back toward the vanity mirror and caught her reflection again, but this time, the version of her that peered back smiled, tilting its head just slightly.

Startled, Rue let out a clipped scream and pushed herself back with as much force as she could muster, trying to get as far away from the mirror as she could. She covered her face with shaking hands, closing her eyes and trying to will away whatever that *thing* was staring back at her.

"This isn't happening. None of this is real. I'm just exhausted," Rue chanted the words like a mantra, simply wanting to believe that her lack of sleep was the cause of this and not some unseen sinister force. Grabbing her robe and tossing it over the mirror for good measure, Rue climbed into her bed and pulled the duvet up over her head.

She squeezed her eyes shut and continued muttering the same things over and over, praying that she would fall into a dreamless sleep. However, when sleep finally came to claim her, dragging her into its undertow once again, those prayers had fallen on deaf ears.

The dreams came anyway, but this time, she wasn't falling. Rue stood in the same empty void room, only this time it wasn't so empty. The baneful black iron door stood before her. Only the door alone, disconnected from the rest of the library around it as she had seen it before. The air around her felt thick in her lungs. A disgusting miasma.

"*Ruby...*" Something called to her from the other side of the door. It was not a single voice, but many, layered one over another, each with a different emotion. Some whispered, some screamed, some sobbed.

Rue took a single step closer to the door, arm outstretched as it had been before, fingertips almost touching the iron of the door.

Again, the legion of voices spoke, but this time their speech blurred together into an unintelligible cacophony of whispers. Although she couldn't understand their words, she knew what the voices asked of her. Rue felt the pull of an unseen force behind the door, urging her closer. Pressing her hand fully against the iron slab, she pushed it open, revealing nothing but more inky darkness. A yawning maw of emptiness.

Rue took another step forward into the abyss beyond the threshold, but before she could be fully swallowed, the pendant around her neck burned against her sternum. In an instant, the dream melted away, leaving her there in the familiar dark once again.

"Sleep. I will protect you."

It was the same soothing voice that she'd heard in all of her dreams. Rue closed her eyes and let out a deep, calming breath. For some reason, even though she couldn't see whomever the voice had belonged to, she knew she could trust it.

Unable to keep herself upright any longer, Rue dropped to her knees, swaying for a moment before falling down onto her side. This time, sleep took mercy upon her, finally letting her fall into a dreamless slumber.

CHAPTER FIVE

GAINST HER OWN JUDGMENT, Rue decided to heed Ryker's words and took the next few days off. Most of which were spent in a strange place that sat between waking life and sleep. Fortunately, during that time, the only thing behind her eyes was endless darkness. No more dreams plagued her, finally allowing her blissfully restful sleep.

When she was coherent enough to rise from her bed, a bright red envelope bearing only her name sat in the center of her kitchen table. She didn't remember getting up to check the mailbox or if anyone had come while she was in her delirious state. Rue slipped the flat end of her teaspoon under the flap and broke the seal, unfolding the letter.

Rue -

I'm writing this letter for you to find when you wake, since it seems you've come down with some kind of illness and weren't lucid enough when I came by to have any kind of conversation.

I have found what you asked of me. An alchemist by the name of Whitlock in Bellmare. She will have what you're looking for. I also brought you back a jar of the tea you like and left it with the others in your cabinet. I'll come back in a few days, but as always, don't wait up for me.

-J.

Her heart swelled when she saw Jasper's initial at the bottom of the page. She folded the letter back up and tucked the corner beneath her teacup. Dipping the spoon back into her cup and gazing into the swirling dark liquid, Rue considered the new information her brother had left.

An alchemist seemed like the right person to have answers for her. She knew of some that created potions and medicines in the apothecaries; others dabbled in magic as well. Ryker had commissioned several alchemists in the past for binding spells he used on sales and contracts, but Rue had never seen exactly what they did since learned magic like that was seen as taboo by common folk, and she had to admit her curiosity.

The small neighborhood of Bellmare sat on the opposite side of the isle and took a short train ride to reach. Known as the merchant district to most, Bellmare was home to any and all kinds of trade. She'd traveled there multiple times but couldn't recall ever seeing an alchemist's shop or apothecary. Rue took a sip of her tea — blanching slightly as it singed her tongue — and considered her options.

She could go back to the library and keep searching, or she could continue her short leave of absence and use the time away to travel to Bellmare and meet with the alchemist. The thought of going back to the library after the last incident made her stomach churn with unease. She wasn't ready.

"Suppose that makes up my mind then."

Rue wrapped a thick, knitted scarf tightly around her neck and shoved her necklace into her blouse underneath. A sheet of rain poured down, pelting her windows in fat drops. She frowned with a small sigh, accepting that no matter how many layers she wore, she was going to end up drenched and cold anyway.

All roads between Penrith city proper and Bellmare had been flooded with deep water, making it impossible to reach by carriage or on foot, effectively separating the district from the main city. Rue snapped open her plum-colored umbrella and raised it over her head. Surprisingly, despite the dreary weather, a few small slivers of blue sky seeped through the white and grey clouds. If only the sun would join, too.

Rue's heeled boots sloshed through the deep puddles that gathered in the uneven bits of crumbling road. Thankfully, the hour was early enough that the usual bustle of the city was replaced with quiet chatter. The fewer eyes on her the better.

The train station wasn't so much a station as it was a simple bench with a pole affixed with a sign indicating that a train would stop there. She took one look at the bench and her nose crinkled at the thought of sitting on the wet boards, so instead she opted to stand.

The few hints of blue autumn sky had returned to their usual grey. Darker clouds rolled over the horizon and obscured the last shreds of muted sunlight that remained. Despite being alone, a feeling of dread sank into her gut. Each gust of wind carried the sound of a whisper; every rustle of leaves sounded like footsteps. Rue's chilled fingers curled around the necklace hidden under her collar, thumb running over the smooth citrine stone in an attempt to calm her nerves.

Alone with nothing but her thoughts and the sound of quiet rainfall around her, Rue's mind drifted to the voice she'd heard calling her to the iron door. Was there someone — or something — beckoning to her? Or was it just her overactive imagination playing tricks on her? Trying to brush aside the creeping feeling of anxiety that was now permanently wedged under her skin, Rue glanced down the tracks and hoped for a sign that the train was near.

She squinted and pushed her glasses up the bridge of her nose and noticed a hunched figure shambling its way down the tracks in the distance. Alarm bells rang in her mind. Something wasn't quite right about whatever this was. The figure moved closer and closer with each passing moment. Rue kept her eyes trained on it, hands clenched so tightly around her pendant that the tips of the sun rays dug into her palm.

She turned away. Perhaps if she didn't look, it would go away. This had to be in her head. Rue tried to convince herself there was nothing there, only a figment of her paranoid imagination brought on by stress.

"Go away...please, just go away..." she pleaded under her breath to whichever of the gods might be listening. Pleas went unanswered as the figure, which she now could see was an old woman, was nearly to the bench. But the way it— she, Rue supposed— moved was inhuman.

She swallowed thickly, throat constricting with fear. The wizened woman continued lumbering toward her with eyes set straight ahead. Whether unseeing or ignoring, Rue couldn't tell. The woman looked as though she might walk past Rue without sparing a single glance. However, much to Rue's dismay, the woman abruptly stopped before her. Bile coated the back of her throat. She tried to swallow it down, reasoning with herself that this was nothing to be afraid of, even if her senses were all screaming at her to run.

The woman smelled of death. A sharp scent of rot and decay with an undertone of sickly sweetness, layered with something like a perfume oil or incense to mask it. The stench stung Rue's nose and made her eyes water. It took everything in her not to clap a hand over her mouth and nose. The woman turned her head, and milky white eyes met Rue's forest green gaze. The hag's mouth curled into a sinister grin, exposing yellowed, rotten and jagged teeth from behind her peeling lips.

"Your scent is...familiar, child." The woman's voice came out in a hoarse rasp, so quiet Rue had to strain her ears to hear. Rue's throat was too tight to reply. The woman faced Rue now, her clothing nothing more than tatters of different fabrics layered atop one another in a way that reminded Rue of a bird's nest. Dirt, grime, and only the Gods only knew what other filth covered her withered face, the line between where the skin ended and the muck began completely indistinguishable.

The hag sniffed the air around Rue, "Lemon and verbena flowers on spring wind. Like old parchment and ink." She paused for a moment, reaching a gnarled hand between her many layers of fabric and produced a single raven's feather.

"Take this. He will come." The woman's face pulled into another grotesque grin. Rue hesitantly accepted the feather with shaking hands. She knew it was probably a bad idea to accept anything from this woman, but something compelled Rue to take the feather anyway.

"T-thank you...but who will come?" Rue asked. Her skin suddenly felt like a live wire where it made contact with the feather.

The woman said nothing and walked to the opposite side of the tracks, the sinister smile never budging from her lips.

"Excuse me, um, madam! Please, tell me who is coming?" Rue called to the woman, desperation fueling her. The sound of her anxious heart thrumming in her ears drowned out all other noise around her. The woman continued in the same inhuman shuffle across the mossy old tracks. Rue opened her mouth to speak again and reached out for the woman.

Before she could touch her, the train rolled in, breaking her line of sight as her head whipped in its direction. Rue nearly jumped out of her skin, not having heard it approach, too focused on getting an answer about the remarkably pristine raven's feather in her hand. She rolled the feather between her fingers. Faint bits of overcast light caught onto the iridescent shine, exposing the hidden blue and purple undertones.

Rue boarded the train and took a seat on the far side of the car where she last saw the woman. However, through the window was nothing but empty rain covered streets. Her brow furrowed in confusion. How could she have gotten so far so quickly? She sat back against the seat as the train began to move and tried to push the odd encounter from her mind.

The soothing rumble of the train had Rue dozing. Even with the catch-up sleep she'd been getting, her body still screamed for more. Her head rested against the cool glass of the window, the feather still held tightly in hand. Bellmare was only a short distance from her neighborhood, but she would take any small moment of solace she could. Even if it was on a rickety old train.

Rue was still shaken but tried to ignore the nausea that sat in the pit of her stomach. It was just some odd coincidence, she told herself. The raven's feather didn't *mean* anything. There were plenty of ravens around Penrith that shed feathers. The logical explanation was that the woman was just insane, but somehow, that didn't feel quite right, either.

The hag's words stuck in her mind. Who would come for her? Her mind wandered to the faceless man that had continually appeared in her dreams. The feather had the same oil slick hues of the wings that protruded from his back. Surely the woman couldn't know about her dreams. These days, however, Rue was more inclined to believe that anything was possible.

Rue's brows knit together as all the threads of unanswered questions wove through her mind. She wasn't dozing anymore, but it was more comforting to keep her eyes closed than to open them and find some other horrid abomination had potentially joined her.

A bell dinged, indicating the train's arrival at her destination and pulling Rue from her feigned sleep. She rubbed her hands over her eyes, pushing back against the dull but constant ache that had begun to develop behind them. Stepping onto the gravel walkway, she moved quickly, with purpose. Determined to at least get *something* answered. Provided Jasper's insight was correct, anyway.

Rain or shine, the merchant's district was always bustling with shoppers. Some flitting back and forth between stalls and some haggling for the best price. A large cream colored overhang kept the main thoroughfare clear and dry. A few coal braziers were nestled between booths to keep patrons and merchants alike warm and comfortable.

Sellers called out their wares and prices, promising the best deals and fresh goods with voices booming over the cacophony of shoppers' chatter. Strolling down the center aisle, Rue took note of all the various commodities for sale. Nothing looked out of the ordinary, just handfuls of old trinkets and stacks of lovely handmade candles, soaps, and oils. No sign of the alchemist Jasper had spoken of.

Feeling suddenly overwhelmed by the amount of people crowding around her, Rue pulled her hands to her chest and tucked her elbows in tightly to avoid accidentally hitting anyone. Her restless thumbs caressed the soft vane of the feather, giving her worn old necklace a break.

The sensation of the plume against her fingers felt oddly comforting, seeming to help ground her. Rue didn't think too hard about how this feather was suddenly affecting her and kept moving. With only precious few daylight hours left, she pushed forward with steely determination.

The scent of buttery baking bread filled her nostrils, making her stomach rumble. She hadn't eaten anything before she left and the singular cup of tea she did have wasn't nearly enough. The baker's stall was set up in front of a brick and mortar shop. The sweet smell of jammy pastries made her mouth water.

Tenderly, Rue slid the feather into her coat pocket — doing her best not to bend or damage it — and dug out the few coins she'd brought with her.

"Excuse me, Madam," Rue called to the portly woman behind the stall. The woman turned, greeting Rue with reddened cheeks and a motherly smile, wiping flour-covered hands on a stained apron,

"Oh yes, dear, what can I do ye for?" Her accent was thick and not familiar to Rue.

"Could I get one of those small loaves, please?" Rue asked, handing over the coin and nodding toward a steaming loaf of bread that had been brushed with butter and sprinkled with flaky salt.

"Here ye are, darlin'. Anythin' else?" The baker handed the loaf to Rue, the smile never fading from her face. It was almost eerie to see someone so jovial and so...*normal*. At least in comparison to the things she'd been experiencing over the last week. This woman, more likely than not, wasn't going to know anything about the book, but she might be able to lead her in the right direction,

"Yes, madam. Could you tell me where I might find an alchemist's shop nearby?"

The woman's smile fell immediately and was replaced with a look of sheer annoyance. That couldn't be a good sign. She took a deep breath and leaned forward, letting out an exasperated sigh as she spoke,

"You'll find a Miss Fia Whitlock down thataway, the alchemist. Keep yer wits about ye; she's always blowin' things up." The baker shook her head, muttering something Rue couldn't hear under her breath before turning back to the brick oven behind her. Rue muttered a small thank you and followed the direction she'd been pointed in.

Rue unwrapped the bread loaf as she walked and crammed it — in a very unladylike way — into her mouth. The first taste of the warm bread on her tongue sent her eyes rolling back. It was buttery, slightly sweet, a little salty, and still warm. She was going to have to grab a few more of these before she left to go back home. Between the food and the calming aura radiating from the feather in her pocket, Rue was beginning to feel much more like herself.

With renewed fervor, she continued toward the alchemist's shop. The scent was apparent before she could make out the shop ahead. An overwhelming odor of sulfur and something else she couldn't place permeated the air.

Rue frowned and wrapped the rest of the bread back into the brown paper, her appetite lost. A sign that looked as though it was barely holding onto its rusted bolts jutted out from the side of the building. Whatever name had been painted on it was fully eroded away.

The shop doors looked as though they'd been ripped from the hinges and subsequently replaced too many times to count. A metal plaque embossed with the name "Fianore Whitlock" was affixed to the brick to the right of the door. The name was correct, so hopefully, this was the right place. Rue took one last deep breath of fresh air, bracing herself for whatever else might lie beyond the door.

Inside the shop was even worse than the exterior. Half-empty bottles were strewn along the countertops — some without stoppers or corks in them — with gods knew what dripping out of them onto the warped wood and down to several colorful pools on the floor. The few that were corked seemed a bit too precarious for comfort.

Messy stacks of parchment paper and old books littered several of the tall bookcases behind the counter, all with tired shelves that sagged under the weight. Rue could see no rhyme or reason to the...organization. Everything seemed to be shoved into whatever empty space remained.

The walls were stained with splashes of various colors of unknown substances. Thick grey smoke drifted out from a tiny room that was only closed by a flimsy, moth-eaten curtain. That couldn't be safe. Rue understood the baker's warnings now. The alchemist was nowhere to be seen but judging from the noise coming from the room behind the curtain, it was apparent she was there.

"Hello? Miss Whitlock?" Rue craned her neck, trying to catch a glimpse of the alchemist.

After a moment of silence and no answer, Rue opened her mouth to call out again, but the words died on her tongue as the sound of shattering glass and panicked swearing interrupted her.

"J-just a moment! I'll be right with you!" A squeaky, exasperated voice called from the back room.

Rue's brows shot up in a mixture of shock and concern. She could hear the alchemist fumble and knock a few more things over on her way out.

The woman — who she assumed to be Fianore — was breathless by the time she finally made it past the curtain, swatting it out of the way and grumbling a few more obscenities under her breath.

She was small, standing at just barely over five feet, with chestnut hair that was tied back into two messy buns on either side of her head, resembling mouse ears. She wore a pair of large goggles around her neck and had an outline of where they had previously sat clearly visible on her face. Dust, dirt, and whatever else coated the rest of her face. Fianore pulled her thick leather gloves off one finger at a time and slapped them against the wooden counter.

"Sorry about that, I got a little carried away back there." The woman ruffled her hair nervously, avoiding Rue's gaze.

A pair of symbols with thick black ink lines were tattooed on Fia's hands, each a circle with a triangle in the center, one pointing up and the other down. Rue had seen those symbols in one of the books she'd found in the duke's library. The marks of an alchemist associated with learned magic. She had never seen them on anyone else before, and her stomach flipped with excitement. This had to be the person Jasper spoke of.

Rue shook her head, waving her hand, "It's quite alright. The baker said I might find the alchemist Fianore Whitlock here?" She paused for a moment, "Would that be you, Miss?"

"Fianore Whitlock, at your service!" Fianore's face pulled into a wide grin, showing off her slightly crooked teeth, "But you can just call me Fia; everyone else 'round here does."

Rue couldn't help but return the smile. Even as frazzled as the woman was, she had a certain charm about her. It reminded Rue of her brother. She took a step closer and extended her hand,

"My name is Ruby Umberwick, but everyone calls me Rue."

Fia took Rue's hand, shaking it firmly. That grin never left her lips, "Good to meet you. What brings you to my humble little shop here in Bellmare, Miss Rue?"

"I was told you might have some information I'm looking for."

CHAPTER SIX

FIA'S DEMEANOR CHANGED IN the blink of an eye. She eyed Rue suspiciously for a long moment before speaking again, "What kind of information?"

"Old folktales. Information about the Old Gods, that kind of thing," Rue said plainly. Fia didn't seem like the kind of person she needed to tiptoe around.

"What kind of folktale is it that you're looking for? Must be some pretty dark stuff if it forced you to seek out someone like me." Fia leaned forward over the dirty counter, holding her chin in her hand, and raised an inquisitive brow, waiting for Rue's answer.

"It's about a book. A book that is said to contain passages for rituals —" Rue began but quickly held back, unsure just how much information she should give right away, "rituals that have the power to essentially end the world."

Fia regarded Rue suspiciously for a moment longer. Her eyes screwed up in thought as though she were combing an internal catalog for any recollection of this particularly heinous tome of forbidden knowledge.

"Yeah, I've heard of something like that. Heard it was lost to the abyss hundreds... or maybe even thousands of years ago, and no one has seen it since." Fia's expression was bored, gaze focused on her nails as she spoke, avoiding looking at Rue directly.

"But the book exists?" Rue blurted, hope swelling in her chest.

"I didn't say that. I said what I heard," Fia countered, "but why are you so interested in something like that?" The suspicion in her voice returned. Distrust shone in her eyes, the bubbly, irreverent mask had vanished. How many others had come to her with questions regarding things not meant to be spoken of? A guilty blush heated her cheeks, feeling dreadful for potentially adding another mark to the score.

Deciding to show a little vulnerability, Rue leaned in closer, speaking barely above a whisper, "When I was young, my older brother Jasper used to tell me stories about this Cataclysm, and of course, I grew up thinking it was just that. A story. I never believed in any fairy tales or Gods given magic — or even the Gods themselves, if I'm totally honest. I believed in what I knew to be true. Things I could see and touch. But the strangest things have been happening to me. Each day only gets worse. Things that neither logic nor science can explain, and it all just feels like a sign something truly terrible is going to happen if I can't find this book."

Rue continued on, ignoring the anxiety creeping back into her as Fia continued to stare at her blankly, "But I do know that some alchemists are rooted in science, and then some," she paused, eyes dropping to the tattoos on Fia's hands, "Like you, are rooted in learned magic."

Fia's eyes widened in alarm as she pulled her hands back and hid them beneath the counter. Rue placed her hand on the counter, palm facing upwards, wordlessly asking for Fia's. Fia considered Rue for a beat as though she was calculating the risks, but eventually, she hesitantly placed her hand in Rue's palm.

With her other finger, Rue traced over the symbol tattooed on the back of Fia's hand gently and offered a small smile before covering the other girl's hand with her own. Fia's shoulders slumped slightly as she relaxed under Rue's touch and nodded for her to continue.

"I had hoped that you might know something that could help me find this book...and destroy it. Before it falls into the hands of someone who might use it for a more nefarious purpose."

Fia said nothing, a long silence wedged between them. The alchemist's eyes focused on where her hand still lay pressed between both of Rue's. She chewed her lip, peeling away bits of dried skin with her teeth before she spoke again.

"I don't know much myself, but my sister can tell you more. If anyone, she would have more of the answers that you seek," Fia said, eyes dragging away from their hands to meet Rue's gaze.

"Really?" Rue breathed, an excited smile tugging at the edges of her mouth, "is she here? Can I speak with her now?" Rue was getting ahead of herself but the relief she felt after finally getting somewhere after this hellish week propelled her forward without hesitation.

Fia shook her head with an apologetic frown, "My sister, she won't leave the house anymore. Not after what they did to her," she explained. Rue tilted her head curiously, her lips curving downward.

"These are marks of magic, yes," she explained, showing Rue the tattoo on her other hand, "I was marked when the villagers found us — my sister and I — in the woods. She was only trying to help, but of course, they couldn't see that." Fia's face contorted into a look that was equal parts rage and sadness, "They didn't want to see it."

Rue's heart ached for Fia and her sister. Most of the people who lived on the isle were afraid of magic. There were two different kinds of magic — some that was learned and some that was given to chosen individuals by the now lost pantheon. This gods given magic was something of legend. Something that may have existed once but with the disappearance of the pantheon, the only bits of it left were nothing more than legends in story books.

That sort of power became something to be feared. The stories told of what great and terrible things magic from the gods could do and therefore the majority of folks left on the isle saw any and all magic as unnatural. Forbidden.

Some braver sorts dabbled in it, learning spells from old tomes but kept quiet about their studies, but learned magic always came at a price, and there was no telling what that cost might be. Even for the simplest of spells. Only the rich and powerful — people like Ryker — could afford to employ these self-taught mages.

"I am so sorry, Fia. Some people out there," Rue shook her head, "are monsters. Attacking what they fear because they do not understand, but I can promise you that I intend no harm to you or your sister. I just need help to do the right thing, and right now, I think you are the only one who can help me."

Fia nodded, "Alright. I will explain everything to my sister and convince her to speak with you. Come to my home in one week, but until then, I expect you'll keep this quiet."

Rue's stomach sank. A week? She had no time to waste, but at this point, it wasn't as though she really had another option, so Rue agreed and kept her arguments to herself.

"Yes, of course. Thank you. Truly, Fia." Rue squeezed Fia's hand between hers tightly before letting go. Fia pulled a scrap of paper from below the counter and, with a pencil that had been hidden in one of her messy buns, scribbled something on it before sliding it over to Rue.

"My address. Vesper sleeps during the day, so you'll need to come at night."

Rue took the scrap and carefully folded it before sliding it into her pocket alongside the feather. Fia tugged the leather gloves back on and adjusted her apron, spinning on her heel to return to the other room.

"Fia," Rue called out to her once more. The alchemist paused but didn't turn back to face her.

"I said it already, but thank you. For trusting me when you didn't have to. I appreciate it more than you know."

At that, Fia glanced over her shoulder at Rue, a warm smile gracing her lips as she nodded in understanding and walked away.

The next week went by in a nervous blur. Rue returned to the library, continuing her search for any information about the book, but found nothing more than she already knew. Despite the library's perfect organization, Rue was at a loss of what to even look for anymore. Her eyes burned with exhaustion, and her body ached from climbing up and down the ladder what felt like hundreds of times. Resting her head against the shelf, Rue let out a frustrated groan and finally accepted her loss for the day.

Tonight was the night she was to meet with Fia's sister. Worry had flooded her every day since her first meeting with the alchemist. Fia had said she would convince Vesper to speak with her but there was always the chance the other woman would decline. This was the only opportunity she had at her disposal to get some kind of direction of what to do next.

She wrapped her cloak around her shoulders and tied her boots tightly around her ankles before heading out to the train, following the address Fia had given her.

The moon was nearly completely obscured by the thick clouds in the sky, leaving only a faint glow of light to guide her way. This only added to the unease that had permanently settled in her stomach. Rue didn't know what to expect from this meeting, though she hoped it would provide a breakthrough after hitting dead end after dead end.

At this time of night, the streets of Bellmare were dark and empty, a stark juxtaposition from the raucous crowds that swarmed them during the daylight hours. The path before her was lit by a scant few lamps at the edges of the sidewalks. The roads steamed from the sharp drop in temperature, and the smell of wet earth and asphalt hung heavily in the air.

Glancing at the scrawled address again and looking between the buildings, Rue finally located the correct number that Fia had given her.

"Alright, this is it..." she spoke softly under her breath, steeling her nerves. The tall townhouse before her looked dark and empty, but she knocked on the door anyway. Rue rapped her knuckles against the peeling red paint on the door, waiting for any indication that someone might be inside.

Rue pressed her ear to the door but heard nothing. Biting her lip to quell another wave of nerves, she lifted her hand to knock again, but before her hand could connect, the door swung open.

"H-hello? Fia, is that you?" Rue called as she leaned in, squinting hard and adjusting her glasses trying to make out if anyone stood in the open doorway. Whoever was on the other side didn't answer, but the door opened a bit wider, squealing on its hinges in a way that made her teeth ache. Rue took it as an invitation to enter and stepped over the threshold. The foyer was dark, save for a few old and yellowed candles that burned on a small wall-mounted shelf, seeming to only be held up by the growing pool of wax around their bases.

The person that had answered the door stepped out from behind it. They were completely shrouded from head to toe in black garments. Rue opened her mouth to speak but closed it again, deciding it would be better to wait until she knew Fia was here and this wasn't some kind of elaborate setup that she was walking into.

A soft voice made her jump, "Fia will be down in a moment. Please make yourself comfortable." This person must be Vesper. The woman motioned with a wave of her hand to one of the moth-eaten wingback chairs that sat facing an unlit hearth. Rue muttered a soft thank you and carefully sat in the chair that looked as though her weight might break it. The two of them sat in a stiff, awkward silence as they waited.

The rhythmic ticking of an unseen clock was the only sound that filled the space. Time seemed to drag on as she waited. Rue shifted in the uncomfortable chair, cringing as the wood groaned and cracked with her movements. Vesper hadn't seemed to move an inch, her head cast downwards to hands crossed over her lap. Her face was completely hidden by the combination of a dark, nearly opaque veil and shadows of the low candlelight in the room. The musty scent of *old* clung to every surface, as though the house had been forgotten years ago despite the people still dwelling inside.

A sudden heavy thumping of footsteps coming down stairs broke the reverie and snapped Rue from her thoughts.

"Oh, Rue! I didn't know you were here yet! I thought I had heard the door, but Vesper didn't call for me..." Fia's words trailed off apologetically.

Rue smiled and stood up from the chair, causing it to creak loudly again, "It's fine. I'm in no hurry at all."

"Sorry for the mess in here. We really don't use this room anymore since our parents..." Fia shook her head. She cleared her throat, gesturing toward the woman in black.

"This, as I am sure you have guessed, is Vesper. She isn't too warm to strangers but she has agreed to talk to you tonight and tonight only. So make sure you ask whatever it is you need because you won't get another chance," Fia informed her with a voice that was more authoritative than when they'd first spoken at her shop.

Rue nodded, understanding Fia's protectiveness of her older sister. She had done the same for Jasper and hoped that if the situation was reversed, he would do the same. But there was no telling with him.

Rue turned to Vesper with hands clasped together in a gesture of gratitude, "Thank you so much for allowing me this honor, Vesper. I can't even begin to express to you just how much this means to me."

Vesper said nothing but slowly nodded her head, indicating she understood. Rue glanced at Fia with her brow creased in worry, but Fia simply offered a reassuring smile. "Come with me. We can do this in the kitchen, and I can make some tea."

"I would love that."

The kitchen was a stark difference to the sitting room they had just left. Almost as though they'd moved into a different house entirely. Signs of life covered every inch of the space. Oil lanterns hung from the ceiling and illuminated the space in a cozy, warm light. Dirty dishes sat piled in the sink from a recently finished meal. Smells of fresh bread and cooked meat filled her nostrils. The scent made her mouth water. Rue mentally chided herself for not eating a decent meal before she left.

Fia rummaged through the cabinets behind her, producing a ceramic teapot and a small, dented brass tin affixed with an old and faded label. Vesper slid in behind her with silent steps. She practically glided across the floor. Rue couldn't help but find her almost ethereal, the mystery of her hidden face only adding to her allure. The clanking sound of the kettle drew Rue's eyes away from Vesper and back to Fia.

"Thank you again. I sincerely appreciate you inviting me into yours and Vesper's home."

Fia only offered a weak, tight-lipped smile. It was obvious she was nervous about the entire situation, and Rue couldn't blame her. They barely knew each other, and Fia was taking an enormous leap of faith in trusting her. Fia pulled out one of the chairs and slid into it next to her sister.

Reaching into her bag, Rue produced a small hand bound leather journal and pencil, placing them both on the table in front of her as though asking permission to take notes. Fia gave her a nod and in return, Rue offered a grateful smile before untying the leather strap from around her notebook.

Vesper took a deep breath and leaned forward, placing her unadorned hands on the table. Her fingernails were chewed down to the quick, making Rue glance down to her own mutilated fingernails. Silence lingered for a long moment between the three of them. Rue cleared her throat and started to speak before it became too awkward.

"Fia tells me that you may have some information about a...relic of sorts that I am seeking." Rue paused, waiting for Vesper's acknowledgment before continuing. It was comforting, knowing Fia was there with them. The older woman's affect seemed so delicate. Like one wrong word would send her fleeing from the room.

Vesper nodded but remained mute, waiting for Rue to continue before offering any information of her own.

"A book..." Rue began again, "A book that supposedly has the power to end the world, in the most plain terms." Rue chewed her lip, pausing again to allow Vesper a chance to cut in if she wished.

Vesper's hands reached for the heavy veil covering her face and slowly pulled it back to expose what lay beneath. Rue barely managed to hold back a gasp at the shocking sight of Vesper's face. Her left eye was missing from its socket, completely scarred over, much like the rest of the left side of her face. However, Vesper's remaining eye, nearly black in color, held such a deep and profound sadness that Rue could almost feel the sorrow like a stone in her gut.

"I don't know what Fia has told you about me," Vesper began, her voice hoarse and raspy from disuse. "When I was just a child, I was granted the gift of sight. A sight that could see into the future and allowed me to predict things that had not yet come to pass. As well as a sight that could peer into the past, showing me things that had already been in great detail." Vesper indicated to the scars over her face, "But part of that gift was taken from me when it was no longer useful to the people of this town."

Vesper's right eye fell on Rue. A shiver ran down her spine as though she were peering directly into her soul — like she was looking past her; searching somewhere deeper within. Rue's entire body tingled with the sensation of being watched by something unseen despite Vesper being right across the table from her. Was Vesper inferring that she was someone who still possessed gods given magic? Rue was unsure but didn't think it wise to ask, so instead, she gave an almost imperceptible nod to continue. "But, my story is not the one you came to hear tonight, so I will not tell it." Vesper turned her head away. "Instead, I will tell you about this tome you seek. It is an old relic that once belonged to the pantheon of gods and goddesses that the people of Penrith, long before this isle had a proper name, worshiped."

Vesper's gaze flicked behind Rue. Fia set down a steaming teapot, placing mismatched mugs with whimsical patterns before each of them.

Rue muttered a quick thanks, taking a cup in between her palms, leeching the heat from the warmed ceramic into her hands.

"I am sure you heard of the lost pantheon when you were a child. Your parents must have told you stories that sounded little more than fairy tales." Vesper wasn't asking, but she didn't need to. It was common knowledge that most of the children that grew up on the isle knew the stories, but no one truly believed them anymore.

"But unlike you believe, they were not just stories. They are history. The pantheon did exist. Some of them still exist even today. Walking among us, cloaked in unassuming human disguises. Watching us as if we were lowly rats in a cage, meant to be studied.

"The gods of the pantheon were forced to leave their hallowed home as the land had become infested with rot and disease that could not be cured. And so they came to the mortal plane to continue their greedy, parasitic existence instead of dying with the land as they should have." Vesper said bitterly. It seemed she might have a personal vendetta with these Gods.

"But of course, before they could fully abandon their plane, they sought to store the wealth of knowledge they'd accumulated. This task was entrusted to a single goddess. Solira."

"The goddess of wisdom," Rue added. Vesper nodded, a barely there but impressed smile curling on her scarred lips.

"Solira was the only one among them that could be trusted with something of this magnitude. With her power, she created an infinite dimension in which the Grand Vault was erected." Vesper paused for a moment to take a sip of her tea, humming softly as the warm steam caressed her face. "The Grand Vault housed each and every soul of all beings. All that they were, every accomplishment and failure, their sorrow and their joy, perfectly condensed into a single volume. It is incredible just how insignificant we all are at the end of it." A somber smile tugged at her mouth but fell away quickly. "This relic you seek. It came from there. It is a tome of secrets. A tome that was supposed to be sealed away, only to be opened by Solira herself and only ever in dire circumstances."

Rue scribbled furiously in her small notebook, demarcating the key points of the story. She just hoped she could read her chicken scratch handwriting later on.

"But of course there was one god that coveted that power above anything else. Vaion. god of chaos and destruction."

Rue looked up from her notebook, meeting Vesper's eye and tilting her head curiously. That name had never come up in the stories before.

"Vaion coveted the power Solira kept locked away. He desired to be a tyrant among gods and would stop at nothing to get what he wanted...but Solira would die before allowing him to take something of that proportion from her archive. The goddess created a key to lock the tome away and hid it. Only to be recovered when the time was right." Vesper pulled her hands back into her lap and said nothing more.

Rue waited for her to continue but was met with only silence and the sound of a ticking clock.

"And do you know where she might have hidden it? Either the book or the key?" Rue asked, hoping her clarifying questions would lead to something more.

Vesper shook her head, "This is all I know. However, if I had to speculate, I believe the tome will be in the last place you would consider looking, but also the most obvious one."

Rue fought to keep the disappointed look from her face. It was something but not nearly enough, in her opinion. She closed her notebook and slid it back into her bag before standing and smoothing out her skirt, "Thank you for allowing me to come and meet with you. Your insight has been incredibly valuable." She knew it sounded like a lie the moment she said it, but Vesper didn't seem bothered and nodded all the same.

Fia stood and waved her arm at Rue, "Let me walk you out," she said with a look that suggested she had more to say but didn't want to include Vesper in that conversation. Rue nodded and said her goodbyes before following Fia out.

The tension in Fia's shoulders melted as they stepped outside. "I can tell you're disappointed. I know Vesper can come off as...cryptic, but really think about what she said, and maybe there's more information between the lines that will lead you to something you haven't found yet," she said.

Rue deflated but forced a smile to her face, "It's alright. This whole thing is just...one big jumbled puzzle that's missing too many pieces. And for whatever reason, I am in charge of figuring out where those pieces ended up."

"If there is anything I can do to help you, I will. I'm sorry I came off so harsh when you came into the shop, but after what happened to us...it's hard to trust people, y'know?" Fia explained.

"What *did* happen to her? You don't have to tell me, but her face was..." Rue shook her head, the image of Vesper's scars materializing in her mind again.

Fia was quiet for another moment. Clearly muddling over what she wanted to disclose, if anything, and twisted her hands together almost nervously.

"It isn't my story to tell, but just know she revealed the wrong thing to the wrong person, and they hurt her," Fia told Rue with a clenched jaw that quickly softened into a sad expression. Rue nodded in understanding. A thinly veiled warning. They both knew that this thing she was delving into was not just some small curiosity or trinket, and Rue would be wise to hold it close to her chest.

"Thank you again, Fia. I'll come to you if there is anything else I find and need your help with." Rue gave her a small smile and turned to leave when Fia's hand took her elbow, gently pulling her back again.

Rue turned back to face the brunette girl, her eyebrows pulling down into an inquisitive look.

"Please be careful with this. I have a bad feeling that something horrible is going to happen..."

CHAPTER SEVEN

B ACK IN THE COMFORT of her room, Rue's mind began to settle. She changed into a thin nightgown and sat before her mirrored vanity, avoiding her reflection and brushed windblown knots from her hair. Her eyes lost focus as she fell into her thoughts, arms still moving in a stiff and methodical way.

A gentle tapping came from the window behind her, bringing Rue back to the moment. A large raven sat on the sill outside her window, pecking against the glass. She placed the brush back on the vanity table, rising from her seat, and moved toward the window with hesitant steps.

Could this be the same raven from before? Ravens were intelligent creatures that were known to remember the faces of people who were kind to them, but the last time she would have seen one was when Ryker pounded on the glass to scare it off.

"What are you doing here?" she asked through the glass. The raven tilted its head in the same way the first one had. But before she could say anything more, the raven took flight and disappeared into the dreary night sky. Rue continued to search through the window, trying to follow where the bird had gone but it was impossible to see after long.

The next morning, Rue sat behind her desk, mindlessly shuffling stacks of papers in an effort to keep her hands busy while her mind ran in circles. A thick fog of exhaustion rolled over her. The dreams never ceased, only alternated between a handful of different recurring scenes that she still did not fully understand.

On some nights, she stood before the black door, staring as it called her name over and over again. Other nights she was falling into the deep, unfathomable darkness only to be saved by the same man with raven's wings and a soothing voice.

Out of the possible options, she preferred the falling dreams. At least they gave a small reprieve by the end.

Unable to feign focus any longer, Rue packed up her things and headed back to the main hall of the manor. Delnan stood before the door with the same sour look pinching his wrinkled features as always.

"Finished already, Miss Umberwick?" he asked, despite already knowing the answer.

Rue didn't have it in her to grin and bear his attitude today, "Why don't you tell me, Delnan?" The butler opened his mouth to speak, brows knitting incredulously, but whatever he'd planned to say to her was cut short as Ryker stepped into the hall.

Rue's spine straightened instantly, pulse suddenly jumping. She hadn't seen Ryker since the day he'd found her standing in front of the black door and it looked as though something was taking a toll on him as well. His normally pristine dark hair was unkempt and hung over his brow. Deep, bruised circles sat beneath his eyes. Rue frowned sympathetically, he must have not been sleeping well either.

"Delnan, leave. I need to speak with Miss Umberwick alone for a moment."

Delnan gave a nervous bow and departed without another word.

"Are you feeling alright, Rue? Have you recovered since we last spoke?" Ryker asked, placing a hand on her shoulder, his thumb caressing soft circles over her blouse.

"I could ask you the same thing," she said plainly, taking a step closer to him.

"Ah, well, as they say, there is no rest for the wicked," he winked, repeating a phrase he often used, "I do hope you're feeling well enough for our...meeting this evening?"

A warm blush crept into her cheeks, "Yes, I'm still planning on it."

"Very good. I'll see you tonight, then." Ryker's hand moved from her arm to cup her chin, moonstone eyes piercing hers.

Rue's mouth went dry as her eyes flicked to his lips, remembering how dewy and soft they'd felt against hers. Her lips parted of their own accord, but before the gap between them could close, a maid burst through the double doors behind them, a tower of folded linens stacked high on her arms.

Reality crashed back in, breaking the trance Ryker always seemed to hold her in.

"I'm sorry, I should go. I've got some things to take care of before we..." Rue babbled, shaking her head, and pulled back from Ryker's grip. She could see irritation flare in his gaze—whether at her or from the interruption, she didn't know—but tried her best to ignore it as she grabbed her coat and quickly pushed through the front doors of the manor.

Rue sat up with a jolt, sending tepid bath water sloshing over the edge of the bathtub and onto the floor. In hindsight, it seemed like the combination of warm water and the soothing scents of her rose and lavender oils hadn't been the best idea when she was already so tired.

"Shit! Shit!" Rue cursed, hurriedly pushing herself out of the porcelain tub and reaching for the fluffy white towel that hung over the sink across from her. She wrapped the too-small towel around her ample figure, pinching the bottom closed with her other hand as she shuffled down the hall and back into her bedroom. How long had she been asleep? If the clock next to her bedside was correct, she'd been in the bath for over an hour.

Rue tore her nicest dress from the hanger in the back corner of her closet and tossed it onto her bed. Quickly drying her body, she wrapped the towel around her hair, hoping and praying for a miracle to tame her wild orange curls. She slid into her undergarments and plopped into the chair before the vanity, applying whatever creams and pastes she could to quell the heated flush in her cheeks. It wasn't much, but it would have to be enough.

Rue twisted the towel from her head, squeezing the remaining bits of water from her thick tresses. Applying a generous amount of hair oil to the frizzy nightmare of half-dried curls that stuck out in all directions, Rue quickly realized this was not going to be enough. The only thing that would make it look halfway decent was going to be an up-do.

She deftly twisted the strands together, trying to make it look as intentional as she could. Rue reached for the small box she kept on her vanity, digging through it for one of the hairpins her mother had left her.

"This will have to be enough." She held it out before her, letting the light catch it. The comb was made from abalone and gold, with an intricate pattern of leaves and vines swirling around the top. A large white pearl in the shape of a teardrop sat nestled in the center. Her mother had always worn it for special occasions, so it only felt fitting to wear it tonight.

Rue slid the comb into her hair, winding the teeth through her curls to secure it. She took a moment, looking at her reflection in the mirror with sudden trepidation, remembering the reflection that wasn't quite her looking back.

"That's better, at least." Rue gave herself an affirming nod and quickly dressed before rushing out of the house into the night.

Rue had forgone her usual walk and instead opted for a carriage in an effort to get to the manor as quickly as possible. She would still be late, but her tardiness still teetered precariously between being fashionably and offensively late. Her fingers managed to find their way to her teeth as Rue nervously picked and gnawed at her nails and skin. It was a less than lady-like habit, she knew, but unfortunately something she defaulted back to when the nerves became too much.

The carriage hadn't even come to a full stop before she was pushing through the doors and running as fast as she could in her heeled shoes. She slid through the open iron gates and ran through the courtyard to the towering double doors at the manor's entrance. Mercifully, the rain had stopped. Rue's heart hammered in her chest from the mix of adrenaline and physical activity she wasn't used to.

"Miss Umberwick! You're here." The maid she knew to be Beth called to her.

"Yes, so sorry I'm la—" She began but Beth had cut her off with a shake of her head.

"Never you mind that now, nothing we can do. The duke has been waiting for you." Beth reached for Rue's hand, fingers wrapping tightly around her wrist as she pulled. Rue said nothing, having no other option than to follow the plump maid as she was dragged to a second set of double doors that sat nestled under the twinned staircases at the back of the foyer.

Rue had never been in this room before. It was generally reserved for dinner parties with the other wealthy elite of Penrith, and she certainly did not fall into that category. The maid pushed open the door and gave a short curtsy before waving her inside. Rue could have sworn she saw an almost apologetic look on Beth's face before she absconded.

She stepped through the door and jumped when she heard it slam behind her. Rue squinted in the near darkness, waiting for her eyes to adjust to the difference in lighting from the rest of the manor, but didn't see anyone else in the room.

Rue moved into the room, and even after all the years she'd spent working here, she would never not be completely awed by the manor's opulence. Each of the walls were covered with frames of different sizes and shapes, spread out artfully over dark filigree patterned wallpaper, punctuated by an occasional decorative suit of armor or some other priceless art piece displayed in a sturdy glass case.

The room was rectangular, as though it was built around the table in its center. The table itself was carved with intricate floral detail and stained in a dark ebony hue. Matching chairs lined the edge of the mostly empty table, sitting flush against the wood. Soft candlelight and a gentle glow from a fireplace illuminated two place settings near the head of the table.

On the opposite wall from where she stood were two long windows. Framed by heavy, black upholstery drapes that were held back by braided gold ties, they stretched from the edge of the ceiling down to the floorboards. They faced the courtyard statuary that she walked through each morning, though it was too dark out to see much now.

Rue moved toward one of the table settings and reached to pull out one of the chairs when a door she hadn't noticed in the back corner of the room burst open. She nearly leapt out of her skin, hand flying to her chest in an attempt to calm her thumping heartbeat.

"My apologies, Rue. I didn't mean to frighten you." Ryker stepped into the room, unbuttoning the cuffs of his shirt and rolling the sleeves to his elbow. Rue swallowed nervously, mouth going dry. He looked so...casual. She suddenly felt overdressed but knew Ryker was far too polite to say anything about it.

"It's no trouble. I was just admiring your decor," she said. Ryker gave a small smirk and moved toward her. His long legs quickly consumed the gap between them, and before she could take another breath, he stood within a few inches of her. Rue prayed Ryker couldn't hear the sound of her heart beating wildly against the inside of her chest. Thankfully, he didn't seem to notice.

"You look beautiful," he complimented, teeth dragging over his lower lip as his eyes raked over her. She hadn't thought her dress to be anything fancy; A top embroidered with gold patterns and a long black skirt that brushed the floor, but it was clear Ryker approved of it. He stepped around her, pulling a chair out, and gestured for her to sit.

The chair was uncomfortable and her wide backside spilled over the edges of it. She shifted, trying as best she could to get under the low table, but her belly made it a little difficult to do so. Ryker took his place at the head of the table, his slim frame sliding into his seat with ease.

"Thank you for coming. I'm sure you have many other places you could be tonight, but I appreciate you taking the time to spend the evening with me," Ryker said, holding up his glass without even looking whether or not someone was behind him to fill it.

Rue smiled and nodded. "You're very welcome. I am honored you asked me to come," she replied, grateful he hadn't mentioned her tardiness. Another servant she'd never seen before came through the door behind Ryker and poured the amber liquor she knew he favored to the brim of the glass. Ryker nodded his thanks, and the servant disappeared again.

"Would you like a drink, Rue? I have a large collection of wines and spirits you're more than welcome to sample," he asked, turning slightly in his chair, sipping on his own glass.

"Just water should be fine for me, thank you. I have a busy day tomorrow."

"Of course." With that, Ryker tapped two fingers on the table, and like a well-oiled machine, another servant appeared, this time holding a carafe of iced water instead. He filled Rue's glass and left the rest next to her. She gave a grateful smile before the servant nodded and left once again.

They both sat in a stunted, awkward silence for a moment too long before Ryker broke the tension with a hiss coming from his lips as he took another long drink.

"You're nervous," he stated. It was painfully obvious he was correct, but even so, to be called out so plainly on it made her stomach clench with embarrassment.

"I'm sorry, it's just that I don't think I've ever dined so formally," Rue admitted.

"It's nothing formal, Rue. It's just you and I here. The servants will just bring food and refreshments and leave us be," Ryker assured her, leaning forward on his elbows. A grin curled at the corners of his lips, making something in Rue's stomach drop. It was almost predatory, the way he looked at her.

Ryker's eyes were still tired and bloodshot, the dark circles under them seemed worse now than before. It was clear something was wrong, but Rue kept those thoughts to herself, continuing instead to pick at her cuticles beneath the table where he couldn't see.

"I've selected a special menu just for you," Ryker mused, turning his empty glass in a circle on the tabletop, the droplets of condensation forming a wet ring on the wood. Rue internally cringed and wanted to say something about ruining the table, but it was clear Ryker either didn't notice or didn't care.

"Thank you. That was very thoughtful of you." Rue busied her mouth with the glass of water. This was such a far cry from the easy-flowing conversations she normally had with the duke. Rue worried her bottom lip between her teeth and glanced back at his glass. How many had he downed before she showed up? Was he also nervous, and this was just his way of coping?

Rue cleared her throat and tried her best to change the tone between them but was saved by the sound of the door opening once again. She breathed a soft sigh of relief and let her shoulders slump a little now that Ryker's attention wasn't so focused on her.

"The first course, madam." A tall man with a large port wine stain over his face placed a plate before her, covered in a metal cloche. The scent that wafted out from under it was divine. Rue's stomach rumbled, making her realize much too late that, once again, she hadn't eaten much all day. The man removed the lid, revealing a portion of some kind of meat with a thick brown sauce. The portion was barely befitting a child. Before she could open her mouth to thank him, he'd already disappeared.

"Wow, this looks..." Rue swallowed, trying not to let her disappointment at the meager morsel shine through, "delicious." The same plate sat before Ryker, but he was much more interested in the refilled glass in his hand.

"I do hope it's to your liking," he said, finally picking up a fork and taking a bite. Rue reached for the napkin in her lap and dabbed what remained of the sauce from her lip, nodding.

"Yes, it's amazing. I don't think I've ever tasted even half of these flavors before," she admitted.

"I wanted only the best for you, Ruby."

The sound of her full name on his lips made her appetite vanish immediately. He never called her that. Ryker's eyes were on her — glazed over as they were — like a hawk.

She set her fork down and reached for the glass of water at her side, hoping it would disguise the clearly uncomfortable look on her face. If he wasn't before, he was definitely drunk now after downing at least three glasses of liquor since they sat down and who knew how many he may have had before she even arrived.

They sat in stilted silence. Rue continued picking at pieces of her meal, pushing things around on her plate more than anything. Ryker seemed to have noticed and let out a groan that almost sounded like a growl before dropping his fork onto the plate with a loud clang.

"Is there something wrong?" he asked bluntly, irritation laced his voice with eyes still trained on her like a predator watching his prey.

"N-no, I'm just not feeling well suddenly..." she replied quietly.

"Perhaps we should cut this short then." Ryker stood from his chair, legs scraping against the wooden floor. Alarm bells rang in her mind. Something was very wrong here. More than just his obvious inebriation.

Ryker slammed his hand down on the table in front of her, caging her in before he slid a finger under her chin, tipping her head up to face him. His normally beautiful and clear eyes looked hazy and distant.

"Are you afraid of me?" All traces of sweetness left his voice. Rue felt a cold chill run down her spine.

"No."

"Then why do you deny me?"

"Ryker, I didn't—"

He tilted her head back and brushed his thumb over her lower lip, dragging it down. Rue's pulse quickened, but she kept silent as his eyes raked over her.

"Before you give me any excuses, let me tell you this, I do not give up so easily. I will win this little game of cat and mouse you play with me, Ruby Umberwick. Trust and believe." He released her chin and stepped away, dragging a hand through his already disheveled hair and left the dining room without another word. Rue watched his retreating back, eyes wide with disbelief.

The fork in her hand dropped down onto the plate, startling her. What just happened? Rue thought back to earlier that day, trying to come up with some kind of explanation for his behavior. Did he perceive her pulling away from him in the foyer this afternoon as a slight or rejection? She was sure she wouldn't have the answer to that question no matter how long she sat there and thought about it.

Pulling the napkin from her lap and dabbing her lips, Rue threw the cloth over her plate and rose from the table.

"Thank you for the meal," she said quietly, unsure if anyone was even listening.

CHAPTER EIGHT

FOLLOWING THE DISASTROUS DINNER date, Rue did everything she could to avoid the duke. Coming into the library earlier and leaving later took its toll on her, but it was a better alternative to facing him again after their awkward exchange. On the bright side, the extended hours meant more time to dedicate to searching the shelves for more information, though it felt meaningless. With such a massive collection, she would need years to pore through each one of the texts with only minimal hope of coming across something useful.

Today was no different; she'd left her home before the sun had even crested over the horizon. An endless stream of yawns carried with her as she trudged sluggishly through the foggy, early morning streets of Penrith. Rue had all but given up on sleeping soundly. The dreams that plagued her only grew worse with each passing night.

Cyclical nightmares repeated yet gave no answers. Only creating an ever-growing list of more questions instead. Occasionally, the mystery man's voice would cut through the terror. Only on those nights did she find peace in her slumber, but unfortunately for her, those were few and far between.

Rue pushed open the manor's heavy iron gate. The squeal of its rusted and corroded hinges seemed louder in the somber quiet of the early morning. The sound set her teeth on edge.

A dense fog rolled through the courtyard statuary, curling around her battered brown boots in a gentle caress as she walked. Morning dew clung to the closed eyelids of the weeping statues, adding to their already dark tear streaks.

Despite the permanent exhaustion that clung to her, Rue grew to appreciate the early mornings. She enjoyed the quiet, the slow rise of the sun behind her, and the soft cawing of ravens. Since that night at the manor, it seemed at least one raven was constantly at her heels, becoming another odd sense of comfort for her in these even odder times.

Rue slowed to a halt, taking one last moment to appreciate the scenery before entering the double doors of the manor. Crumbling gargoyles lined the perimeter of the roof, spouting water from their mischievous mouths, while moss and vine covered grotesques sat along the base, watchfully observing any visitors that came through. The duke's manor was oddly morose in its outer decor, but Rue still found it beautiful none-the-less.

Taking the wide but short set of steps up to the double doors, Rue let herself in as she always had. She hadn't been hanging her coat by the door as she did before, not wanting the garment to betray her presence to the duke. Instead, she went directly into one of the passageways and headed straight down to the library.

She slid the door shut behind her, doing her best to avoid making too much unnecessary noise, when she saw the foreboding black envelope atop her desk. It didn't have a name on it, but she knew who had left it. She flipped it over and slid a finger under the edge of the flap, breaking the wax seal. Familiar handwriting greeted her as she unfurled the parchment inside.

Rue,

Please meet me in my study after you read this. I'll be waiting for you.
-R.A.

Rue's hand shook as she read over the note several more times. Trying to find any hidden meaning in his message, but with so little to go on, she found nothing. Had Ryker learned about Jasper? About the book? Or was it about what had happened at their last meeting? The last thing she wanted to do right now was face him — especially if this meeting had anything to do with the book or her brother — but if she wanted to avoid suspicion, the choice was already made for her.

The sun had fully risen, sending threads of buttery golden light through stained glass window panes, painting the white marble floors of the foyer with a kaleidoscope of color. Sounds of the early morning bustle in the manor sang behind every door she passed. Rue ascended the steps of the westward staircase, dread sinking lower and lower into her gut with every step. The west corridor was mostly dark, with only a few low-burning oil lamps to light her way.

Rue tried not to think about the dark and how it reminded her of those dreams, but with her nerves on edge, it was hard to think of little else. She had been in Ryker's office plenty of times before when she was still acting solely as his personal assistant, but this time was different.

Walking in a daze, Rue stopped short when she thought she saw something lurking from the corner of her eye. "Hello?" she called softly. She was sure it was just an unhelpful combination of anxiety and exhaustion, twisting things and making her believe something was there when it wasn't.

Rue stood in the corridor for several long minutes, waiting for something to move again. Her eyes darted around the walls, to the floor, and back up to the ceiling, watching for any small movements. She breathed a sigh of relief when she saw nothing. Just her mind playing tricks on her once again.

Continuing down the next long corridor toward the office, Rue picked up the pace of her steps. This hallway was even darker than the last, making her heart race in her chest. Although she didn't see anything move when she stopped, she was not entirely convinced something wasn't there. She wrapped her hand snugly around the pendant that rested against her collarbone, immediately feeling a sense of calm wash over her.

She'd almost reached her destination when she felt a puff of hot breath at the back of her neck. The sensation sent a chill skittering down her spine. Rue stopped again, her other hand clapped against the back of her neck as she turned on her heel to look behind her.

"I am in no mood for jokes! Whoever's out there had better come out right now!" Her voice was no longer soft and frightened. Now, she was just angry. This had to be someone playing a trick on her. Perhaps one of the younger servant girls following her down the dark halls hoping to spook her.

Rue continued to search the darkened corners of the hall with squinted eyes behind her glasses. The feeling of anxious unease was swiftly replaced by irritation. A door opened behind her, snapping her neck in the opposite direction, hoping to catch the culprit of these childish games.

"What's all the commotion out here?" Ryker stepped out of his office. Rue stared at him, dumbfounded for a moment before an embarrassed blush crossed her cheeks. Great. Now she'd made a fool of herself on top of everything.

"Nothing. I just thought..." She trailed off, looking behind her once again before shaking her head, "It's nothing. I'm sorry. You wanted to see me?"

"If you wouldn't mind." Ryker took a step back, gesturing for her to enter the open office door. Rue entered with tentative steps, teetering between sitting down and hearing him out or running back down the stairs, never to be seen again.

As easy as the latter option would be, she had no real choice and took a seat in one of the oversized chairs before Ryker's desk. The decor of his office was minimal compared to the rest of the house. A few framed documents along the walls and a single shelf with only a handful of boring business-type books in a corner were the only things that stood out. Ryker's desk, however, was littered with papers and ledgers. Another pile of what she assumed were more ledgers and important documents sat on the floor in a haphazard stack.

Ryker slid between her and the desk and leaned back on his hands. Rue slowly raised her head, meeting his gaze for the first time since she'd entered the office. The bags under his eyes were still there but weren't nearly as dark as they had been previously. His hair was back in its usual perfect style, clothes crisp and fresh from the laundress without a single thread out of place.

"I called you here," he paused, seeming to carefully choose his words before speaking, "Because I wanted to apologize for how rudely I behaved the other night. It was very unbecoming of me."

Rue blinked slowly. Well, that was definitely not what she thought he was going to say.

"Things have been extremely overwhelming with the upcoming annual ball. The musicians I'd hired to perform have backed out at the worst possible time, and finding a replacement this close to the event is proving more difficult than I would have hoped. However, this is not an excuse, merely an explanation."

The annual masquerade ball was something the Ashworth family had done for generations. One night every year, the manor was opened to anyone and everyone on the isle, regardless of status or station. A single night of the year for the duke to show his appreciation to the people who kept his family in power for centuries. The Ashworth family had always been a benevolent family, helping the common folk of the isle when they needed it, and so the people of Penrith never had any qualms with the way they ruled over them.

Rue nodded in understanding. Her tongue went dry and felt like sandpaper against the roof of her mouth. Sure, it made sense that he would be busy and overwhelmed with the preparations, but a nagging feeling inside her knew there was more.

"Again, it doesn't excuse my behavior. You didn't deserve the ire I gave you, and it was extremely inappropriate of me to drink as much as I did." He cleared his throat at the mention of alcohol, reaching behind him for the water pitcher and two glasses. He filled both to the top, offering a glass to Rue. She tried to say thank you, but only her lips moved without the words to accompany.

Ryker downed the entire glass just as easily as he had knocked back the glass of liquor before. She watched as his Adam's apple worked up and down his throat as he drank. Rue averted her gaze, becoming suddenly fascinated with the crystal glass in her hand instead.

"Rue..." Ryker's voice was soft, almost desperate. Rue slowly pulled her eyes from the cup and looked up at the duke. He was so incredibly beautiful. Beautiful in the same way an object in a glass case would be considered beautiful. Captivating but untouchable.

"You have become someone of great importance to me. More than just the title you hold under my employ." Ryker set his glass on the desk behind him and moved closer to her, "When you're near, I can't seem to control myself." His hands settled on the armrests of the chair, caging her in.

Rue lifted her head, meeting his eyes. Hunger like never before radiated from him, making her pulse quicken and her stomach clench. Rue had taken lovers in the past — never anything long-term — but no one had ever looked at her like this.

Ryker moved his hand up the arm of the chair, his fingers brushing against her arm and blocking her in further. He leaned in, swallowing what little space was left between them. His breath brushed her ear as he spoke, "Please don't make me beg."

The words dripped like honey from his lips, making the small hairs on her arms rise. Rue's eyes closed as a sudden rush of need coursed through her body. She knew what he was asking.

"But Ryker, what if someone—" she tried, but a scrape of his teeth against her earlobe cut her off before she could complete the thought. And then it was gone.

"No one is here but you and I, Rue." Ryker's lips moved down her neck and over the small bit of her clavicle that was exposed. Rue closed her eyes, unable to argue when his kisses were so enticing. She pressed her hands against his chest, half-heartedly pushing him away, but Ryker didn't budge.

With the quickness of a lightning strike, his hands moved from the chair to her wrists. His long, delicate fingers encircled them so tenderly. He nipped at her jaw, pressing soft kisses against the tiny hurt.

"I'll only ask once. Please?" His voice was rough against her skin, breath hot as he spoke.

Rue was quiet for a moment longer as he continued trying to convince her to submit. Ryker pinned her hands back down to the arms of the chair, trapping her wrists against the plush upholstery.

"Y-yes." Her voice broke. "Yes," she said again with more certainty.

"That's a good girl."

And with those four simple words, Rue melted in his grasp.

Ryker didn't hesitate. He'd gotten the permission he so desperately desired and needed no further coaxing. His lips moved from her throat to her mouth. This kiss was not like the others they had shared before, but something more. Something deeper.

The duke's tongue swiped across the seam of her lips before pressing past them. Not asking permission, instead giving warning. Rue let out a soft moan and screwed her eyes shut. His kiss tasted smoky yet sweet. The scent of his spiced cologne overwhelmed her senses, leaving her mind empty of everything but him. Every touch was electrifying, and she longed for more.

Ryker's hands held her firmly in place, even as she tried to move against him. She wanted to touch him desperately, to feel his bare skin against hers. To rip open the buttons of his pristine white shirt and feel his heartbeat against her hand.

When he finally pulled away, breathless, a grin split his lips open, exposing rows of perfect white teeth.

"Absolutely delectable," he muttered, pushing a knee between hers and parting her thighs. Rue's entire face burned. She didn't need a mirror to know she must have been beet red to the tips of her ears. To hear him talk about her this way... It was downright sinful.

"Ryker—" she said his name but quickly forgot why as he sank to his knees before her, pushing the heavy skirt of her dress up and out of his way. With her hands free, Rue sunk her teeth into her knuckle, trying to keep quiet.

Ryker's hands ran up and down her thighs, over her long stockings, "You don't have to keep quiet. In fact, I want to hear you." He pressed a soft kiss to the top of her stocking, where the fabric ended and her skin began.

Rue hesitantly removed her hand from her teeth, doing as she was told.

"Good girl," he said again. The words made her thighs clench. Ryker smirked. He knew exactly what he was doing. The prick.

Ryker pushed her thighs open with little grace and hooked her legs over each arm of the chair. Rue's face deepened even more with the way she was now exposed to him. At least her panties left something to the imagination.

Ryker licked his lips and swiped a single digit over the already damp satin of her panties, circling slowly over her clit. Rue's head fell back, and her body jerked as a shock of pleasure ran through her, lips parting in a soft moan once again.

"Beautiful," he mused — mostly to himself — hooking the same finger into the gusset of her panties and tugging them aside. Rue's head shot back up, a protest ready on her tongue, but Ryker's lips on her center had that notion fading before it was fully formed.

His tongue followed the kiss, lapping at her slowly. His hands held her thick thighs open on either side of his head as he devoured her. Rue could do nothing but submit, heavy breaths and moans falling from her lips. Heat swirled low in her belly, a fire igniting within her as Ryker's tongue swirled over her clit, only stopping to suck the small bud between his lips every so often.

"I'm c-close..." she whispered, digging her fingers into the chair to stop herself from clapping a hand over her mouth as more, louder moans and whimpers filled the room. Ryker took her admission as a challenge, his pace going from agonizingly slow to fast and hard. Rue's thighs shook under his hands, but he held her like a vise, not allowing her to move a single inch as he continued, dragging her ever closer to the edge.

"O-oh, oh gods!" she cried out, her entire body shaking now as the first wave of her climax crested over her. Ryker did not stop. In fact, it seemed her cries only made him more ravenous. His fingers dug into her skin, leaving red welts in their wake as he lapped and sucked and kissed her core. Rue's back arched, and her fingernails scraped for purchase on the velvety chair as she cried out once more.

Ryker's tongue finally slowed, and he pressed one last kiss against her clit. He sat back on his heels, hands still clutching her thighs. Rue's chest heaved as she tried to catch her breath, coming down from the high of her orgasm.

She lifted her head, shyly meeting his gaze. Ryker's eyes were still full of that hunger she'd seen in him before as he licked the last drops of her arousal from his lips.

Ryker stood, dabbing at his chin and neck with a handkerchief he'd pulled from his breast pocket as though he'd just finished an evening meal. Rue quickly pulled her legs back down from the armrests, tossing her skirt back over her thighs.

Ryker chuckled darkly, "Oh I hope you don't think I'm finished with you just yet."

CHAPTER NINE

RYKER TORE OFF HIS vest and shirt, tossing them aside without care. His lips crashed into hers. Rue immediately matched his urgency, throwing caution to the wind as she plunged her hands into his perfect hair. She tugged gently, and Ryker groaned softly as she did. Finally, she had something to use against him.

Rue tugged again, pulling him impossibly closer. Her still-clothed chest met his bare one, heat coming in waves from his skin. The heat between them began to rise, sending beads of sweat dripping down the back of her neck.

Ryker's hands moved to her waist, tugging at her dress. "Off," he demanded against her lips. Rue didn't need to be told twice. She stood and spun around for him, wordlessly asking for his help with the long row of buttons running down the back of her dress. Instead of slowly unhooking each button, Ryker's impatient hands tore through the stitches, sending a mass of buttons flying in all directions around the room.

Rue gasped. Well, it was a good thing this dress wasn't one of her favorites. Ryker spun her to face him again. Her concern for the dress instantly vanished as he tugged the garment up and off of her. Static electricity clung to her hair, zapping her face and shoulders.

"Oops," she let out a girlish giggle that was more nerves than humor. Rue was not prudish, but having Ryker's eyes and hands on her body was something else entirely. She had never been a thin woman, her body was soft with ample curves along with a protruding belly. While she'd never considered herself unattractive, she couldn't help but think of how Ryker might see her now with every inch of her body on display.

Her dress joined his shirt in a heap on a forgotten corner of the floor, leaving her standing before Ryker in nothing but a nearly translucent slip that clung to every dip and curve of her body. Heat painted her cheeks once again. She took her bottom lip between her teeth nervously. But Ryker's stare as it raked her body was ravenous. Moonstone eyes drank her in like a fine wine. Slow and savoring.

Their heated moment had begun to simmer, but the fire still remained. Ryker moved to her, one arm wrapping around her waist again, pulling her body to him. His lips latched to her throat once more. Rue closed her eyes, holding onto his arms to steady herself as he lavished her. Ryker's other hand moved to her breast, caressing her softly through the thin fabric of her slip. Her nipple pebbled beneath his touch, the sensation nearly torturous.

Rue let the thin straps of her slip fall, baring her chest to him. Her breasts were modest in comparison to other, more voluminous curves of her body but full enough to perfectly fit against Ryker's palm. She sighed softly as he teased her, alternating between pinching and rolling her hardened bud between his fingers.

His lips and tongue were still affixed to her neck and jaw. With his hips pressed into hers, Rue was suddenly very aware of how she was affecting him. She let out a sound that was somewhere between a moan and a gasp, finding herself surprised at the size of him. Ryker let out a dark chuckle against her neck.

"Are you intimidated?" he asked.

"N-no. Not at all."

"You don't sound convinced." Ryker rolled his hips against hers again, pulling another small moan from her throat. His hand slid from her breast to her thighs, coaxing them apart with a nudge. Rue opened easily for him, wanting anything and everything he was willing to give.

Expert fingers stroked over her lips, dipping in and caressing her. Rue wrapped both arms around his neck, spreading her thighs more for him.

"That's good. You're so good for me, Rue," he whispered against her neck, hot breath sending a shiver over her. His fingers pushed inside, slowly stretching her. Rue let out a soft, affirming groan, rolling her hips slowly against his hand as she adjusted to the size. Ryker's long fingers stroked her deeply in all the right places. Unable to help herself, she fisted a hand in his hair, tugging harder than before.

"P-please." Rue found herself pleading without meaning to. Ryker was more than happy to oblige as he began thrusting his fingers in and out of her, fingertips still curling against the most sensitive parts of her as he did. Rue's breath came in short, hard bursts, moans twining with each one. She could feel the tell-tale swell in her abdomen again; she was so close already.

Before the wave of pleasure could fully overtake her, Ryker pulled his fingers back, making her whine at the sudden loss. Ryker smirked as if the sound of her frustration was amusing to him.

"The only way I'm letting you come is with me buried inside of you." His tongue darted out, swiping some of her arousal from his fingers, "You want that, don't you?"

She wanted that.

Gods, did she want that.

Rue couldn't trust herself to form something coherent, nodding fervently instead. His words shot directly to her core, making the flame inside her burn brighter than ever. Ryker moved decisively, stepping behind her. He placed a hand at the back of her head, gently pushing her forward.

"Bend over the desk."

Rue did as she was told, sliding her hands gingerly between the stacks of papers and notebooks to hold herself steady. Ryker's hands brushed down her spine, making goose flesh rise on her skin in their wake.

"Spread your legs."

His words were not suggestions but commands, and Rue blindly followed. Ryker pushed her slip up and over her rear before tugging her panties down her thighs, letting them fall to the floor where they pooled at her ankles. Rue closed her eyes, leaning her head forward onto the desk, the anticipation killing her.

"This is your last chance to change your mind, dove," he cooed with a hand stroking over her backside tenderly.

"I'm ready. I'm sure," she told him, voice low and wanting.

Ryker didn't hesitate after that. One hand gripped her hip, holding her still while the other guided his length into her. Rue's fingers curled against the wood of the desk, nails raking a trail over the surface. He didn't bother taking anything slowly. His hips snapped hard against her plush backside, each thrust pulling a string of incoherent moans and obscenities from her lips.

Both of Ryker's hands held her hips now, pulling her back to meet each of his thrusts. She was already so sensitive from his fingers and tongue earlier; she knew she wouldn't last long. It was clear Ryker also knew this as his movement began picking up pace to a brutal speed.

"Ryker!" she called out in warning, but he did not stop, only angled himself to hit her where it counted. Rue arched into the desk with a sharp gasp, nearly biting her tongue at the sudden explosion of nearly overwhelming pleasure. Her stomach tied in knots as she held out for as long as she possibly could.

"That's right, dove. Come for me." Ryker demanded between heavy breaths, squeezing her delicate skin hard enough to bruise. Rue began to move her hips back against his, taking what she wanted.

In an instant, the flame in her seemed to explode into a raging inferno. She reached forward, gripping the edge of the desk, doing her best to hold on while he fucked her relentlessly. Rue was falling over the edge and a supernova of pleasure was bursting through her. Her thighs shook as her orgasm washed over her. Ryker pulled out and quickly followed behind, spilling himself over her ass and down the back of her legs.

He slumped forward over her, pressing exhausted kisses to her shoulders and spine. Rue lay there, unable to move and trying to catch her breath.

"You were incredible. Such a good girl for me," he muttered against her skin, sending shivers down her spine once more.

They stayed like that for a moment, allowing the heat of the moment to inevitably gutter and die out. Ryker straightened and collected his shirt from where he'd thrown it, pulling it back on expressionlessly. After the hazy cloud of lust had subsided, the atmosphere between them felt...off. Like he'd gotten what he wanted and no longer had the need to keep up an appearance.

Rue pushed those thoughts away and collected her ruined dress from the floor. A deep frown tugged at her mouth when she realized she would have to figure out a way to secure it without the buttons. It wasn't like she could just leave and walk the streets of Penrith in nothing but a thin slip.

"Sorry about your dress. I'll have one of the staff bring you something to wear home," he told her dismissively, buttoning his own shirt back up. Rue nodded, sliding the ruined garment back over her head, feeling oddly exposed even after all they had done.

Without another word, Ryker left the office, leaving her alone with her thoughts. The stickiness at the back of her legs made sitting uncomfortable, so instead, she stood, pacing back and forth as the first bits of regret began to flood her.

Rue didn't see Ryker again after he'd left. A maid came to her instead, presenting her with one of the plain dresses they'd worn as a uniform. The maid in question asked no questions, but Rue could tell by the judging look on her face that she knew exactly what had transpired.

Rue used her already ruined dress to clean herself up and slid the clean garment on before making a quick exit out of the manor. There was no way she was going back to the library after that.

As she walked, sore and exhausted, she couldn't help the nagging feeling that settled deep in her gut. Of course, she had dreamed of such a moment with the duke over the years she had worked for him, but this... something about it didn't feel right. Rue somehow felt as though something was taken from her despite the fact that she'd been more than willing.

She wrapped her arms around her chest in a self-soothing gesture, far away eyes trained on the murky puddles under her feet as she walked. The cold water seeping into her boots and drenching her stockings didn't even phase her.

Despite the busy mid-afternoon, sounds of the city around her were muted, coming to her as though her head was underwater. When she finally arrived home, Rue locked the door behind her and checked it once again before immediately drawing herself a bath. She felt unclean. Unclean in a way that even the scalding water couldn't wash away.

Rue slowly slid into the water, not even blanching when the heat scalded her skin. Her eyes were still hazy and unfocused, trapped in an unending cycle of unpleasant thoughts. She wrapped her fingers around the pendant at her throat, clutching it tightly against her palm, thumb tracing patterns around the citrine stone.

Letting out a deep breath and closing her eyes, she plunged her head under the water. The world around her faded away as she lay flat against the bottom of the large tub. Her hair floated around her, its ends caressing her skin so softly, reminding her of the ways her mother would soothe her as a child when she had a bad day.

When her lungs burned, begging for breath, Rue finally surfaced. Sounds of the world rushing back in all at once. She wiped her eyes and pushed her hair back from her face, taking a moment to refocus.

Not for the first time, Rue wished she knew where Jasper had gone. She couldn't fully explain to him what happened, but even having him around would have been a much needed comfort.

Rue sat in the tub until the water went cold and the skin on her fingers wrinkled. Finally, she convinced herself to rise from the water and sighed when she saw the mess she'd made on the floor.

"What's one more mess today," she groaned under her breath as she stepped out of the tub. The water soaked into her curls drenched the floor even more and Rue couldn't find it in herself to really care all that much. It was just water. It would dry and the floor would go back to normal. Like it had never even happened.

She wished she could say the same for some of the other things that she'd done. That given time, it would go back to normal. Everything would be as it once was, but she knew that wasn't an option.

What happened had happened.

There was no going back now.

After a halfhearted attempt at drying her hair and dressing in her nightgown, Rue climbed into bed despite the last bits of sun that still lingered in the sky. She was too physically and emotionally exhausted to do much else with her day, and her bed seemed like the perfect escape from the rampant thoughts that still ran on a loop in her mind.

Rue lay curled on her side, staring out the uncovered sliver of her window and watched the sun set. As it sank, dipping down below the horizon, it painted the sky with a myriad of reds, oranges, and purples. Deeper, more saturated colors than the soft pastel hues of the sunrise. She pulled her fluffy down comforter under her chin, letting her lack of glasses blur the colors together in a fuzzy mural.

Tomorrow would be better.

Tomorrow would be different, she told herself, pushing the blame for her heightened emotions on as many external and out-of-reach factors as she could. Control was slipping through her fingers, taking everything else along with it. The peaceful, almost monotonous life she'd been living up to this point was being upended into nothing but chaos. Rue never thought she would wish for a boring life, but it was sounding better and better by the moment.

The sun had fully vanished, bathing the sky in an inky darkness that blended in with the heavy curtains over her window. The day was over, and there wasn't anything she could do now. She would sleep — hopefully without any more dreams — and wake up in the morning before sunrise just like before, and she would continue her work like nothing ever happened.

She hoped it would be that simple. Her eyelids grew too heavy to keep open, each blink leading to the monumental task of reopening her eyes. Not having the strength to keep fighting, she let them slowly drift closed, falling into sleep's embrace once more.

CHAPTER TEN

Unfortunately, sleep brought no reprieve.

Again, Rue stood in that same empty, dark room. But unlike the last time, the room was different. The iron door was no longer there, instead replaced with a person. A person she could only see from behind, but even so, they bore a striking resemblance to herself. Rue took a tentative step forward, pulling her nightgown up above her ankles so as not to drag it through whatever substance coated the floor and stuck to her bare feet.

This doppelganger sat crouched on the floor before her, hands clawing into something Rue couldn't quite make out from where she stood. She took another step forward, angling her head to look around the other's shoulder to get a better look.

It looked like a patch of wooden flooring, disconnected and standing out against the dark. A single section removed from where the boards had originally sat, now transported here to her nightmare abyss. The doppelganger's hands frantically dug into those floorboards, ripping them out and tossing them with a splash into the thick liquid that covered the floor.

Rue took another step forward. She craned her neck, trying to see exactly what was under the destroyed floorboards that this other version of herself was so eager to get to.

But before she could make it out, the doppelganger's head snapped toward Rue. She let out a horrified gasp and covered her mouth. The face before her matched her own but was so, so wrong. The other's eyes were fully swallowed by a thick, umbral ichor — that almost looked like candle wax — dripping from the edges of her lower eyelids and down her cheeks like tears.

Rue recoiled slightly as she stared into the profane reflection of her own face. Slowly, she reached out to the mirror image in front of her, but before she could make contact with the doppelganger, its mouth contorted into an ear-splitting scream.

Rue clapped her hands over her ears and dropped to her knees. Fiery pain coursed through her entire body. The scream was deafening, her eardrums feeling as though they were about to burst. The doppelganger spun and crawled toward her on all four limbs like a rabid animal, mouth still hanging open. Its hands were covered with the same inky black liquid as its face.

The dark substance dripped from its fingers and down its arms. Rue felt the viscous liquid coat her skin as the thing's icy hands gripped her face. The scream quieted and faded into nothingness, leaving behind a sudden and disturbing silence that left her ears ringing as it hung in the air between them.

"What are you?" Rue whispered, slowly moving her hands away from her ears.

The doppelganger didn't answer her right away, only stared with those haunted black eyes that seemed to look through her. Rue felt the substance from its hands dripping down her neck and onto her night clothes. The room plummeted into an unbearable icy cold as the other leaned in, breath coming out in a plume as she spoke,

"It's calling to you, Ruby. From under the floorboards."

Rue opened her mouth to speak, wanting to ask what exactly was calling to her, but before she could utter a single word, she was thrust back into reality.

A scream died on her lips as she returned to the waking world.

Rue's hands immediately went to her face, feeling for any signs of lingering residue that had coated her face in the dream. She breathed a small, relieved sigh when she found none. Her entire body was covered in a layer of sticky sweat, leaving her nightgown nearly adhered to her like a second skin.

She was safe.

In her bed.

She pulled herself fully upright and tried to comb her fingers through her matted and tangled hair. A dark laugh bubbled up from her chest like she found it silly how her life could go from being perfect to a living hell so quickly.

Everything she ever wanted had suddenly been burned away with the strike of just one match. One small and seemingly insignificant action had pushed her down the path of a living nightmare at alarming speed. Nothing was the way she'd hoped it would be. There were so many more questions than answers. Even sleep had stopped offering her an escape.

How wonderful, she thought.

Rue laughed again, the sound quickly morphing into a sob.

There was no humor in the strangled sound she made.

After Rue had spent her next few hours crying her eyes dry and mourning the life she thought she'd had, she forced herself up and out of bed. The sky outside was still dark. She couldn't have been asleep for more than a handful of hours.

Quickly dressing and tossing on a dark cloak, Rue decided that she was done waiting for Jasper to come back. She was done waiting for things to fall into her lap. She would go find him on her own. There were only a few places he could be, but the most likely of which was Fool's Hope. The thought of going to the thieves' town on her own in the middle of the night was frightening, but after all she'd experienced in the last month, what could possibly be worse?

Rue was relieved to see that despite the late hour, carriages were still out and ready for a fare. Tossing the driver a bag of coins and giving her destination, she climbed into the back and closed the door before he could ask anything else.

The ride to Fool's Hope wasn't a long one, but the road into the town hadn't been repaved in who knew how long, making her jostle about in the back of the carriage as the wheels rolled over the cragged and broken streets.

The boundary between Penrith proper and Fool's Hope was marked by a thickening tree line. A forest that had no name but had been dubbed 'The Wicked Hollow' cut a line between the two. The idea of walking through those trees had once scared her, but Rue was finding that now, little truly scared her anymore.

She leaned her head against the small window, keeping her face buried in the hood of her cloak. Watching the stacked buildings of the city fade as they neared the Hollow. The large expanse of woods that always felt like some kind of barrier between Penrith and another world. There was only a single dirt road through the Hollow. Thick trunks of trees were illuminated by slivers of pale moonlight that poured through the sparse autumn leaves.

The carriage came to an abrupt stop, hurling her forward onto the bench across from where she sat, "That was completely unnecessary," she grumbled under her breath, pushing herself up.

"Your stop, Madam," the man called gruffly, turning his head and spitting into the dirt. "Town's just ahead there," he indicated with a jerk of his chin.

Rue trudged forward without looking back, holding her cloak tightly to her in a feeble attempt to cut the biting cold of the wind that whipped around her. At least — by some small miracle — it wasn't raining tonight.

It was a bit of a walk to the gates of the town itself, but determination pumped through her veins, spurring her forward. She had no idea where she would find Jasper here, but she was sure his vibrant orange hair would stick out like a sore thumb.

Rue stopped before a broken and bent sign with fading paint that indicated she'd made it to the right place. She steadied herself with a deep breath and kept her head low as she walked through tall, open wooden gates.

The first thing she noticed was the smell.

Gods, what was that smell?

It reminded her of the pungent sulfur smell of Fia's shop, but infinitely worse. She pulled her cloak up over her nose and pressed on. Fool's Hope looked a lot like Penrith in terms of architecture, except everything looked as though she was peering through a dirty brown lens.

Rue walked through the streets, cobblestones rough and uneven under the heels of her boots. From a building behind her, the shouts of men arguing and something about cheating could be heard. Probably some card game with a hefty sum on the line, if she had to guess.

Rue kept moving, picking up her pace. From the next alleyway she passed, sounds of pleasured grunts and soft moans echoed into the night air. A lady of the night plying her trade for the promise of a few coins. Rue felt an embarrassed blush creep into her cheeks at the thought of doing something like that somewhere so open. She quickly moved on.

From the corner of her eye, Rue could see a dim, warm light glowing against a stone wall at the end of the long strip of broken road she was on. She ran toward it, hoping it was some kind of tavern where most of the miscreants of this town spent their nights, drowning in booze and...whatever else it was that people did here.

A much nicer sign than the one she'd passed at the gate hung over the door and read "The Devil's Due".

"Might as well start here," she mumbled and pushed the door open with her shoulder. The sounds of breaking glass, rowdy patrons, and several different conversations hit her all at once. It was so overwhelming she had to hold onto the wall to keep herself from running back out again. Rue had always been more suited to quiet places, and something like this was so far out of her depth, she could hardly breathe.

He had to be here. This was the perfect place to casually overhear a conversation without making it obvious. Rue carefully stepped between the rows of tables, narrowly avoiding a slosh of ale that a hefty drunk man launched from his tankard as he animatedly swung his arms about.

Another group of men sat with their heads inclined in a circle towards one another, speaking in hushed tones. They eyed her with menacing looks of distrust as she passed by. She quickly snapped her head away from them and kept moving.

Rue was surprised to see a woman behind the bar. She looked to be around Rue's age and stood tall with a similarly curvy frame. Her skin was a deep brown that glowed beautifully in the amber light of the lanterns around the walls. She had long dark locs that were adorned with beads and golden rings. Her décolletage was on full display, spilling out of her white top, leaving very little to anyone's imagination. Her hazel eyes met Rue's and a smile curled on her lips.

"Oy, girl! Come 'ere!" The woman called to her in a thick accent she'd never heard before. Rue scurried to the bar and lowered her cloak from her face.

"You look like someone I seen before. You got a brother maybe? Red-head, doesn't know when to shut his mouth, ah?" The woman leaned over the bar, getting a better look at her. Her eyes flicked up to Rue's head, and her hand reached out, tugging gently on a single red curl. "This a unique color. You must be related." The woman gave her a little wink and a knowing smile.

"How do you know...him?" Rue stopped herself from giving too much information. She didn't know this woman, and knowing her brother as well as she did, it wasn't out of the question that he may have scorned her in some way and taken off. Typical Jasper.

"Ah, ole boy is in here often, trying to strike up deals and playing too many card games he can't afford." She shook her head, but her expression remained fond as she spoke.

That definitely sounded like her brother, and it seemed this woman also knew him well.

"Do you know where he is?" Rue pushed back the curl that had fallen out of her hood and adjusted her glasses.

The woman nodded and pointed with her chin to the opposite side of the room, "He's there now. Come in just a little 'fore you did."

Rue turned, pushing herself up on the balls of her feet to scan over the crowd, looking for any sign of Jasper's unruly curls. Her eyes locked onto him where he stood, leaning against one of the back walls. She raced toward him, suddenly not so concerned about her hood falling back.

"Jasper!" She nearly choked on his name as she threw her arms around him.

Jasper's eyes blew open wide as he returned the embrace. He looked frantic.

"Rue, what are you doing here? You shouldn't have come here." His arms gripped her protectively. She was about to pull away, but the feeling of holding him like this was so incredibly comforting after the last few weeks of constant fear and anxiety.

"I needed you. I needed to find you, and you never came back." The sting of impending tears burned in the tip of her nose. She blinked rapidly, trying to push it away.

"Jasper, everything has changed. I've been so scared." She squeezed him tighter, nuzzling her cheek to his chest, trying to soak up every bit of warmth in his body.

Jasper looked around the room, eyes settling on a door behind them. He pulled Rue along as he slipped through one of the doors next to the bar. Once they were outside, he took one more glance around, making sure no one else was out there with them.

"What do you mean everything changed? Did your boss find out?" he asked, concern lacing his tone.

Rue shook her head, "No, no, that's not it. I heard a voice. I heard someone calling my name in the library. I heard it again in my dreams... and then there was this woman at the train station, she gave me a raven's feather and told me someone was coming and I jus—" Rue's mouth was going a thousand miles a minute. Jasper cupped her cheeks in his hands and shushed her quietly,

"Hush, darling, take a moment to breathe. I'm not going anywhere, so just...speak slowly and tell me what's going on."

Rue did as her brother asked, taking in a deep breath through her nose, letting it out slowly from her mouth. Once she was able to string a coherent sentence together she recounted everything from the beginning to the most recent dream she'd just woken from. Jasper listened intently, his hands never leaving her — which she very much appreciated.

"So you're telling me you know where the book might be? Under some floorboards?" He repeated, making sure he was getting all the facts straight.

"Yes, I just don't know where." Rue sighed, scrubbing a frustrated hand down her face. Jasper was quiet for a moment longer, thinking.

"What about this black room? You said you felt it call to you, right? What if it's somewhere in there?" he suggested. Rue gnawed her lip. Jasper made a good point. If something this horrendous *was* in the library, it would make sense for it to be in a place that was hard for just anyone to reach. But Rue wasn't just anyone.

"I can check when I return, but I can't guarantee that it's there."

"It's a solid lead, at the very least," Jasper said, pulling her back against him in a tight embrace, "but for now, let's not think about that and go back inside. It's fucking freezing out here."

Rue agreed, her teeth nearly chattering as the frigid wind cut through her cloak.

Jasper slid back through the same door they had come out. The sudden change of temperature from the chill outside to the warmth of the pub made her whole body shiver as she adjusted. She had no other answers yet, but at least she had her brother at her side. Despite how infuriating he could be at times, his presence was still a balm to Rue's frazzled soul.

She recalled when they were children, if she'd had a nightmare, she would sneak into his bed at night, burrowing herself against his chest, using the warmth radiating from his body to soothe away her fear. It seemed at least that part of their relationship hadn't changed over the years.

"Lydia, dearest, would you get my darling baby sister a drink?" Jasper asked the woman behind the bar.

"Of course, love." The woman — Lydia — grabbed a tankard from the rack behind her and began filling it. Rue tugged down her hood slowly, the unease of this place leaving her now that she had Jasper with her. The blur of different voices and sounds in the bar still clamored all around her; the sheer volume made it hard to think.

Good.

Rue accepted the tankard, thanking Lydia before guzzling down the bitter ale, hoping the alcohol would help dull her senses just enough to let her relax a bit. Jasper looked to her with disbelief before a goofy grin spread over his face.

"Wow, my little Ruby. I've never seen you so...improper!" He barked out a laugh, clapping a hand to her back. She glared daggers at him, turning her head defiantly, and pushed the tankard back toward Lydia.

"I'll take another, please. On his tab." She jerked her head toward Jasper, not bothering to face him.

Lydia threw her head back in a laugh that shook her shoulders and gave Jasper a wink, filling Rue's tankard.

"I like her." She leaned on the edge of the bar, her arms crossed in front of her.

Jasper rolled his eyes and slid onto an empty stool next to her, "Everyone likes her. She's definitely the better of the two of us." his arm wrapped around Rue's shoulders, pulling her next to him. Ale sloshed in her cup, white foam sticking to the tip of her nose as she tried to drink.

"Damnit, Jas, you're going to make me spill all over my cloak, you oaf." Rue huffed and slammed her tankard back onto the bar, glaring at her brother once again. Jasper only laughed, tugging at her shoulder again. Rue couldn't help the surge of relief that spread through her despite wanting to be annoyed with Jasper.

It was so nice to just take a breath for a moment and let go of the constant dread she'd been holding onto for the past several weeks. She wrapped her fingers around the large tankard and pulled it to her lips to take a sip. For the first time in what seemed like an age, Rue smiled.

Chapter Eleven

Rue stayed with Jasper in the tavern for a bit longer but knew the time to head home was upon her.

"I've got coin for a carriage home if you'll come with me tonight..." She looked to her brother, hopeful he would agree to go with her. She couldn't bear the thought of losing his comfort already. Jasper gave her a nod and moved to stand, digging in his pocket and producing a few dented pieces of silver.

"Lydia, dearest, thank you for your hospitality as always. I should hope to see you again soon." He slid the stack coins across the bar. Lydia picked them up, dropping them into her cleavage.

"Don't you go gettin' into no trouble, you hear me?" Lydia gave him a stern look, squinting one of her eyes.

"I can't promise anything, you know that," Jasper replied with feigned arrogance in his tone.

Lydia rolled her eyes, waving him off with a shoo-ing motion of her hands. Rue followed behind her brother with fists balled into the back of his shirt. The alcohol sitting in her empty belly made the world feel soft around the edges. She couldn't say it was an unpleasant or unwelcome feeling. Truthfully, it was nice to have a break from the hard edges of life.

"So...are you seeing Lydia?" Rue asked, breaking the lingering silence between them as they walked.

Jasper let out a humorless bark of a laugh and sighed, "Oh gods no, I wish. Alas, she is a very happily married woman...and her wife doesn't like me much."

Rue couldn't recall seeing a ring on Lydia's finger, but she supposed she wasn't really looking for one either. "She is rather beautiful." Rue shrugged but didn't press the subject. She had a feeling Jasper was a bit guarded about it. He murmured an affirmative response and kept walking.

Come to think of it, Rue couldn't recall a lady ever being in Jasper's life. She supposed that with his transient nature, a long-term relationship was hard to hold onto. Rue herself had had a few gentlemen in her life, but nothing that was ever so permanent. No one had ever felt quite right. She thought about Ryker again and visibly crumpled. She'd thought he could be the right one but came up disappointed in the end.

Rue was quiet for too long, the combination of alcohol, lack of sleep and proper meals hitting her all at once. Her head hurt. The pain pounded mercilessly behind her eyes and made it hard to think. Her feet moved of their own accord, carrying her along without even knowing where they were going.

"Rue? Hello?" Jasper waved his hand in front of her face, trying to bring her back to the moment. She hadn't noticed the carriage already arrived and was waiting for the two of them to board. She blinked slowly for a moment, recalibrating herself before digging into her cloak pocket and pulling out a small purse. Rue tossed the coins to the driver and climbed into the back of the carriage. Jasper held her steady, making sure she didn't slip, and followed in after her.

"What're you thinking so hard about?" he asked once they settled into the benches. Rue just shook her head, pulling her cloak hood up around her face, and leaned into her brother.

"Nothing. It's just been a very odd couple of weeks, and I feel like I could sleep for years."

Rue returned to the library the following day. After spending the evening with her brother. Waking to the familiar sight of his long limbs dangling from the arms of her tiny sofa, she felt a deep sense of calm. She knew she was ready to find out if her dreams were just dreams, or if they were in fact, premonitions.

Rue stood before the tall iron door to the black room and closed her eyes, straining her ears to listen for the same voice that compelled her before to speak again. As the minutes stretched on, Rue was met with nothing but silence. Of course she didn't even know if this would work, but it was the only plan she had.

The grandfather clock behind her chimed. Its toll ringing sonorously through the hush of the library. Now she was beginning to feel silly. Standing here, waiting for something that may never come. She took a deep breath through her nose and released it slowly through her mouth. Maybe she just needed to be receptive. Let her guard down for a moment.

The tension she'd felt in her shoulders slowly ebbed as she released her breath.

"Open," she murmured to herself, "I need to be open."

She focused on the rhythmic ticking sound of the clock behind her, letting it pull her into a hypnotic state. Rue didn't know how much time had passed, but eventually, the library melted away around her, leaving her in a trance-like state. Her body seemed to float, suspended there between space and time.

Weightless.

Calm.

Free.

A confident peace overtook her. Without thinking, Rue stepped forward and placed her hand on the door in the same way it had been before when Ryker found her. Maybe actually touching the door would spark something, anything, to happen.

The metal was cold and rough under her smooth hands. She focused on each scratch and dent along the iron as she dragged her fingers down the door, eyes still shut tight. At her sternum, the pendant began to warm once more. Unlike the fiery burn before, this was a gentle warmth, like wrapping a thick blanket around her shoulders on a cold winter night.

Rue placed her other hand on the door now, fingers searching for anything unique that stood out against the grain of the slab. The warmth in her pendant grew, still not to a burning heat, but definitely warmer than it had been with only one of her hands on the door. She felt like it was telling her something.

Rue stood there for what felt like a short eternity.

Listening.

Waiting.

And then, she heard it. The same legion of voices that spoke to her before.

"Ruby..."

Rue's brows knit together with determined focus as she strained even harder to listen.

"Come to me, Ruby..."

The pendant's warmth turned to a scorching burn against her skin and she pulled her hands back as though they'd been burned as well. This had to be it. The book was here. Something deep within her felt its presence. Calling to her, beckoning her.

Rue dug the keys out, fumbling through each one as she undid the locks with shaking hands. That feeling inside her intensified with each snap of the locks coming open. After the final bolt was released, Rue dropped the keys and wrenched open the door. She knew she had to do this quickly. The doppelganger's words came to her mind again.

The floorboards.

That's where she needed to look. Thankfully, the room was small enough that even if she had to pry open every single floorboard, it still wouldn't take very long.

Rue stepped over the threshold, and suddenly, the 'something' inside of her seemed to take over, pushing her aside within her own mind. The voice calling her had dulled and become a buzzing hum. She was trapped within herself, but for some reason, she trusted whatever this force was implicitly.

With each step she took, that hum grew louder and louder as though it were leading her. The pull towards the center of the room was strong, like a string tied around her sternum.

Rue dropped to her knees, wrenching up the corner of the old, thick woven rug that stretched out over the floor and exposed the pristine wood beneath. Her arm moved as though it had a mind all its own, hand slamming down against the boards, feeling for the buzz below.

Closing her eyes, the rest of her senses flared to life. Rue slowly raked her hand over the boards, searching. A violent jolt of energy shot up through her palm and rooted her to the spot. Her eyes immediately flew open.

"Here!" Rue cried out breathlessly, fingers immediately clawing at the ground, searching for a loose board.

"Come on, damn it!" She tugged hard, the tips of her fingers aching with the amount of force she exerted trying to pry the wood panels out of the floor. Finally, she found purchase, wrenching the board out and tossing it away just as her doppelganger in her dream had done.

The dark, empty space under the boards revealed what looked like a metal chest.

Rue began to yank on the few boards around the one she'd taken out, tossing them into the pile with the first one.

The chest was small and rusted, its surface etched in what looked like some kind of foreign script she didn't have time to look too closely at. Planting her knees on either side of the hole for balance, Rue reached in and hoisted the box up and out of the hole.

The chest was much lighter than it looked.

Rue's entire body was thrown backward, crashing into a shelf and nearly knocking one of the many display cases atop it to the ground. The chest hit her square in the stomach as she toppled over. She released a winded grunt but didn't lose her grip on the box.

"Well, I'll be damned," she panted out. A shocked and almost manic grin spread wide across her face.

Unable to linger on her discovery for too long, Rue hastily placed the floorboards back into place and tugged the rug back over them. She made sure nothing else in the room looked disturbed before scooping up the chest and securing the door's locks back into place.

She couldn't believe she'd actually found it. Granted, she didn't yet know what was inside of this box. For all she knew, it could very well have been empty. But with all the coincidences, it was a chance she was willing to take.

Rue gathered her things. She wrapped the chest with her coat and used the sleeves to tie it up. She knew she had to leave immediately. But making it out of the manor without anyone seeing her go was another matter entirely. It would be tricky with the servants essentially patrolling the hallways, but luckily for Rue, she knew the tunnel system in the house's walls like the back of her hand.

Rue climbed out of the wall into an empty room. It must have been used for something at one point in time, but now its only purpose was to collect dust.

She carefully nestled the box under her arm, holding it tightly to her body as she slowly opened the door and peeked down the hallway. Rue sighed heavily with relief when she saw no sign of anyone and heard no footsteps. Carefully, she tip-toed out of the room into the long corridor. All she needed to do now was make it a few more yards down the hall and through another unused door that led out into the statuary garden.

Rue's heart hammered in her chest. Adrenaline and nerves tied up like a knot around her heart. She didn't dare breathe too loudly as she walked along the darkened hallway, checking behind her every few steps to make sure no one was there.

Just a few more steps.

When she reached the door to the garden, she let out a long breath. The door was bolted from the inside, and once she left, she knew there was no way to lock it, but without any other choices before her, that was a risk she was going to have to take.

Slowly, Rue turned the deadbolt, and the door unlocked with a loud snap that echoed down the empty hall. Her breath caught in her throat, eyes darting around to make sure that no one was there to hear it.

Once she was sure she was alone, Rue gingerly turned the knob and pried the door open. It took a bit of strength to get the strike plate to detach from its resting place on the wall, set firmly with years of disuse and the elements on the other side. But she managed to open it just enough to slide through the gap before wedging it gently back into place.

Rue stepped out into the garden and slid along the perimeter of the wall, trying to stay out of view of any windows that faced the part of the statuary she stood in. Thankfully, it hadn't been raining, but the breeze still chilled her to the bone without her coat. Her teeth chattered together as a gust of wind whipped through her.

The outside of the manor was surrounded by a high wall. Too tall for her to even entertain the idea of climbing. She swore under her breath. Rue hadn't considered that when she'd come this way, but it wasn't as though she could walk through the front gate, either.

Determined to find another way out, Rue searched the high walls for some kind of opening. A crack in the foundation or a few loose stones. The manor was old and though it was maintained well, with its expansive grounds, there had to be some spot that had been overlooked.

Rue clutched the box to her chest, holding onto it like a life raft as she scanned for any openings. Her gaze fell on thick ropes of ivy that climbed over the stacked bricks. Perhaps the small bits of greenery could guide her out. Crouching down, she slid between the statues, using them as cover. She tucked her hair into the back of her dress, silently thanking her past self for thinking to style the unruly curls into a smooth plait today.

Inching closer to the wall, Rue noticed a crack in a patch of bricks cleverly hidden behind a cluster of small imp-like statues.

She dropped down to her knees, unconcerned about the mud and grass stains that were seeping into her dress, and began pulling the statues away from the wall. Rue groaned with the force it took to move the solid stone and rolled each of the figures out of the way. The crack looked like it may be just large enough to wedge herself through with some careful maneuvering. Rue peeked through the hole to see where the path led before looking in both directions to make sure no one lurking was nearby.

Tossing the box through first, Rue climbed through the hole. Sharp edges of broken brick scratched and scraped against her skin as she wiggled through. She ignored the pain and kept moving. Stopping wasn't an option. Her dress tore open in a few places, but she managed to make her way through to the other side with minimal damage.

Stopping only for a moment to catch her breath, Rue reached back through the hole and pulled the few imp statues she could reach back into place, concealing her exit once again.

The manor backed up to a small copse of trees. Rue raced through them as fast as she could with the box clutched to her chest. Branches scraped at her face and snagged her hair as she ran, but she didn't care. She needed to find a carriage on the other side of the trees, and she needed to do it fast.

Rue rushed to her flat after departing the carriage. Adrenaline, fear, and — oddly enough — excitement propelled her forward.

She had to tell Jasper.

She needed to know what to do next and couldn't bear to do it alone. When Rue reached the flat, she pounded on the door, not wanting to let the chest go in order to reach into her pockets and get the key out.

"Jasper, it's me! Please help me with the door!" Rue shouted through the closed door. A moment later, Jasper's hurried footsteps approached. The door swung open quickly, causing her to fall through the threshold and onto the chest.

"...Ow."

Jasper couldn't help but laugh as he reached down to help his sister back to her feet.

"Are you alright? What's got you in such a tizzy?"

"I found it. I found the book! It was under the floorboards. It was hidden, and I..." She was spiraling again. Jasper reached out and held her shoulders, shaking her gently.

"Hey, hey, slow down, I can't keep up. What do you mean you found it?" His eyes locked on hers, trying to get her to focus on him and calm down. Rue just pointed to the sad-looking metal chest on the ground where she had fallen,

"The book! It's in the box."

Jasper's eyes widened in fearful astonishment as he finally realized what she was telling him.

"By the gods' breath...you really did it."

Chapter Twelve

J ASPER PUSHED HIS HAIR off his forehead, heaving a sigh, "I don't even see a lock on this thing, but it is sealed tight."

The box sat on the table before them. It felt surreal. Rue slid her fingers around the dented edges, trying to feel for some kind of seam where the chest might come apart. On the front end of it, she noticed a small recessed design coated with dirt and dust. Unable to make out what it was, she grabbed the tea towel hanging over the stove and began scrubbing the grime out.

"What's that?" Jasper bent down, hands on his knees with his eyes squinted, trying to get a better look at what Rue was very aggressively rubbing at.

"I'm not sure, but it's the only thing on this box that might give us a clue about how to open it." She used her fingernail covered by the cloth to scrape at the edges, getting the last bits of dirt out of the recess. Blowing away the last bits of debris, Rue leaned closer to get a better look at it.

"Wait...I recognize this symbol. It's— " Her hand flew to the pendant around her neck.

She tugged at the necklace, breaking the clasp in the back and holding it out before her.

"Mama's necklace..." she paused, turning back to face her brother. "But why...?"

Jasper eyed the necklace in stunned silence. With shaking hands, Rue detached the pendant from the chain and carefully placed each pointed end into the matching slot.

The citrine stone in the center began to pulse, emitting a soft glow. A mechanical sound of metal grinding together came from under the lid.

Rue was flooded by so many more questions that she didn't have time to think about, electing to focus on the single task at hand instead.

A gust of air hissed out from between the seam of the lid as it popped open. Rue's pendant fell from the hole onto the table, the glow in the stone at its center slowly fading away. Both of the siblings stood there, staring at the chest in awe and disbelief, but neither of them made a move to fully open the lid.

"Open it," Jasper finally said, nudging his sister with an elbow.

"You open it!" Rue snapped, "You're the one that got me into this mess in the first place!"

Jasper muttered something unintelligible under his breath, but moved to open the box. Rue took a step back, fingernails between her teeth as she watched him with dread laden anticipation. Jasper gently tugged on the upper lid of the box. It slid off with ease. He set it aside, hesitantly leaning forward to peer into the box.

"It looks so...normal." Jasper almost sounded disappointed.

"It's the normal-looking ones that are the most dangerous..." Rue muttered in reply, speaking of more than just the book.

Jasper moved to reach into the box, but before he could even get close to it, Rue reached out and slapped his hand away.

"Don't touch it!"

"Well, what are we going to do, just stand here and stare at it?"

Rue narrowed her eyes and glared at her brother, placing her hands on her hips. She swore Jasper had no self-preservation left in him.

"No, you idiot, but you can't just touch it with your bare hands. What if it has some...something coating it for protection?" Rue waved her hands around incredulously, unable to fathom how her brother was this dense.

Jasper opened his mouth to say something, but Rue leveled him with a scathing glare. She knew she was right, and if the defeated look on his face was anything to go by, he knew it too. He shoved his hands into his pockets and cleared his throat, trying to detract from the embarrassed reddening of his cheeks.

Rue grabbed the dirty towel she'd used to clean out the locking mechanism and wrapped it around her hands, gingerly reaching into the box to pull the book out. The dark leather bound cover was in perfect condition, still glossy and well oiled with not a single scratch nor speck of dust to be seen.

Rue had no idea how long it had been in this box under the floorboards of the duke's manor, but judging by the condition of the metal chest itself, it might have been anywhere from decades to potentially centuries.

Although, now, so many things that didn't make sense nagged at her as she looked the book over, turning it reverently in her hands.

Had Ryker known it was there?

Was it something that his father, grandfather, or even great-grandfather had put there? She was fairly certain she wouldn't ever know the answers to these questions.

Jasper slid into one of the chairs at the table, watching Rue as she inspected every inch of the tome. His leg bounced anxiously, waiting for her to say something. Her face pulled into a look of discontent.

"When I was looking for the book, I felt this...instinct take over my body, like something was trying to show me where it was." She gently set the book back down in the box and sat next to Jasper. "I saw it in my dream before that. And now, holding the book, I can feel power coursing through it. Like lightning in my hands." She looked down at her hands, flexing her fingers. So much had changed in such a short time, and she was finding it difficult to wrap her mind around.

Rue let out a soft sigh and leaned into Jasper, head resting on his shoulder. She didn't say anything, but hoped he knew how much his presence meant. It was sad to think that it took something so incredibly dangerous to finally pull the two of them together. Jasper reached out, picking up the fallen sun pendant and twisted it around in his fingers.

"Mama's necklace was the key to opening the box. That might be the first step in explaining why you've felt this connection to it...why I, of all people, just happened to overhear someone talking about it in Fool's Hope." Jasper spoke quietly, suspicion thick in his tone. His eyes never left the pendant between his fingers.

"There's something more to this than either of us knows." He set the pendant back down on the table, sliding it back towards Rue.

"There are so many things I wish I could ask her..." Rue chewed her lip to keep the tears that threatened to spill over at bay and rubbed her finger over that smooth citrine stone, hoping it would bring her even a modicum of the comfort she had once gotten from her mother.

They had always been close with their parents, but as Rue was learning, even that closeness didn't stop the deep well of secrets her family managed to keep hidden from her and Jasper. It was too much to wrap her mind around on top of everything else that had happened today.

"Let's just close this up for now until I figure out what the next step is. This isn't going to simply be something we can toss in a fire and be done with."

Rue gave Jasper's arm a quick pat before he could object. Then, she stood, grabbing the lid of the box from the table and sliding it back on. The fit of the two pieces were so perfect that the seam line between them became nearly invisible. She picked up the pendant-turned-key and pressed it back into the recess, locking the box once again. The grinding sound of metal clicked, assuring her it was secured.

"I'll have to make another trip to Bellmare and see if Fia can brew me some kind of acid or something to take care of it," Rue said, mostly talking to herself as she scrubbed a hand over her face, exhaustion settling deep in her bones. "However, I have had an extremely emotionally charged day, and I am going to eat everything I can find in my cabinets and then go to bed."

Jasper nodded and pulled her into his chest, wrapping her in a tight hug. "I have some things to take care of, but I'll be back in a few days. Don't do anything stupid while I'm gone, you curious cat." He gave her a pointed look and tapped his finger against her nose.

Rue glared, narrowing her eyes at him. "I swear on everything I love, Jasper, if you leave this apartment and go off to tell someone about this, I will actually kill you and bury you in the Hollow."

Jasper just stared back at her with wide eyes, "Gods, Rue, no need to get violent now!" He threw up his hands in mock surrender.

Rue grumbled a few choice words under her breath but ultimately conceded; her mind was too tired to continue to pry. She walked Jasper to the door, making sure the deadbolt was firmly locked behind him.

"Maybe I'll just put this here, too. For good measure," she muttered to herself, sliding a chair under the door handle.

She'd found the book.

That part of it was finished, but now what? Would Fia actually be able to concoct something to destroy something so powerful? And if she couldn't, what other options did she have?

She would have to think about that when she'd had more than a mere handful of hours of sleep, she thought, covering her mouth as she stifled a yawn. Somehow, despite everything, a feeling of calm settled over her.

After eating what felt like her weight in all manner of snacks, Rue opened her bedroom door, the welcoming sight of her bed calling to her. She opened her closet and tucked the box under a stack of old dresses she'd been meaning to get rid of but never managed to get around to. It wasn't the best hiding place, but it would have to do for now until she could deal with it in the morning.

Stripping off her clothes down to her slip, Rue tossed them into a pile to be dealt with later. The ever-growing mountain of laundry was the least of her concerns.

Rue shuffled over to her bed, taking off her glasses and rubbing her tired eyes before setting them on the small nightstand. She reached into the single drawer and fished around, looking for another chain or something similar to replace the one she broke in her urgency to test the pendant in the lock. The only thing she could find was a piece of rope, but it would have to do. It was extremely important for her to keep the pendant with her at all times if it was the only thing that kept the box locked tight.

Even with the book tucked away in the closet, Rue could feel its aura calling to her, beckoning her closer with the same pull she'd felt before in the library. A knot firmly tied around her soul, dragging her like the tide to the full moon.

She turned toward the closet, so tempted to answer the call. But instead, she climbed into her bed, tugging the thick, downy duvet up over her head, and cocooned herself in its warmth. The repetitive ticking sound of the small clock on her nightstand eventually lulled her into a deep sleep.

Rue stood in the middle of a long corridor that seemed to stretch out endlessly on either side. A shiver ran up her spine. It was freezing wherever it was that she stood, wearing nothing but her thin night dress and no shoes on her feet.

"Ruby..." A faint but stern voice called from the darkness. Panic immediately rose in her chest, making her skin prickle uncomfortably. She had to run. Something inside of her was telling her, screaming at her to run. Without another moment of hesitation, Rue bolted in the opposite direction of where she'd heard the voice call her name.

She had no idea where this hallway would take her, but she knew she needed to get away. She pumped her legs as fast as she could, feet slapping hard against the wood floor beneath her. A deep, quaking rumble shook the ground under her as the unseen pursuant's footsteps grew closer.

Rue dared to glimpse over her shoulder but saw no one. It only pushed her to run faster. The walls were lined with identical doors on either side of her. The spaces between each one painted with complex patterns she couldn't make out as she sped past.

It took her a moment, but she began to realize everything around her was familiar, like she had been here before.

She was dreaming again.

Rue stopped in her tracks, panting heavily from the exertion. She turned around slowly and faced the direction the voice was coming from. She braced herself for what might be coming, but the rumble of footsteps stopped, the entire hall going silent.

"It's not real... This isn't real!" She whispered at first, but her voice grew louder with more conviction as she chanted the words over and over again. She would not succumb to this dream again. She was going to fight. She closed her eyes, pulling her arms to her chest trying to center herself and find calm.

"You will submit to me, Ruby Umberwick."

The voice in the darkness was the last thing she heard before she found herself sitting up in bed, panting hard. Rue turned and looked at the clock on her nightstand, squinting to try and read the numbers.

It was still early morning. She fell back against her pillow, closing her eyes once more. What was that? She had never been aware of being in the dream before, and she definitely hadn't been able to wake herself up like that.

The dark aura from the book behind her closet door still pulsed through the walls. Something about it made her skin feel sticky, though part of that could have been the thin sheen of sweat coating her body.

She just needed to go back to sleep. She didn't want to deal with this right now; her day had been plenty eventful yesterday. With a few deep breaths, she felt herself regain calm once more, and the world around her turned fuzzy at the edges as she fell back into a blissfully dreamless sleep for the next few hours.

CHAPTER THIRTEEN

The following morning Rue was awoken by an insistent banging at her door. Rubbing the sleep from her still tired eyes, she slid on her glasses with practiced ease. "I'm coming," she mumbled groggily. She pulled her robe around her and headed down to see what this sound coming from her front door was all about.

It hadn't occurred to her sleep-addled mind, until now, that it was odd for someone to be here first thing in the morning as not many people knew where she lived in the first place.

She pushed up on her toes, squinting to peek out the tiny hole on the inside of her door, trying to see who stood on the other side.

"Rue, open the door, it's me, Fia!" A squeaky voice called from the other side of the door. Rue's eyes went wide and she wrenched it open, the surprise on her face more than a little obvious.

"Fia? What are you doing here so early? Did something happen? How did you even know where to find me?" Rue reached for her friend's arm, pulling her inside and closing the door behind her. It wasn't like Fia to venture away from her own home in Bellmare, so whatever it was...couldn't be good.

"That's not important right now. What is important is that Vesper told me to come; she said she felt like you were in trouble." Fia's eyes were wide and full of concern. Rue rubbed the last bits of sandy sleep from her eyes, desperately trying to wake herself fully.

"What do you mean trouble?"

"I-I don't know, she just said that she felt a shift and that there was a strong presence here that she couldn't sense before."

Rue stared blankly at Fia, processing what she was saying. Was it the book? Had Rue opening that box caused some kind of change? "Did she say when it happened?"

"Just before midnight, I believe," Fia confirmed, her features turning slightly suspicious.

Right around the time she'd opened the book with Jasper. She chewed her lip nervously and debated on how much information she should give Fia. But the reality was that Fia was the only other person she *could* tell about this.

"I found the book. It's here." Rue said quietly, looking around the room like the walls might be listening to her. Fia's eyes went wide as she pulled back from Rue.

"Are you serious? Why did you bring it here!?" Fia whisper-screamed, the incredulous tone in her voice making Rue feel that guilt even more now.

"I don't know! I didn't know where else to take it!" Rue admitted, pushing her hands through her hair and tugging at it.

Fia leveled her with a look that was an equal parts disappointment and concern, "Alright. Well, there's not much we can do about that now, but you need to get it out of here and fast. I doubt Vesper was the only person in the whole isle to feel something. There are plenty more," Fia hesitated for a moment, struggling to find the right word to use, "gifted people in hiding."

"I was planning on bringing it to you anyway," Rue admitted, rubbing her arm sheepishly.

"Me? And what am I supposed to do with it?"

"You're an alchemist. I thought you might have some kind of magically imbued acid that would melt it."

Fia barked out a short laugh. Rue couldn't help feeling somewhat offended by it.

"What? Why are you laughing?" She asked, her brow knitting together in annoyance.

"A book like this is not going to be easily corroded by some kind of caustic substance. Magical or otherwise," Fia deadpanned, like this information was common knowledge Rue should already be aware of.

"And how was I supposed to know that? I don't know a damn thing about this book other than it's not good," Rue snapped, "All I know is that it has something to do with the necklace my mother gave me."

Rue's hand moved to her neck of its own accord, fingers wrapping around the sunburst pendant. Fia's eyes tracked her movement, her head tilting curiously.

"What about it?" Fia asked, lowering her voice.

Rue took a deep breath, slowly letting it out to ground herself before answering. She didn't even know half of what was going on, but she hoped that telling Fia would give her another perspective on the situation at the very least.

"The box the book was contained in had a lock on it. And this necklace fits perfectly in the slot." Rue held up the pendant for Fia to see, "And since opening the box, I can feel some kind of powerful aura coming from the book. I feel it calling out to me. Like there is some kind of string tied around my heart dragging me closer."

Fia nodded with concentration on her brow, urging Rue to continue.

"I've been having nightmares for a while," Rue continued, "While I'm in the dream, everything feels so real, and I don't realize it's a dream until I wake up. But, last night... it changed. I was able to realize that I was stuck in the dream again, that none of it was real."

"And you think that has to do with the fact that you've got the book now." Fia surmised. Rue nodded, suddenly feeling vulnerable, wrapping her arms around herself.

She hadn't given herself time to think too much about all of this before exhaustion overtook her the night before, but now that she'd said everything out loud, she didn't know what to make of it. It felt so out of place. Like some horrible prank that she was the victim of.

Rue still didn't know what her role in any of this was.

Fia sighed softly and placed her hands on Rue's shoulders, "Okay. I don't know what all of this means, but why don't you bring the book to Vesper? We can see if there is anything she can pick up from it."

Rue nodded. She knew Vesper was their best option. It wasn't as though she could ask Ryker for anything.

Ryker.

Her thoughts drifted to the duke. Amidst the chaos of the situation, Rue hadn't thought about Ryker's involvement in everything. Doubts had already begun washing away the rose-colored film she once viewed him in, but her lovesick heart stopped her from fully accepting those doubts. And now, it was impossible to deny them.

"Alright. I can bring the book to Bellmare tomorrow. I just really need some time to wrap my head around everything, or I might implode," she groaned, pressing her fingers into her temples.

"Please be careful. Hold onto that book like your life depends on it," Fia warned.

"Everyone's life depends on it," Rue countered. It was still much too early to be having this conversation. "Well, since you're already here, why don't you stay for breakfast?"

Fia hesitated for a moment. Rue turned back to her with a single raised brow, questioning.

"I dunno. I—"

"You don't have to stay if you don't want to, but it would be nice to have some company other than my brother for once."

Fia's eyes lit up, and the nervous reluctance seemed to fade from her features. Rue had never had many friends. Other than her university acquaintances, but even then, they were just that — acquaintances. She hadn't known Fia for very long at all, but something about the mousy girl was so inviting. They'd skipped the entire awkward beginning phase and gone straight into confidants. Although Rue supposed that was most likely in part due to the complex situation they stood to face.

"Sounds good to me." Fia shed her coat and hung it over the back of a chair, sliding in and making herself comfortable like she'd been here dozens of times before. The tension that filled the room dissipated, replaced by a comfortable camaraderie.

Rue put the kettle on and dug through her cabinets for the replenished jar of tea Jasper had brought her. "Hope you like it strong," she said, dumping a few hearty spoonfuls of tea leaves into a sieve. Fia just murmured an affirmation and busied herself with a letter Rue had left on the table.

"Pen pal of yours?" she asked, turning the envelope from Orionna's last letter in her hands.

"Kind of. We went to university together. She lives on the mainland, but we try to send letters a few times a month."

Rue thought about Orionna, a frown pulling her lips. She still hadn't heard back from her. It was out of her usual character to take this long to respond, but who knew what was happening on the mainland. Rue usually didn't bother herself with the news from over there. It was normally incredibly depressing headlines, and she already had enough to contend with here on the isle.

"Ah, I see," was the only response Fia gave. She set the letter down and huffed a sigh.

"What's wrong?"

"Oh, nothing. I just..." Fia hesitated. She wrung her hands in her lap and chewed on her lip again. Rue clocked the nervous habit and hid her fingers away in her robe pockets.

"I don't really have any friends. I mean...I have Vesper, but she hardly counts."

Rue's mouth pulled into a deep frown. It seemed she and Fia were more alike than she thought. For as long as she could remember, Jasper had also been her only friend, and even now, history had repeated itself.

"I'm your friend." Rue reached her hand out, placing it palm up on the table. An invitation.

Fia stared at it for a long moment as though deciding if she wanted to take it or not. Rue stayed silent, allowing Fia all the time she needed.

"Thanks," Fia's nervous expression melted into a warmer, more comfortable one, "I'm your friend, too." she said and slid her hand into Rue's. She could feel the other woman's hesitation, but couldn't blame her after what she'd known about Fia's past.

"Whatever happens...we're going to fix all of this. Together."

Fia's mouth turned into a brilliant, wide grin, "Together. You're stuck with me now."

"Wouldn't want it any other way."

She wasn't going to do it.

Rue had already promised Jasper she wouldn't do anything stupid while he was away, and reading from this book was *the* stupidest thing she could do. She paced back and forth across her kitchen floor, gnawing on what was left of her fingernails.

Oh, she wanted to so badly.

"It's just a book...it can't be that bad, right? It's not like I'm going to *do* any of the rituals inside." Rue tried to reason with herself as she approached the box where it sat on the table. Something about it continually drew her in, like there was a metaphorical finger curling and beckoning her closer.

Despite what she'd cautioned Jasper before, Rue ran a bare finger over the cover. This was no ordinary book. Rue felt its power pulsing through the beautifully crafted leather cover. She reached into the box, carefully grasping the tome with both hands, extricating it from the box.

"What secrets do you hide?" She whispered, eyes raking over every part of the cover's design. Despite its age, the cover only showed minimal signs of wear. There weren't any intricate designs or embellishments other than an embossed sun motif in the center, similar to that of her necklace. Otherwise, the book looked fairly plain.

Rue took a deep breath and held it, steadying herself before curling her fingers around the edge of the book's cover. She leaned in closely, trying to catch a glimpse of what might be written into its pages without fully opening it. A sly loophole in her sworn promise to both Jasper and Fia.

Her brows knit in confusion when she realized — the inside of the book was completely blank.

"Well, that can't be right..." Rue mused aloud, opening the book fully now and flipping through the hundreds of empty pages.

Was this a trick? Or some kind of invisible ink that only worked with a solvent or heat? Rue wasn't daring enough to try and figure out if either of those were the case, but there had to be something she was missing.

She slid her fingers down the edge of one of the pages slowly as she rolled the possibilities around in her mind. A sharp pain pricked the tip of her middle finger and broke the cycle.

"Ouch!" she hissed, pulling her hand away from the page. The thick paper had given her a nasty cut, leaving a steady stream of crimson dripping down her finger.

Rue quickly stood, shoving her fingers under the running tap to rinse the blood from her hand, leaving the book wide open on the kitchen table. As she washed and wrapped her injured finger with a bit of cloth, the coppery tang of blood permeated the room. Rue raised her finger to her nose, inhaling. She was certain such a small cut couldn't smell so pungently.

Behind her, the sound of rustling paper caught her attention. Rue spun on her heel, eyes wide as she watched the book come to life on its own. Pages flipped wildly back and forth as though guided by an unseen hand. With tentative steps, she approached the table once again with disbelief.

The pages began to fill. Words, charts, diagrams, and drawings spread over the pages in a deep crimson ink. It looked like blood.

Her blood.

With pages now filled, the book finally stilled. Stationary once again. Rue leaned in, glancing at the page that had been left open. Words of a language she had never seen before filled every inch of the paper. More unknown symbols and other drawings filled the margins.

Although she knew for a fact she'd never seen anything like this before, somehow, the text began to make sense. Not the words themselves, unlike a normal written or spoken language, but the meaning of these things were clear to her.

Deep in the pit of her stomach she felt that same sense as before. Something inside of her that made her feel as though she were nothing but a guest in her own body. Her lips parted of their own accord and before she could stop it, words began to form on her tongue. A voice that was not her own spoke the words of the ancient text before her.

"No. We are not doing this." Rue's better judgment had finally taken the reins. She snapped the book shut before this thing inside of her, whatever it was, could cause even more trouble. Chucking it back into its metal prison before slamming the lid on, Rue slid the pendant from the neck once more and locked the box tightly.

Rue wrapped the box in her plain white tablecloth, gathering it into her arms. She just needed to take it to Bellmare. Everything would be fine. Vesper would know what to do.

Or at least she hoped that was the case.

Rue slid into her boots and pulled her arms through her coat, trying not to focus on the raw dread settling heavily in her gut. She knew opening that book was a bad idea, but her curiosity had managed to convince her otherwise. The words had already come out but the best she could hope was they were nothing serious. Maybe just an introduction or something equally harmless.

Just as her hand touched the doorknob, a loud banging followed by a horrendous scratching sound came from upstairs. Rue stood frozen and waited to see if the sound persisted.

Another bang, more scratching, now followed by the sound of cracking glass.

Rue's heart leapt into her throat, nearly strangling her. She held the wrapped box firmly against her chest and slowly moved toward the source of the sound.

Pushing open her bedroom door with her elbow, Rue realized the sound was coming from the window. The curtains were still drawn closed over it, obscuring whatever it was that might be on the other side.

She carefully set the box back in her closet, making sure the pile of clothes she'd hidden it under fully covered it.

The sound at her window grew louder, more urgent now. With shaking hands, Rue hesitantly pulled back the curtain.

The face that met her other side wasn't human.

The creature snarled, snapping its long, needle-like teeth at her. Its face looked almost like some kind of bat with long ears that curled behind its head and an upturned snout-like nose. Its teeth seemed to dig into the flesh around its mouth, creating a grotesque maw dripping with blood and foamy saliva.

Rue screamed. The shock of what she saw made her fall backward into her vanity table as she tried to get away. Bottles of lotions and perfume fell to the ground, shattering against the wood floor.

A long, forked tongue rolled out from behind the creature's sharp teeth and licked up the glass of the window. The scraping of its talons had created spider web fissures along the pane of the glass window.

Rue could swear it was smiling at her. She wanted to vomit. She had to get out of there. She didn't know if she would be able to run, but she had to try. Staying here with this *thing* looking in on her like a piece of meat — and the only barrier between them threatening to break — was not an option.

Rue pushed herself up from the floor and almost slipped on the liquid that spilled but caught herself before she could completely topple. Bellmare was too far away to run to, leaving only one person she could think of to help her. As much as that option made her stomach sour, there was no time to consider any other options.

Before she could convince herself otherwise, Rue bolted out the door and ran.

Chapter Fourteen

R ue ran as fast as her legs would take her. She didn't know if the creature would follow her, but she wasn't going to take any chances and find out. Her thighs and lungs burned with exertion, but she couldn't — wouldn't — stop until she reached the manor.

Rue could only pray that she had been fast enough to create space between her and whatever it was that had been lurking outside her window. From the edge of her vision, she swore she saw something in every darkened alleyway she passed. But she shoved those thoughts from her mind, focusing only on the destination.

The windows of the manor were dark at this late hour, but she pushed on anyway. Flinging open the heavy gate and slamming it closed behind her, she didn't slow for even a moment.

Rue reached for the handles of the main doors, swearing colorfully when she realized they were locked. She beat her fists against the door, hoping it was loud enough that someone — anyone — inside would hear her. Anxiously hopping from foot to foot as she waited, Rue dared to glimpse behind her, making sure she was still alone.

Seconds passed like hours as she waited for a response. She slammed her fist against the door again, this time calling out.

"Hello? Hello, is anyone there? Please let me in!" Her voice came out in a strangled cry, but she kept pounding, not bothering to wait again.

The sound of the lock sliding open with a click stopped her in place. She took a step back, waiting for whoever came to open the doors and let her in.

A sob of relief ripped out of her. Rue never thought she would be happy to see the old butler, Delnan, standing there, regarding her with his usual judging eyes.

"I need to see Ryk— Duke Ashworth. It's urgent," she told him, pushing her way past the threshold. She closed the door behind her and threw the lock shut again without waiting another second longer to be invited in. Delnan continued to stare, but Rue found that she couldn't care less about what he thought of her at that moment.

"Now!" she barked. The relief of seeing the butler had already faded.

Delnan scoffed but did as she asked, climbing the staircase toward the duke's office. Rue turned to make sure the door behind her was indeed locked shut when it hit her.

She'd left the book in the house.

"Fuck!" she swore, slapping a hand against her forehead. She'd been too scared to think of anything other than getting away from the creature that she'd completely forgotten.

Rue began pacing back and forth over the entryway rug, chewing one of her less abused nails down to the quick. Of all the things she could have forgotten, it was, of course, the one thing that she absolutely needed to remember. The only small comfort she had was the one and only key to get into that box currently hung around her neck.

Too lost in her self chastising, Rue hadn't noticed Ryker come downstairs until his hand was on her shoulder, startling her out of her spiral.

It only took one look into his piercing, opalescent eyes for her to realize it had been a mistake to come here. There was no way she could tell him about this. Not when doubt was the only thing she felt as she held his gaze.

He said nothing and placed both of his hands on either side of her face. Rue blanched at how wrong his touch suddenly felt on her skin, barely tamping down the urge to jerk out of his grip.

"What's the matter, darling?" he asked, voice quiet and laced with concern that didn't meet his eyes.

"T-there was something outside my window," she started, choosing her next words carefully, "It looked like some kind of beast or monster." Rue kept the description intentionally vague, waiting for his reaction before giving him any more information.

Ryker's brow furrowed, "Are you sure you didn't just have another nightmare, dove?"

The pet name made something in Rue's stomach curdle. What did he mean 'another'? She was fairly certain she had never mentioned anything about her nightmares before.

Rue pulled his hands away from her face, nodding her head, swallowing down all that she wanted to say in favor of simply agreeing with him.

"I— I think that might have been it."

"I thought so. Why don't you just go home and get some rest? Take some time off. Clearly, you need it."

Rue stood before the duke, his callous smile grating on her nerves.

"Yes. I think that will do the trick." Her voice sounded far off and unconvinced. She could tell Ryker was suspicious, although it was clear he thought he was doing a good job of hiding it.

"Sorry I came to you like this, I was just scared and didn't know where else to go." Rue tried to look shameful, but wasn't sure she was really selling it, either.

They stood there like that for too long. Simply staring at one another with no words exchanged. Eventually, the sound of Delnan clearing his throat behind them broke the awkward stand-off.

"Miss Umberwick, shall I call a carriage for you? Although, I'm not sure any will be running at this time of night."

"No, it's fine. The cold air will be good for me to clear my head."

"Very well." The butler didn't push any further and took his leave.

Ryker took a step closer, closing what was left of the small gap of space between them, "Take all the time you need, sweet dove. I'll be waiting." He slid his finger under her chin, tilting her head up to look at him again. The moonstone eyes she'd once wanted nothing more than to drown in suddenly looked on her with a certain cruelty, as though they hid some kind of twisted secret about her employer.

"Of course. I should go." Rue cleared her throat and turned her head, breaking his heavy stare.

"Be careful out there. This town has been going to hell lately." Ryker opened the door for her and watched her leave. Rue reached for the pendant at her throat, partly for comfort and partly to make sure it was still there. Something wasn't right with the duke, but she wasn't going to stay and find out what that something might be. Instead, Rue walked through the darkened streets of Penrith back to her flat, suddenly not as terrified as she was before.

Rue sat before the fireplace, the raven's feather spinning back and forth between her fingers. She'd left it on the mantle and had forgotten about it until now. The comfort it brought before came again as soon as the plume touched her skin. The tight knot that had formed in her chest loosened, finally allowing her to breathe again.

The house was quiet, with only the sounds of her soft sniffles punctuated by the occasional crackle or pop of a log in the hearth. Rue wiped her face, a salted crust already forming on her cheeks from the endless river of tears she shed. She couldn't help but blame herself. She knew she should have left that book well enough alone. But now, with the knowledge that her blood had inked the book's pages, there were even more layers to this bottomless mystery that she hadn't even really begun to unravel.

Rue thought of Jasper and how her actions could have hurt him. She thought of Fia and Vesper and everything they had already been through. The tears came once again, a choked sob caught in her throat. How could she be so naive? So stupid to think that it was just a book and therefore harmless. So stupid to think that nothing would happen.

"Whoever was supposed to come for me," she whispered to the feather in her hand, feeling a bit silly, "I could really use some help right now." Rue pressed her lips to the soft, oil-slick, iridescent vanes of the feather, tears falling like tiny dew drops on the surface before rolling off to the floor.

Rue closed her eyes and held the feather there against her lips, whispering over and over again the same plea.

Please... please help me.

She sat there like that for a long time.

Minutes or hours, she didn't know. Time felt irrelevant.

She turned her glassy stare back to the fire, confused to see it had suddenly pittered out to nothing. The once glowing embers had gone cold, leaving charred black wood in the grate. She sat up quickly, eyes wide with panic. There was more than enough wood to burn; how could the fire have simply...gone out? Rue's breath became a vaporous cloud before her. Between the sudden drastic drop in temperature and the renewed sense of fear, her entire body shook uncontrollably.

Had she done something wrong again? Gods only knew what might be coming for her now.

Rue's eyes darted around the room, looking for any sign of another horrible creature creeping around at the dark edges of her home. Fear gripped her and held her rooted to the spot she sat in on the floor.

A rustling came from the chimney above her. The sound of scraping claws or talons against brick echoed down the shaft. She sat there still and silent, not daring to breathe for a moment while she listened. The sound seemed to vanish shortly after she'd heard it. She leaned forward, daring to look up the flue.

Not again.

This could not be happening again. Not so soon after that last one. Her heart slammed erratically against her sternum, adrenaline spiking and making her forget about the cold.

A single black feather floated down, shooting out of the hearth, and landed at the edge of the fireplace grate. She blinked, momentarily confused as to what she was looking at. Another followed...and another, and another before the horrible scraping sound returned, and a single giant black wing jutted out from the hearth.

Rue leapt back with a scream, tripping on her nightgown and slamming her head backwards into the wood floor. She groaned from the pain but sat up, rubbing the back of her head.

"Ouch..."

The shock of pain nearly made her forget what was happening. Her eyes snapped back to the hearth, her hand still resting on the back of her head as she froze in place. The wing was undulating and almost looked as if it were pulsing. Rue couldn't bring herself to look away even though she desperately wanted to.

Time seemed to crawl as she watched the blue-black sheen of the wing shine in the low light. After what felt like a short eternity, the wing began to slowly pull back, revealing a head of shaggy hair that matched the color of the feathers. Everything stood perfectly still — and then moved all at once.

An entire man's body rose from the small hearth. He seemed to unfold as he came through. Once he stood at his full height, his head nearly touched her ceiling. The man opened his eyes, revealing irises of melted gold that gave off an eerie glow in the darkness. His broad shoulders dipped down into a narrow waist. Even through his layers of solid black clothing, she could make out a defined silhouette.

Behind him, Rue could see the massive black feathered wings that protruded from his back. It was at that moment she knew exactly who this man before her was.

He was her savior. The one from her dreams whose hands had cradled her so gently night after night.

And he was beautiful.

She could see all the most defined parts of his face with how the shadows lit him like a work of art on display in a gallery. His jaw was sharp and his nose long and straight, leading to full lips that looked sinfully soft.

His dark hair was shaggy and curled around the ends, with half of it tied up. Rue was sure it was an extremely inappropriate thought to be having at that moment but she couldn't help thinking about what it would feel like to run her fingers through it.

He took a step forward, tucking his wings back and looked down to her. His eyes called to Rue and she felt her body answer, gaze immediately locking with his. It was like a spark of lightning shot down her spine. She let out a gasp and arched her back at the pain. The feeling left her nearly as quickly as she'd felt it.

"W-who are you?" She pushed herself up from the floor, knees wobbling dangerously beneath her. Her hands fumbled for purchase on a nearby wall to hold herself steady.

The man didn't respond but took a step closer. His long legs swallowed the space between them in a single stride. She couldn't convince her feet to move and if she was honest...she didn't want to. Something about him radiated a feeling of safety. The same comforting feeling she got from the feather.

He stood before her, no more than a breath away. Rue had to look up to him as he stood at least two heads taller than her. She swallowed, coating her dry throat before asking again,

"Please tell me who you are..." Her voice came out in a pathetic, raspy whisper.

His molten eyes widened in a look of shock just long enough for her to notice, but his gaze quickly hardened. He didn't quite look like the pure-hearted savior she had expected, but what was another thing gone wrong when it seemed like everything was melting out from beneath her feet anyway?

"Where is the book?" he asked, and Rue felt her entire body stiffen.

His voice.

If she hadn't already been certain that this man before her was the one from her dreams, that voice would have convinced her. It made her stomach clench with a feeling she could not name.

Rue took a step back but hit the wall behind her. "H-how do you know about the book?" She was on the verge of breaking down again but used every bit of strength left in her to shove the panic down and stand tall.

"You were able to summon me with that feather. That means the book has been activated. And I need it. Now." He pointed at the feather still dangling between her fingers and took another step closer, pinning her against the wall.

"I— It's upstairs put away safely." Rue swallowed nervously and pulled her arms to her chest, feeling very vulnerable under his intense stare.

"Somehow, I doubt that." The man pushed past her, large wings ruffling behind him as he looked around for the stairs.

Chapter Fifteen

RUE WATCHED INCREDULOUSLY AS this stranger pushed his way through her apartment like he owned the place.

"Excuse me!" She scoffed indignantly and moved her hands to her hips, the anxiety she felt now fully replaced by annoyance, "You can't just come out of my fireplace and make demands from me without even telling me your name or why you're here in the first place. I have half a mind to summon the authorities!" Rue threw her hands up and followed after him.

Who did this man think he was? Gone were her delusions of him being some perfect gentleman with her best interests at heart. Men like that only existed in storybooks; she should have known better.

"I don't think any *authorities* are going to be able to do anything about the hoard of creatures running rampant around the city right now." He continued up the stairs without looking back at her, boots leaving sooty prints behind as he walked over her wood floors.

Rue's brows knitted as a wave of anger rose in her chest. Reaching out and grabbing the back of his shirt, she tugged as hard as she could, using what little strength she had left to stop him.

"I have no idea who you are or where you came from, but you can't just show up in someone's house and rifle through their things. I mean, look at the floors!" Rue gestured to the trail of boot prints left in his wake, "Now, before I let you go any further into my home, I need some questions answered." She leveled him with a withering stare, summoning every ounce of bravado she possibly could.

He huffed out a heavy, irritated sigh and rolled his eyes. Crossing his arms over his chest and widening his stance, the man waited for her to ask whatever it was that she wanted to know.

"First off, do you have a name? And why are you here now suddenly and not when I opened the book in the first place?" She crossed her arms over her chest, mirroring his posture.

"My name is Corvus. I'm here now because you asked me to come." The man — Corvus' eyes slid back to the feather she was still clutching, "I don't know how you got it but it's good that you did. Otherwise, you would have a lot more to contend with than me getting your floors dirty."

Rue huffed. She couldn't disagree with him, but his answer didn't make her any less annoyed.

"Lovely to meet you, Corvus. I'm Ruby, but I would prefer if you called me Rue...but judging by the situation we are in, you probably already knew that," she rambled before clearing her throat and getting back to more important matters, "I was given this feather by some...old hag at the train station. She didn't say anything other than 'he will come,' and it seems she was correct." Rue curled her fingers delicately around the feather before tucking it back into the pocket of her night dress.

Corvus' eyes narrowed suspiciously at her mention of the hag, but he didn't press further.

Rue cleared her throat, changing the subject. She was finding it hard to concentrate when the air around them felt tense and charged.

"You know, instead of just pushing your way in, you could have just asked me, and I would have been more than happy to show you where it is." Rue pushed past him just as he had done to her and opened the door to her bedroom, waving a hand to usher him inside.

Corvus kept quiet but kept that stoic look on his irritatingly handsome face. Rue followed behind him, moving to the closet and digging under a pile of clothes she'd hidden the box in.

Her heart nearly stopped in her chest.

No, no, no. It was here. It had to have been here. She'd felt the power of it as soon as she walked in the door. Rue began to frantically dig through the piles of fabric, tossing them behind her while shaking out others, hoping it had simply gotten lodged into one of the dresses.

She spun to face him, eyes blown wide with panic.

"I-i-it's gone..." Rue bit her lip and awaited whatever insulting thing he was going to say, but he said nothing. Corvus looked at her for a moment longer and blinked slowly as though he hadn't heard her correctly.

"What do you mean it's *gone*? You just said it was put away safely." Corvus pinched his brow and shook his head, mumbling something she didn't quite catch under his breath.

"It was here when I got back. I still felt it. It was here."

"Well, now it is very much not here. Where did it go?"

"Do you think I know?" Rue stood and squared up to him, jabbing a finger in his chest, "If I knew that, I would have told you where it was."

Corvus' brow creased with fury as his eyes fell to where her finger dug into him. He grabbed her hand and shoved it aside, taking a step closer to her. He opened his mouth to say something but seemed to decide against it at the last moment.

Rue ignored him and searched her bedroom, looking for any signs of entry. She hadn't heard anyone come in but that didn't mean it was impossible. She turned to the window, staring at the closed curtains. Panic arose in her once as she thought of the creature at the window and the cracks that had splintered the glass.

"There was one of those creatures at my window earlier. After I opened the book and...activated it, as you said." She pulled the curtain back slowly, fully expecting to see a broken window, but breathed a sigh of relief when she saw it was still intact.

"Maybe it came back when I was downstairs and sneaked in without me hearing it." It seemed like a flimsy explanation, but it was the only one she had. Corvus shot her a look of disbelief but still kept his mouth shut. His face said everything for him anyway.

"If you have any better explanations, then please! By all means, I would love to hear them," Rue snapped in retort to his silent judgment.

"Does anyone else know that it was here?"

"Yes, but no one that would have taken it without me knowing."

"Great. So not only is it gone, but more than just you know about it."

"I'll have you know the few people who do know about it happen to be incredibly trustworthy!" Rue crossed her arms defensively, the volume of her voice rising. She would hear no slander of her friends.

"Again, I hardly believe that," Corvus replied with a scoff. This man had been in her home for less than an hour, and she already wanted to kick him in the shins repeatedly.

"It doesn't matter either way," he continued, "If the book is activated and missing, we need to leave. You aren't safe here anymore. Pack whatever essentials you need, and I will take you to—"

"First of all," Rue raised her hand, cutting him off before he could finish, "I am not going *anywhere* with you until I find my brother."

"We don't have time to worry about your brother. He isn't my problem. You are."

"I am about to become much more of a problem if you try and take me somewhere against my will. Believe that."

They stood there in a silent standoff. Rue was not going to back down on this. Jasper was the only family she had left, and she would be damned before she lost him, too.

"The book might be gone, but I still have the only key to get it out of the box." She pulled her pendant from where it sat inside of her night dress, showing it to him. Corvus' eyes widened again, the same way they did when he first saw her. He knew something about the necklace, but she was sure he wasn't keen on telling her anything.

"So, if you would like me to cooperate with you, I suggest you escort me to find Jasper, and then I will go wherever it is you need to take me. Deal?" She dropped the necklace back into her dress and held out her hand. Corvus stared at her open palm for a moment as though considering what she said. Rue impatiently jabbed it toward him again.

"Deal," he said finally, taking her hand and shaking it firmly. Rue felt a hot, tingling sensation shoot down her arm like her nerves were on fire.

"What did you just do!?" she screeched, jerking her arm back to her chest. Corvus was looking at his own hand, clearly having felt the same thing. Rue watched his Adam's apple bob as he swallowed.

"Looks like you and I are locked in a contract now."

Rue looked at her palm. An imprint in the same eight-pointed sunburst shape as her necklace was now imprinted into her skin.

"When I said 'deal,' I meant it figuratively! I didn't mean this!" she whined, trying — and failing — to rub off the imprint on her hand. Corvus turned his palm toward her, showing the same imprint. Rue groaned and stopped rubbing at it.

"Pack your things, and we'll head out immediately," Corvus conceded, but judging by his tone, it was obvious he still didn't like the idea.

"There is no way we are walking through the Hollow right now! It's the middle of the night, and like you said, who knows what's out there waiting for me. We can leave at first light." Rue crossed her arms over her chest, trying her best to exude some kind of authority. Considering Corvus towered over her by at least a foot and was much more broad, it wasn't easy, but she stood her ground.

"We don't have that luxury. Either you go through the woods to get to your brother now, or you stay here and let whatever's out there kill you. Your choice, sunshine." The nickname dripped from his lips with a particular kind of venom. Anger bubbled up in her stomach. Who did he think he was to talk to her like that?

"Excuse me? How dare you call me some condescending little pet name. You don't know me." Her hands moved to her hips again, and her brow knotted with frustration. Corvus lifted his chin defiantly and looked down his nose at her, crossing his arms and effectively closing himself off.

"Honestly, you don't even have a choice. This deal between us prevents me from just leaving you here, so if push comes to shove, I will drag you out of here kicking and screaming if I have to." His tone left no room for argument. Rue knew he was right, but she didn't like it one bit. She threw her arms up, conceding to him.

"Fine. But I don't like it." She jabbed her finger into the part of his chest that was exposed above his crossed arms and gave him a withering stare before turning on her heel to head up to her room.

"Pack light," he called after her. She didn't reply and just threw up her middle finger in lieu of an answer. Rue could hear him muttering — probably some more insults — under his breath as he walked out of the room and back down the stairs. It didn't matter; she didn't care what he had to say about her, anyway.

Rue snatched an old bag out of her wardrobe, slamming it on her bed, and wrenched open the clasps. This brute of a man decided to show up in her home and practically accused her of being the catalyst for the potential end of the world.

Even if it was partially true, how rude!

"What an asshole," she grumbled under her breath and ripped the simplest of her garments off their hangers, shoving them into the bag.

She didn't even care how wrinkled they became. Rue slammed the wardrobe doors shut with more force than was necessary, but she was so angry she couldn't find it in herself to care about that either.

This really couldn't get worse. Not only did she unleash some kind of hellish demon army due to a stupid lapse in her own self-control, but now she also had to deal with this giant prick of a man whose sole purpose was to make sure no one ever unearthed that particular book.

"Why couldn't this be another one of those dreams?" Rue sighed, slumping against the edge of her bed, head resting in her hands. Her temples were pounding and the pain wasn't helping her mood in the slightest.

The thumping sound of Corvus' heavy footsteps pulled her attention. Gods, what did he want now?

"Speed it up; we need to go," he shouted from the hall outside her door. Rue shot a glare over her shoulder at the closed door. She knew he couldn't see her, but it made her feel a little better anyway.

"Go away. I'll come down when I'm finished," she bit out as she grabbed a few of the unbroken bottles from the vanity shelf, carefully wedging them between the soft clothing, hoping nothing would break on their journey.

There was no sound of retreating footsteps, meaning he was most likely standing there outside the door, waiting for her. Rue swore he was doing everything possible to annoy her further. She let out a breath from deep inside of her chest before closing the clasps on her bag and hoisting it over her shoulder.

She pulled the door open and nearly jumped out of her skin when Corvus was much closer to her than she thought he would be. This close, she could see long, thick lashes that rimmed his eyes. As much as he pissed her off, he was indeed gorgeous...and somehow, that just made her more mad. She tried to brush off those thoughts, attempting to elbow her way past his hulking form in the doorway.

Corvus didn't budge an inch. His smoldering eyes made her stomach clench again. They stood there for a long moment, locked in a strange battle of wills. Rue refused to back down. She wouldn't concede again; she'd already done so once tonight and wasn't keen to make it a habit.

"Look. We have to work together, whether either of us likes it or not. I am trying to do what is best for you as well as for my own mission, so please, for the love of the Gods, try not to make this harder than it needs to be." His voice rumbled in his chest, dropping an octave as he spoke.

Rue didn't know what to say. She definitely hadn't expected *that*. She knew he was right, as much as she was loath to admit it. She let her shoulders fall and gave him a small nod of agreement.

"Alright. Let's just go before I change my mind."

Corvus gave her a small appreciative smile that made the ever-present clench in her stomach turn into a swarm of butterflies. He had the tiniest dimples in the middle of each of his tanned cheeks that only added to his allure. It definitely pissed her off more.

She pushed past him, but not with the amount of force she'd tried the first time. He moved aside, letting her by. and closely followed behind her as she marched to the door. Rue's hand hesitated on the knob, emotion welling up in her throat. It was hard to imagine leaving behind this place that she had worked so hard for. All of the things she'd collected, all the memories she'd made.

All of the worst-case scenarios plagued her thoughts, but Corvus was right. They had to leave before any of those things had the chance to happen.

Chapter Sixteen

T HE TREE LINE THAT separated the edge of the Hollow from the rest of Penrith was a few miles away. Rue was already regretting her choice of footwear as they walked, but of course, she didn't complain. The last thing she needed was to give Corvus more things to nag her about.

The city streets around them were quiet and empty in the late hour. Like a still-life painting. Smoke rose from chimneys high above, and dim golden light glimmered through the windows. Rue thought about the people who lived in these old buildings and how easily they went about their lives. None the wiser to her own life crashing down around her.

How she envied them.

She wished she could go back in time. Back before she'd ever heard of such a book and could live her life in peace. Part of her wanted to pin the blame solely on Jasper for all of this, but she knew that was unfair. He didn't read from the book. He didn't even touch it before he'd left. She'd gotten into this mess all on her own.

Rue also knew, somewhere deep inside her, that all of this was inevitable. It had to be. It was no mere coincidence that she was somehow so deeply interconnected with so much of what was happening.

Corvus' massive wings shivered behind him, catching tiny beams of moonlight that peered through the clouds above them. She was grateful no one was out on the street to see him. He looked so...*other*, and the people of Penrith weren't exactly the most welcoming to outsiders.

She'd had to jog a few times to keep up with his long strides. Damn her and her short legs. He hadn't even bothered to look back the entire time they walked. Rue scowled at his back, pursing her lips together tightly to stop herself from saying anything. It wouldn't matter if she did, anyway. He would just keep walking, telling her to keep up or threaten to carry her again if she fell too far behind.

The last thing she wanted was to be thrown over his shoulder like some kind of sack of potatoes. The thought of it was too humiliating to even consider.

Corvus stopped before her without warning, and she slammed into his back, too lost in her thoughts to notice.

"Oof!" Rue gasped out, cheeks instantly flaming with embarrassment. This wasn't helping her case at all. He didn't even acknowledge her, simply holding his hand up, a warning for her to keep quiet.

Rue took a small step back, chewing her lip nervously as he surveyed the area around them. Did he hear another one of those creatures? The image of the snapping teeth and a maw dripping with muck came to mind again, freezing her in place.

Corvus lowered his hand, but his stance was still on high alert. Rue wrapped her shaking hands around her bag's straps to keep steady. She knew in her gut that Corvus would never let one of those things hurt her, but it still didn't help the way her pounding heart nearly exploded from her rib cage.

"We aren't alone." His voice was barely above a whisper, but with the empty silence around them, Rue heard him loud and clear. The fact that he confirmed her suspicions didn't help, either.

She swallowed hard, trying desperately to ignore the nausea that swirled in her stomach. Without thinking too much of it, Rue reached out and held on tightly to Corvus' arm. She could feel him tense under her touch.

Their tandem breathing was the only sound around them, coming out as clouds of vapor in the cold night air. Rue tried to make out what it was that Corvus was seeing, but nothing stood out.

"I don't see anything," she murmured, throat still feeling tight.

As if her words summoned whatever it was Corvus had heard, the air around them plummeted into an even more bone chilling cold. Rue's teeth chattered, clacking together as she gripped his arm harder, nails digging into his skin beneath the sleeve.

A deafening, inhuman screech echoed from the alley to her left. Her eyes blew open wide with terror. Those things, those...creatures, they had come for her, just like Corvus said they would. He pushed her behind him with a strong arm, the other reaching for the scabbard nestled between his wings.

The sword glowed with an ethereal ultraviolet light. Rue had seen that sword in her dreams, just as she'd seen Corvus. It was hard to process any of what that might have meant when the threat of danger lurked in the shadows not ten feet from her.

"Stay here. Do not move. And whatever you do, do not make any sound," he commanded. Rue could only nod, slapping a hand over her mouth to keep quiet. She didn't like the thought of him leaving her here defenseless but something told her to trust him and he would never let any harm come to her.

A split second later, he had vanished from her side and barreled down the alleyway with his sword held high. His movements were graceful and looked more like a dance rather than a battle stance.

The creature hidden in the alley moved into the small slivers of light. Rue gasped against her hand. It was like a nightmare come to life. The demon at her window was nothing compared to the beast before her now.

It was an abomination. Colossal with multiple spider-like limbs that it used to hold itself upright. Her eyes raked over the beast, trying to fully comprehend what it was that she was looking at. Each of its legs ended in sharp points, giving every step it took a metallic echo that shook from the cobblestones below.

Its eyes were a deep abyss that dripped with the same dark ichor that rimmed the eyes of her doppelganger. The thing's mouth stretched open, showcasing rows upon rows of needle sharp teeth that glimmered with more of the black sludge. It snapped those teeth together and a serpentine tongue darted between them.

"Give us the girl," it said in a distorted layered voice. The sound alone made Rue's stomach clench in terror again.

"Or suffer the consequences of your refusal."

Corvus stood before the hideous creature, sword drawn up in defense. Rue could only watch in horror from where she stood. She crouched down behind him, trying as hard as she could to remain unseen.

"Try me, you ugly piece of shit," Corvus taunted. A soul-piercing scream came from its mouth as a barrier of darkness encased both her and Corvus within it. Rue slammed her hands against her ears, trying to block out the sound, but it was no use. The pitch rattled in her eardrums, sending shooting pains through her entire being.

It reared back and raised its sharp, talon-like legs, preparing to strike Corvus. He flipped the sword around in his hand, tightening the grip on it, and swung wide, colliding with the creature's abdomen, slicing cleanly through.

Violet flames burst from the blade and seemed to cauterize the wound instantly, leaving it smoking instead of gushing whatever blood might be flowing through its veins.

Rue's eyes welled with tears from both the intense terror as well as her sudden inability to blink. She couldn't take her eyes off what was happening before her. The simple grace Corvus managed while he cleaved this beast apart was more than just a little impressive. The way he moved was without fear, instead radiating confidence. She just hoped that it wasn't unfounded.

The creature let out a pained growl but didn't let the giant, smoldering gash across its midsection slow it down. Corvus leapt back, dodging a tight swing of one of the thing's spindly limbs. Rue could see the pointed ends of its legs now oozed a sickly green substance. Could it be some kind of poison? Or acid? She hugged her arms to her chest and hoped she wouldn't find out the answer before Corvus could dispatch it.

Corvus gripped the pommel of his blade, swinging it up over his head and cleaving down into the beast's hide. It let out another equally horrendous screech of pain that reverberated against the dark walls of the barrier around them.

Corvus whirled around the creature with a practiced ease. This was nothing for him. He dodged to the right, narrowly avoiding a collision with another long limb. He ducked down, sweeping his sword out in front of him, trying to reach the thing's back legs to throw it off balance.

The tip of the blade grazed the flesh of its leg before the thing figured out what was going on and reared back out of Corvus' reach. She heard him bark out a curse. He rolled his shoulders back, shaking out his wings, and straightened out his posture. The creature lurched forward, snapping its jaws dangerously close to Corvus' face.

Rue wanted to scream, but Corvus' arms moved faster than she could even see. He pulled his blade up to block the sharp teeth from gnashing into his face. Corvus steadied himself, pushing his foot back to hold his balance and used a combination of his body weight and the strength of his wings flapping out behind him to push the thing back, with the sword taking the brunt of the assault.

"Would you just fucking die already?" he shouted, flicking the blade back around and shoving it through the thing's mouth and up through its skull. In an instant, the beast's entire body went limp, collapsing in the street before him.

The shadowy dome around them faded in a puff of smoke and the creature's limbs twitched and writhed as though it had been struck by lightning. Rue turned her head away, unable to continue looking at it now that the threat was gone.

The sick crunch of bone was as good a death knell as any. Rue turned back just as Corvus plunged his blade into the beast's body, and a flash of ultraviolet light illuminated her periphery. The purple and blue flames enveloped the corpse and burned it away into nothing but a pile of ash.

Corvus shook the last bits of gore from his sword before sliding it back into the scabbard on his back with a tiny click. He panted hard, and his face was splattered with black ichor. Rue let out a long, shaky breath of relief. He was alright.

"Are you okay?" He offered his hand, which she took gratefully, and nodded, completely dumbstruck.

"Good. Let's keep going." Corvus tugged her hand, pulling her body closer to him, and continued walking like nothing had even happened. Rue looked back over her shoulder at the pile of smoldering cinders left in the street, wondering what she would have done on her own.

She was suddenly very glad she had chosen to be cooperative and go with Corvus. Despite his promise to drag her with him no matter what choice she'd made. They walked in silence for a while longer, the tree line of the Hollow coming into view. Rue's heartbeat eventually returned to normal, and her mouth no longer felt glued shut in fear.

"Thank you," she said so quietly she was unsure he could even hear her. But the grunt he gave in response told her he did. There were a multitude of things she wanted to ask him, but she knew now wasn't the time for it, so she kept quiet and continued following her guide into the dark trees of the Hollow.

It was hard to tell where they were going in the pitch-blackness of the forest, but Corvus seemed to know the way. The canopy of tall pine and fir trees obscured any remaining moonlight that might have lit their path. Rue squinted, trying to make out her surroundings.

The strap of her heavy bag dug into her shoulder, weighing her down. Wrapping her hands around the thick strap, Rue prepared to heave it up onto her shoulder for the umpteenth time since they'd started walking when the weight disappeared altogether.

"Give me that, you're just going to slow us down," Corvus grumbled, taking the bag and sliding the strap over his shoulder with ease, holding it like it weighed nothing. For someone as strong as him, it probably was nothing. Rue's cheeks heated with embarrassment, suddenly grateful for the darkness.

Overcome with nervous energy and now having nothing to occupy her hands, Rue's fingers made their way back into her mouth, teeth gnashing at her fingernails once more. Corvus' hand was suddenly around her wrist, pulling her hand from her face.

"Don't do that; you're going to destroy your fingers. And it's a disgusting habit." He wrapped his fingers firmly around her hand, holding her close to his side.

"I can't help it. I've done it as long as I can remember," Rue muttered under her breath, embarrassed by his comment. He didn't say anything else but kept her hand firmly in his.

"You don't need to hold my hand, you know."

"I do if I expect you to keep it out of your mouth."

She stuck her tongue out where he couldn't see, silently mocking him, but couldn't help the warmth that spread through her stomach when she thought about how large his hand was and how it completely enveloped hers.

Touching Corvus was so different than how it had felt to touch Ryker. Corvus' hands were rough and bore the scars of hard work, whereas Ryker's hands were soft and delicate, a man of money who'd never done a day of real work in his life.

Rue's heart clenched painfully when she thought about Ryker and the way he'd reacted when she told him about the creature in her window. She knew she shouldn't have expected much from him, but it still hurt. She gave him so much of herself — too much, if she was being honest — and he couldn't even be bothered to return a fraction of the favor.

She let out another long sigh and let her posture slump slightly, relaxing more the farther they walked. Corvus glanced down at her periodically, his stare sometimes lingering on her for longer than she thought was strictly necessary. Rue pretended not to notice, but the feeling of his eyes on her made her stomach flip.

"Why do you keep staring at me like that?" she asked, brows knitting in equal parts confusion and irritation. He shook his head and pressed a finger to his lips, wordlessly telling her to keep quiet. That small gesture had her nerves flaring up again. What was he hearing that she wasn't? She pushed her glasses up the sweaty bridge of her nose with her free hand and tried to keep her breathing even.

"I need you to be very, very quiet." His voice held a dire warning, and she knew she would be stupid not to heed it. Rue nodded and curled her lips inward. Of course she was terrified, but having a very strong and capable man with her definitely alleviated the fear, at least marginally.

Corvus' eyes were unnaturally bright in the darkness. He scanned their surroundings, gaze sharp and predatory. Seeing him like that reminded Rue that he wasn't entirely human. It was easy to forget when she felt so safe standing here next to him.

Corvus' eyes were still combing the area around them, his body rigid and on alert, making her increasingly more nervous. She wanted to ask him what he saw or heard but thought better of it and tightened her grip on his hand.

"Whatever was here is gone," Corvus breathed out, the rigidity in his shoulders fading after a moment. They continued walking with nothing but the sound of the occasional snapping twig or crunching leaves under their shoes. Abruptly, Corvus stopped, lifting his face to the sky and closed his eyes. Rue watched him curiously. A cold gust of wind blew out at them, whipping around her face. Her hands wrenched away from his and immediately flew to her hood, holding it on as best as she could.

"What's happening?" Rue asked, body subconsciously pressing into his, seeking the warmth it offered against the frigid wind.

"The ravens in the woods speak to me," he said plainly, like it should have been obvious. Rue's brow creased as she considered what he was saying. Was that why those ravens kept showing up around her? Yet another strange not quite coincidence to add to the tally.

"Like...a familiar?" She pressed.

"Yes, something like that."

"Interesting."

She didn't press any further and tucked the information away for later as they continued to move. The earthen floor of the woods was covered in twisting vines, thorny brambles, and broken branches. Rue squinted hard, trying to watch where her feet were going, but found it increasingly difficult to see anything, even as her eyes began to adjust in the darkness.

"Ouch!" she gasped out as her ankle twisted into a briar bush. She stopped and squatted down, trying to quickly disentangle herself from the thorns. Her hands shook too much to be useful. She let out a frustrated groan, feeling the prick of angry tears behind her eyes, making her nose sting.

She would not cry. Not here. Not like this.

Corvus stopped, realizing she was no longer following him. He made a noise of annoyance but still knelt down to help her out of the thick vines anyway.

"Watch your step next time," he chided, wrapping his large palm around her upper arm, helping her back up.

"We can't all have fancy glowing eyes that can see in the dark like you."

Corvus chuckled softly at her words, and the sound made Rue's chest tighten.

It wasn't fair. He had the grace and balance of a cat, and here she was, walking around like she had the legs of a baby deer. Frowning, she pushed him away halfheartedly.

"Glad you find me so amusing," Rue grumbled under her breath, eyes still on the forest floor.

"Amusing is one way to describe it."

"What is that supposed to mean?" she barked at him, but he just brought a finger to his lips, reminding her to keep quiet.

Jerk.

CHAPTER SEVENTEEN

They arrived at The Devil's Due just before sunrise. Corvus had cloaked his wings somehow, drawing a slew of half-formed and incredulous questions from Rue before Corvus simply settled on 'magic' punctuated with a shrug by way of an explanation.

The last of the night's patrons stumbled out into the early morning, reeking of stale beer and gods knew what else. Corvus eyed them all with suspicion but said nothing. Rue's body tingled with the last dregs of adrenaline. It staved off the exhaustion, but she knew that, now that they were in relative safety, any moment, it was going to hit her like a bag of bricks.

She pushed open the door and craned her neck, trying to find either Jasper's tell-tale orange head of hair or Lydia's booming voice behind the bar. The tavern was still decently full despite the hour, but Rue supposed these people must have had rooms upstairs. She didn't see Jasper, but Lydia was where she had seen her before, standing behind the counter and wiping a stein with an old rag.

"Lydia!" Rue called out, waving her arm at the proprietress. Lydia stopped and jerked her head with a smile, wordlessly calling Rue over.

"Welcome back, girl. And with a friend this time?" Lydia's lilting accent was musical as the words came off her tongue, bringing a strange sense of comfort to Rue's tired heart.

"I'm looking for my brother. Have you seen him? It's very, very important," Rue told her, ignoring Lydia's comment about Corvus. Lydia set the stein on the counter and shook her head with a sad expression.

"Sorry, ya just missed him. Left not but an hour ago."

"Did he say where he was going?"

"Nah, nah. I'm not his mama," Lydia laughed and shook her head, "But he did say he would be back in a day or so to gimme that money he owe me."

Rue opened her mouth to respond, but before she could speak, Corvus stepped in and cut her off.

"We don't have a day or two for your brother to *maybe* show up."

"I already told you. I am not going anywhere until I find him. I can't just leave without knowing—" Rue stopped herself before the emotions brewing in her gut could get the best of her. The mix of fear and exhaustion made for a caustic cocktail. Corvus leveled her with a glare that said he would make good on his promise of dragging her with him if he was forced to.

"Please. Just let me have two days. If he doesn't show up, we can go," Rue conceded, even if the thought of potentially leaving Jasper behind made her stomach fold into knots. Corvus continued to stare at her as though considering. Eventually, his shoulders slumped with a defeated groan.

"Two days, nothing more. That's all I can give you."

Rue nodded, giving him a wide, toothy grin, showing off the tiny gap between her front teeth.

"Thank you." She wrapped her fingers around his forearm, giving a small squeeze. Corvus said nothing and turned his head, suddenly focused on anything other than her face.

"Lydia, I need a room, please."

Rue was grateful that Lydia had one room left, but in an unfortunate turn of circumstance, there had only been a single bed available. Corvus' face said more than his words could. He was unimpressed by this development. Rue rolled her eyes and kicked off her heeled boots.

"It's just a bed. We're just sleeping. Don't make a big deal out of it," she told him, massaging her aching heels with a small relieved moan. Corvus stood still as a statue in the corner with his arms crossed. She almost laughed. He looked like such a petulant child.

"I'm not going to bite, you know. I might snore, however."

Corvus shook his head and crossed the room over to her. The unimpressed look was still plastered onto his face.

"You're more than welcome to sleep on the floor if that would offend your obviously very delicate sensibilities less, but I will be sleeping on this very —" Rue pushed down on the mattress and cringed at the amount of lumps in its old springs "Comfortable mattress."

That earned a small chuckle from Corvus. Rue smiled at him and scooted over, patting the now empty spot on the bed.

"There's plenty of space for both of us."

"I'll sleep on the edge just in case something happens and I need to get up," Corvus told her, like he was trying to justify it somehow.

"Whatever you have to tell yourself."

Rue fell asleep almost immediately after her head hit the pillow. She awoke the next morning feeling more rested than she had in the last month. No dreams, no nightmares. Only deep and refreshing sleep. She rubbed her eyes to see Corvus sitting at the edge of the bed, eyes trained on her like if he blinked, she would disappear. He had slept next to her all night, but she hadn't felt him move to get up. She must have been sleeping harder than she thought.

"Good morning," she mumbled, rubbing the last grainy bits of sleep from her eyes.

"Morning."

"You didn't sleep, did you?"

Corvus shook his head and pushed his shaggy fringe from his fore-head. She could tell he was exhausted. Trained warrior or not, everyone needed sleep.

"I'll go downstairs and get some food," he said, moving to stand, but Rue caught his hand and tugged him back down.

"I'll go. I can manage on my own for a few minutes."

They held each other's gaze for too long. The sound of Corvus clear-ing his throat broke through the trance. Rue decided to ignore whatever the feeling in her gut was and jumped out of bed, still dressed in her clothes from the night before. She darted out the door, leaving before Corvus could change his mind and in an attempt to conceal the heat that painted her cheeks.

Options for food this early were limited. Lydia hadn't even come downstairs yet. Instead, her wife — who Rue knew to be called Theo — stood behind the bar, slicing into a loaf of brown bread. Theo didn't seem much for conversation, likely just having woken up herself. They exchanged quick pleasantries before Rue took a plate of bread, cheese, and some kind of dried sausage back to the room with her.

When she returned, Corvus was fast asleep on the bed, shoes still on but hanging over the edge. Rue felt a smile creep into her cheeks as she set the plate down on the scratched night stand beside him. She knelt down next to the bed, and pushed a single onyx curl from his forehead. Corvus didn't stir, sleep had fully claimed him.

This close, Rue could now see all the faint scars that ran over his tanned skin, like a myriad of lightning bolts flashing through a dark sky. Rue's chest tightened when she thought of all the different battles he may have fought and what terrible things he must have gone through to earn these scars. She realized just how little she actually knew about this man, and yet, his presence felt so comfortable and safe. Familiar, even.

Rue pushed that thought aside before she could linger too much more on it. She stood up, moving to the bathroom, and closed the door behind her.

The room they stayed in sat at the back of Lydia's tavern was and was much more spacious than most. It included an en suite bathing room with all of the basic necessities. But the large ostentatious claw foot tub that sat in the center of the room was the true highlight.

Rue sat on the edge of the tub and turned the tap, letting it run for a moment to heat up while she got undressed. She slid out of her now sullied dress, letting the thin fabric pool at her ankles before stepping out of it and kicking it away.

Catching her reflection in the full-length mirror made her cringe. Her face was covered in small scrapes from the countless times she'd walked into low-hanging branches, and her hair was in knots instead of curls. She'd really looked worse for wear and was positive she didn't smell much better either. Steam rose from the now hot water streaming out of the tap. Rue reached down into the deep tub to stuff the stopper in the drain, allowing it to fill.

Rue sat at the edge of the tub again and tried to tame the knots in her hair as the water rose. Hot steam wrapped around her leg, coaxing her into the water like a siren's song. She quickly gave up the futile endeavor with her twisted locks and slid into the half-filled tub instead.

The moan she let out was downright indecent. The water was a little too hot, but she didn't care. The immediate relief she'd felt in her sore muscles was worth a little scalding. She stretched out her legs, leaned her head back against the tub, and closed her eyes. She wanted to savor this small moment of peace before she was thrust back into the waking nightmare she was currently stuck in. No, all that awaited her on the other side of these doors could wait for an hour or two.

Rue wiggled her toes into the running water as it came out of the tap, her skin beginning to adjust to the heat. Next to the tub was a tray of bottles full of various lotions, soaps and oils. She reached for one and popped its cork open, bringing it to her nose inhaling the sweet scent of lavender and sage.

Tipping some of the viscous substance into the water, the scent immediately permeated the air as it mingled with the hot water. In the last few weeks, quiet had begun to unnerve Rue, but now, the solemnity was comfortable. She leaned back against the porcelain again and let her head sink further into the water. Hot water saturated her curls, gently cradling her scalp, pulling a low, appreciative sigh from her chest.

Between the lovely, calming scent of lavender and the water's warmth cocooning her, Rue felt herself drifting into a gentle doze. It had been a long time since she had felt at peace like this, and she was going to let herself enjoy it for just a while longer.

Rue awoke with a start without any idea how long she had been asleep in the tub. She dunked her head under the now cool water, sluicing it off her face as she arose. The lantern in the corner of the room had gone out and the windowless bathroom was now blanketed in darkness.

Slowly, she pulled her knees to her chest and wrapped her arms around them. Her eyes darted around the room as she tried to make out anything at all in the dark. Something wasn't right. This had to be another dream. She was still asleep in that tub, and this was all in her head.

The comfortable quiet of the room had turned unsettling. Rue's pulse thrummed in her ears as she strained to listen for anything out of place. Was Corvus still asleep on the other side of the door? Would he hear her if she screamed for help? Her eyes weren't adjusting to the darkness at all, exponentially ramping up the feeling of dread in the pit of her stomach.

Suddenly, the sound of slow, clunky footsteps broke the silence. Rue's head snapped so hard toward the source of the noise, she was surprised she didn't hurt herself. Her grip on her legs tightened, nails digging into her skin as she tried to keep quiet. Hoping whatever was making that noise wouldn't find her if she stayed silent. Someone — or something— was in here with her. She wanted to scream for Corvus, but the rising terror she felt held her voice in a choking grip.

The sound of those footsteps grew closer and closer with every passing second. Panic sunk its claws into her, and she hid her face between her knees, trying to take a few calming breaths. Trying to will away whatever nightmare was encroaching on her now. The sound of nails scraping against porcelain rang in her ears. She clenched her teeth tight, holding in a scream that was desperately clawing up her throat.

Please leave me alone...please go away...

She chanted those words over and over in her head, rocking her body in the now nearly freezing water. Hot tears streamed down her face, but she refused to raise her head from her knees. She did not want to see whatever horror was facing her down.

Rue didn't need to see it to know it was getting closer. She could hear the snapping of teeth and smell the rotting stench of its breath. Bile rose up the back of her throat and coated her tongue, leaving a horribly bitter taste behind.

A bony hand thrust into her hair, gripping like a vise as it wrenched her head back. Two lambent orbs stared into her from above. Most of the creature's face was still hidden by the shadows around her but its sharp teeth dripped with a foul smelling substance. It opened its mouth, lowering its face to hers as a long serpent-like tongue caressed her cheek, dragging the stinking ooze along with it.

Fresh, hot tears flooded from her eyes as she opened her mouth to scream. The creature's other hand grabbed her chin, holding her head in place. Sickening chartreuse eyes bore into her, pulling her into its hypnotic stare. Her mouth hung open, a scream dead on her lips. The creature was so close now she could finally see it clearly. Its tongue raked over thin lips that pulled back over too-long teeth, more of that grotesque sludge dripping onto her face.

"Your warrior isn't here to save you now," it said with a voice that sounded strangled and pained. Rue tried to pull her head out of its grasp but when the creature didn't budge she took a deep breath and bellowed as loud as she could.

"Corvus! Please!" His name came out in a strangled cry. She prayed he would hear her even through his deep sleep. Prayed he was even still there. She didn't stop and began thrashing with all her might against the creature's grip.

She couldn't be helpless. She would not go down without a fight. She lifted her arms, trying to feel around for the glass bottles. If she could just grab one and break it against the side of the tub, she would have at least a modicum of a chance to defend herself.

"Yes, scream for him. Your fear is delicious," the creature gurgled out. Rue's searching hand eventually made contact with one of the glass bottles. She reared it back, slamming the side of it against the porcelain tub as hard as she could. Rue swung her arm and thrust the end of the broken bottle into whatever part of the creature she could reach. It released its grip on her, hissing in pain. For just a moment, she internally thanked herself for years of lifting heavy books.

Rue moved, trying to pull her body from the tub, but her foot slipped out from under her, sending her sliding right back down. "Shit!" she swore, trying again to right herself. Before she could even think, the bathroom door burst open, nearly flying off its hinges. Corvus was barreling through the door, sword held high over his head.

Violet light flooded the room, and the creature hissed even louder. The smell of burning meat was suddenly overpowering. Corvus' sword cleaved through the creature's rotting flesh, acrid smoke rising from its body.

Rue tugged her knees back against her chest, her eyes wide and fixated on the gruesome scene before her. The burning blade engulfed the now-dead beast in deep aubergine flames. Corvus stood to his full height and slid the sword back into its sheath behind him. His eyes slowly dragged from the pile of ash on the floor to Rue's face.

"Are you alright?" His brow creased with worry.

"Yes, I am now." She nodded, still breathing hard. Corvus' eyes flicked down to her exposed chest and quickly back up to her face.

"Good. I'll, uh, let you get dressed then." He turned hard on his heel and walked out of the bathing room. Rue could have sworn she saw his cheeks tint pink. When she was certain he wasn't looking, she stood from the bath, letting the excess water drip off of her before stepping out and grabbing one of the clean towels from the pile near the door.

CHAPTER EIGHTEEN

I T WAS CLEAR THEY couldn't stay here and wait for Jasper any longer. Corvus began packing Rue's things back in the bag she'd brought with her, and she tried not to think about him handling her unmentionables.

"You don't need to do that. I can manage, thank you." Rue nudged him away, snatching the last remnants of clothing from his hands. Corvus moved without argument, but she still felt his eyes practically burn into her back. Rue bent forward to pick up one of her skirts that had fallen without thinking of the indecent length of the robe she'd hastily pulled on after the bath incident.

That was a mistake.

She let out a yelp and stood up straight, tugging down the edge of the robe as she felt the breeze of the room practically kiss her backside.

"Don't look! Turn around!" Rue screeched in a panic.

"You give yourself far too much credit, sunshine," Corvus barked out a laugh. Her cheeks flared with embarrassment, but her stomach did a flip at the nickname.

"Jerk," she muttered under her breath and slid a pair of panties up her thighs under the robe, letting it fall to the floor once she was sure Corvus' back was to her. Rue pulled on one of the lightweight dresses she'd brought, feeling much more secure as the fabric brushed against her ankles.

She perched on the edge of the bed and bent down to pull her boots on and lace them. Corvus turned to face her again, a look of relief on his face when he saw she'd finally put on something more proper than a skimpy robe.

"If you're ready, we should leave. Before we lose more daylight." He picked up her bag, hoisting it over his shoulder, standing straighter. Rue nodded and pushed herself from the mattress, standing only a few inches from him.

"Thank you." Her eyes locked with his, "For coming for me. I don't think I could have taken that thing down alone."

Corvus' eyes softened, and his posture relaxed, "Stabbing it with a glass bottle was pretty impressive, if I'm being honest." He shook his head with a small smile that showed his dimples.

Damn that smile.

Rue swallowed, trying to maintain her composure. How could a single being be so infuriating yet charming at the same time?

"You said there was a place you were going to take me?" Rue questioned, rubbing her hands together and fighting the urge to put her fingernails between her teeth again.

"Yes. There is a temple of sorts deep in the forest." He affirmed with a nod.

Rue had never heard of such a thing despite living on the isle her entire life, but as she was finding out, there was a multitude of things she had never heard of. It seemed the small isle she'd always called her home was drenched in secrets as well as rain.

"Alright. I'll have to leave a word with Lydia for Jasper whenever he returns..." Her voice fell with a sadness that Corvus seemed to sense. His hand slid into hers and gave it a reassuring squeeze.

"He's going to be alright."

And for whatever reason, she believed him.

Rue stood with renewed determination, "Let's go before I lose my courage."

With all of her things packed, Rue and Corvus left the Devil's Due after leaving a note with Lydia to pass along to Jasper whenever he deigned to return. Corvus held her bag, this time without asking, as they made their way through the Hollow.

The sun had crested over the horizon, and tiny fragments of light wove their way through the thick canopy of trees, making their journey much easier than the first time they'd ventured through the forest.

Being inside the heart of the Hollow was like stepping into another world. No evidence of the city on the outside could be seen through the endless sea of bark and leaves. The Hollow did make a good place to hide a secret temple, she supposed.

As they walked, Corvus' hand found hers again and Rue reminded herself it was more likely to keep them from being separated than him actually wanting to touch her. She tried not to let that thought bother her.

"You said there are others at this temple?" Rue finally asked, hating the way the silence hung between them.

"Yes. Other Veridae like me."

Rue thought about the word, rolling around a few possibilities in her mind, "They have wings like you then? Is that why the ravens speak with you? Is it some kind of magical link?" She began rattling off more questions rapid-fire before she could stop herself. Corvus huffed, sounding slightly annoyed, but answered her anyway.

"In a way, yes. The wings we are born with are a symbol that we have been chosen by the Goddess. We are the protectors of Solira."

"Wait, so you mean you actually knew her?" Rue questioned, "That means you've got to be hundreds of years old!"

Corvus shot her an offended look, "Yes, that's exactly what it means."

Rue's mind was spinning, diving through all the different possibilities. She began linking the connections between what he was saying and what she already knew of the pantheon. There were still a great number of holes in these theories but she hoped she could get more information once they reached the temple.

Without realizing, Rue must have gone quiet when she retreated into her mind. Corvus' eyes were trained on her with equal parts melancholy and confusion.

"W-why do you look at me that way?" Rue stumbled over her words, feeling scrutinized.

"It's nothing." Corvus shook his head and turned his gaze back to the path in front of them. Rue's brow creased with irritation as she dug her heels into the dirt, tugging on his hand.

"I know I'm probably not what you expected, but I will have you know I am plenty capable. I may not have muscles, and I most *definitely* cannot use a sword in any way, but I have what counts!" Her voice rose as she defended herself, "I have the power of knowledge! And no one can take that away from me." Rue closed her eyes and turned her nose up in a slightly snotty gesture, but then, instead of another argument, she heard laughter.

"What? Why are you laughing at me?" Rue pulled her hand out of his and placed both of hers on her hips.

"Nothing, nothing, sunshine."

That nickname again.

"All of this is just starting to make a bit more sense, is all." Corvus didn't elaborate further and simply turned away from her and continued walking. Rue stared at his retreating back, dumbfounded. What was making sense? What had she said? In any case, she didn't have time to think about it too deeply as Corvus was now getting farther and farther away from her.

"Wait for me!" Rue called out, hurrying to catch up to him, her face still in a scrunched expression.

"You know if you keep making that face, you're going to get wrinkles," Corvus said in a very matter-of-fact tone.

"Are you always this charming, Corvus?"

"Just for you, sunshine."

"Don't call me that."

Corvus scoffed, "What? Sunshine?"

"Yes. I have a name and I would prefer if you used it," Rue stated, trying her best to sound stern but her tone was half hearted at best. She wouldn't tell him, but she was actually beginning to enjoy hearing the nickname. If nothing else, it matched her tangerine hair perfectly.

"Fine, Ruby."

"No! Not that one, you jerk! I told you to call me Rue."

Corvus rolled his eyes and shook his head, muttering 'Rue' in a condescending little voice under his breath. Rue couldn't help but smile at how this giant boulder of a man could be so childish.

The early morning hours had passed, the sun sat high in the sky but was mostly obscured by heavy dark clouds that promised rain once again. The temple had to be close by now, Rue felt like they'd been walking for an eternity.

Before them, the tree line began to thin, creating a wider path than the one they had been walking on. In the distance, Rue could see a blurred outline of what looked like it might be some kind of house, but certainly not the kind of temple she had in mind.

"Is that it up there?"

Corvus nodded, "Not too much farther now." He tugged on her arm gently, urging her to pick up the pace. He must be exhausted, she thought, between staying up all night while she slept and then being interrupted when he did finally have the chance to get some shut-eye. Traveling had to be taking a toll on him.

"How many others will be there?" Rue asked, suddenly feeling nervous. Corvus had told her that others were there, but she hadn't thought to ask how many. Imagining a room full of more broody, curt men wasn't exactly inviting.

"Last I heard, it was just three of them."

Three. That was manageable. Or at least she hoped it would be.

"When we get there. Do not speak until I do. They do not know who you are; they only know about the book," Corvus told her, his voice low and stern. Rue nodded despite the fact he wasn't looking at her. She got the feeling that he knew anyway. He seemed to have some kind of strange sixth sense when it came to her.

"Walk behind me and stay close," he added as the temple came into view. The small structure she had seen in the distance was breathtaking once they got close enough to make out all the details. Although the outer walls looked as though they'd seen better days, the architecture was still a wonder.

Edged in red brick trim and carved with intricate designs that seemed to tell a story, the temple walls were made from rough hewn stone, laid in a way that made the mortar holding the mismatched stones together look like a spider's web. Each place where the stone met created a thread that connected to the rest of the design.

A single steeple stood directly above the only door she could see. In the center of the long column was a single stained glass window that looked like it hadn't been cleaned in centuries, but through the dirt and grime, Rue could make out that the panes were colored like fire. Reds, yellows and oranges reflected in the glass against whatever bits of light could reach.

Atop it was a symbol that matched the pendant around her neck. Rue wrapped her hand around it as she stared up at the large citrine gem that sat in the center of the sun, the same way her necklace did.

"Is that symbol for Solira?" she asked quietly, though she could probably guess the answer.

"It is. She was the Goddess of many things, but the sun was what we associated her with," Corvus replied. His vague answer made Rue want to press for more, but before she could even formulate the words on her tongue, Corvus turned and faced her, pressing a finger to his lips, reminding her to keep quiet as they entered.

Corvus pushed the doors open. Whatever trick he'd used before to cloak his wings faded, bringing the soft feathers back into view as they stepped over the threshold.

The inner walls of the sanctum were covered with beautiful and complex murals depicting scenery and other abstract bits of art. They were painted in muted colors – or maybe they'd been vibrant once and had simply faded with time. The main room was lined with candle lit sconces, bathing the area in a soft, serene light. The temple was sparse, with no pews or other seating, leaving the floor completely open and empty.

A man slightly shorter than Corvus stood at what looked to be some kind of altar. His hair was a dark, ruddy brown, pulled into a quick, sloppy bun behind his head. He definitely looked younger than Corvus, with a more round and boyish face. His cheeks were tinted a soft peach color against his paler skin.

"Oliver." Corvus nodded his head in a greeting to the younger man.

"Welcome back. Who is she?" the man, Oliver, leaned to the side, peeking around Corvus' side.

"The vessel."

Rue's brow pinched in confusion. What did he mean she was a vessel? She started to open her mouth to ask, but Corvus' warning came back to her, making her shut it immediately instead.

Oliver's eyes went wide with shock for a moment, but he quickly shifted back to the casual demeanor he'd had before.

"Truly? It's her?" His voice sounded hopeful, which only confused Rue more. Corvus had made it sound like the Veridae were hostile and unaccepting of outsiders, but Oliver seemed eager, almost excited, to see her there.

Corvus gave a curt nod, moving aside and putting Rue directly in Oliver's line of sight. She swallowed nervously, raising her head up, trying as she might to project an air of confidence she didn't feel.

Oliver took a step toward her, his deep blue eyes raking over every inch of her. Rue resisted the nervous urge to push her glasses up on her nose.

"The resemblance is really kind of uncanny," Oliver commented, rubbing his chin pensively with his thumb and forefinger, "Curious."

"Where are the others?" Corvus moved past Oliver toward the altar. It was a simple fixture consisting of a single long table and adorned with various stones, herbs, candles, and other scattered random offerings. Corvus dropped to one knee before it, touching his fingers to one of the stones in the center of the table, bringing them to his forehead.

Rue made a mental note to ask him about it later, even though he would probably give her another non-answer like any of the other times she tried to ask him anything about his life.

An echoing sound of footsteps rang out in the quiet of the temple. Rue turned toward the sound and saw another man step out into the main room. He looked older than both Oliver and Corvus, his hair long and streaked with silver. His face was long with sharp angles, but his eyes were the same fiery color as Corvus'. Rue wondered if they were related somehow.

"Corvus, you've returned...and with a guest." The man's voice was deep and gravelly, making her think of smoke and whiskey.

"She's..." he began, his eyes widening the same way Oliver's had and his head snapped toward Corvus who simply gave an affirming nod.

"Yes." His voice was curt, almost warning. Like he was urging this man not to say anything more. Anger rose in Rue's chest. What were they even talking about? What was all this nonsense about a vessel, and why did everyone keep looking at her like that? She couldn't hold her tongue any longer.

"Can you all *please* stop talking about me like I'm not standing right here?" Her words came out more accusatory than she'd meant, but she kept her features stern. The older man crossed his arms over his chest and a small amused grin flashed across his face.

"Oh. I understand," he chuckled, looking back to Corvus. Rue turned to face him too, tilting her head in question.

"Am I missing something?" She snapped, throwing her hands up in frustration. Corvus sighed and pinched the bridge of his nose. Did he actually expect her to stay quiet and just listen to these strangers essentially gossip about her to her face?

"Now is not the time to discuss this. We will talk later." He walked back toward the center of the room, turning toward the older man.

"There is a problem, Ardeth. The book is gone. By the time I got to her, it had already been taken." Corvus explained. The man, Ardeth, muttered something that sounded like a curse in a language Rue couldn't understand.

"Vaion's probably sent one of his little minions to retrieve it now that she's completed the catalyst ritual." Ardeth sighed.

"It's more than likely. We just have to find where he's hiding it before he can take the next step." Corvus confirmed. Rue wasn't sure what to think about this new information she was hearing. She'd heard the name

Vaion from Vesper but didn't yet know much about this God. From what it sounded like, whatever he was up to was not good.

Chapter Nineteen

"I will alert Sabrien. He can contact the others and send a search party through the city," Ardeth said.

As if called on cue, another tall man stepped out from another door on the opposite wall. He reached his hands above his head in a stretch, wings spreading out behind him as he nearly yelled a yawn.

"Someone talking about me — Oh, Corvus, you're back already?" Sabrien, she assumed, looked to Corvus in confusion. He was the same height as Corvus, but his build was more on the slim side. His golden blond hair cut into a shaggy undercut with curls that toppled over his brow. Green eyes cut away from Corvus as he caught hers.

"Well, I'll be damned," he muttered, "It really is her."

Again with this. Rue was going to grill Corvus until she got answers, but she pushed that aside for now.

"Does she have the book then?"

"No, if you'd been here earlier, you would have heard everything, and I wouldn't need to repeat myself now," Corvus grumbled, glaring daggers at Sabrien.

Sabrien shrugged, "It's not like we were expecting you back so quickly, don't get all pissy now."

Rue wanted to laugh. She immediately decided that she liked Sabrien. Corvus' face flushed for a moment, but he took a breath and collected himself before speaking again.

"The book was already gone by the time I'd reached her. The creatures had already found her, so Vaion's already awakened, and he's probably sent some of his lackeys to fetch it," Corvus explained again, summarizing for Sabrien.

"Nothing can ever be easy, can it?" Sabrien rolled his eyes as he dramatically sagged his forehead into his palm, "I suppose you're going to send me out, then."

"Right you are, seeker," Ardeth answered this time, pushing his way between Corvus and Sabrien before they found something else to bicker about.

"Ugh, fine. I'll go as soon as I greet our lovely guest." Sabrien turned to Rue, shooting her a wink with a small grin.

"Oh, don't be so cheeky," Oliver chimed in, pushing Sabrien so he could wedge himself into the sort of half circle they had begun forming around her.

"I'm very confused about all of this..." Rue finally said, "But, I'm really sorry for causing all this trouble, I didn't think it would really..." she trailed off. She didn't think, and that was the real root of the problem. Rue chewed the inside of her lip nervously as she thought about the look Corvus had given her when he'd first appeared before her. The look of contempt. Of anger and rage so plain on his face.

"It was bound to happen eventually. It was just a matter of time for the right vessel to be chosen, I suppose." Ardeth was the first to speak. Rue didn't know what he meant by the right vessel, but she didn't bother asking as she was sure she still wouldn't be getting any answers.

"We have prepared for something like this to happen, and though it won't be easy, we will prevail as always," Ardeth continued, not speaking to Rue at all anymore. His eyes jumped to each of the other men before him. He continued speaking, but Rue couldn't hear him anymore. The room was spinning around her, and she suddenly felt lightheaded.

Everything caught up to her all at once. Her vision swam, the walls around her blurred, and her stomach lurched with nausea.

"I need to lie down," Rue interjected, cutting off whatever Ardeth had been saying. Corvus' gaze cut to her, his brows knitting together with concern, but he nodded once, turning to Oliver.

"Take her to the bunks."

"Of course." Oliver took a step forward toward Rue, jerking his head in the direction of one of the doors down the hall, "Come with me, please."

The temple was much larger than it had initially appeared from the outside. The door Oliver took her through stretched into a long hallway lined with more doors on either side. Rue was completely enraptured by the delicate artwork along all of the walls.

"This temple is beautiful," she whispered as they walked.

"It is. It's the work of many generations of Veridae."

"Do you know how long it's been here?"

Oliver shook his head, looking a little sad, "I'm honestly not sure. It's been here for longer than any of us can remember, I think."

"Are you the youngest of them?" Rue asked as Oliver seemed more inclined to answer her questions than Corvus.He nodded, "Yes I am. So I am, unfortunately, not the most reliable source for any questions about the history of the temple." Oliver gave a soft apologetic laugh and Rue felt herself begin to relax. He was so different from Corvus, it was almost alarming. "It's fine; I shouldn't be asking so many questions anyway. You all probably want to keep all this secret society stuff quiet, I'm sure."

Oliver laughed again, louder this time, and shook his head, "We aren't a secret society."

"You live in an old temple in the middle of the woods. That sounds pretty secretive to me." Rue tilted her head toward Oliver, offering him a playful smile.

"Well, I suppose when you put it like that…" he sheepishly rubbed the back of his neck.

When they approached the end of the hall, Oliver opened one of the doors and ushered her inside. The room was small but comfortable. There were four simple beds, with metal frames, adorned with a single pillow and blanket.

"It's not the most lavish of accommodations, but you can at least get some rest in here without anyone bothering you." He gestured to one of the beds. Rue bowed her head in thanks and walked toward one of them, sitting at the edge.

"Thank you, Oliver."

"Of course. Rest well."

Oliver bent in a sketch of a bow and left, closing the door behind him.

Rue wasn't sure how long she'd slept for. There were no windows in the room she'd been led to, so the perpetual darkness left no indication of what time it might be. She sat up slowly, rubbing sleep from her eyes, looking for her glasses that she'd set beside her before passing out.

A tray of food and a pitcher of water had been set next to her. Someone must have left them while she slept. She took a cursory glance around the room, looking to see if any of the others had joined her.

"Hello?" she called out weakly, throat dry from disuse (and probably snoring). Rue reached for the glass of water and chugged every drop down. Relief coated her throat immediately, "Hello?" she called out again, louder this time. She threw the blanket over and swung her legs over the side of the bed, standing up.

"Corvus?"

Rue stretched her hands out in front of her, the darkness of the room making it hard to see where she was going. Before she could get much farther, the door swung open, causing her to jump back with a squeak.

"Devil be damned, you scared me!" She clutched a hand to her chest and huffed a humorless laugh. Oliver sheepishly rubbed the back of his neck again, bowing his head apologetically.

"Sorry, I thought you might still be asleep," he explained as he lit an oil lamp, immediately brightening up the room.

"How long have I been out?"

"About a day." Oliver shrugged, but Rue's eyes went wide. How had she managed to sleep for an entire day? Without dreams, no less.

"Wow," She breathed, "I must have needed it then."

"From what I hear, you've been through quite a bit recently." Oliver stepped forward into the room, lighting one of the other hanging lanterns on the wall. Rue could feel her anxiety begin to fade once the room came into view.

"Where is Corvus?" She asked, turning to Oliver.

"He's here. He's speaking with Ardeth in the main hall."

Rue nodded but didn't ask anything else. Oliver gestured to the uneaten plate of food next to her bedside. The tray consisted of mostly different dried items. Nuts, jerky, and some fruit.

"You must be starving. Please, eat something. Corvus insisted."

Rue had the feeling Oliver was just saying that last bit about Corvus, but she was certainly grateful for the rations anyway. She sat back down at the edge of the bed, selecting a few different things off the tray, and nibbled on them.

"Have you all found anything else out?" she asked once she swallowed. She still didn't really understand what was happening, but from what she knew, they'd planned to dispatch Sabrien to find the book. She doubted they'd come back so soon with any information, but the uncertainty grated on her.

Oliver shook his head, "Not yet, unfortunately."

Rue frowned, shoving another piece of the cured meat in her mouth. The door swung open again, Corvus' hulking form striding in.

"Oh good, you're finally awake," he said, giving her a small smile, but his tone was still snarky.

"Well, good morning to you, too." She rolled her eyes and popped a couple of dried apricots in her mouth.

"How are you feeling?" He leveled her with a look, tone shifting into that protector voice he'd used with her before.

"Fine." She shrugged.

"Good. We need to talk."

"We most certainly do."

Oliver turned on his heel, using that as his cue to leave them. He joined Ardeth in the hall, closing the door behind him and leaving only her and Corvus. He took a seat on the bed across from her, perching at the edge to give his wings space to spread out. Rue couldn't help but think about how magnificent they looked. The low light of the room shimmering across them, bringing out that iridescent shine once more.

"There is a lot that I haven't told you," Corvus began.

"I'll say," she snapped. Corvus took a steadying breath, like it was taking everything in him to stay calm and not snap back at her.

"Please just...listen to me. Let me tell you everything and if you still have questions, I will answer them. I promise you." He looked directly into her eyes now. It made something under Rue's skin prickle. It was too intense. She averted her gaze, biting her lip and gave him a nod, busying her mouth with more of the dried fruits on the tray.

"Many, many centuries ago, when the pantheon still existed as we knew it then, our world was falling apart. I won't bore you with the details since I'm sure you know at least the basics, but what most of the stories don't tell you is that the reason it began to crumble was because of the God of Chaos. Vaion. He coveted power so much that he was willing to do anything to take it for himself. Including tearing apart the pantheon and the world itself."

Corvus paused, mulling over what to say next, "Solira, the Goddess we Veridae serve, knew that no matter what, she could not allow Vaion to take her power. She alone held the infinite wisdom of the world in a vast vault. Each and every book on its shelves contained secrets, souls, and much more. But there was one tome that, above all else, could not fall into his hands."

Rue didn't need him to spell it out further; she understood exactly which tome he spoke of.

"She locked it away in the box you found it in. As well as her soul into that stone right there," he pointed to her necklace, "If her soul continued on, even without corporeal form, he could never assume complete power. The stone was given to Veridae priestesses to be passed through generations until the chosen vessel came to be." Corvus paused and raised his head, eyes locking with hers, sending a shock down her spine.

"Me?"

"You."

"But...why?"

"The Veridae are also chosen. We are born into normal human families with a mark on our backs where, eventually, our wings grow. No one knows what makes the Goddess choose us, but we accept our fate without question. Solira must have chosen you because she knew you would be the one to face Vaion and defeat him once and for all."

Rue's head spun, all of the information threatened to overload her. She wrapped her hand around the pendant at her neck, rubbing her thumb over the stone. If she had heard this a few weeks ago, she would have insisted that he was crazy but with everything that she'd experienced, Rue knew that he was telling the truth. What reason would he have not to? It was in his best interest that she cooperated.

"I don't understand. Why didn't Solira just destroy the book when she had the chance?"

"The book cannot be destroyed. It contains so much more than just the destructive spells Vaion wants. It must be contained and kept. It has been lost for a century, but now, you were able to find it," Corvus pushed his shaggy hair back from his forehead, "How *were* you able to find it anyway?"

"I saw it in my dreams. Another version of myself led me there," she said, leaving out the part about the doppelganger's bleeding abyssal eyes.

"He knew it was there. He had to have led you to it." Corvus' tone turned hard.

"Who? Vaion?" Rue asked, confused.

Corvus nodded, folding his arms over his chest, "The man you worked for. He's not who you think he is."

Rue's eyes widened. Was Corvus actually insinuating that the duke of Penrith was actually part of the lost pantheon? Immediately, she wanted to disagree, but when she took a moment to think about it, what Corvus said made sense. Ryker must have known who she was from the very beginning.

Rue's fingers came to her lips again as she turned all of these revelations over in her mind, but before she could sink her teeth into her fingernails, Corvus' hand pulled hers away once again.

She heaved a sigh and held onto his hand, "What about Jasper, then? Is he also some kind of vessel for a God? Or is it only me that got lucky?" Sarcasm dripped from her tone.

"As far as I know, it's just you, sunshine." He gave her a shrug and she chose to ignore his use of that nickname she loved to hate.

"That bastard would get off easy." Rue crossed her arms over her chest and sighed. "Well, there's no use being upset about it, I suppose. I'm here now, and what's done is done, so what do we do now?"

Corvus looked at her, brows raised damn near to his hairline and eyes wide with surprise.

"What? Why are you looking at me like that?" she spat, giving him a withering glare. Corvus laughed. The bastard was laughing! The nerve he had.

"You're just taking all of this remarkably well; I didn't expect it to go over this easily, given how livid you were before."

The corner of his lips pulled up into a grin, that tiny dimple he had showing again, making her feel some kind of way.

"What do you suggest I do, Corvus? Just keep pouting and crossing my arms like a petulant child?" Rue threw her arms up in an exasperated gesture.

Corvus' smile widened, but she kept her face stern and serious. She wasn't done being annoyed with him just yet.

"You know," he leaned back on his elbow, looking entirely too casual for the situation, "The longer I'm around you, the more of her I can see in you."

Rue blinked and dropped her arms, tilting her head at him inquisitively, "What do you mean? The Goddess?"

Corvus nodded. "She had such a fiery soul, never took any shit from anyone." He laughed softly, looking a bit wistful as he spoke.

"Sounds like you were quite fond of her." Rue's eyes landed in her lap. She couldn't look at him, her nerves like a rope around her heart.

"I was the head of the Veridae guards."

"Was? As in past tense?"

"Yes, past tense. I passed the title to Ardeth a long time ago."

Corvus still wasn't looking at her, and her eyes were still glued to her hands like they were the most fascinating things she'd ever seen in her life.

"I see. I'm sure you don't want to talk about it, so I won't even bother."

Corvus sat up straight again, pushing himself off the bed to stand, and offered her a hand.

"Now that you're awake, would you like a tour?"

Chapter Twenty

T HREE DAYS PASSED WITHOUT word from Sabrien or his team of ravens. The idle days were starting to get to Rue, making her restless without anything to keep her mind otherwise occupied. Corvus wouldn't let her wander far out of his sight, which only made her even more batty.

He'd given her a tour of the temple when they'd first arrived. The space was amazingly detailed but held little to no personal effects. Corvus had explained that it was more of a base of operation than an actual home for the Veridae that cycled through, so it wasn't necessary to keep any non-essential items around.

"It must be lonely," she'd said, thinking back to her apartment that was full of little meaningless trinkets that she'd collected over the years. They'd held nothing but sentimental value, but having them around brightened up her space anyway.

"You can't really miss something you've never had. The Veridae are a mostly nomadic group, so we don't tend to get attached to things," he explained, and while it made sense, it didn't sound like the kind of life Rue herself would like to live.

"My friend Fia's house would probably horrify you. She's such a mess." Rue gave a sad laugh. She missed her friend but knew it was best for her to stay away after what happened back at Lydia's tavern. Rue hated the thought of putting anyone in danger, and right now, she was essentially a walking beacon for trouble.

Corvus gave Rue a small nudge when she went quiet, "She's fine, I'm sure," he said as though reading her thoughts.

"I know...I just miss her. We haven't been friends for long, but she's been one of the only people in my life that I've felt like I could truly connect with. Someone I didn't need to wear a mask around." She sighed and hoisted herself onto a chair that had been dragged out to the main hall, "I've always kind of been the odd one out in friend groups. When I went to university, I had people I might consider a bit more than an acquaintance, but none that I was particularly close to."

Rue's thoughts drifted to Orionna again. All the other things that seemed like strange coincidences had proven to be anything but. She hoped with every bit of her that Orionna wasn't involved in any of this but found it more and more difficult to hold onto those thin threads of hope.

Corvus sat beside her and quietly listened while she spoke. Rue turned toward him, feeling her chest pinch when she noticed the frown that crept into his features.

"Oh, don't give me that look." She waved her hand at him, "I'm a big, tough girl, I'll get over it." Rue gave him a forced smile, but the gentle downturn of his lips told her he remained unconvinced.

"This will all be over soon, right? I'll be fine." She nudged his shoulder the same way he'd done to her earlier.

"Yeah...of course." Corvus bobbed his head and moved to stand, "Come on, let's get you some food." He offered his hand. Rue stared for a moment, debating whether or not she wanted to accept it.

Corvus was such an enigma. His moods were constantly switching from hot to cold and back again so fast it made her head spin. One moment, he's chastising her like she's some meddlesome child, and the next, he's doing this. Offering his hand like an olive branch.

She slid her fingers into his hand, feeling the roughness of his calluses and somehow finding it comforting. He hoisted her up from the chair, letting go of her hand as soon as she stood fully. Rue smoothed out the wrinkles of her skirt and adjusted her glasses.

"Lead the way."

The normally quiet halls were filled with quiet chatter and the occasional peal of laughter. It was more lively than Rue had heard it since they'd arrived.

"Sabrien's back." Corvus made a face.

"Not a fan, hm?"

"He's just...loud." Corvus' frown deepened, and Rue shook her head at him.

As Corvus had suggested, Sabrien was sitting in one of the few plush chairs now in the main hall, his head tipped back in a full bellied laugh. Her eyes slid to Corvus, trying to gauge his reaction. His arms were crossed over his chest and a muscle in his jaw jumped as he clenched his teeth.

"You're going to give yourself a headache if you keep clenching your jaw like that. Loosen up a little," Rue whispered, prodding his side with her elbow and walking away before he could say anything else.

"Ah, there she is," Sabrien called out when he noticed her walking toward them. Rue gave a sheepish little wave, feeling uncomfortable with everyone's eyes on her. She definitely wasn't used to being the center of attention in a room of people.

"What's your name this time?" he asked, folding his arms behind his head.

"Ruby, but please don't call me that. Call me Rue."

"Rue... cute." Sabrien grinned, making her cheeks warm in an instant. This boy was going to be trouble, she could already tell.

Oliver kicked Sabrien in the shin from where he sat on one of the other chairs.

"Quit being a flirt."

"What!? I'm not! I just said her name was cute," Sabrien said with a look of mock offense. "I am just a gentleman. You could stand to learn a thing or two, Ollie."

Oliver didn't say anything but rolled his eyes and went back to whatever he was reading. Rue felt her lips curl into a smile. It was odd, but she already felt so at home with these boys. Something about them felt like she had known them forever, and if what Corvus had told her was actually true, in a way, she had. Their playful banter reminded her of Jasper.

Gods, did she miss him.

Rue plopped down into one of the empty seats, curling her legs under her. Oliver looked over to her, his bright blue eyes sparkling.

"Did you sleep well, Rue?" His voice was soft and quiet — such a contrast from both Sabrien and Corvus, who were currently arguing over who knew what, but she wasn't listening to them anymore.

"Yes, I did. Thank you." She offered a small smile and felt her heart warm at how pleased he looked with her response.

Rue shrugged the thick cloak off her shoulders and let it fall to the floor. Between the body heat and the roaring fire in the hearth at the front of the room, it was comfortably warm.

Corvus turned away from whatever Sabrien was still saying to him, eyes locking with hers for just a moment, like he'd sensed her movement and had to make sure she was still here.

Rue shot him a disapproving glare. She didn't need his eyes on her at all times, deal or not. She was a grown woman, and she could handle herself just fine without his babysitting. He broke eye contact. Her wordless chiding rang loud and clear.

"I am absolutely starved. Where the hell is Ardeth with our dinner?" Sabrien groused, flopping back on the chair, his wings splaying out under him.

"You could have gone with him, you know," Oliver muttered, nose still firmly wedged between the pages of his book. Sabrien shot him a glare and groaned, sitting back up.

"I spent the last three days doing non-stop recon. I deserve a break."

"Then don't complain."

Rue sat up straighter, clearing her throat and speaking up before this could break into another pointless argument.

"Did you find anything?" She clasped her hands together in her lap, anxiously awaiting his answer. Sabrien turned to her, a small frown tugging at his features.

"Unfortunately, no. Some of the ravens are still out keeping watch, waiting to see if they can hear anything around the city."

Rue's heart fell. She'd really hoped he would come back with at least some kind of heading. They couldn't just sit idly by at the temple until something came up either. She gave Sabrien a nod, turning back to Corvus. He leaned against one of the tall pillars with his hands shoved into his pockets and that near-permanent scowl on his face.

"We have to go back to Penrith soon," she said. Not a question, not a request, but a command. She needed to find Jasper and see what he'd found — if anything — since they'd left Lydia's.

Corvus eyed her with a look that said absolutely not. She could see it in the way his body shifted when she spoke. He opened his mouth once, closing it again, taking a moment to think before saying anything.

Smart.

"There may be a way into the duke's manor. There was a door I left unlocked. Hopefully no one noticed it," Rue told them. Sabrien perked up at the new information.

"Maybe we could try and sneak in again and have some of your raven friends scope the place out?" Rue offered.

"Oh, I like this one. She's got the right idea." He gave her another little wink. Rue knew she shouldn't inflate his ego anymore, but she couldn't help it. Anything to get a rise out of Corvus.

"Thank you, Sabrien. Finally, someone appreciates me." Rue raised her chin triumphantly and flicked a stray lock of hair behind her shoulder. Corvus' brow furrowed, and he let out a loud, unimpressed groan.

"It's not a bad idea," Corvus grumbled, pinching the bridge of his nose with irritation.

"Did that hurt to admit?" Rue shot him a wry grin. She could see annoyance rippling from his head like steam from a tea kettle. Corvus snapped his head in Sabrien's direction, jabbing an accusatory finger at him,

"Don't you go rubbing off on her. She's already enough of a headache without your help."

Sabrien scrunched up his face and mimicked what Corvus was saying under his breath. Rue rolled her eyes at both of them.

"Play nicely now, children."

Before either of them could get another word out, the sound of doors cracking open echoed through the room. She felt herself tense, hands gripped tight at the edges of the chair. Her eyes immediately darted to Corvus, silently asking him what was happening. His features softened when he saw the fear in her eyes.

"Ardeth is back," he assured her. Rue slumped in relief, releasing her vise grip on the chair, and settled back down into the cushions. She glanced over her shoulder, and just as Corvus had said, Ardeth strode into the main hall with his hands clasped behind his back and a somber look pulling at his features.

Corvus stood up straighter, looking to Ardeth, seeming to silently ask him something. Ardeth gave a small shake of his head, and Corvus let out a relieved breath. Rue's brows tugged together as she glanced at Corvus.

"What is it?" Rue asked quietly.

"Nothing. Just wanted to make sure none of those creatures found the temple," Ardeth explained, assuaging Rue's concern. She nodded and settled back down into her chair; the urge to bite her nails was nearly overwhelming, but she knew Corvus would just pull her hand away from her mouth again as he'd already made a habit of doing.

The room went quiet. Even Sabrien had halted his endless chatter and was chewing on his lips nervously. Rue took a deep breath and stood up from her seat. This wouldn't do at all.

"Well, if there is nothing going on out there, then we have no reason to be so morose in here, now do we?" She had her hands on her hips, trying her best to look authoritative. Her eyes swept over the four men, and she noticed a tiny smile curl on Oliver's lips before he closed his book and set it aside.

"Rue's right. Let's enjoy our last night here and a good meal before we all have to part again," he suggested, standing and joining Rue where she stood.

Sabrien sat up quickly, clapping his hands together. "Yes! Don't we have some rum hidden around here somewhere?" He hefted himself from his seat, using his wings as a counterbalance. Corvus gave him a disapproving look but didn't say anything.

Rue wrinkled her nose at the thought of the liquor. She'd never been a fan, but maybe it wouldn't hurt to have a little and calm her nerves. Sabrien disappeared into one of the many rooms in the halls of the temple, coming back not a moment later with a dark green glass bottle, shaking its contents.

"I knew I left it here," Sabrien murmured, popping the cork out of the bottle and lifting it to his lips, but before he could take a swig, Oliver snatched the bottle from his hands.

"I thought you were a gentleman, Sabrien." Oliver shook his head and offered the bottle to Rue first, an apologetic look on his features.

"Ladies, first."

Chapter Twenty-One

R UE DEFINITELY DRANK MORE than a few sips like she'd planned. They had all been passing around the bottle, laughing and sharing stories, the alcohol warming her blood and loosening her lips. Corvus had been the only one to abstain, stating someone had to babysit the idiots. Rue rolled her eyes and took another swig before passing the last few dregs in the bottle to Sabrien.

He was splayed out on the floor, limbs like a starfish. He was probably the most drunk of the bunch. "Ah, thank you, my dear!" He sat up and snatched the bottle from Rue's hand, knocking back the last of the fiery liquor. His face pinched, making Rue laugh so hard she snorted. Her hand immediately flew up, covering her face in embarrassment. Sabrien let out another hearty laugh of his own.

"You sure can drink, little Ruby," Sabrien mused, wiping his lips.

"I normally don't even like the stuff, but this was actually quite nice," Rue confessed, a little hiccup bubbling up as she spoke. She glanced over her shoulder to where Corvus stood in one of the dark corners of the room. His face was tight with annoyance and irritation, and it was starting to seriously sour Rue's good mood.

She pushed herself up from the floor, wobbling as she stood. She was much more inebriated than she had thought but was determined to walk over to Corvus and give him a good what-for.

A single dark brow raised as he watched her struggle to toddle towards him. Even with her blurred vision, Rue could see the amused smirk he was trying desperately to hide by wiping a hand over his jaw. She narrowed her eyes at him and put her hands back on her hips again.

"What's so funny, Mister Broody Bird."

Corvus couldn't contain it anymore and laughed, shaking his head at her. She was swaying where she stood with the occasional hiccup but was determined to be stern.

"Nothing at all — just observing." His voice was smooth, and the sound of it felt like being wrapped in silk. It made the tiny hairs on Rue's arms stand, and if her cheeks weren't already glowing red from the alcohol, they definitely were now. She dropped her hands and prodded him as hard as she could right in the middle of his chest, just like she had done on their first meeting.

"You are so..." Rue paused, all the words she'd planned to say died on her tongue before she could get them out. The way his eyes fell on her made her stomach twist in a not wholly unpleasant way. She hated this hold he seemed to have on her. No matter how angry she wanted to be at him, all he had to do was give her that look and she melted.

"Ugh, never mind," Rue turned on her heel and walked back to Sabrien and Oliver on the other side of the room. They were better company than he was, anyway. She could hear Corvus chuckling behind her as she walked away and chose to ignore him the best she could. Rue plopped down unceremoniously in the middle of the floor between the other two.

"Sabrien, I have a question for you."

Sabrien sat up on one elbow and pushed his golden hair back, "And what might that be?"

"How could you tell that I was...the vessel?" She swallowed. Those words still felt so foreign on her tongue, and her inebriated state didn't help as much as she'd hoped it would.

Sabrien blew out a breath, glancing at Corvus in the corner with a look that might have been worry in his eyes. She didn't know what that was all about, but she let it go anyway.

"Part of it was your aura. Being a seeker, I am acutely attuned to things like that," Sabrien began, rubbing his chin thoughtfully, "The other part of it is that you look more or less the same. Of course, there are some things that are different, but your hair is unmistakable."

Rue rubbed a stray curl between her fingers, letting herself smile at the thought. She had always been different because of her hair, sometimes even the center of ridicule when she was younger. To hear that it was a trait she shared with a goddess made her feel like it might actually be something she should be proud of instead.

"I always thought my hair was strange, honestly," she admitted, "Jasper's is the same but it's not nearly so bright, so of course he got off easy there too." Rue smiled, glancing back up to Sabrien. "Can you tell me more about her...me? Not *me* me but Solira?" Rue scooted closer to him, speaking quietly like they were sharing secrets.

Sabrien sat up taller and crossed his legs before leaning in closer to her. His eyes were glazed with drink, and his cheeks glowed with the effects of the alcohol. Rue wanted so badly to reach out and pinch them but stopped herself.

"She was a lot like you. Which makes sense considering you've got her soul in there." He poked her chest right above her heart, "She had that same fight in herself that you do."

Rue found herself smiling wide. She'd never liked how women in stories she'd read always seemed so helpless. She didn't want to be like them, she wanted to hold her own and stand tall. She may be no trained fighter or a master of espionage but she was clever and had a wealth of knowledge and as she learned recently, she would stab a horrifying eldritch abomination in the face with a broken bottle if the occasion called for it.

"Was he always like that too?" Rue tipped her head toward Corvus, who still hadn't moved from his proverbial perch in the corner. Sabrien's expression saddened as he considered his answer.

"Hmm, no. Not always." Sabrien shook his head. Rue got the feeling Sabrien was being purposefully vague about his answer. Sabrien's eyes flicked to Corvus and then back to Rue. A shiver ran down her spine, and she swore she could feel his heated stare boring into her back.

"Oh. Did something happen?" she asked, voice barely above a whisper. Sabrien's eyes left hers again, shifting behind her instead. The rumble of Corvus' boots preceded him, effectively cutting off any answer she might get.

"We need to get some rest. We leave early, and you have quite a bit of alcohol to sleep off." It wasn't a request. She knew he was going to stand there, looming over her, until she stood up and returned to her borrowed bedroom in the other wing.

"Ugh," She pushed herself up from the floor with a beleaguered groan, purposefully knocking her shoulder into his arm as she stomped away. She honestly didn't even know why she was so angry about his interruption. She knew it wasn't Sabrien's story to tell and Corvus didn't owe her any of his life story but still, it still felt like being rejected in a way that she couldn't explain.

Rue pushed the door open and slammed it shut with more force than was actually necessary before flopping onto the bed and shoving her face into the pillow. She didn't know if she was more upset with herself or with Corvus. She needed to keep reminding herself that this partnership was purely professional, and even though he was...incredibly attractive, he was absolutely infuriating, and her lonely heart was just playing games with her.

Rue rolled over onto her back and stared up at the ceiling in the darkness of the room. Before she could spiral too deeply into her thoughts, the tell-tale creak of an opening door had her springing back up to a sitting position.

"Gods, you scared me!" Rue whined as Corvus moved close enough for her to see him in the dark. He grumbled a half-hearted 'sorry' under his breath as he crossed the room to one of the other beds, and sat on the edge. Rue spun herself on the bed to face him. She regretted the motion.

"Oh no. I shouldn't have let Sabrien talk me into drinking more." She was talking to herself more than anything, letting her head drop into her hand and closing her eyes as she tried to quell the nausea rising in her stomach. She heard Corvus stand again, the sound of his footsteps moving closer to her. What did he want now? To chastise her some more?

He picked up the water pitcher from her bedside, pouring what was left into the glass, handing it over to her. "Drink this." It was a soft command, but a command nonetheless. Rue reached up for the glass without looking, a familiar electric buzz running up her spine as the tips of her fingers brushed against Corvus'.

"Thanks," Rue muttered, trying to ignore the feeling that still tingled across her fingers, and chugged the water. Corvus sat beside her, so much closer than she'd needed him to be.

"Did you hear me talking to Sabrien?" She asked quietly, rubbing the rim of the glass against her lower lip. Corvus didn't answer, but Rue heard the quick intake of his breath through his nose. He definitely had.

"I'm sorry. I know I shouldn't have pried but..." Rue set the glass down on the table, turning to face him. "You're such a mystery to me. You make me absolutely mad, but then there's just something about you that is so endearing to me...and now knowing about this whole vessel...thing, it's starting to make sense."

Corvus gave her his full attention. The intensity of his crackling flame eyes made her pulse race. She took a deep breath and buried down her nerves, letting the lingering effects of the liquor burn away the last of her inhibitions. Rue reached forward and slid her fingers under his jaw.

"It feels like my soul remembers you."

Corvus blinked once, a look of shock dawning on his face for a moment before it faded...softening his features. He held her hands where they met his skin. The intimacy of his touch and the way he looked at her with something like reverence was almost too much. Rue felt the way he tugged at her hands, beckoning her closer. Her heart beat wildly against her sternum like a battering ram, and her breath shook.

"Please remember me, sunshine," he whispered, moving to close what little space remained between them. Rue's eyes fell closed instinctively as she leaned her head forward, answering his call.

A breath later, his lips were on hers, and it was as though a bolt of lightning shot down her spine. The same sensation she'd felt when he first stood before her. A flood of images raced through her. Memories, she realized. She was seeing someone else's memories.

Was this Corvus' mind? Or was it...hers?

She pulled back from him, pain blossoming behind her eyes and in her temples. Corvus' eyes were wide with concern. His hands immediately cupped her face, tilting her head toward him.

"What's wrong? Rue?" His voice was suddenly frantic.

Rue reached up, her hands resting atop his, "I'm fine, I just... I saw memories. I think? Flashes of them, at least." She opened her eyes, suddenly feeling stone-cold sober. She couldn't bring herself to look directly at him, almost afraid to meet his gaze again. It should have felt like it was too much, too fast, but something inside of her had changed. Shifted.

"Can you tell me what you saw?" he asked, thumb tracing small soothing circles against her cheek. His cool touch was a welcome relief against her heated skin. She could see the protector in him coming out and it made her smile as she allowed herself to rest against him.

"It was too much to see anything clearly but..." She bit her lip before speaking again, "I could see you...and what looked like Solira if what Sabrien said is true about her hair looking like mine."

Corvus tensed for a moment but let out a breath he must have been holding deep inside his chest.

"Is that why you didn't tell me before...about being her vessel?" Rue asked, voice sounding almost too loud in the quiet of the room.

"Yes," he answered simply. He didn't really need to say more, but part of Rue had hoped he would. He was obviously feeling enough to kiss her and to ask her soul to remember him in earnest.

"You called her sunshine, didn't you?" Rue took his hand in hers, lacing their fingers together while they talked, hoping that maybe the familiar touch would help him open up to her, even just a crack.

"I did." He swallowed. His voice was tight, like he was trying to hold back the emotions he was now feeling.

"Corvus, please don't do this. Don't give me these stilted answers while also holding me this way...looking at me the way you do." Rue sat up, locking her eyes with his. The air between them seemed to thicken.

"I don't want to lose you again." His words came out like a plea, a prayer, and she could feel the hurt. "Back then, you always promised me you would come back when the time was right, and I never stopped waiting. I never stopped dreaming of the day you would come back to me."

Corvus turned his body fully to face her, tucking his wings tightly behind his back. Rue didn't know what to say. Words stuck in her throat like thick honey. She knew there was a connection between them when he appeared to her in her apartment. Something that made her trust him implicitly.

"You won't lose *me*, Corvus. I am going to stay here by your side." Rue grasped his shoulders and leaned backward, trying to tug him down with her. He sighed and held fast, not allowing himself to be coaxed by her siren's song.

"You've been drinking..."

Rue frowned, feeling the harsh sting of his rejection more acutely than she probably should have. He was right, and no matter how sober she might be feeling from these revelations, she knew it wasn't a good idea to act on any kind of impulse right now.

"I'm sorry, I didn't mean—" She blushed, scooting out from under him, and tried to move to the other side of the bed.

"Don't be sorry. I shouldn't have kissed you." He combed his fingers through his hair and huffed another deep sigh. She could tell he was disappointed by the situation. Rue silently cursed herself once again for drinking so much.

"I liked it..." Her lips curled into a tiny grin, facing him again. Corvus met her gaze, and she could see the faint glow of a blush on his cheeks. It was ridiculous how such a small thing could make her feel so much.

Corvus stood up from the bed and started toward the door. He stopped just as his hand reached the knob, pausing for a moment before looking over his shoulder at her once more.

"Goodnight, Rue."

"Goodnight, Corvus."

Chapter Twenty-Two

R UE SLEPT FITFULLY THAT night. The newly recovered memories plagued her dreams with a series of disjointed moments she couldn't piece together or make much sense of. She woke the next morning with a splitting headache pounding in her temples.

She sat up in the dark and reached for the water pitcher, letting out a small, distressed noise when she realized it was empty. "Shit," she grumbled under her breath. The door creaked open slowly, and she turned to face whoever it was.

Unsurprisingly, she recognized Corvus' outline. His build was much bulkier than any of the other Veridae. Rue grabbed her glasses, sliding them on, and offered Corvus a tiny, awkward grin. The image of their kiss and the subsequent embrace came to mind again.

"Good morning," he greeted her, moving closer to where she sat, "Did you...sleep alright? I heard you whimpering." His brows knit with concern.

Rue just shook her head, not really wanting to talk about the memories while her head still felt like it was going to split in two.

"I'm fine. I just need some water." She stood and grabbed her cloak from where it sat at the foot of her borrowed bed and wrapped it around her. "But, I figure we need to be going anyway, so we can get some on the way out."

Corvus nodded and led the way back out the door. Why was he being so standoffish again? She thought they'd be past this after what they'd shared the previous night.

Rue pursed her lips and jogged a little to catch up with his long strides. She slipped her hand into his and tugged on it to force him to keep pace with her instead. Corvus' fingers tightened around hers, bringing a small, accomplished smile to Rue's lips.

"Please don't fold in again, Corvus." She was practically begging. He halted like he was thinking of how to answer her.

"It's been a long time since…I was able to be close to someone like this. You're going to have to cut me some slack." He turned to face her, his free hand cupping her cheek. Rue felt her skin warm under his touch.

"I understand. We can take time to figure out what this is…between us, but you can't close up on me again," she said. He gave a single nod and let his hand reluctantly fall from her face, his other still holding hers in a firm grasp.

"Thank you," Rue whispered, giving his hand a small squeeze. She didn't know what to expect from the next leg of their journey together, but she knew that whatever it was, they were meant to make it together.

They rejoined the rest of the Veridae in the main hall once again. Rue was surprised to see them all looking bright-eyed and bushy-tailed despite the amount they had all drank the night before. It didn't escape her notice that Sabrien's eyes were firmly locked on hers and Corvus' clasped hands. Corvus shot him a look that clearly said, 'Say anything, and I will kill you.' And to Rue's surprise, Sabrien actually kept his mouth shut.

Ardeth was the only one missing from the group, but he'd been elusive since she'd arrived, so his absence wasn't anything alarming. Corvus led Rue to the same spot she'd sat in the night before and helped her down.

"Stay here, I'm going to find Ardeth and get you some water."

Rue nodded and curled up on the soft cushion. The main hall of the temple was made of some kind of marble, making the room unbearably cold without the fire that had been roaring in the hearth before.

"I'm guessing something good happened?" Sabrien asked as soon as Corvus was out of earshot. Rue laughed out loud but quickly clapped her hand over her mouth. She should have known Sabrien was going to say whatever he wanted as soon as the imminent threat was out of the room.

"That is for me to know." Rue stuck out her tongue playfully. As much as she wanted to tell Sabrien everything, she figured it would be better to respect Corvus' wish for privacy.

"You're no fun." Sabrien pouted and crossed his arms.

Rue turned to where Oliver sat quietly in the corner of the room, his nose firmly lodged between the pages of another book. She bent her neck and tried to make out the fading gold letters on the spine, but they were too far gone to comprehend.

"Reading anything good?" She asked.

Oliver looked up with an adorably embarrassed look of being caught on his face. He snapped the book shut and slid it between his hip and the cushion of the chair.

"Just trying to do some last-minute research. Most of the books containing any sort of information on the tome have been long lost," he told her with a frustrated sigh. Oliver was truly a boy after her own heart, as he seemed to be constantly in the pursuit of knowledge.

"Anything useful in there?" She nodded to where the book was stashed next to him. Oliver frowned and sadly shook his head.

"Nothing more than what we already know, unfortunately."

Corvus had returned with Ardeth in tow, along with a large pitcher full of water that she had never been more grateful to see. Corvus sat next to Rue, poured a glass, and handed it over to her. Ardeth took his seat at the front of the room by the fireplace.

"Now that we have a solid lead on where the book has been taken, we need to come up with a way to get it back," Ardeth announced. No one spoke up for a long moment as they all collectively thought out just how they could pull something like this off.

They must have sat there for hours, bouncing ideas off one another, though none of them stuck enough to formulate an actual solid plan.

"Are there any other entrances to the manor?" Ardeth offered, but Rue just shook her head.

"There are, but he will have them all watched now. Even the door I left unlocked is probably shut tight. I can almost guarantee it...especially with his annual masquerade coming up." Rue's eyes blew open wide. That was it! This was the thing they needed. She snapped her fingers in an a-ha! Moment.

"The masquerade! I don't know why I didn't think of that first. I could sneak in disguised as a guest since it's an open invitation for the whole city."

They all looked at her with disbelieving looks.

"Hear me out. I know the manor like the back of my hand. Every hidden wall, every nook and cranny. I can wear something over my face so Ryker doesn't recognize me and slip into one of the hidden passages to get down to the library and—"

"No." Corvus spoke first, his brows pulled down into a stern expression once again.

"No? What do you mean no? I don't see anyone else coming up with anything more viable at this point!"

"I don't want you going in there again. I don't want to risk you getting caught and leave us with no way to get to you."

Rue huffed a sigh and deflated into her chair. Of course he would shoot down the only idea any of them had come up with in the last hour. Surprisingly enough, it was Oliver that spoke up in her defense.

"What if we all dressed up and snuck in with her?" he suggested. Corvus turned, giving him one of the cold glares that were usually reserved for Sabrien. But he knew as well as she did that they didn't have another option that was better than this one.

"What makes you think he would put the book back in the library, though? That would be too easy," Sabrien chimed in, making an excellent point.

"It is too easy. Which is why he would do it. We would just be letting her walk into a trap," Corvus countered.

"We have no idea where he could have put it. But the library seems like the best place to start," Rue rubbed at her chin thoughtfully, "All of you could run a distraction while I slip down there and check? It will be faster if I do it since I know where to look."

She turned to Corvus. His hardened expression said he wasn't convinced. Rue took his hand between both of hers and held his gaze, "Please. You have to trust me. This is the best and potentially only chance we have at getting the book back before something terrible happens. The entire city will be at the ball; it would be the perfect time for him to do something heinous. We have to stop it before it starts."

Corvus' eyes searched hers. She channeled every scrap of confidence she had into him. Rue needed him to believe she could do this. As usual, Corvus was completely unreadable. His face was set as stone, and it didn't seem like he was going to budge.

"Corvus, she's right. We really don't have anything else better. We can't just fly into his windows and break in that way." Oliver was the one to break the silent standoff. Corvus turned to the younger Veridae with fire blazing in his eyes. Rue could see Oliver practically start to sweat under Corvus' scrutiny.

"Why don't we take a while to think on this," Rue interjected, putting herself between Corvus and Oliver. It was obvious tensions were running high, and she needed to do something to stop the momentum before everything crashed and burned. She had seen how many times Corvus had nearly gone to blows with Sabrien for more minor things in just the short amount of time she'd been here with them.

Rue turned to Corvus and placed her hands on his chest, "Why don't we go for a walk outside." It wasn't a suggestion, and the look she gave him said as much. Corvus blew out a breath and deflated at her touch.

"Fine. Let's go."

Outside the temple, it was another frigid morning. The isle really only had two seasons — cold and colder. Rue pulled a borrowed cloak up around her chin and rubbed her hands down her arms, trying to use the friction to warm herself faster. Unsurprisingly, Corvus — who ran as hot as a furnace — wore nothing but his usual leather armor.

"Why are you so opposed to this? It's not like you're throwing me into the lion's den alone. You're all going to be there." She cut right to the chase, not bothering with any useless preamble. She had learned in her short time with the Veridae that it was better to just say what you meant. He wasn't interested in any of the double-speak she had grown accustomed to from the elite of Penrith.

"I know, I just..." he paused, kicking a pile of leaves. Rue had to stop herself from giggling at how much he looked like a small child doing something like that. "With the amount of people who are supposedly going to be attending this ball, it's going to be a lot more difficult to keep my — our eyes on you."

Rue knew he meant well, but the fiercely independent part of her was offended that he was implying she would even need him to watch her the whole time. "There is no plan we could come up with that wouldn't have some potential of going horribly wrong. We all know that," she reminded him, "I also think you owe Oliver an apology. He was just trying to help."

Corvus rolled his eyes and stopped in his tracks. Gods, he really was such a baby sometimes. "He may have meant well, but there are still ranks among us, and he can't just ignore that and—"

Rue cut him off with a finger to his lips. Without saying another word, she stood motionless, waiting for him to collect himself. "You're deflecting. I can tell. What is *really* going on?" She asked, moving her hand down to his chest, right over his heart. He was nervous.

"It's just you, me, and the ravens out here. Tell me why your heart is beating like this."

Corvus huffed and slid his hand over hers, pressing it down more firmly against his chest.

"If this man is truly Vaion as I suspect he is, I cannot in good conscience allow you to put yourself in his way again."

Again? What did Corvus mean by that?

Rue stood quietly, gently pressing her hand against his chest, and urged him to continue.

"There are a lot of signs that point to him being one of the Gods. Just like you. However, the difference between him and you is that his power wasn't sealed. He knows exactly what he's doing." The crease in Corvus' brow deepened.

"Does this have anything to do with what I asked Sabrien?" Rue's eyes locked with his. Burning embers swirled within his irises. He was so closed off, but she wanted in so badly. She wanted to know him.

Rue knew that the goddess inside her was very dear to him before, but she wanted to know who *she* was to him and what she could become. She moved her hand to his cheek, cupping it gently. Her thumb brushed against the tiny bits of stubble and the faint trails of scars on his skin, trying to calm his nerves and get him to open up, even just for a moment.

"It's a complicated answer, but the shortest version is yes." Corvus finally conceded. A tight grip held her heart firmly in a perfect combination of both excitement and anxiety.

"Come with me, and I will tell you." Corvus took her hand in his and led her deeper into the forest.

CHAPTER TWENTY-THREE

AN ENDLESS SEA OF trees towered over them, blocking out what little sun fought to shine through dense and heavy clouds that seemed a permanent fixture in the sky. At least it wasn't raining. The forest floor was littered with dead, soggy leaves, fallen branches, and scattered remnants of old animal bones that had been picked clean by whatever creatures inhabited this forest. Normally quite a macabre sight, but Rue found there was beauty in it even still. The Hollow didn't seem so foreboding now that she knew what lay in its center.

Corvus continued leading her deeper still. He faced straight on, making a bee line for the destination and not once bothering to look around him. Rue frowned and tugged on his hand. His head immediately snapped in her direction, that same worry from before engraved into his brow.

"What's the matter? Why are you stopping me?"

"It's just... I noticed you don't look at anything around you. You're so focused on the goal you can't enjoy the journey." Rue rubbed her arm, feeling a bit bashful suddenly. Corvus' brow softened first, with the rest of his body following a moment later.

"We don't know what's going to happen, and as much as we hope all will go well, who knows when we will be able to just walk freely through the woods again. Alone." She almost didn't add on the last word, but she wanted to make a point.

Rue swore she could see the faintest bit of a blush coloring his tanned cheeks.

"We aren't in a hurry. Let's walk like it." She wrapped her small hand around his larger one and gave it a squeeze, emphasizing her words. Corvus scrubbed a hand down his face, trying — and failing — to somehow wipe away the flush in his cheeks. Rue smiled to herself and led the way this time.

They continued walking, more slowly now in the comfortable silence she had come to expect from the Veridae. The colors on the trees began to shift from deep emerald-green hues to fiery reds, yellows, and oranges. It was beautiful to see the change from the inside for once.

Penrith never had many colors, the same washed-out greys and blacks blanketing most of the buildings and streets. The forest was more than that. It seemed almost alive, and in a way, she supposed it was. The tiny critters skittering under their feet felt so different than the first time she walked these woods with Corvus. The more she thought about that first time, the more she realized *they* were different this time.

Before, Corvus couldn't wait to be rid of her, or so he'd made it seem. Rue almost chuckled to herself but thought better of it. She remembered just how terrified she'd been to walk through these trees after the first night creature found her, but now, the forest felt serene. Welcoming, even.

"I can practically hear the cogs whirring around in your head. What are you thinking?" Corvus finally asked.

"Oh, nothing. Just...how different things have become after such a short time." She squeezed his hand again and left her answer purposefully vague. She didn't want to allow Corvus to use her own thoughts as a distraction from his promise to share his own. He didn't press, as it seemed they had reached their destination.

Before them stood an ancient and gnarled tree. The thick trunk was nearly as wide as she and Corvus combined. Its bark was a deep mahogany with rope-like vines that climbed and twisted around the trunk. An array of different fungi grew from between the bark's thick plates. Colorful mushroom caps of all shapes and sizes, along with tufts of spongy verdant moss, decorated the barren branches that reached for the sky in an almost supplicating gesture. It was otherworldly, ethereal.

Rue felt compelled to take a step closer and reached to touch one of the vines. Under her hand, what she expected to feel rough and fibrous felt like...skin. Soft and warm and pulsing with life.

"What is this place?" she asked quietly. Reverently.

"Our own tree of life. This is all that's left of the majority of the Veridae people," Corvus told her, a sort of melancholy apparent in his words.

A harsh pang of sadness flooded her. What was left of them?

"Are there none left but you and the others, then?" she asked, not sure she really wanted to know the answer. Corvus shook his head and shrugged.

"There are a few other groups left, but we've all become so spread out that we don't meet often...or at all, if I'm honest."

Rue nodded in understanding but hoped that one day she would have a chance to meet the others. Her people. That must have been why she'd felt as though it were calling to her, beckoning her closer with a warm welcome. It was similar to the pull she'd felt when she found the book under Ryker's floorboards. But instead of the sinister and cold voices, these were warm, inviting. *Loving*.

From what Corvus had told her, the Veridae had been Solira's protectors. She was their goddess. That divine blood that she now knew ran deep in her veins felt its people from inside the tree. She closed her eyes and listened to Corvus speak, hand still firmly on the tree.

"After the last battle... when Sol—" He paused, correcting himself. "When *your* soul was locked away, this tree is where the last of the fallen soldiers were buried. That night I lost you. I lost you to the greed of a God. A God that grew too covetous and wanted more than just his own power. He wanted everything. He wanted you and all that you were. He wanted to corrupt you, but instead of letting that happen, you sealed your soul in this stone." He took her necklace between his fingers more delicately than he'd been before.

Rue opened her eyes at the feel of his hands brushing her skin.

"My mother had this necklace before me, and as far as I know, her mother before her had it. Why did it only work for me?" She pulled her hand from the tree and turned to face him.

"Your family must have been chosen to carry it. Only to activate when the soul felt it had a worthy vessel to return to."

That information struck Rue harder than it should have. Worthy vessel? Did that mean all of this was meant to happen? Surely, that couldn't be what he was implying. Could it?

"There is no such thing as coincidence in my experience. It was always supposed to be you. It was always supposed to be now, but how he planned it..." Corvus' words fell off, breaking his momentum. Rue gently cradled his cheeks, turning his head back to hers.

"Don't worry about that right now. Tell me more about that night. I want to know, Corvus. I want to remember." She tried to keep the desperation out of her voice, but it was difficult when she was practically champing at the bit for more answers.

"I was there with you. I had begged you not to do it, but I knew there wasn't another option that wouldn't end up even worse. I knew it was selfish to want you to stay with me, but I couldn't help it. I was still young and stupidly in—" Corvus stopped himself, that tell-tale flush creeping up his neck and cheeks again. Rue had an idea of what he was about to say but let it go. She waited for Corvus to collect himself. He could say whatever it was when he was ready.

"But Vaion and his army were coming, and there wasn't time. I fought them off for as long as I could before I just...couldn't anymore. I collapsed, and they went straight for you. When I eventually came to, you were already gone. I didn't get to say any goodbyes, I didn't get to tell you anything I should have, and now..." He swallowed hard, fighting with himself to keep talking. She admired his determination to say all of this despite it being something incredibly painful for him to recount.

"Now that I have you again, I don't want to lose you. I know this time, it's not...exactly the same as it was before. You're not exactly the same as you were before. But I can't just let you walk off into danger without at least trying to figure out what all of the options are." Corvus took her hand in his, bringing her knuckles to his lips and pressing a soft kiss against them. Rue's stomach flipped, and she let out a small, surprised sigh at the action. It was such a simple gesture, but somehow, it was everything in that moment.

"Corvus..." she began, but the words stuck in her throat. His eyes were lined with silvery tears. It was the first time she'd seen him so vulnerable, so bare, and so different from the Corvus she'd come to know. Without thinking, Rue flung her arms around him, holding him as tightly as she could.

"I'm not going anywhere. *I*," she emphasized, "am going to be here with you every step of the way, just like I promised. We are going to get the book back, and when all of this is over, maybe...maybe we can leave Penrith. Find somewhere new and start over. Somewhere with sun," she laughed wistfully but didn't loosen her hold. "But right now, I need you to trust me to do this. There is a purpose to all of this, and I am going to see it through, but I don't want to do it alone. I *can't* do it alone, and I need you there with me."

Rue finally let go. Her hands hung loosely at his sides, not quite ready to sever the physical connection between them. "I know this has all been so sudden, but every day you're here with me, the more I start to remember the life I had before. I dream about it. I see flashes of memories when you kiss me... and I know you and I are meant to do this together."

She didn't know what she expected in response, but his lips crashing into hers definitely wasn't it. Although, she wasn't complaining. Rue closed her eyes and let herself melt into his kiss. His hands slid up her back and tugged her body back into him. Just as it had before, a rush of memories found her again. She ignored the pain that throbbed in her skull, not ready to pull away from him yet.

This time it was something different. She saw Corvus just as she had before, but this time there was more. There was fire and screaming and blood. So much blood. She let out a soft whimper as the images behind her eyes shifted again. Rue saw the book. She watched as her past self placed the tome in the same box she found it in. The same necklace she had worn her whole life used as a key to lock it tight. Away from Vaion...

Corvus broke the kiss, his brow creased with concern, "Did you see something again? You said you saw memories when I kissed you, so I thought maybe you would see that night if I tried here." He sounded the slightest bit guilty. His kiss may have held some ulterior motives according to him, but Rue knew there was more to it than that at this point.

"Y-yes, I saw Solira— me, locking the book away with my necklace." Her fingers wrapped around it out of habit, her thumb running back and forth over the stone like she always did when anxiety seemed to overwhelm her.

"I couldn't make out much more than that, though." Rue looked up to Corvus, "Maybe you'll just have to keep kissing me so we can figure out all these deep, dark secrets." She gave him a mischievous wink and turned on her heel to head back to the temple.

"Come on, broody bird, let's head back before they start worrying about us."

"Don't call me that."

When they arrived back at the temple, the rest of the Veridae were scattered around, finding other tasks to occupy themselves while Rue and Corvus were gone. She didn't see Sabrien or Ardeth but Oliver was no longer sitting on the chair with his book, instead now he paced up and down the hall while reading, muttering little things to himself, lost in his own world with a finger twirling around a stray lock of his hair. The sight made Rue smile again, heart warm.

"Should we let everyone know what the decision is?" She asked quietly, keenly aware of Oliver behind her, not wanting to interrupt by speaking too loudly. Corvus looked around, no doubt trying to locate the others.

"It might have to wait. I think Sabrien and Ardeth have gone out as well." He let her hand go and walked toward Oliver. Rue's throat tightened for a moment but relaxed instantly when she saw Corvus gently tap his shoulder. Oliver stopped in his tracks and looked up at the older Veridae with a start, snapping his book shut.

Corvus said something too low for her to hear and wrapped an arm around the younger boy's shoulders. It looked like he might actually be apologizing to him. Even in the dim light, she could see Oliver's cheeks bloom. Clearly, he didn't know how to react to Corvus' softer side.

"Sabrien left to gather some supplies. He should be back before nightfall," Corvus informed her once he finished his conversation, "However, speaking of supplies, you and I should go back to your apartment and get whatever's left before the masquerade." Corvus' eyes softened, almost apologetically. "It won't be safe for you to stay there anymore after all of this."

Rue knew he was right but it didn't stop the drop of her stomach. She steadied herself with a deep breath, holding it until her lungs burned and let it out slowly. There was nothing else she could do and it was no use arguing for the sake of argument when she would have to admit she knew Corvus was right in the end anyway.

"Alright. When do you want to go?"

"As soon as you're ready."

CHAPTER TWENTY-FOUR

THE JOURNEY BACK TO Rue's flat passed her in a blur. With too many different scenarios running through her mind, it was hard to focus on yet another thing. Corvus had cloaked his wings again and kept her hand firmly in his, silently offering her his support in whatever small way he could. With her hand firmly lodged in his, Rue had to take out her anxiety on something else. Her teeth caught a tiny strip of chapped skin on her lip and tugged.

"Ouch!" She jumped from the zing of pain in her lip. The coppery taste of blood that swirled over her tongue made her wince. Corvus stopped and turned to face her. His calloused hand slid under her chin and turned her face toward him.

"You're so self destructive. What did your poor lip ever do to you?" He chided with good nature but Rue could hear the underlying tone of concern in his voice.

"Sorry... just thinking too much yet again," she admitted sheepishly.

Corvus frowned and stroked his hand over her cheek, and somehow, that small action quelled her nerves from a thunderous cacophony down to a dull roar inside her head.

"You don't have to be sorry. There is a lot happening, and unfortunately, the bulk of it relies on you. Your nerves are understandable," he told her.

Rue narrowed her eyes playfully and pressed the back of her free hand to his forehead. "Are you ill? Why are you being so nice?"

Corvus swatted her hand away, rolling his eyes, but she could still see warmth blooming on his cheeks. It was nice to see him flustered every once in a while.

"Come on, we're almost there."

When they arrived at her apartment, the state of it made Rue want to break down and cry. The lock on the door had been broken, leaving splinters of wood hanging from the door where the strike plate sat. Taking a few tentative steps past the threshold, Rue's hand slowly lifted to her mouth as she tried desperately to keep the sob that was building in her chest from coming out.

"W-what happened?" Her voice was barely audible, but Corvus' hand on her shoulder told her he'd heard. Rue fell to her knees, silently scraping up tiny pieces of broken glass from the picture frames that previously lined the walls, now crushed without care on the floor.

"My home," she whispered, her chest so tight she could hardly breathe. It was like a knife had been plunged and twisted into her heart. Corvus remained stoic and silent. What could he say? She knew that in the end, sacrifices needed to be made, but seeing the destruction in front of her like this. It was a much more devastating blow to her already weary heart than she ever could have imagined.

They both sat in silence for a long while, Rue in mourning and Corvus doing anything he could to comfort her. However, before the reality of the situation could fully consume her, a familiar voice echoed in the now-empty space of her living room.

"Rue!" Fia ran in, tripping over the piles of debris and her own two feet. Rue's eyes widened, finally snapping out of her melancholy as she leapt to her feet and threw her arms around the smaller girl.

"Oh, Fia!" Tears flowed in rivers down Rue's cheeks. Fia's arms wrapped around her were the only thing holding her together. Seeing her friend in the middle of all this chaos was like a dazzling light guiding her across a dark and stormy sea.

"I was so worried about you," Rue managed between her sobs, refusing to let the mousy girl go, "How did you know I was going to be here?"

"Worried about me? I was worried about you!" Fia began, still clinging to Rue just as hard, "I've been coming to check on the place every day since a group of men came to my shop asking about you. I got a really bad feeling about them and told them I had no idea who you were but I don't think they believed me. I was so scared you would come back and get caught up with them and wanted to warn you if I could."

Rue pulled back, her hands still firmly gripping Fia's upper arms as she looked her in the eye.

"Asking about me? What did they look like?"

"Well, I couldn't see their faces. They were wearing hoods and masks."

"Shit."

They had to have been some goons working for Ryker. Most likely trying to find the key to open the box. Considering the duke held the entire isle in his pocket, it wouldn't be too far a stretch to assume he would hire some thugs to come and collect her.

"Woof." Another familiar voice broke the tension.

"Sabrien!"

"You!"

Rue's head snapped back to Fia.

"You know him?" Rue asked, brows shooting clear to her hairline.

"He's been coming to the shop for the last couple of weeks. Buying different tinctures and potions." Fia's face blazed more red than a ripe tomato. Slowly, Rue turned back to the blond, who still stood, now frozen in the broken doorway.

Sabrien's cheeks and ears were glowing with a soft blush of his own, and despite the tragedy of her current situation, it made her smile.

"Funny meeting you here," he said, eyes never leaving Fia's. Rue could feel the younger girl tense beneath her touch. As desperate as she was to ask both of them a thousand questions, it would have to wait.

"We will talk more about this later," Rue stated, pointing back and forth at each of them, "but right now, I need to go salvage what is left of my clothes," she took a deep breath and let it out forcefully, "maybe cry some more and get out of here before whoever was looking for me come back. If whoever it was catches wind I'm here, it would be in all of our best interest to be long gone by the time they show up again."

She let go of Fia, gently nudging her towards Sabrien with a coy grin.

"You two keep each other company," she murmured to Fia, giving her a wink and another nudge with her shoulder, "Corvus, can you help me upstairs, please?"

Corvus' eyes darted between Sabrien and Fia, who were now awkwardly standing together, greeting each other in simple pleasantries before turning back to Rue with a small, knowing grin of his own before following her up to the bedroom.

"Did you know he was going to Bellmare for things?" Rue asked as she folded a dress into thirds, placing it into a bag with the rest of her clothes.

"We sent him to grab a few things, but it seems he made it a point to go back on his own," Corvus replied from where he sat on the edge of her ruined bed, holding the bag open for her.

"You know, I adore Sabrien, but I will not hesitate to kick him in the teeth if he decides to play around with her heart."

"I would actually pay to watch you do that regardless."

Rue laughed and shook her head. She wouldn't tell Corvus, but part of her was happy to see them together. They could be good for each other. Even if part of that was just her selfishly wanting her friends to be close to each other as well as her.

"Alright. I think that's everything I can salvage," Rue concluded with a sad sigh, shoving the last of her unmentionables into the bag, not caring if Corvus was looking. She turned to the vanity table, her lips pulling into an even deeper frown when she took in the cracked mirror and spilled bottles. How many times had she sat there, brushing her hair or writing letters to Orionna? It was a clear sign that every last piece of the life she'd lived until now was gone, shattered along with the mirror's glass.

"I'm gonna miss this vanity." She trailed her finger over a long fracture in the glass.

"We'll get you another one." Corvus hefted the bag over his shoulder, taking a step closer to her, and pressed a small kiss to the crown of her head.

"Ready?"

When they returned to the main room, Sabrien and Fia were still standing together, but without anyone's prying eyes on them, they'd drifted closer. Rue stood at the bottom of the landing, watching the two of them quietly for a moment longer before alerting them of her presence.

"I'm glad you're okay. I was really worried when you stopped showing up to the shop," Fia told him, meekly folding in on herself.

"If I had known you knew Rue, I could have told you more," Sabrien said, reaching out to tuck away a lock of her chestnut hair behind her ear, a soft smile on his lips.

Rue cleared her throat gently, effectively ending their moment. With a start, they both jumped back from each other, facing in opposite directions.

"I'm ready. Let's go find Jasper."

With that, the group filed out, Rue taking up the rear. She stopped, pausing for a moment to look back at the small flat she'd lived in for so long. Without the distraction of her clothes or the relief of her friends being safe, the stinging prickle of tears behind her eyes and tip of her nose returned.

Rue's eyes combed over what was left of her through the wreckage and remembered all the times Jasper had come here when he had nowhere to go. Rue thought of all the times she would come home from the manor late in the night but somehow still found the energy to dance around her kitchen singing far too loudly and off-key while she made herself a meal.

The more she tried to tear herself away, the deeper the roots beneath her feet seemed to hold her firmly in place. This place was more than just a simple dwelling to her. This place had become her safe haven, her *home*. And now – everything was gone. There was nothing left for her here. No more safety, no more comfort. All that was left was a mausoleum for the life she once had.

"Rue?" Fia's hand gently tugged at her shoulder. "Are you alright?" She asked.

"I'm not now, but I know I will be." Rue wiped a single tear from the corner of her eye and took a deep breath, finally finding the courage to turn away.

"Jasper will most likely be at The Devil's Due. We could probably expedite our search if we start there," Rue said, facing the group.

"In Fool's Hope?" Fia asked, looking a little nervous at the prospect of going into the proverbial belly of Penrith's beasts.

"Yes, and somehow, it's probably the safest place on the isle right now," Rue told her, frowning at her friend's obvious discomfort.

"Thought it would be a cold day in hell before I ever considered that."

"You and me both."

Without any argument from either Corvus or Sabrien, Rue nodded. It was decided. They would venture back to The Devil's Due first to find Jasper before finishing any of the other errands they needed to before the masquerade.

They all walked in a sort of melancholy silence. The reality of the situation was beginning to weigh heavily on everyone's heart. Fia kept pace with Rue, but stayed quiet as they crossed through the tree line onto the broken road that led to Fool's Hope.

Fia slid her hand into Rue's, gripping her fingers tighter than was strictly necessary. Rue turned to face her, brows knitting together in concern.

"What's wrong, Fia?" Rue returned the grip, hoping to pull her friend back to ground.

"I'm just...so scared, Rue. I don't want you to get hurt, and it feels like you're running headlong into waiting jaws."

"I'll be honest with you. I'm absolutely scared out of my wits. This isn't at all what I had in my future plans, but sometimes, the future doesn't really care what you plan. If I don't do this, then there might not be a future, so as terrified as I am of all of this, I have to do it," Rue paused, turning to meet Fia's gaze, "And I would really love it if you were here with me for it. To see all this through to the end."

Fia didn't respond for a long moment. She turned away from Rue, staring down at the array of fallen leaves scattered over the craggy road instead.

"You don't have to say anything, Fia. You being here right here with me at this moment is more than enough."

They walked the rest of the journey in comfortable silence before reaching the gates that lead into Fool's Hope. Taking in the sight of cracked and splintering wood with paint peeling off in strips, Rue thought of the first time she'd come here to find Jasper, desperate and horrified. She couldn't help but laugh to herself. How wrong she was to think that coming to a place like Fool's Hope was the scariest thing she could do.

"What's got you laughing?" Corvus asked from behind her.

"Oh, nothing. Just reminiscing," Rue answered.

Corvus crossed in front of her, reaching out to push open the gate, "Reminiscing, huh?"

"Just thinking of how scared I was the first time I came here to find Jasper, but now I don't think anything in this place could truly frighten me." Without any further explanations, Rue walked past Corvus, her head held high as she walked through the nearly empty streets of the Thieves' City.

Chapter Twenty-Five

WITH THE PARTIALLY OBSCURED sun still cradled in the clouds, the normally bustling tavern stood empty. Like it was fast asleep and would only awaken at the stroke of midnight. Rue cupped her hands against the darkened windows and searched for any sign of Jasper or Lydia inside. Anyone, for that matter.

"I can't see anyone."

"Does the owner live here?" Corvus asked, taking it upon himself to peek inside as well.

"Why don't we just knock?" Fia suggested.

"I suppose we could," Rue agreed. She approached the door and rapped her knuckles against the splintered grain of the wood.

"Hello? Lydia? Theo?" she called, knocking again, harder this time. Desperation to find her brother and make sure he was still alive overcame her.

"Hello?" She cried out, the silence within maddening. Corvus pulled her back from the door before she could start kicking her feet against it. He wrapped his hands around hers, holding her body against him.

"Don't panic yet, sunshine. I'm sure he's fine."

"You obviously don't know my brother. He's a master of getting himself into sticky situations, and I really don't need that right now."

Before Corvus could offer another counterpoint, his mouth snapped shut at the sound of a window opening above them.

A clearly irritated voice boomed, "Why you bangin' on my door, girl? I'm tryin' to get some sleep before I gotta get the tavern ready."

"Lydia! It's me, Rue! Please, I'm looking for my brother. Do you know where he is?"

Lydia blinked a few times before rubbing the leftover sleep from her eyes, "Jasper? He was here last night. He might still be up in a room," she groaned, scrubbing a hand down her face, "Gimme two shakes and I'll open the door."

The window slammed shut. The knot coiled tight in the center of Rue's chest began to loosen. She just had to hope he really was still there. Lydia took her time getting down to the door, leaving the group standing there, awkwardly shuffling around.

"You are a very lucky girl, Rue Umberwick. Anyone else come knockin' on my door like this wouldn't get any kind of welcome from me." Lydia stood there, clutching a silk robe over her chest. She was beautiful even in her just-roused-from-sleep state.

"Thank you. I'll make it up to you somehow." Without thinking, Rue threw her arms around Lydia's neck and felt the woman soften beneath her.

"Upstairs, last room on the left. Go on now before I change my mind."

Leaving the rest of the group downstairs, Rue lifted the edge of her skirt and stomped up the stairs. She hadn't seen Jasper in what felt like a small eternity. Excitement warred with fear in her chest, both emotions clawing at her with equal fervor.

Rue took a deep breath and, with a shaking hand, she turned the brass doorknob slowly. "Jasper? Are you here?"

"Rue?" a tired but frantic voice rasped from the darkness that blanketed the room.

Rue's heart leapt into her throat.

He was here.

He was alive.

Without a second thought, she burst through the door, not caring if it closed behind her, and threw herself onto the hazy outline of his body.

"Oh gods, Jasper, I—" Her words were cut off by an unbidden sob that tore through her. No matter how much she seemed to play the responsible sibling between them, in the end, Jasper was still her older brother, and she would always turn to him for comfort in these moments.

"Shhh, darling. You're alright, I'm here now," he cooed, rocking her in his arms and stroking her tangled curls. Rue let every ounce of her pent-up emotions flood over her. With her brother's strong and soothing hands holding her, putting her back together slowly but surely, she finally felt safe enough to do so. Jasper continued to murmur and placate her, allowing her to weep into his shirt without complaint.

"Everything went so wrong." She lamented, wiping her eyes.

"I kind of figured that, judging by your state here."

"Ryker managed to get the book from me and now we have to steal it back. Again. So, I need you to take Fia somewhere safe," she summarized in the most basic way she could. Unable to summon the energy to explain further. Jasper didn't argue, only nodded his acceptance of his sister's desperate request. Rue sniffled and hiccuped, her emotions finally beginning to simmer down.

"And what do I do if you don't come back?" Jasper asked somberly.

It was a possibility neither of them wanted to acknowledge. Especially not right now. But she could no longer deny the likelihood of it rang more true than not.

"I..." She paused. What did he do? What could she tell him? "You take whoever is left, and you get the hell out of Penrith. I don't care where you go, but take them and go as far away as you possibly can to somewhere safe."

With another solemn nod, Jasper agreed.

The pair joined the rest of the group back in the main hall of the tavern. Corvus paced a dent into the floorboards while Fia and Sabrien sat close together in another corner of the room. Lydia seemed to have retreated back to her room, leaving them to do whatever it was they came for.

"Alright. Now that we have Jasper, we can finish getting the rest of what we need," Rue announced with a clap of her hands. Corvus barreled across the room toward her, his eyebrows pulled together in his usual mix of concern and irritation. His golden eyes flicked toward Jasper, looking him up and down, clearly judging every part of him.

"Jasper, this is Corvus, my—" she paused. What exactly was he to her? Neither of them had really spoken of it, and in all honesty, she wasn't ready to talk about it either, "My companion." Rue caught Corvus' gaze, waiting to see his reaction to the description of their relationship she gave. His eyes flashed with something she couldn't recognize, but he quickly turned to face Jasper before she could really discern what it was.

Corvus held out a hand to her brother, "Good to finally meet you, Jasper. Rue has spoken of you quite extensively." Jasper laughed and took his hand, shaking it firmly.

"I hope 'extensive' doesn't mean she's only told you all of my many, many shortcomings."

Rue chimed in, hands on her hips again as she looked to her brother with incredulity, "Jasper, please! What kind of sister do you take me for?"

"Just one that's dealt with my tomfoolery for much too long."

Rue couldn't even deny that. She shook her head and pinched the bridge of her nose, "Well, no matter. We have other things to handle, and we are very rapidly running out of time. We can have this chat later." Rue turned to where Fia and Sabrien still sat, fully engrossed in conversation with one another, and allowed a small smile to soften her features.

"Come on, you two," she called out finally when it seemed like they hadn't heard her a moment before.

"Oh, right. Sorry, Rue." Fia quickly stood, creating space between her and Sabrien. The apples of her cheeks pinked with embarrassment. Sabrien stood, stretching his long limbs, expression still as cocksure as it ever was.

"What's next then?" Jasper asked.

"I'll need a dress for starters. Even if my flat hadn't been ransacked, I never owned anything nice enough to attend a ball."

Fia spoke up, raising her hand, "I could go get you one! I know a nice place in Bellmare that has a good selection, and I can get Vesper while we are there, too."

Rue considered this for a moment. Splitting up wasn't her first choice, but they could all cover more ground and get the things they needed in half the time.

"Alright. I trust you to get me something appropriate for the occasion," Rue nodded.

"I'll go with her. To make sure nothing happens," Sabrien volunteered before Rue could continue. She knew there was more to it than simply making sure Fia stayed safe, but she wasn't going to say anything. She nodded again, agreeing to Sabrien's terms, and turned toward Jasper and Corvus.

"Jasper, I need you to scout around the city and see if you can get any information about the masquerade and the duke. You're good at eavesdropping." Rue gave her brother a playful wink. Jasper rolled his eyes but agreed nonetheless.

"Corvus will send a raven to guide you back to where we are staying later tonight," Rue continued, now turning to Corvus, "As for you and I, we'll go back to the temple to tuck away what's left from my flat and let the others know what's going on."

Rue's expression turned sorrowful as she thought about the paltry handful of items left from her flat. Like he was attuned to her, Corvus noticed the shift in her mood and stepped closer, placing his hand on her elbow gently in an attempt to comfort her.

Jasper seemed to have noticed Corvus' attention and raised a questioning eyebrow at his sister. Rue shook her head almost imperceptibly before facing Corvus again with a forced smile.

"Alright, let's get out of here before we waste any more time. Everyone, meet back at the temple after sundown."

"So, this man is your 'companion' then?" Jasper nudged Rue with his elbow.

Rue brushed him off and huffed, "Yes, that's all."

"Seems like he might be a bit more than that, dear sister."

Rue glared at Jasper, "Seems like you should really mind your own business, dear brother."

Jasper laughed and shook his head, "What good would I be as an older brother if I didn't make sure my sweet baby sister was being taken care of by some tall, brooding man that very obviously has some secrets."

"He is brooding alright. Rude and bull-headed, too."

"Hmm, definitely nothing to like there at all, then."

Rue's cheeks flushed. She knew Jasper had already figured out that something was happening between her and Corvus, even if he didn't know what exactly.

"I see the way he looks at you. The way he touches you without thinking of it," Jasper continued, speaking quietly, "As long as he takes care of you and treats you well, he'll have my blessing. Even if it seems he's not entirely fond of me."

"He is...good. He's gotten me this far without much incident," Rue told her brother, thinking back on all the times Corvus had stepped into the line of fire to protect her. She didn't say that it was most likely because she was some kind of reincarnation of a Goddess as well as his past lover. That would have to be a conversation for another time.

"Then all is well," Jasper stopped for a moment, taking Rue's hand in his own, "But this is where I leave you for now, sister. I promise I won't be gone long this time, okay?" He pressed a soft kiss to her forehead, and Rue felt a pang of anxiety at the idea of being separated from her brother again, but she knew it was necessary, and they needed him to gather as much information as he could before the ball.

"Alright. Please, stay safe and don't get yourself into any trouble." Rue leveled him with a serious look and Jasper crossed his hand over his heart in an 'x' and bowed his head.

"I promise."

The siblings embraced once more. Rue hesitantly released her brother, chewing the inside of her lip to keep from calling him back as he began to retreat.

Before he got too far, Jasper spun on his heel and called back, looking at Corvus, "You better keep her safe. I'm counting on you."

Rue's head snapped toward her companion, and much to her surprise, Corvus simply bowed to him.

"You have my word," he said, stealing a glance toward Rue before facing Jasper once again.

"Good man." Jasper gave a mock salute before shoving his hands into his pockets and heading out into the city.

Rue watched his back until he disappeared. She wanted him to stay despite knowing that he couldn't. She closed her eyes and took a deep breath, trying to maintain her composure. A hand at the small of her back pulled her back to ground. The warmth radiating from Corvus' palm was comforting. Rue leaned into him and slid her arms around his waist, resting her head against his chest.

"Thank you," she muttered. Corvus held her tighter to his chest and pressed a soft kiss to the crown of her head.

Chapter Twenty-Six

With less than a full day before the masquerade, Rue was unsure if the disguise they'd procured would be enough to fully obscure her. Ryker was sure to recognize her regardless, considering he had seen her every day for the four years she'd worked for him. She didn't even want to think about the small remaining fact that she and Ryker had been...intimate. An exasperated groan rumbled out from her chest as she dragged her hands down her tired face.

"This whole endeavor suddenly feels impossible," she whined. Corvus stood against the wall, arms crossed over his chest as usual, with a scowl on his face. He wasn't helping matters at all.

"Alternatively, you could just stay here and let us handle it like I wanted you to in the first place," he muttered under his breath. It was a lesson in futility, however. He knew as well as she did that they didn't have time to change the plans now. Rue's knowledge of the manor was the best chance they had to get in and out as quickly as possible, and they all knew it. She tilted her head, leveling him with a stare that said, 'I don't think so.'

Corvus sighed and ran his hand through his hair, leaving some of it stuck up at odd angles. Rue chuckled softly at the sight before crossing the room to him and smoothing it back down. This close, it was easy to see the crimson tint that dusted his cheeks.

"I know you're worried about me, and I am grateful that you are, but this whole debacle is my fault to start with, and I have to fix it. There isn't any other way."

Corvus closed his eyes and let out another heavy sigh, "I know… I just wish we didn't have to put you in the line of fire. I have a bad feeling he's going to pull some kind of stunt." He unfolded his arms and wrapped them around Rue, pulling her closer. She let out a small, surprised squeak but quickly melted into his embrace. He was so warm, like her own personal furnace. She nuzzled her cheek against his chest and slid her hands around his back.

"As long as I know you are all there for me, I won't be afraid of anything."

It was odd how this group that she hadn't known for much longer than a month or so felt like family to her. She supposed part of it had to do with the fact she was currently acting as a vessel for the soul of a forgotten Goddess, but even so. It struck her hard in these moments that she had been so alone for so long.

After her mother died and Jasper went off on his own, she did everything she could to protect her peace. The only friend she'd really had since university was Orionna, and even that wasn't as fulfilling a friendship as it had once been since she'd returned to Penrith. Rue sniffled softly, trying as hard as she could to reign in her emotions. She would not cry. Not here where Corvus could see her. But it was too late.

"Hey, hey sunshine…" he slid a hand under her chin and tilted her face up to look at him, "Why are you crying?" His brows furrowed with concern as his eyes raked over her face, trying to figure out what was wrong.

"It's nothing," She said, reaching up to wipe a stray tear from her eye before it could fall, "I just don't want to lose any of you. Now that I have you, I can't imagine my life without you."

Corvus was silent for a moment, seemingly contemplating his words before he spoke. Silences with Corvus had gone from awkward and stilted to comfortable and serene. It wrapped around her like a cozy blanket. Simply being near him was enough to put her at ease.

"I will do whatever it takes to keep you safe. Believe that." He moved his hand from her chin to her cheek, cupping it gently and stroking his thumb over her soft skin.

He started to say something else but was abruptly interrupted by the sound of the door opening behind them. Corvus tried to pull away from her, no doubt trying to keep up the appearance of his usually gruff attitude, but Rue tugged him closer and cleared her throat.

"What do you want?" He turned his head toward the door, seeing Sabrien standing there with a look that meant he would absolutely be pestering Corvus about this later.

"I was just coming to see if Rue was ready for the uhh," Sabrien paused, scratching the back of his head, "preparations for tomorrow."

"Preparations?" Rue questioned

"Mmhm. We have to hide that lovely mane of yours, and our dear baby boy Oliver has come up with a hopefully foolproof plan."

Rue narrowed her eyes at the word 'hopefully.'

"So, if you don't mind, I'm here to steal your girl for a little while." Sabrien held out his hand, offering it to Rue.

She looked back to Corvus and held his gaze for a long moment, wordlessly assuring him that they would finish this conversation later. He nodded in understanding and hesitantly released her from his grasp, fingers lingering on hers as they separated. Rue took Sabrien's hand and turned to follow him out.

Sabrien led Rue into a room at the back of the temple that she hadn't seen before. The walls were covered from floor to ceiling in a beautifully intricate mosaic of deep ocean blue and tide-green tiles.

As she walked forward, Rue noticed that some of them glinted with iridescence against the dim light like the inside of an abalone shell. The whole room was breathtaking. Rich, saturated colors hidden away like a treasure trove.

"Wow, this is..." Rue spun on her heel, trying to take all of it in at once, "Incredible." She breathed. Sabrien smiled, holding his hands on his hips and looking at the walls. His expression didn't seem nearly as impressed, but Rue supposed that when you look at something this beautiful for so long, it might start to look plain.

"There used to be a lot more art like this but..." Sabrien frowned as he spoke, not finishing his thought. Rue didn't press for more; she was plenty content to just look at what was left and appreciate it thoroughly.

"So what's this big plan Oliver has for my disguise?" Rue asked, changing the subject. Sabrien smiled softly, clearly grateful for it.

"He's got a recipe for a temporary dye that should disguise your hair to a deep brown. It won't stay forever but it will take a few washes to get out." He tapped his chin, eyes raking over the mess of Rue's fiery orange curls, "As well as a mask that should fully cover your face."

Rue tugged at a stray lock of her hair, twisting it in her fingers. She'd always wondered what her hair would look like in another color that wasn't so...vibrant.

"It will be strange to be someone else for a while, but who knows, maybe it will make this whole situation a little more fun and a bit less end of the world." Rue laughed humorlessly, tossing her hair behind her shoulder, "Well, no time like the present. Let's do this."

Rue had stripped down to her slip — which was barely more than a satin scrap of fabric — but for whatever reason, she didn't feel uncomfortable being so undressed in front of Sabrien and Oliver. Wrapping her arms around her chest, she smiled to herself. They both reminded her of her brother in different ways. Sabrien was all of the parts of Jasper that drove her up the wall but she loved anyway. Oliver was all the softer parts of Jasper she wished she saw more. It was such a comfort to have them both here with her when Jasper couldn't be.

Oliver's hands in her hair broke her out of her reverie, "You looked like you were thinking about something sad," he said as he sectioned out parts of her hair. Rue sighed softly and swallowed down the tears that stung behind her eyes.

"I was just thinking about my brother." She didn't look up at either of them as she spoke. Seeing any amount of pity in their eyes would tip her off the edge, and the dam she had been holding together would break. "He and I haven't always gotten along. Especially after our mother died. He didn't know how to deal with his pain, so instead of coming and talking to me, he crawled into the bottom of every bottle he could." Rue picked at the fraying laces of her boots, focusing her attention on each one of the woven strands so she kept talking without breaking down.

"He would only come to me when he wanted something. Money, food, a place to stay — and I gave it to him every single time. I always thought he was ungrateful and selfish, and most of the time, I was right, but then he told me about that book." She took a shaky breath, pulling particularly hard on a thread, snapping it away from the rest of the lace, "I was so angry. I was so livid that everything that I had worked so hard for had gone to hell so fast. I lost my dream job, the man I thought I was in love with turned out to be a monster, and on top of all that, I had to deal with Corvus!" She laughed with a bit more mirth this time. "But, as irritating as all of that was, I'm grateful for it."

Oliver raised his brows and turned his head, reminding her of the way the curious raven's heads would turn when she offered them trinkets, "What makes you say that?"

"Because all of that led me here. Led me to find out I had a life before this one and you were all a part of it. To unlock these memories that have been dormant in me this whole time. No matter what happens tomorrow, I am just grateful I got to have an adventure worthy of a storybook."

The room went quiet. The hands that were in her hair stilled and before she could turn around and ask what was wrong, both Sabrien and Oliver's arms were around her. Rue froze in place, her mind taking a moment to catch up and understand what was happening, but she hugged them back the best she could.

"G-guys, it's alright. You really don't need to do this—" Her words were cut off by Sabrien,

"For once in your life, please just accept this," he chided playfully. Warmth bloomed deep inside of her. Their arms around her felt like the soft warmth of early summer. It reminded her of a time when she still saw the sun.

"Thank you." Was all she could get out before the tears she'd tried so hard to hold back tumbled down her cheeks. Oliver gave her one last squeeze before letting her go again. She knew in that moment, no matter how chaotic everything around her became, she was going to be just fine.

It took a few more minutes of pinning and piling her hair onto her head before Oliver produced a bowl with a thick brown paste that looked more than just a little suspicious. Rue eyed it, unable to keep the disgusted wrinkle from forming on her top lip.

"Please tell me that isn't what it looks like."

"That depends on what you think it looks like," Sabrien said without any hint he might be joking. Oliver rolled his eyes and elbowed the older Veridae.

"It's a mixture of ground tree bark, wild mushrooms, acorns, and a mixture of a few different kinds of flowers."

Well, that didn't sound too bad, at least. Rue took a deep breath and squared her shoulders, mentally preparing herself.

"Alright, do it before I change my mind." She closed her eyes and pulled her knees to her chest. She heard Sabrien chuckling behind her as he grabbed one of the sectioned locks of her hair and began to apply the paste.

The three of them sat in silence while they ran the mixture through all of her hair. It was the same comfortable silence she'd had with Corvus. Sometimes, it was nice to just enjoy the quiet for a while. After the mixture was applied to all of her hair from root to tip, Rue turned to the others. "Thank you for going through all this trouble for me."

"You don't need to thank us. Really, we are here in service to you." Oliver reassured her with a smile.

"You mean the old me. Solira." Rue corrected him, trying to keep the sadness out of her voice and hugging her knees a bit tighter to her. Oliver just shook his head, placing a hand on her shoulder.

"No. You." His tone left no room to brook disagreement, so Rue nodded but still did not feel fully convinced.

"No matter what your name is now, you are still our Goddess."

Rue nodded again with a bit more conviction, she knew he was right but it was still hard to wrap her head around at times.

"Are you lot done yet? I need to talk to Rue." Another voice joined them, making Rue jump in her chair. She hadn't even heard the door open.

"Bloody hell, you didn't want to knock?" Sabrien exclaimed, hand on his chest in mock terror. Corvus didn't say anything and just cut him with a look. That was all he needed to do to get the other two Veridae to leave the room. Rue felt more exposed in her slip now with just Corvus in the room; she could feel her cheeks heat with embarrassment, but his eyes stayed on hers.

"You look..." he paused, a rare grin tugging at the corner of his lips, "ridiculous." Corvus laughed. A deep and hearty sound that Rue would have paid any amount of money to hear again. Her heart clanged against her ribcage like a prisoner trying to escape.

"Thanks," Rue muttered, resisting the urge to push her hands into her hair. The mixture made her head feel heavy, but at least it smelled nicer than she thought it would.

Corvus took a seat next to her, his leather-clad leg touching hers. Despite the cold of the chamber, Corvus' touch remained warm as always, sending goosebumps up her arms.

"You said you had something to talk to me about?"

Chapter
Twenty-Seven

ORVUS TOOK AN UNSTEADY breath, holding it in his chest for a moment before blowing it out. Was he anxious? She'd never seen him look so vulnerable before. Somehow, it was endearing to see such a fierce warrior look nervous to talk to a woman. Rue slid her hand onto his, squeezing his fingers in a way that said, 'Go on.'

Corvus gave her an appreciative smile and visibly relaxed, "Do you remember when I told you about the bond. When you first summoned me with the feather?"

It seemed so long ago now. When he had first appeared in her hearth after the first of the attacks. It was another lifetime.

"Yes. You said it was so you could find me if we got separated."

"There is more to it. Or, there can be. If you want to make it more." His voice sounded so hopeful, it made Rue's stomach flip.

"More? Like...marriage?" she asked, the words coming out before she had a chance to stop them. It was the only kind of 'deeper bond' she could think of. Her cheeks turned bright red, and now, with her hair pulled back and covered in a thick paste, there was no way for her to hide it. She just hoped Corvus didn't say anything about it.

He swallowed hard and took another breath. From the look on his face, she could tell the word 'marriage' had stirred something up inside of him.

"Not quite. If we deepen the bond, it can be felt both ways. You will be able to sense me when I am near to you."

Corvus took her hand in his, twining her fingers between his, and stroked his thumb over the back of her hand. The soft caress of his fingers sent a shiver up her arm and straight down her spine. It was nothing particularly intimate, but between the two of them, but it still felt like lightning in her veins.

"I know you still have so many questions and so many memories that have yet to be recovered, but having you here with me after being absent for so long..." He sighed softly, almost wistfully. "I tried not to, you know. I tried *so* hard not to fall for you again. I didn't want you to think that I was only here for you because of who you once were and what you were to me then." Corvus lifted his head, apologetic eyes locking with hers.

Rue's heart clenched in her chest. He had said he was falling for her, and she supposed it should have been obvious by now with the way he touched her and kissed her, but hearing it from his lips was something entirely different.

She turned her hand against his, threading their fingers together, "I'm here now. I am here with you, and the only way I am going to leave is if I am dead. You make me feel safe. You make me feel like I am capable of really doing something, and I won't give up that feeling for anything." She moved her free hand to his face, cupping his cheek, thumb stroking over the rough bits of stubble he'd grown over the past day.

"Whatever we need to do, I am more than willing, Corvus."

Rue closed her eyes, feeling the moment take her away. She leaned in closer to him, and with their proximity as close as it was, she felt Corvus lean closer, too.

"Hey, no kissing! Wait until after this mess is out of her hair, please," Sabrien burst through the door and waved his hands, trying to shoo

Corvus away. Rue groaned and rolled her eyes; the embarrassment of getting caught like a teen on a first date was more than mortifying.

"Sorry," she mouthed to Corvus, but he simply shook his head and offered a tiny grin.

"We can talk more about everything after you clean all this up." He told her, gesturing to the thick paste coating her hair. "I'll be in the room you slept in before. Come and find me when you're done with the others."

He stood to leave and it took every bit of self control Rue had not to ask him to stay with her. She just nodded instead and squeezed his hand once more before he turned to leave.

"Alright, are we ready to wash this muck out and see what it looks like?" Sabrien's voice cheerfully cut through the silence she'd been left in.

"I'm a little scared, but there's no turning back now."

"You're already beautiful. There's nothing to be scared of," Sabrien told her with utmost sincerity. Rue made a noise of embarrassment. Hearing someone call her beautiful so casually was not something she was used to. Sabrien chuckled and jerked his head, calling Oliver over to help.

When they had fully rinsed the mixture from her hair and dried it, the moment of truth was here, whether Rue was ready or not. She took a deep, calming breath and kept her eyes tightly closed as Sabrien turned her around to face the long mirror on the wall.

"Alright, open your eyes," he told her with his hands still bracing her shoulders. Rue gave a small nod and reluctantly cracked her lids open. It took a moment for her eyes to adjust to what exactly she was looking at without her glasses, but when the focus returned the anxiety drained from her body.

She was still the same but only this time she looked much more like Fia than herself. Her hair had that same brown hue her friend's did but leaned a few shades darker. With a small smile, she ran her hands through her locks. The color was plain, maybe even boring but it wouldn't stand out among the crowd of revelers and that was exactly what they needed.

"I miss the orange already." Sabrien sighed with an exaggerated frown.

"Shame, I think I might stick with this color," Rue teased, knocking him with her shoulder playfully. Sabrien only grinned and shook his head. He knew as well as she did that she would never change her hair color permanently. The orange, as much as it made her stand out, had become somewhat of a signature for her.

"Oliver can help you with makeup tomorrow if you want, even though your face is going to be hidden under a mask."

"I think I'd like that. I've never had my makeup done by someone else, and I'm not very good at doing it myself, so I'd like to see what kind of magic Oliver can work." Rue turned to face Sabrien, who was still staring at her hair, no doubt trying to reconcile this new look with the person he was accustomed to.

"Stop! You're making me self-conscious!" Rue screeched, swatting at Sabrien's chest. Before he could retaliate, Oliver joined them. He fully stopped in his tracks, taking a long moment to look at Rue.

"Wow, that worked so much better than I even thought it would," he mused, clearly impressed with his own handiwork.

"Well, if you are all done gawking at me for a moment, I have an unfinished conversation with a certain broody bird."

When Rue entered the room Corvus had told her to meet him in, he was pacing yet another hole into the floor.

"What do you think?" She asked quietly, approaching him. Corvus stopped in his tracks, eyes widening as he took in her new appearance.

"Sabrien said he missed the orange already, but this is nice, too, right?"

Corvus took a step closer to her, reaching out and running his fingers through her still-damp hair with a small smile appearing on his lips.

"I agree, the orange suits you more, but for me, the color of your hair doesn't matter. You're still just as beautiful." Corvus' voice was low and gravelly as he spoke, making the hair on her arms stand up. It was one thing to hear such a compliment from Sabrien, but hearing it from Corvus...

"T-thank you," Rue cleared her throat, trying to rid herself of the lump that formed there, "I want you to tell me more about the bond. Tell me what we need to do." She jumped right into the matter at hand, not sure if she could endure a single compliment more.

Corvus nodded, dropping his hand from her hair and taking hers instead, leading her to the bed where they both sat at the edge.

"Before I tell you this, I want you to know that you don't have to do any of it. Don't feel obligated in any way. We can still make this work without it," he began. Rue could see he was nervous, but about what, she couldn't tell.

"I already told you, whatever it is, I will do it," she said as firmly as she could, finding that instead of trying to convince herself, she truly meant it.

Corvus let out a deep breath he must have been holding for a while, his shoulders deflating as the air left his lungs.

"This deeper bond requires a blood exchange." He paused, looking at her, like there was more to what he was saying besides the actual words. Rue tilted her head in confusion, not quite understanding why he would be so nervous about something that sounded so simple.

"However," Corvus continued, swallowing hard as his thumb stroked the back of her hand, "when the two people involved in the exchange already have...feelings for one another, things can get a bit more complicated."

Rue sensed he was being purposefully vague as though when she found out exactly what was going to happen she would change her mind and he needed to ease her into it. "Corvus, please just speak plainly. I can handle whatever it is," Rue assured him once again, squeezing his hand in hers.

"Everything we feel for one another will be amplified. It may lead to things that you aren't ready for, and I don't want you to do this without knowing the possible outcomes."

Oh.

That's what he was hesitating about. The feelings she had for Corvus were still new, and there was still so much to consider between the two of them. He had said before he didn't want to fall for her because of who she once was, and though he tried, he'd done it anyway.

Corvus had fallen for her.

For *Rue.*

And for her, that was enough.

She cupped his cheek and turned his head back toward her, holding his gaze. His golden eyes were practically glowing in what little light illuminated the room. This close to him, Rue saw an entire cosmos swirling in his stare.

"Whatever may come, I want to do this. With you." And with her decision made, Rue leaned in, closing the space between them, sealing her words with a kiss. It wasn't the first kiss they had shared, but it was the first one Rue had initiated and somehow it had broken the last unseen wall between them. She hoped that with this kiss, she could show him that she was in this with both feet.

Corvus slid his hand out of hers and wrapped his arms around her, pulling her closer and deepening the kiss. At that moment, everything else seemed to melt away. With only the two of them there, nothing else mattered.

The memory hit her suddenly, like lightning striking a tree in a storm. The force of it pulled her back from Corvus, hand going to her forehead in a futile attempt to stop the piercing pain that clawed at the center of her brain.

Rue could hear Corvus speaking, but his voice was muffled and sounded far away. She opened her mouth to speak, but nothing came out. Flashes of another life played out before her eyes. She saw herself there, but she was different. Her hair was the same, and her build was similar, but her face was just different enough. Could this be Solira? It had to be. There was no denying the resemblance.

Rue gasped, trying to catch her breath. Her body felt heavy, like she was caught beneath the ocean's waves, struggling to find the surface. Warm hands on her arms shook her, trying to bring her back to the moment, but the continuous flood of memories playing like a film reel behind her eyes kept her in a trance.

After what felt like a lifetime, Rue managed to finally catch her breath and resurface into the moment. "I'm sorry, I don't know what happened... I saw more of those old memories." She apologized out of habit, still holding her throbbing head. Corvus brushed off her apology and pulled her body against his.

"I think as you and I become...more intertwined, the memories will surface more."

"I hope they will also stop being so horrendously painful, too." Rue winced, snuggling closer to his chest.

"I think the only way we can test that is with repetition." Corvus' mouth pulled into a devilish smirk as he turned her face to meet his, nose brushing against hers.

"I suppose you're right," Rue agreed and cupped his jaw, pressing her lips to his once more.

Chapter Twenty-Eight

Corvus immediately melted into the kiss, his arms circling around Rue and pulling her closer. Rue let out a soft noise that was somewhere between a gasp and a moan. Bracing herself for the piercing pain that came with each of their other kisses, Rue grasped Corvus' shirt tightly. He seemed to have noticed and tugged her into his lap.

"I've got you, love," he whispered, pressing his lips to her jaw instead. Those words shot straight into her stomach. She remembered hearing his voice in her dreams before she had even met him in this life. The voice that had been the only thing stopping her from answering the call of chaos.

She nuzzled into him, eyes still closed as she awaited the pain. Only to find that this time, it never came. Rue breathed a sigh of relief and tilted her head up to face Corvus.

"I'm alright this time," she said, nodding. Corvus gave a soft smile and brushed a hand through her curls.

"Perhaps this is for the best, then."

"Perhaps."

Corvus took her hand in his, turning her palm upwards. His fingers traced the outline of the sun-shaped imprint stamped there from their first unknowing bargain. He did so with such a tender caress that Rue felt a shiver run through her entire body, like his touch was setting her entire body alight.

"At first, I hated the idea of being bound to you like this," Rue confessed with a nervous chuckle. Corvus huffed a laugh and pressed a kiss to the center of her palm.

"Honestly, I can't even blame you," he said, lips moving against her skin as he spoke.

"But now, I don't know how I could have done any of this without you, Corvus," Rue admitted softly, moving her hand to cup his cheek, pulling him down and nuzzling her nose against his. So many things that neither of them had the words for hung between them.

"Are you ready for this?" Corvus finally asked. Rue nodded, hoping her apprehension wasn't too apparent. The words 'blood exchange' indicated there would probably be pain involved, and although she wasn't nervous about the exchange itself, the idea of having to physically cut herself open gave her pause.

"It will only hurt for a moment, love," Corvus reassured, seeming to sense her apprehension. From somewhere behind him, Corvus produced a small dagger with a curved blade that looked to be carved from a chunk of dark stone. Rue winced and bit down on her bottom lip as she watched him line up the blade in the middle of her palm.

"Take a breath in for me."

Rue sucked in a deep breath through her nose and screwed her eyes shut. The blade burned as it slid over her skin, making her grimace, but mercifully, the cut wasn't as painful as she'd thought it would be.

"Very good," Corvus praised, and Rue's stomach flipped. She cracked one eye open to see the pool of crimson flooding the center of her palm, immediately grateful that the sight of blood didn't make her queasy.

Corvus sliced his own palm in one quick motion before setting the dagger aside. Rue marveled at the fact he didn't so much as flinch. A true warrior.

"Now," He said, using his uninjured hand to turn her face back to him, "listen to me very carefully and repeat what I say exactly as I say it."

Rue nodded, her eyes locked on his.

The words Corvus spoke were in a language she didn't understand, but she repeated him to the best of her ability, coaxing her tongue to form the strange syllables.

Once Rue spoke the last words of the oath, Corvus pressed her bloodied palm against his and laced their fingers together. Rue's entire body was suddenly burning. Every fiber, every nerve ending inside her, flared to life. She swore she could actually feel his blood begin to course through her. Rue closed her eyes tightly once again as a flood of images flashed in quick succession before her.

More memories.

Only this time, there was none of the head-splitting pain to accompany them.

She could see everything now. She watched the rise and fall of the Goddess. Watched those painful and desperate last moments between her and Corvus. Tears flowed like rivers down her cheeks, drenching her blouse as she wept. Every bit of pain, sorrow, love, joy, and everything in between from those memories threatened to consume her. It was a sundering anguish combined with a blissful ecstasy she'd never felt before and, with any luck, would never have to feel again.

"I'm here. I'm here with you, Rue," Corvus whispered, wrapping his free arm around her waist. His touch was an anchor. Without it, Rue was certain she would have shattered irreparably.

"Hold on, love. Just a little more, you can do it," he grit out, clearly having some intense feelings of his own.

Rue sobbed, holding onto Corvus' hand so hard she was sure small crescent imprints from her nails would be embedded in his olive skin.

After another eternity, the scenes playing behind her eyes began to fade. Her tears began to slow, and her breathing eventually became even and steady once more.

"It's over. You did so well." The gentle feeling of Corvus' lips on Rue's neck had her body igniting once again, but this time, the sensation was completely different. His words of praise stoked the flames of passion in her stomach. Rue tilted her head, offering more of her neck, and Corvus descended.

"I need you," she managed to choke out. Her fingers thrust into his hair and removed the leather tie holding it back. Corvus immediately obliged, sliding his hands under her backside and pulling her over him as he laid back.

"I've needed you for so long," he murmured, capturing her lips in a heated kiss. His tongue slid between her lips, and Rue breathed a soft sigh of approval. Corvus' hands moved to her waist, gripping her wide hips. She didn't care if he got blood on her dress as long as he didn't stop touching her for even a moment.

Kissing Corvus felt a lot like coming home. He tasted like something she'd once lost but was now so keenly familiar, and she vowed never to forget it; she wanted to imprint it onto her memory.

Corvus broke the kiss and gripped her hips tighter before rolling their bodies so he was above her. His raven-dark hair cascaded over his forehead and cheeks, and Rue was awestruck by how incredibly beautiful he was.

"Are you certain this is okay?" he asked breathlessly. Rue saw concern tangled with need in his expression. She held his jaw between both of her hands, holding his gaze directly.

"Yes. More than."

Rue pulled him down, her lips pressing softly to his. The buzzing energy that rippled under her skin intensified once again, pushing her to deepen the kiss. Corvus matched her fervor instantly. His hands caressed her sides, gently squeezing at her ample curves as he moved downwards. Rue pressed her hands against Corvus' chest, and a soft moan tumbled into their kiss.

She hadn't realized how badly she wanted to touch him all this time. To feel his skin against hers. She pulled back from the kiss and spoke in a heated, breathy whisper.

"Take this off. Please." Her words came out like a needy whine, but she was too far gone to care. Corvus didn't need to be told twice; he stripped off his leather vest and tunic in one swift motion, tossing it over his shoulder.

Rue's hands immediately found his now naked chest. Her fingers dragged over each of the raised scars that were scattered over his skin like stars. Corvus took her injured hand and pressed a tender kiss to her palm. With the pain from the cut already subsiding, Rue closed her eyes and focused on the feel of him. All of him.

Corvus rolled his hips, and Rue met his advance, pressing herself into him. Corvus let out a soft moan against her palm before moving his lips back to hers. Rue's body blazed with lust-filled fire. Every minute touch only served to immolate her further.

"I want more," she mewled softly. Corvus was quick to comply, rolling their bodies once again so she straddled his hips. Without a second thought, his hands were already deftly undoing the row of buttons down her back.

Rue's dress slid easily from her shoulders, exposing her chest under the practically sheer chemise she wore beneath. Normally, her modest demeanor would prompt her to try and cover her skin, but with Corvus, it didn't matter. She wanted him to see all of her.

She already knew he loved every inch.

Corvus sighed with admiration, eyes trailing slowly over her freckle-dappled chest as if he was savoring it, committing the sight to memory. Gently, he pushed the dress down further and Rue shimmied around to slide out of it, letting it fall into a heap on the floor next to his discarded garments.

"You..." he paused, expression shifting, softening with the flurry of emotion between them, "are absolutely radiant in every way imaginable."

Rue was taken aback by the sincerity in his voice, a familiar burn creeping into her cheeks. Before she could even utter so much as a thank you, Corvus pulled her back down to him, kissing her deeply. Rue's eyes fluttered shut once again as she allowed herself to escape into him once more.

His hand pressed against the back of her thigh, parting her legs even wider. She opened easily for him, silently granting permission. Corvus' thick fingers traveled up her leg to her backside, giving it a firm squeeze as he continued to slowly roll his hips against hers.

Rue moaned into the kiss, and Corvus let out a growl of approval in return. His touch grew bolder as he slid his hand between her legs, caressing the softest part of her over her already damp panties. Rue pushed her hips down into his hand, wanting so much more than he was giving.

Corvus broke the kiss, moving his lips to her jaw as he spoke in a breathless whisper.

"Tell me if it's too much."

Corvus' lips moved across her neck and throat as his fingers carefully slid beneath the thin material. His hands were warm, and the pads of his fingers were rough against her. Rue's mouth fell open with a quiet gasp, eyes still screwed tightly shut as a single digit circled around her throbbing clit. His touch felt like a strike of lightning through her, but Rue bit her lip, forcing herself to keep quiet.

Between whisper-soft kisses and his gentle stroking, Rue's body was an overload of sensations. His touches were tender and slow but torturous. Her entire body felt as though it were dangling off the edge of a precipice high above ground.

"Y-yes, like that," she whispered. Corvus' teeth grazed her collarbone, nipping gingerly as his fingers continued exploring her. Rue pushed herself up, holding her weight on her knees to give him more access, but it seemed Corvus had another idea. He pulled his hand away — much to Rue's dismay — and rolled them once more so Rue lay flat on her back, legs still spread wide.

"I need to taste you, love," Corvus said as he slid from the bed and dropped to his knees before her. His strong hands wrapped around her thick thighs, pulling her body closer. Rue let out a surprised yelp but didn't fight him. How could she?

Corvus hooked his fingers into the waistband of her panties, now completely soaked, and slid them down. Rue lifted her hips before propping herself up on her elbows to look at him.

The sight of Corvus on his knees before her was almost enough to make her faint. His smoldering eyes were dark and clouded with a mix of lust, adoration, and something else she wasn't sure if she was quite ready to name just yet.

She slid her hand into his obsidian hair, tugging at his locks with a tiny movement that was more encouragement than anything. Corvus descended on her and held her thighs open wide. Rue moved her hand from his hair, spreading her lips open with delicate fingers, framing herself for him. As if to show him exactly where she wanted those perfect lips of his.

"Fuck," was the only thing she heard him say in a deep, gravelly tone that made her toes curl before his mouth was fully on her. Rue threw her head back, teeth digging into her lip so hard the skin threatened to split in an attempt to keep quiet.

Corvus' tongue rolled over her clit, flicking gently before sucking it between his lips. Rue swore she could have died right then and there and been perfectly fine with it. She'd never felt ecstasy like this before. Every nerve in her body was so perfectly aware of him as he tasted her. Feasted on her.

Rue barely felt it as he let go of one of her thighs, but she couldn't miss the feeling of his fingers sliding inside her. His mouth never once faltered as his digits curled back toward him in a 'come hither' motion. Rue tried to raise her hips from the bed, but Corvus held her down, pinning her to the mattress.

"I-I'm going to—" She started to say, but before the words could leave her tongue, a sensation so hot it was almost cold shot through her whole body. Corvus didn't stop, however. His fingers still pumped in and out of her, still curled into just the right spot, making the icy heat swirling in her abdomen fully engulf her.

Rue's hand flew to her mouth. Her teeth sank into her knuckles while her entire body shuddered and writhed from the intensity of the orgasm that erupted through her. Corvus groaned into her as she came, eagerly lapping up every drop of her arousal.

His fingers eventually slowed before stopping completely. He slid them from her core, rubbing the last bits of her orgasm over her oversensitive clit, making her jerk against him.

Rue blew out a heavy breath, letting her head fall back against the bed. Corvus crawled over her. Thick, muscled arms caged her in as he looked down at her with the most irritatingly beautiful smile.

"I told you things might get intense," he muttered, dropping down to lie down beside her. Rue immediately snuggled into his chest, not ready to let the feeling of him go just yet.

"I hope being with you always feels that amazing," she murmured against his chest, throwing her arm over his abdomen. Corvus chuckled under his breath and tugged her closer.

"I can't make any promises, but I can certainly try to make it just as magical for you next time and every time after that." He pressed a kiss to the crown of her head. Rue's eyelids grew heavier with each blink. Her hand moved down his abdomen, toying with the soft trail of hair that led lower.

Corvus caught her hand in his, moving it away, "You don't need to do that. Just rest now."

Rue pouted and whined in soft protest, but she knew there was no way she could give him the attention she deserved with how drained she felt now.

"Just sleep. I've got you, love." Corvus' now familiar words wrapped around her like a lullaby, and before she could respond, dreamless darkness fell over her once again.

CHAPTER TWENTY-NINE

RUE SAT ON WHAT was probably the most uncomfortable stool known to man while Oliver painted her face. She had never worn this much makeup in her entire life; the weight of it felt suffocating. Had she not known Oliver and believed in his skill, she might have thought she was going to look like some kind of marionette doll once he finished.

"Seems a shame to waste all your artistry by hiding it under a mask," Rue mumbled, trying to keep her lips still as he swiped a smooth brush over them. Oliver's face was full of endearing concentration, and it took every ounce of her control not to smile.

"Rub your lips together for me, please," he said, taking a step back to admire his work. With a pleased grin, he tucked away the brushes and snapped the case shut. Rue was eager to see how she looked after watching all of the different expressions Oliver had been making for the last hour.

"Can I look now?" She asked, excitement mixing with a streak of anxiety. Rue had never been a very glamorous girl. Always opting for comfort over whatever was fashionable at the time. Oliver gave her a nod and stepped out of her way, allowing her access to the mirror behind him.

"Oh, Oliver..." Rue whispered in awe, her hand moving to her face on instinct before she realized and dropped it, not wanting to smudge a single line out of place.

"I had no idea you were so good at this. Where did you learn?" Rue asked, turning on her heel to face the boy again.

"Well," He rubbed the back of his neck sheepishly, like he always seemed to when he was shy or embarrassed, "I had a sister that would let me practice on her when I was young. I always loved to draw and paint back then, so she figured why not let me paint her face."

Rue's heart sunk into her stomach. She had never really thought about their families before all of this. She immediately felt guilty for not asking. With all the worrying she had done about Jasper and the way her worries would seep into everyone else, she felt selfish. Rue took another step back toward Oliver, throwing her arms around him. He was so small, he reminded her of Jasper when he was just a teenager. It made Rue feel protective over him, although she would never tell him that.

"I'm sorry," she finally lamented. Oliver gently returned her embrace, letting out a small relieved sigh.

"It's alright. She left us a long time ago. But it's nice to talk about her again."

Rue pulled away after a long moment, giving the young Veridae's cheek a loving pat.

"I know it's not a perfect substitute, but you can consider me your sister if you'd like. I know I already have Jasper, but just between the two of us, I like you more," she admitted coyly, punctuating her words with a wink. Oliver gave a mischievous grin of his own and knowingly returned the wink.

"I suppose I should go get into my dress. We don't have much more time before we have to get the carriage to the duke's manor," Rue sighed, the reality of the situation crashing back into her all at once. Between her talk with Corvus earlier and the lovely moments she'd spent with Sabrien and Oliver, she allowed herself to forget the purpose of their plan. Soon, all of this would be over, she reminded herself, letting that single thought bolster her courage.

The dress Fia chose wouldn't have been her first choice, but Rue couldn't deny that the silhouette it made was incredibly striking. The gown was black with a bodice laced tight around her middle, disguising the figure that Ryker knew so well by now.

The trim of the long sleeves was wreathed in an elegant floral lace with beautiful appliqué over a thin mesh that crawled like vines up her arms. The collar of the dress was high against her throat with a delicate black silk ribbon that sat right in the dip between her clavicle. Rue's look was finished off with a mantle of raven's feathers — lovingly donated by all of the Veridae as well as a few of their familiars.

The long tiered skirt reached the floor, covering her feet completely, making it much easier to wear a sensible pair of shoes, rather than the tall stiletto heels that were in vogue among the elite. Rue opted for a simple petticoat over a larger hoop skirt, allowing for more mobility in the — hopefully unlikely— event she had to run.

Turning to look at herself in the mirror, Rue took in her completed ensemble and expertly painted visage. Her hand flew to her mouth, tucking a surprised gasp back between her lips before it could fully come out. Despite not looking much like herself, she had to admit she looked... stunning. Oliver stood there behind her, admiring quietly. Rue turned to face him, a nervous smile tugging at the corners of her lips.

"I know we chose black to make you blend in more, but I have to say, I think you'll end up pulling many eyes your way," Oliver admitted with a small snicker. Rue was thankful that the thick layer of paint over her face obscured the blush she could feel radiating over her cheeks. She'd been the object of people's stares her whole life, but it was never because she was someone who possessed extraordinary beauty.

"Oh, I don't know. My whole face is going to be covered, so maybe they won't be too distracted." At least she hoped they wouldn't be.

Corvus sat on the edge of the bed with his forearms resting over his knees, looking like he didn't quite know what to do with himself. Rue held back a laugh at the almost pitiful sight. His wings were magicked away once again, and instead of his usual attire, he wore a beautifully decorated jacket.

The lapels were covered with a gilded filigree design that twinkled in the low light, eye-catching but subtle enough to let him blend in with the other revelers. His hair was a bit more artfully mussed than normal, and he wore a pair of half gloves that — for whatever reason — Rue found very attractive.

"What do you think?" Rue whispered, not wanting to disrupt the peaceful silence Corvus had been sitting in. His head jerked up as though he was snapped out of a trance. His eyes roamed over her face, taking in all the changes she'd made.

"You look..." He paused, standing and moving closer to her, trying to get a better look, "Incredible. I...wow." He put his hands on her hips gingerly. Rue sighed softly, and the nervous energy that buzzed through her vanished in an instant. Corvus' touch grounded her in a way she couldn't explain. Then again, she didn't really need to explain it, did she?

Rue knew from the look in his eyes that Corvus felt the same calming energy between them.

"And you don't look too shabby yourself, I suppose," she teased, sliding her hands over his shoulders. Corvus' lips pulled into a tiny grin as he leaned closer to her and tucked a stray lock of her now brown hair behind her ear. Rue pulled his head down, pressing her forehead to his. Words were not enough to convey what she knew they were both feeling.

Worry.

Fear.

Doubt.

Neither of them knew if this plan would actually work, but they had to try. For the sake of the world around them and for the newfound solace they had in one another.

"I want to kiss you so badly but I think If I ruin your lipstick, Oliver would cry," Corvus admitted, sliding a hand under her jaw, cupping it with such tenderness, she felt like a precious piece of porcelain that would crumble under the slightest pressure.

"Well then, you'll just have to be extra careful." Rue leaned in, pressing her chest against his. There was no way she was going to allow him to just skate by without that kiss. Corvus' grin stretched into a full smile, showing off his pearly white teeth and those damn dimples she loved so much. Rue closed her eyes, and her lips parted eagerly.

The kiss was nothing but pure bliss. At least for the first few seconds before another memory slammed into her. This time, she anticipated it, along with the pain that was sure to follow. Her head pounded with another rush of images flashing behind her eyes. Corvus' hands held her tighter, keeping her anchored to the moment.

These visions were new. Unlike the horrible things she saw by the tree, these memories were pleasant. She saw Corvus, filled with joy and smiling in the sun. His hands were full of sunflowers, arranged into a bouquet and tied off with a bit of twine. There was something so simple about it, yet she knew this memory held power. Rue let out a soft whimper and pressed deeper into him. Seeing him so bright and carefree was something she swore she would do anything to see again in this lifetime.

Reluctantly, Rue pulled back. As much as she wished she could stay here with Corvus and forget about the world outside of the temple walls, the time to leave was rapidly approaching. If they didn't catch the carriage, everything would be thrown off, and there was no secondary plan if this one failed. Her lips pulled into a frown as Corvus pulled her hand into his, pressing a soft kiss to her knuckles.

"This is it," he breathed. She could tell there was so much more he wanted to say, but the words seemed to stick to his tongue before he could get them out.

"Whatever it is you want to say, you had better say it now," Rue pressed. Now was not the time for shyness and tip-toeing around things they both already knew to be true.

Corvus blew out a heavy breath and pushed a hand through his hair. His nerves were clearly getting the best of him. "I've never been too good at words, especially when it comes to...feelings," he said, crinkling his nose. "But I need you to make it out of here. I need everyone to make it. I know everything between us is still fresh, and there is still so much more to learn but..." He paused, gnawing on his lip, like he was warring with himself to get the words out.

"Yes?" She leaned into him again, wanting desperately for him to finish his sentence. Corvus started to speak again, finally gaining the courage to say whatever it was that he held so close to his heart, but before the words could fall from his lips, the door to their shared room burst open. Both of their heads snapped toward it, partially in panic and partially in annoyance — at least on Rue's behalf.

"We have to leave right now. If we miss this window to arrive at the edge of the forest at the same time as the carriages, we are fucked. So sorry to spoil whatever moment you two were having, but we have a party to crash," Sabrien warned, expression not showing the slightest bit of remorse for interrupting. Corvus looked back to Rue with an apologetic frown as if to say this conversation would, unfortunately, have to wait.

"Be safe. We will meet you there." His hand was still fully wrapped around hers, reluctant to let go.

"I will," She promised. There was so much more she wanted to say, more she wanted to tell him, but they were out of time. She would have to use this as her motivation to get in and out of the manor as quickly as possible without getting caught. Rue gave Corvus' hand one last squeeze before finally letting go and following Sabrien out.

"Wait!" Rue spun around and tugged her necklace from where it sat against her collarbone.

"I don't think it's a good idea to take this with me just in case the worst happens." Her fingers wrapped around the pendant, and though she felt like a piece of her was suddenly missing without its comforting weight around her neck, Rue knew she had to leave it behind. Sabrien nodded and handed the piece off to Oliver. The pair exchanged glances, and the younger left to secure the pendant somewhere far from the duke's hands.

Rue let out a deep, anxious sigh, trying to convince herself that this was the right choice and it would be here for her when she came back. But more than anything, keeping the way to access the book away from Ryker was absolutely essential.

Rue hurried out into the courtyard, trying to keep up with Sabrien's long strides. Normally, carriages wouldn't come this close to the hollow, but on the night of the masquerade, drivers would go to every inch of the city to catch a fare. Sabrien led them through an opening in the tree line that opened out to one of the more neglected roads of Penrith.

Sabrien produced a watch from the pocket in his vest, opening it with a tiny click. "Right on time," he murmured before snapping the timepiece shut again and tucking it away. Nervous energy washed over Rue in a wave that threatened to drown her. She knew it was too late to back out now, but her mind only supplied all the worse-case scenarios anyway.

"You alright over there?" Sabrien asked, a hint of concern in his tone. Rue shook her head and gave him a small grin. "Not entirely, but I don't really have a choice, do I?"

There was nothing more he could say to that. They both knew it. So instead, Sabrien just nodded in agreement. The sound of clopping hooves echoed off the cobblestones as the carriage approached them.

"Mask on. We can't be too trusting of anyone at this point," he said in a voice low enough for only Rue to hear. She let out one last steadying breath, clutching the mask in her hands with a vise-like grip. It didn't do much to calm her nerves, but it was worth a try anyway.

The mask she chose reminded her of an old theater mask, but instead of a gleeful grin or anguished cry the expression it wore was completely blank. The lower half was plain and porcelain white, save for the lips that were painted in a soft shimmering gold.

The top half boasted an intricate lace pattern of black and gold with a crown of more raven's feathers to match her dress. The eyes were fitted with thin mesh panels, enough for her to see through but dark enough to hide her eyes. She could barely see through them — especially without her glasses — but she would have to make do.

Rue slipped the mask over her head, turning to allow Sabrien to fasten the ribbons around the back of her head to hold it in place. Once her mask was secured, he pulled on his much less obscuring counterpart.

A simple domino mask with winged edges that pulled upward at the corners. It was decorated with small glass jewels and false pearls, giving it just enough to look expensive despite being bought cheaply.

The carriage came to a stop before them. The driver said nothing and held out his hand for the fare, which Sabrien tossed to him in a small velvet pouch. The man grunted and jerked his head, wordlessly telling them to get in.

Sabrien held out a hand and bent in a small bow — ever the gentleman — and helped Rue in first, quickly following behind. They sat in silence, not daring to speak lest they be overheard during the ride. The city's gas lights burned blurred streaks across her vision as they passed. She thought of all the times she'd walked through the streets, going to and from the manor without a care in her mind. Now, everything was different. Every second they drew closer to the duke, Rue's stomach clenched with unease. Despite all they had done to disguise her, there was still a chance that Ryker would recognize her in an instant. Especially if what the Veridae had said was true and the duke really was another God of the lost pantheon.

All of these thoughts spiraled, and her vision blurred, turning the street lights into nothing but softly twinkling stars. Without her necklace to use as a worry stone, she tugged at the delicate lace of her sleeves, and the delicate fabric threatened to tear. Sabrien pulled her hands apart, wrapping his fingers around hers, stroking softly. She let out a small sound of relief and turned away from the window.

"Thank you."

Sabrien gave her a warm, reassuring smile, squeezing her hand gently.

After what felt like an eternity, the carriage finally slowed to a stop outside the familiar gates of Ashworth Manor.

CHAPTER THIRTY

T HE MANOR WAS MORE lively than Rue had ever seen it. Even in the previous years that she had attended, she couldn't remember the ball being this opulent. The normally dreary and dark walkways were lit with portable oil lamps that danced with flickering flames. The statuary garden had been cleaned, the overgrown vines trimmed away, and statues scrubbed, turning the manor's entrance into a breathtaking scene.

Revelers walked along the lit pathway were dressed in lush finery and dazzling jewels. Even with the lovely gown and mask she wore, Rue couldn't help feeling underdressed. Though it was probably for the best that everyone else shared that sentiment. Sabrien held fast onto her arm, and she was grateful for it. He was the voice of reason that kept her there despite every other part of her screaming to run away.

He gave her arm a gentle squeeze as they approached the doors. Immediately, Rue caught sight of Delnan standing behind the threshold, welcoming each of the guests. She took a sharp breath and held it in her chest as they stepped through the doorway.

"Welcome to the Ashworth Manor. Proceed into the ballroom, and enjoy your evening." Delnan repeated the greeting to each group of partygoers, waving them forward without sparing Rue or Sabrien a single glance. She let out the breath burning in her lungs slowly and closed her eyes under her mask, basking in the momentary relief.

In the main hall, a few couples and groups lingered, admiring the series of Ashworth family portraits that lined the walls. As she walked by, she heard the same whispers that came every year. Talk of how handsome Duke Ashworth was and how surprised they all were that he still remained unmarried. Rue rolled her eyes and tugged on Sabrien's arm, pulling him away from the crowd and into the ballroom.

She had been in this room before, but her memory did it no justice. The domed ceiling was covered from edge to edge with a fresco painting of the perfect sunset, casting the entire room in soft orange and pink hues.

A large crystal chandelier hung in the center of the dome, speckling the walls in a kaleidoscope of colors. However, the lack of any other light source left plenty of dark corners for them to hide away in without being seen.

These masquerades were mostly an excuse for Ryker to flaunt his wealth and remind the people of Penrith just who it was that kept their fair isle afloat. Most of the attendees used it as an excuse to drink on his dime and forget about their lives — for a few hours, anyway.

On the opposite side of the room, a quartet of musicians played a melancholy waltz while the guests danced around them. As they twirled, glittering jewels and swirls of color from their clothes created an almost hypnotic scene. Rue hadn't realized she'd been rooted to the spot, completely enraptured, until Sabrien tugged on her arm and broke her focus.

"We can dance later."

She nodded and moved to follow his lead. Rue hadn't been back to the manor in weeks, leaving without a single word to Ryker. She knew it was him — or his lackeys, rather — that had stolen the book from her apartment, but would he expect to find her here? Did he think she would be so bold? It wouldn't be the first time he'd underestimated her.

Anger rose in her chest, and Rue pulled her gaze away from the throngs of dancers, turning to wherever Sabrien was leading her.

"Have the others made it yet?" she whispered close to his ear. Sabrien craned his neck, searching around the room before shaking his head.

"Not yet. Unless they didn't come in. Ardeth said he would be waiting outside to keep watch."

"I really wish Fia and Jasper could be here, too," Rue said, nudging his shoulder at the mention of the former. She couldn't see his face under the mask as it came down far enough to cover his cheeks, but she felt him tense up under her jab.

Rue enjoyed a private chuckle to herself at the way he'd reacted to her friend's name but decided she could wait to tease him after they finished what they'd come here to do.

"So, fearless leader, what is your plan now that we're here? Is there a secret door in a wall that no one knows about that you plan on sneaking through?" he asked with good humor.

"Actually. There is," she replied, tipping her chin up at him. Sabrien was gobsmacked at the fact that it was indeed that simple, but Rue didn't linger to give him the satisfaction that he'd actually impressed her with his deduction.

Before she could get too far across the floor, the tinkling sound of someone tapping a glass interrupted her.

Ryker.

He wore an ostentatious half-mask that resembled a hawk. A porcelain beak and a crown of tawny feathers — much like the ones on Rue's mask — adorned his head.

He stood there, before the quartet, holding a half full glass up to the light. A small stream of light shone through it like a magnifying glass, threatening to annihilate a small colony of ants. That was all the people of Penrith were to the duke, his own personal ant colony to toy with.

"Welcome one and all to this year's annual masquerade ball." His voice boomed in an echo now that everyone had fallen silent.

"Please enjoy the many refreshments and dance to your heart's content. This event is for all of you, lovely citizens of Penrith, after all," he added with a coy grin that exposed fang-like teeth.

Rue's hands curled into fists, nails leaving behind deep crescents in her palms. How she ever thought she could love him was beyond her. He was nothing more than a sycophant with a God complex. A spoiled child who wanted the world served to him on a silver platter. Ryker lowered his glass and disappeared back into the crowd. After seeing him, Rue was more on edge than before. The persistent itch of anxiety under her skin was replaced with a fiery rage.

Sabrien must have noticed because as soon as everyone returned to whatever it was they were doing before Ryker interrupted, he leaned down and whispered, "You can't worry about him right now. He will get what he deserves in the end." Rue huffed and nodded in agreement. She could only hope he was right.

They spent the next hour meandering around the ballroom, sliding between guests to get a closer look at the walls. The hidden door had to have been just like the ones that led from the library to different parts of the house.

All of the doors that led to these inner passages had a tell-tale seam where the wallpaper split. To an unfamiliar eye, it would be nearly impossible to notice, but Rue had spent the last four years creeping in and out of the walls of Ashworth Manor and knew exactly what to look for. Unfortunately, finding the seam was infinitely harder without her glasses to aid her.

Sabrien kept watch while Rue slid into one of the darker corners of the room. She casually ran her hand along the wall, trying to feel for the split where her eyes could not quite see without drawing anyone's attention. After a few empty searches, there was only one option left.

"It must be on the west wall," she told Sabrien, who was currently on his third flute of champagne.

"Now the only problem is getting to it. Looks like everyone's decided to congregate there," he lamented, nodding his head to the gaggle of bodies blocking the way.

"I wonder if he put the refreshments over there for a reason." Rue rolled her eyes under her mask, thankful no one could see it. They were going to have to find another way to sneak into the main house if this was going to work.

Suddenly, an idea occurred to her. With everyone so focused on the endless array of booze and hors d'oeuvres, this could be much more of a help than a hindrance.

She turned to tell Sabrien, but the words died before she could fully formulate them. From the edge of her vision, Rue thought she'd seen a familiar silhouette.

Orionna had moved to the mainland years ago, but not for the first time, Rue could have sworn she saw her among the crowd. She must be losing it. There was no reason she would come all the way here just for a party, or at least, Rue didn't think so.

Shaking off what she chalked up to a manifestation of anxiety and lack of proper eyewear, Rue swallowed thickly, dislodging those lost words from her throat.

"I have another idea, but I am going to have to do it on my own. I need you to stay here and make sure no one follows me out." Rue knew Sabrien was not going to like this plan, but in the end, he didn't have any other choice but to concede and let her go. He stood there, still and silent for a long moment before nodding in reluctant agreement.

"Find the others and wait for me in the statuary. I will find a way out through the library once I find the book." Rue reached out and took his hand in hers, giving it a reassuring squeeze. She could tell he was nervous, but whether it was because he feared for her or he feared what Corvus would do once he found out she was allowed to split off on her own was anyone's guess.

Before she could change her mind, Rue spun on her heel and slid through the crowd, leaving Sabrien behind. Now, she had to figure out what exit would be easiest to slip through without anyone noticing. The east wall was nothing but a solid row of arched windows, and the main entrance was to the south, leaving no other choice but to try and find a way out somewhere on the north end of the room.

She meandered slowly through the crowd, trying not to draw attention to herself. As ostentatious as she thought her gown and mask were, they seemed almost plain in comparison to some of the things others were wearing. She sent up a small silent prayer of thanks for her dark gown's ability to blend in.

A couple that had one or three too many drinks bumped into her from behind, sending her flying forward. A small, surprised yelp escaped her as a pair of strong hands caught her upper arms, bracing her fall.

Slowly, she raised her head, making sure her mask was still securely in place before facing her savior. A smile tugged at her lips, and her heart was alight in her chest.

Corvus.

She had already seen him in all his garb before they left, but now, with that simple, jewel-encrusted domino mask over his eyes, he truly was a sight to behold. His plush lips and those perfect dimples were on full display as his mouth pulled to one side.

"Are you alright, Miss?" He asked, his voice low and gravelly, making her toes curl in her shoes.

"Y-yes, thanks to you, kind sir." Rue bent at the knee in a polite curtsy. It felt strange being so formal like this with him, but it was the easiest way to keep up appearances. Corvus extended his hand to her, dipping into a short bow.

"Would you like to dance with me?" he asked, voice edged with hope. Red roses bloomed wildly on her cheeks under her mask, and once again, Rue was thankful no one could see. She knew they didn't have time for this. Especially not when Ryker was still making his rounds, stopping here and there to mingle and engage in some mindless chatter. Rue knew he was watching everyone like the hawk his mask boasted. She bit her lip nervously. What harm could just one dance be?

"I would love to," she acquiesced, sliding her hand into his. The familiar warmth and the gentle scrape of his callouses sent a wave of calm over her. She sucked in a deep breath in through her mouth, letting it out slowly through her nose, and took a step closer to him. Corvus' arms wrapped gently around her waist in an almost reverent way.

The quartet had changed the tone of their song from melancholy to something a bit more uplifting now. Corvus led the dance, his steps following the tempo of their strings. Rue felt as though she were floating along with him, the rest of the room around her fading into black. The only thing left was the smolder of his eyes from behind his mask, like the last bits of burning embers in the hearth.

"I know I already told you, but you look beautiful," he said so quietly the words were almost lost in the commotion around them. She knew he couldn't see her face, so she gave him a small nod, letting him know she had heard the compliment. Corvus spun her around the room with fluid grace. He danced the same way he fought, each step smooth and practiced. Rue made a mental note to herself to ask him where he learned to dance after all of this, but for now, she allowed herself to melt into Corvus for the brief moment she had him.

The masked party goers around them faded away and for just a moment it was only the two of them drifting across the marble tiled ballroom. His fingers twined with hers, pulling her impossibly closer as they spun.

Everything became a blur of softly glowing lights and the muted twinkle of a sea of luxurious gowns adorned with stones and sequins. Rue wanted so badly to stay here in his arms for the rest of the night and forget about her missions, but before she could change her mind, Corvus dipped her low and whispered close to her ear.

"I don't want to let you go, but I think I see your window," he told her, leaning in closer. Once again, she nodded, squeezing his hand. She followed his gaze to see Ryker thoroughly distracted by a group of fawning women crowding around him.

"Go."

And she did.

Chapter Thirty-One

Slipping through the familiar halls of the manor, Rue made her way to the closest secret wall entrance she knew would lead her directly down into the library. She had to move quickly; she'd had a nagging suspicion that Ryker was indeed aware of her presence. He was much too keen not to have noticed.

Rue glanced over her shoulder as she approached the wall, making sure no one had seen her leave the ballroom and run down the halls. With the coast clear, she ran her hand over the busy patterned wallpaper and felt for the seam.

"Gotcha," she muttered when her finger found purchase at the edge of the near-invisible separation in the wall. Rue pushed against it, activating the spring mechanism that popped it open, fully separating it from the other side of the wall. With one last quick glance over her shoulder, Rue ducked into the passageway, pulling the wall shut behind her.

She swore under her breath when she felt resistance tugging her back as she tried to walk away. The hem of her gauzy gown had been caught in the mechanism. Carefully, she tugged it out, cringing when the sound of the fabric ripping hit her ears.

"Shit!" she swore again, trying to pull the bits of fabric out of the crack. She was running out of time and just had to hope that she was able to get most of it out before moving on.

The passageway was dark and cold, making it hard to see even just a few feet in front of her. Rue's hands clung to the walls, using them to guide her way. She followed her feet along the familiar route, her heart hammering against her ribs with a volatile mix of adrenaline and fear.

Each creak and groan of the old manor settling along every small thud of someone moving around in another part of the house gave her pause. Narrowing her eyes and squinting to try and see through the cumbersome mesh eye holes of her mask, Rue sighed and pulled it from her head, tucking it under her arm.

"There, much better."

Once she finally reached the end of the passageway, she pushed on the mechanism once more. The wall popped open and led directly into the heart of the library. She stepped through and quietly closed the wall again. Rue stopped to take in the mysterious beauty that was the duke's library for what was most likely the last time.

She'd spent countless hours within these walls; it had become like a second home. But now, the library only felt like a tomb. Her eyes slowly moved to the ominous black room, but instead of the thick iron door being closed and bolted shut, it hung open.

Every alarm bell within her screamed *trap*. Rue took a few hesitant steps toward the door and though the strange voices no longer called to her, the empty, ringing silence was somehow worse.

Bracing herself on the door frame, Rue peered into the room cautiously, taking in what remained. Each of the covered display boxes still lined the walls of the small room. Everything looked the same as she'd left it the day she found the box beneath the floorboards.

She stepped over the threshold and entered the room. Her entire body was on high alert, listening for any sign that she'd been caught.

Maneuvering around a tall cabinet in the center of the room, Rue noticed another display. One she couldn't remember having seen before.

Delicately, she reached out with shaking hands and tugged the cloth away, exposing what lay underneath. Just as she had suspected. The dented metal box sat closed upon a short pedestal, looking completely unassuming.

Rue reached out for it, overcome with elation and relief from being able to find her prize so easily but something stopped her before she could touch it. The sound of footsteps outside the room.

"Ahh, it's good to know that you're still so predictable, Ruby."

Before she could take the chance to grab the book and make a break for it, the heavy iron door swung shut.

Gods, she hated it when she was right.

"RYKER! You motherfu—" she screamed, throwing her body into the door and banging her fists against it. She knew it was futile, and the door wouldn't open until Ryker allowed it. That didn't stop her from trying. She would fight until she couldn't. Beat down the door until her knuckles were bloody and bruised.

Through the door, she heard the faint tapping of Ryker's perfectly polished shoes approaching. Burning anger rose in her chest, and she struggled to keep her breathing even. She raised her chin, looking into the metal of the door defiantly, even if he couldn't see her. Rue refused to allow herself to crumble. Not when she was so close to the finish line.

"Open the door, Ryker. I just want to talk," she tried.

"Just to talk, hm?" His voice was muffled, but she heard his condescension clear as crystal, "Doesn't sound like you have anything nice to say."

Rue took a deep breath and tried to calm herself before she proved him right. Slowly, she let the breath out through her nose, but before she could regain her composure enough to speak, the door popped open.

She pushed it open the rest of the way, revealing Ryker standing before her. He wasn't wearing the outfit she'd seen him in earlier in the ballroom. Her brows knit with confusion, but without any time to mull it over or hesitate with her next actions, Rue took a few reluctant steps forward. Something was amiss, but what, she couldn't place her finger on.

"How did you get down here so quickly?" Rue's chin remained high, false confidence and adrenaline the only things keeping her from shaking like a leaf.

"Who do you think built the passages in the walls, my dear? You didn't think you were really going to get a leg up on me, did you?" His lips curled into an arrogant smile that only served to make Rue's blood boil even hotter. She clenched her hands into fists, keeping them tightly against her sides. She couldn't believe there was ever a time she found him handsome. All she wanted to do was punch the smug expression right off his face.

"But you were...I saw you wearing something completely different."

It wasn't impossible that he could have shed his entire costume on the way here but there was no evidence of disheveled hair or clothes that would indicate him having done so.

Her eyes combed every inch of him from head to toe, trying to figure out what was so *other* about him. Was this just a trick her mind played on her? Or something sinister in the library's walls conjuring him as a product of her own fear?

Taking another step closer, Rue reached out to touch him. He didn't stop her, only stood with that irritating grin on his lips. When her hand connected with him, instead of finding a solid, corporeal form, there was nothing.

"You're not real. You're an illusion," Rue revealed with a pleased smile. But as soon as the apparition faded, the library around her fell into darkness. Apparently, touching the illusion was a very bad idea. Without the slightest glimmer of light, Rue was trapped. She clutched her hands to her chest and tried to make herself as small as possible.

"Rue!" A voice she was sure to be Corvus called to her from the depths of the dark library. She spun on her heel, turning toward the source of the sound.

"Corvus? Is that you?" She squinted, trying to make out his form to no avail. Without thinking, Rue rushed toward his voice, arms reaching out blindly as she tried to find him in this abyss she'd been plunged into.

"Corvus, please answer me!" she called out again, panic rising in her chest. The library seemed to have disappeared around her, leaving her in an endless void. Just like her nightmares.

Before she could move, a heavy force pushed her to the floor. She toppled over, her head slamming into the ground. Rue screamed, but no sound came out. Like it was also swallowed up by the dismal darkness.

"Sleep," a whispered voice commanded.

Her eyes began to close against her will. She tried to fight it, but her body became too heavy to struggle against the unseen force that held her.

"Sleep, little Ruby." Was the last thing she heard before succumbing to the spell.

Rue opened her eyes, blinking rapidly to clear the fog that settled in them. She winced as she tried to open her mouth. Her jaw throbbed with pain, and the inside of her mouth was coated with the taste of bitter iron.

Every one of her muscles protested as she moved, and what was worse, she didn't know where she was, nor could she remember how she had gotten there.

The room slowly came into view as her eyes adjusted to the darkness. It was a round, rough hewn chamber with nothing adorning the walls nor any kind of furniture she could see. She squinted hard, trying to tell if anyone else was in the room with her but was only met with emptiness.

Panic cut through the pain. Her hand immediately flew to her throat, checking for her necklace, but she breathed a sigh of relief, remembering she left it back at the temple. The last thing she could remember before everything went black was reaching for Corvus' voice and the sudden force that ripped her away.

Rue attempted to sit up but immediately regretted that decision when a shock of dizzying pain lanced through her entire body. Thick twine rope held her wrists in place, rubbing her skin raw with each and every minute movement.

"Don't panic. Don't panic. Do. Not. Panic." Rue whispered to herself in a mantra through her short breaths. It was much easier said than done, but she needed to keep a level head if she had any hope of getting out of here in one piece. Before she could think too much harder about her predicament, the sound of approaching footsteps echoed to her right. Her head snapped in the direction of the sound, and she had to hold back a groan of pain at the sudden movement.

"Ah, good. You're finally awake." A familiar voice crooned from the shadows.

Ryker.

Rage pushed away the pain. He had brought her here. She tried to stand again as he came into view, still looking as pristine and polished as ever. Rue's legs wobbled and gave out under her, sending her face-first into the filthy stone floor.

"Tsk, tsk, Ruby. That's no way for a lady to behave," Ryker chided, squatting down before her and reaching for her face. Rue snapped her teeth at his hand. The condescension in his tone only added more fuel to the inferno of her anger.

"Don't you dare touch me, you mother fu—" Her words were cut off by a sharp slap across her cheek. Her head cocked back with the force of his hand. The coppery tang of blood flooded over her tongue and teeth again.

"Watch your tone with me, girl." His hands gripped her chin tightly as he forced Rue to look at him. The false sweetness was gone from his voice, replaced with a dark malice that was reflected in his eyes. It should have frightened her. It would have under normal circumstances, but Rue was done being scared. She was tired of playing nicely. She rolled her eyes back to him, tongue darting out over her lips to lick away the blood that had dripped out of her mouth.

"I am no girl, and I think you know that. You always knew that, didn't you?" Rue's lips curled into a hateful, bloody smile. She wanted nothing more than to free her hands of their rope bindings and sink her thumbs deep into those moonstone eyes she'd always looked into with such longing. He'd held her under his spell for years, and she'd fallen for it. She'd fallen for him. But now, all she could feel for him was contempt. Hatred.

Ryker tapped her nose with his index finger, "You were always so clever, Ruby. It's a shame it had to be this way..." he paused, features softening for just a moment before he leaned in closer. He loosened his grip on her chin and curled his finger under her chin, tilting her head up to meet his eyes. Rue kept the blinding hatred and rage she felt for him in her stare. She refused to let herself falter.

"It would have been so much easier if you would have just submitted to me."

Rue jerked her chin back and spit in his face before she could even think better of it. Ryker's stormy eyes darkened, but the rest of his features didn't betray his emotions. He dragged a gloved hand over his cheek, wiping away her saliva.

"I will never, *ever* submit to you. I would rather die," she spat with as much venom and bravado as she could muster.

"Such a pity. Truly. But not to worry." His lips pulled into a devious grin, "You won't die here, Ruby." Ryker leaned in, so close she could feel his breath on her skin, "Breaking you will be so much more rewarding." He tapped her cheek in a mock slap and stood back up, turning on his heel to return to the darkness.

Rue let out a labored breath that threatened to become a sob and let her shoulders slump, the last dregs of adrenaline rapidly fading from her body. Her throat tightened, and her nose prickled with the sting of impending tears, but she wouldn't let them fall. She refused to show any weakness. Especially not to Ryker.

Her thoughts drifted back to Corvus. He had to know where she was, and he had to be coming for her. There was no way he would leave her here, and she wouldn't allow herself to believe the alternative.

She pulled her hands to her chest, where she could still feel the bond between them, that cord wrapped around her heart, cradling it with gentle hands within her chest. Even if she didn't know where Corvus was, at the very least the undulating pulse of that bond let her know he was still out there.

Rue carefully pulled herself up, whimpering as she leaned her head back against the bumpy stone wall with a heavy pained groan. She was so tired. Her mind, body and soul were so incredibly tired. Every breath felt like shards of glass in her lungs. Her brows knit together as she tried to will it away, trying to focus on anything but the white-hot sting.

Maybe she could just close her eyes for a moment. The thought of falling into a deep unconsciousness was more inviting than it should have been, but she forced herself to keep her eyes open and stay as alert as possible.

She swallowed, desperately trying to coat her bone-dry throat with some kind of moisture. How long had she already been down here? There was no way to tell the time without any windows or even tiny cracks in the walls that might let in a bit of light from the outside. She was still dressed in the gown she'd worn to the masquerade, though it was now in tatters.

She didn't know how long she sat like that, staring into the foreboding emptiness of the room with its corners shrouded in a thick miasma-like darkness. Eventually, after what felt like a short eternity of blankly staring, her eyes drifted shut, pushing her into a restless slumber.

CHAPTER THIRTY-TWO

THE CLATTER OF METAL against the stone floor jolted Rue from her slumber. She nearly wept at the burn of her stiff and sore muscles as she tried to move. She had no idea how long she had been asleep, but everything around her looked the same as before.

"Eat." A single command barked from above her.

Rue looked up with bleary eyes to see a woman with pallid skin and dark hair that brushed the tops of her thin shoulders. It took her a moment to recognize the woman, her face mostly hidden by shadows, but the eventual recognition shot through her like a bullet.

"Orionna!? Why are you here?" Rue narrowed her eyes, glaring at her.

Orionna scoffed, huffing out a humorless laugh, "What? Did you think you just happened to fall into his lap all by yourself?" She sat perched on a large boulder at the edge of the rounded room, crossing her ankles. The picture of feminine grace while Rue lay on the filthy ground with her once fine clothes in shreds.

"You knew about all of this?" Rue snarled and tried to stand up again, finding the motion much less painful now that she'd had a chance to rest her body.

"Of course I knew! Who do you think led you right into his web, Ruby?" Orionna paused, waiting for Rue to say something but when she was met with no response she continued, "You didn't think he actually had feelings for you all this time?" Orionna barked out a laugh.

Rue still remained silent. This traitor didn't deserve her words. She didn't care if Ryker did or didn't have feelings for her. The bastard could rot in hell for all she cared at this point. What she did care about was finding a way out of here and getting back to Corvus as soon as possible.

Orionna looked at her nails, turning her hands back and forth in the low light. She breathed a heavy sigh and pushed her hair back off her shoulder, "It is a real shame though. He was right; all of this could have been avoided if you would have just gone along with his plans." She shrugged and stood up, "But you've always made things so much harder for yourself, haven't you, Rue?" Orionna sneered and nudged Rue's shin with the pointed tip of her shoe.

Rue didn't look up at her, not wanting to give her the satisfaction of acknowledgment. Her eyes were fixated on the tray in front of her. She hadn't dared to accept anything given to her. Ryker was more than capable of fighting dirty, and she knew it.

Orionna must have grown tired of her silence. She scoffed and muttered something under her breath Rue couldn't hear before leaving the chamber. The sound of a heavy door opening and closing again sounded in the distance, but the echo off the empty walls made it nearly impossible to figure out where exactly the sound came from.

Rue leaned back and blew out a heavy breath. Her hands were still bound in the same thick rope as before. If she was going to have any sort of chance to get out of here, she would need to get the binds off first. Finally having the strength to fully stand, Rue pulled herself from the floor, trying not to lose her balance as she planted her bare feet against the damp floor.

"Okay...step one," she muttered to herself. Rue's lungs still felt like they'd been lined with jagged shards of glass, but she was doing her best to ignore that. She searched the room, looking for anything that could be used to cut herself free. Unfortunately, the room was empty save for a few boulders scattered around with edges too blunt to hack through the fibers.

"Damnit!" Rue kicked the silver tray at her feet in her frustration, all of its contents scattering around the room and splattering against the wall. She moved to the boulder Orionna had been sitting on and leaned against it. Even with renewed strength, her knees still trembled.

She was going to have to come up with another plan. There was no way she was going to get these binds off without the help of some sort of sharp object, and of course, there was nothing at her disposal — something she was certain had been done purposefully.

She didn't move from the rock for a long while. Her eyes cast to the floor as she racked her brain for every possible option she had to get out of here alive. She could lie to Ryker and tell him she was giving up and hope that would be enough to at least get her back to the surface where Corvus might be able to find her easier, but that wasn't a guarantee either.

Ryker was too damn unpredictable; it was impossible to make any decision that involved him. She would have to come up with something that didn't take his help into account at all, and that was where she came up short. She blamed the lack of food and water for her brain refusing to formulate a somewhat coherent plan.

Rue was pulled from her thoughts by the sound of the door she could not see opening again. Someone was coming back. She stood straight, raising her chin defiantly, bracing herself in case it was Ryker walking through that door.

They say if you speak of the devil, he will appear — and so he did. Ryker's form materialized out of the darkness. He'd shed his outer coat and now stood in a simple collared shirt and dark trousers. She watched as his deft fingers rolled back his sleeves. It made Rue sick to think about those same fingers touching her skin in a way she should have never allowed him to.

"My, my. What a rude guest you are, dove." Ryker cocked a brow as his eyes caught the overturned tray, "There are people starving beyond these walls, and yet you waste a good meal." He clicked his tongue, scolding her like a child.

"You know, I waited a long, long time for you, Ruby." He took a step closer to her, and instinctively she stepped back, "I waited a hundred miserable fucking years for a worthy vessel to be born out of your line of Priestesses. A century waiting for your soul to come back to me."

Rue's brow furrowed in confusion. It wasn't a shock to her that he knew about the soul of the Goddess in her, but...

"What do you mean you waited for my soul to be born?"

"Ah, so you don't know everything then. Seems your little bird boy didn't fill you in on all the details." Ryker's face pulled into another one of his nasty grins as he continued, circling around her like a vulture waiting for its prey to die.

"That lovely little necklace you so cherish, an heirloom from your mother no doubt, is what led me right to you. The sun crest was to be presented to the vessel chosen to house the soul of the Goddess Solira. In this case...you." He stopped, leaning in too close for comfort, "Congratulations."

Rue sneered, moving her face away from his. She tried to take another step back to create more distance between herself and him, but her back met the wall. She let out a soft gasp of surprise, earning her a predatory look from Ryker. He knew she was cornered.

"Your friend Orionna is a faithful servant of mine. It was much too easy to get you to trust her; you simply took everything she said at face value and went along with whatever she suggested. You were so pathetic and *desperate* for a friend," He laughed and shook his head, "Really thought my job was going to be just as simple, but we see how that's working out now, don't we." His fingers were around her chin again, digging into her skin and holding her in place.

Rue tried to jerk her chin back from him, but his grip only tightened. She growled and pushed him as hard as she could with her fists.

"I wasn't so pathetic when you were on your knees for me, now was I?" Rue's lips curled into a defiant grin.

Ryker let her go and cocked his hand back again, but when he saw Rue's forest green eyes boring directly into his, unflinching, he dropped his arm. She claimed that victory, no matter how small it might have been.

Ryker flexed his fingers and continued, "All I needed to do then was get your idiot brother to relay the information he'd just so happened to overhear at the Devil's Due. He just needed to get your mind on the right track, and I took the rest from there. It must have been nice for him to finally feel like he was useful."

Her chest tightened with rage, and a growl escaped her lips. How dare he speak about Jasper that way! He didn't know her brother. He didn't know the hell he went through after their mother died.

"Don't you dare speak of my brother that way. He's more of a man than you will ever be," Rue snarled, punching her bound fists into his chest.

Ryker barked out a harsh laugh devoid of mirth, and Rue felt a jolt of crackling energy at the back of her mind. Memories flooded in again, nothing but quick flashes this time, barely enough to make out what she was seeing. In her memory, she had seen Ryker like this before, but he wasn't the same as he appeared now. His eyes were completely black, scleras an empty void between his eyelids. Two long horns curved outwards, protruding from his forehead. This must be Vaion – the man that stood before her in his true form. The images vanished just as quickly as they'd come, Ryker's voice breaking the spell.

"Jasper is nothing but an insignificant, selfish reprobate and always will be. He was not destined for such greatness. Not like you..." He slid his hands behind his back as he approached, "And you have already achieved so much with so little direction, my darling. I'm rather impressed." His wicked grin returned, and it only served to irritate her more.

"The voices guided you to the book. They pulled you where you needed to be, and you obeyed just like the *good girl* you are." He was trying to get under her skin now. Rue refused to show that it was working and kept her jaw clenched tight.

"And just like the curious little cat you are, you had to open the book and see what was inside, didn't you? Poor little clumsy girl sliced her finger on the pages, making a bloody mess inside." His patronizing tone grated on her, making her clench her jaw so hard her molars threatened to crack under the pressure.

"Do you just talk to hear your voice, Ryker? I really don't understand what the point of telling me all of this is," she snapped, thoroughly surprised with herself at the amount of bite in her words.

Ryker sneered and started to say something else but was interrupted by a loud blast that shook the walls, sending a rain of pebbles, dust and debris to rain down on them. He quickly spun on his heel trying to discern the source of the disturbance.

"What in the hell was that?"

Rue's pulse quickened.

Corvus.

He was here; Rue felt him through their bond, the cords around her heart giving a reassuring squeeze. She kept quiet, moving back against the wall, not wanting to alert Ryker of her savior's presence.

Out of the darkness, Rue could see the glowing ultraviolet light of his sword. She could see the look of confusion spread across Ryker's face as Corvus walked through the thick miasma at the edges of the room.

"So you did manage to find a way in after all." Ryker smirked, crossing his arms over his chest.

"Vaion," Corvus taunted.

"Hm, I haven't been called that name in a long, *long* time." Ryker barked a laugh, "It seems my suspicions about you and our little darling were correct after all. You've been bonded."

Rue nearly snarled at the way he'd said "our." She didn't belong to him and never would.

Corvus didn't say anything to confirm or deny what Ryker had assumed. Instead, he stood his ground and waited for his opponent's next move. His amber eyes shifted, locking with Rue's. She could feel him silently questioning if she was unharmed. She nodded almost imperceptibly but knew he saw as his chest seemed to deflate slightly with relief.

"You always did talk too much." Corvus pulled his sword from his back and swung it in a long arc, a trail of violet flames following the motion. Rue curled up against the wall, trying to stay as far as she could from either of them.

"Shut your mouth and fight." Corvus took his stance, readying the blade. Ryker's — Vaion's lips pulled back in a maniacal grin, full of sharp teeth and hatred, as he waved his hand and produced a cloud of smoke between his palms. Two long daggers materialized out of the haze, shining against the low light.

"If it's a fight you want, then let's fight."

Chapter Thirty-Three

RUE'S EYES DARTED BACK and forth nervously between the two men as she tried to pull on her restraints again. They still wouldn't budge. Panic threatened to take hold of her, but she kept herself together. She couldn't afford to crack now.

"You think you can take me this time, crow boy? Or were you just planning to let me beat you into the ground again?" Vaion called with a flick of his wrist that sent the shadow dagger flying. Corvus turned his head just enough for it to miss his face, letting it lodge in the wall behind him instead.

"It's been over a century since you last fought me, Vaion. I think you're sorely mistaken if you think I would let you beat me again." Corvus took a step forward, swiping his blade into the dagger in Vaion's other hand. Vaion was too fast to let Corvus disarm him completely. Rue cursed. She knew this wouldn't be a quick fight, but she hoped Corvus could overpower him at least.

Out of the corner of her eye, she noticed a figure move in one of the dark corners of the room. Without her glasses, she couldn't see too far beyond her nose. The figure crept closer, crouched down and moving silently. The clashing of metal echoing off the chamber walls was too loud to hear much, anyway.

Rue desperately tugged on her binds, even knowing it was a futile endeavor. The figure moved closer and her breath caught in her throat, but the tell-tale sign of reddish brown hair in the small fragments of light in the pit had her nearly exploding with relief.

"Oliver!" She breathed out, careful not to draw attention to herself. Oliver held a finger to his lips, urging her to keep quiet, and reached for the rope around her wrists.

"I'm going to cut you free, but I need you to stay here for just a little longer. Sabrien and Ardeth are coming." He cut the rope with a knife that had been lodged in his belt, and Rue's binds fell to the floor. She rubbed at her raw skin but nodded in understanding and didn't move from her spot on the dirt floor.

Ahead of her, Corvus and Vaion were still going blow for blow. Corvus still stood tall, taking every hit with grace, but Rue could see Vaion begin to falter. His normally perfect hair was disheveled, and his pristine white shirt had come untucked from his trousers.

Corvus swung his sword hard, holding the pommel tight with both hands, but Vaion countered, blocking with the side of his dagger's blade.

"You're getting sloppy," Corvus snarled and pushed Vaion back, swinging his blade upright once again. Vaion's feet slid across the dirt floor as he nearly lost his balance. His chest heaved with exertion, but he wasn't going to give up.

"You can't save her. No matter what, I will have her and that damn book." Vaion cocked his hand back and hurled the other dagger in a last-ditch effort to land a shot on Corvus.

Corvus swung his sword like a bat, slamming the dagger into the ground. Rue perked up, eyes going wide. Corvus had disarmed him! This was his chance.

But, of course, nothing was as easy as it seemed.

Vaion stood, rolling his shoulders and smoothing his hair back into place.

"Very well. I see you're not going to relent." Vaion lifted his chin and pulled his gloves from his hands, flexing his fingers.

Corvus moved back into a defensive position, trying to read Vaion's movements and anticipate the next blow. Rue's eyes were glued to him, heart hammering like a steam piston in her chest.

A hand on hers pulled her eyes away from the scene and onto Sabrien, who had somehow made his way into the underground chamber. The tears she was trying too hard to hold in spilled over. Behind Sabrien, Ardeth and Oliver stood in wait. They were all safe, and even though Corvus was still locked in battle with Vaion, relief rushed through her.

"Save those tears, Ruby Rue. We gotta get you out of here." Sabrien offered his hand, and Rue took it without hesitation.

"What about Corvus? We can't just leave him here to fight on his own!" She screeched as Sabrien pulled her to her feet.

"Don't worry. Ardeth is going to stay and fight with him, but you have to leave here before Vaion can use you."

Rue wasn't sure what he meant by that, but there wasn't time to hash it out now. Once she was fully upright, she tore off the last shredded bits of her skirt to allow her more mobility. She was sure they were going to have to make a break for it to get out of the chamber.

Rue clung to Sabrien, her numb legs wobbling like a newborn calf. Before they could get too far, a thundering boom came from where Corvus and Vaion fought. The god held another dark cloud of energy in his hands. It crackled and created a maelstrom between his palms.

Vaion raised the dark cloud higher, like an offering to an unseen force. His lips moved rapidly, chanting words she couldn't hear or understand on his lips. Rue gasped as the cloud began to ooze a thick, murky, and viscous liquid. It looked like the same inky substance she had seen dripping from her doppelganger's eyes in her dream.

"Corvus!" She called, reaching out for the warrior, but Sabrien pulled her back against his chest, holding her there to keep her from running to Corvus.

"Are you insane? Come on, we have to leave. Now!" Sabrien pulled back on her arms and steered her toward the exit.

She knew she shouldn't fight and just allow Sabrien to take her, but she had to stay and see this fight through. She had to make sure Corvus made it out of there.

The vaporous cloud in Vaion's hands turned completely to liquid, leaving dark muck falling into congealed puddles on the ground. Corvus remained guarded on the other side of Vaion as they both watched the liquid begin to converge into one pool.

The ground beneath them shook, causing Rue to almost lose her balance. Beside her, Sabrien let out a string of curses, "Fuck! The pathway back collapsed." He slammed his fist into the now-closed wall, his bare knuckles bruising with the impact. Loosening his grip on Rue, Sabrien turned back to where Corvus and Vaion stood.

"What the actual fuck are those things?" Sabrien's lip pulled back in disgust. From the dark pool on the ground rose a stream of tall, thin creatures made of abyssal darkness. Rue's hand flew over her mouth to stifle a gasp. It was hard to fully make them out without her glasses, but whatever those things were, they answered to Vaion's every order. A militia of shadow soldiers ready to strike.

"You know Corvus, it really is adorable that you thought you could possibly beat me. I admit, I let you think you had the upper hand for a moment, but you bored me much too quickly." Vaion outstretched his arms and the shadow soldiers followed the motion, rising to their full height.

From the alcove behind Corvus, Rue could make out another figure approaching. She held her breath, panic arresting her again. Ardeth appeared out of the shadows, and she deflated with relief to see the other Veridae.

"I can't see very well, what's happening?" Rue asked, fingers curling into the fabric of Sabrien's sleeve.

Sabrien held her closer, "He's creating what looks like an army to fight alongside him because he's incapable of playing fairly," he scoffed. Rue grumbled an agreement under her breath. Sabrien's humor wasn't helping as much as it normally did.

"You've never won a fair fight. You're only capable of tricks to take the win. Quit talking, and let's get this over with," Corvus demanded. He adjusted his grip on the sword's pommel before swinging it up over his head to charge at the God.

In response, the shadow soldiers lunged for Corvus and Ardeth — who was now wielding what looked like a bo staff. Rue squinted hard to make out more of what was happening. Damn her for not wearing her glasses under the mask.

Corvus thrust his sword forward and sliced through one of the shadows. Its body separated for a moment before knitting itself back together. Rue heard Corvus swear in the distance as he backed up, putting more distance between him and the rapidly approaching group of shadows. He flicked his wrist, the sword in his hand illuminating with violet flames again. He thrust the immolated blade directly into one of the shadow's chest, flames immediately engulfing it. A shrill scream rent the air, causing both Rue and Sabrien to slap their hands over their ears to block it out. The sound was piercing, like a needle being thrust into her eardrums.

Rue's already clouded vision doubled; everything around her swayed and made her stomach lurch. What on earth was that sound? She removed her hands from her ears, unable to hear anything else over the ringing that replaced the scream. Corvus and Ardeth continued slicing through the creatures, leaving the bodies in piles of ash at their feet.

"Go help them!" Rue shouted, pushing Sabrien toward what had become a makeshift arena. He shook his head and held tighter onto Rue,

"I am not leaving your side. If something happens to you, I will be held responsible, and Corvus is going to be pissed off enough as it is. Just stay here and let them handle it," Sabrien screamed back, his hearing also clearly affected by the screeches the creatures made.

Rue was not happy with his answer but knew he was right. She took a deep, shuddering breath and turned back to the fight. Vaion crouched with his back against the wall, biding his time until they had finished off his pawns. Rue squinted again, trying to get a better look at him. Around Vaion's body, she could make out a deep crimson aura that pulsed in time with her heartbeat. The ground beneath her feet began to shake, and she gripped Sabrien's arm tighter to avoid toppling over.

When the last shadow creature fell, Corvus shook off his sword, letting the flames die out. Ardeth spun his bo staff, holding it in a defensive position. Vaion rose from where he was crouched against the wall.

"Very good, Corvus, very good." He stepped forward, clapping his hands mockingly at Corvus, "You are really outdoing yourself this time." Vaion flicked his wrist as a long sword made of shadow appeared in his hand, "Try not to die tired."

"Does this guy ever stop with the villain monologue?" Ardeth grunted out, readying his staff for another round. Corvus growled and shifted himself into a crouched position, using his wings to launch himself into Vaion across the dirt floor. Gravel and dust sprayed up into Rue and Sabrien's faces. She used what was left of the tattered sleeve on her dress to cover her mouth and tried to keep the debris out of her eyes. Sabrien used his arm to fan the rest of the dust away.

"I have a bad feeling about this. He's just going to run Corvus ragged and wait to strike to take him down then." Sabrien's grip on Rue's arm tightened. The anxiety radiating off of him was palpable.

"Go help him! I will be fine here, I promise. I will start looking for another way out," Rue urged him, using every scrap of energy she had left to be authoritative. Sabrien's eyes locked with hers for a moment longer before he gave a quick nod and pulled a short sword from where it rested at his hip. Rue silently thanked whichever of the Veridae had brought something for him.

"Stay out of sight and keep close to the wall," Sabrien told her before using his own wings to propel himself forward and into the fray. Rue stood watching and waiting until Sabrien engaged with Vaion. Beside him, Ardeth fought with the grace of an acrobat. The way he spun his bo staff between both of his hands looked so fluid as he deflected each one of Vaion's swings towards him. Corvus flanked him, but Vaion anticipated his moves too well and dodged away from every swing. Sabrien was right. Vaion was just trying to tire Corvus out. Rue had to figure out how to get them out of there and quickly. She crouched down and slid across the cavern wall, trying as hard as she could to stay low.

On the other side of the cavern, Vaion had materialized another sword, fighting both Ardeth and Sabrien simultaneously without so much as breaking a sweat. Rue bit into her lip and hoped with everything in her that they could overpower him. Sabrien thrust his short sword into Vaion's side but missed when the god spun backward, throwing the Veridae off his mark. Ardeth attempted to follow up with a swing to Vaion's chin, but he bent back just in time to miss the strike once again.

"Tsk tsk, boys. Three on one, and you still can't manage to take me down," Vaion taunted, a smug smile on his face.

Back in the center of the room, Vaion lurched forward, slicing his blades in a scissor motion toward Sabrien. Rue felt her breath catch in her throat, but Sabrien was too fast for him. He pushed his foot into the ground and launched himself up into the air, his giant wings flapping and pushing a gust of dirt and debris into Vaion.

"You're going to have to try harder than that, you cockwart," Sabrien called down, and if the situation wasn't this dire, Rue probably would have laughed, but instead, she was holding a breath in her chest, waiting to see what Sabrien had planned. He raised his blade up, and with a resounding crack that echoed off the walls, the sword transformed. The blade and the pommel split in half and opened up into a bow. Rue had never seen anything like that, and from the look on Vaion's face, he hadn't either.

"What kind of cheap trick is this?" Vaion growled out, but Rue could hear the underlying fear in his words.

Sabrien slid a single arrow from his belt, its tip glowing a sickly green. In less than the time it took her to blink, Sabrien had the bowstring taught and aimed at Vaion. He released it with a hard *thunk* that was followed by an agonized scream. He got him! The arrow was lodged in Vaion's kneecap, pushing him to the ground. It seemed that Veridae would finally be able to get ahead of him. Sabrien slammed the bow back into its original position and fell back to the ground.

"Corvus, now!" Ardeth shouted from across their improvised ring. Rue's head snapped to where Corvus was standing. His sword was once again wreathed in flames as he hurled himself into Vaion, taking advantage of his injury.

"You really thought I was going to go down that easily?" Vaion's voice shifted in that instant. It sounded like a legion of multiple voices. Like the ones she'd heard calling to her in the library before. The sounds overlapped with different emotions. A scream of agony, of anger, of sadness, all creating an amalgamation that made Rue want to cover her ears again. Corvus' entire body slowed, moving as if he were underwater before collapsing into the dirt floor.

"This fight is nothing but child's play for me. You should know that," Vaion called out in his strange new voice. Rue's heart leapt into her throat, strangling her with fear. She didn't know what was going to come next but whatever it was, she was sure it wasn't going to be good. Corvus' body slowly rose from the ground and Vaion stood, seemingly renewed, all signs of pain and injury vanished.

With a sickening crack of bones, Vaion's body began to change. He reached down, yanking the arrow free from his knee without so much as a single drop of blood, before tossing it to the ground. Sabrien and Ardeth were also frozen in place, unable to help Corvus at all. Rue's breathing turned into harsh pants; she didn't know what to do.

From Vaion's back, a set of wings similar to Corvus' broke through his skin. They were tawny in color, similar to a hawk. Just like the Ashworth family crest. All the pieces were falling in place so much faster than she could even wrap her mind around. His body continued to transform before her eyes. His legs ripped through his pants and shoes, revealing bird-like legs and thick, black talons.

"I've had enough of you and your kind, Corvus. Now, I can finally exterminate the last of you and finish the job I should have a century ago." Vaion reached out — the same black talons now jutted from his fingertips — and wrapped his hand around Corvus' throat. The bright line of crimson trailing down Corvus' neck was visible even from where she stood, and it ignited a white-hot fire within her that she'd never felt before. It felt as though she could rip through her own skin. It was like the same sensation that overtook her in the library, but this time it burned with rage. A blinding fury that pushed her into action.

"And this time, she can watch you die," Vaion cackled, turning to where Rue stood. A sick, satisfied smile curled on his lips that only furthered the wrath that was smoldering under her skin, engulfing her. His smile fell quickly, a look of fear replacing it.

"Put him down, Vaion." The demand came from Rue's mouth, but the voice was not her own. The soul of the goddess had taken the reins, born from the flames within. Vaion's hand only dug in deeper, as if he were challenging her.

"Or what? You're powerless." There was doubt lacing those words, making a sinister grin appear on Rue's lips — or was it Solira, now? She stepped toward him, her feet practically gliding across the floor.

"You know you aren't strong enough to beat me. I can see the fear and doubt behind your eyes. Let him go, or you will have to face me," she commanded, the words coming out on their own. Rue and Solira's consciousness intertwined now, forging a bond as hard as steel. They were unbreakable.

They were one.

Vaion stood firm, clearly warring with himself, "I'll let him go," he conceded, "But you will come with me."

"This is not a compromise. You will let him go and or you will face me. There are no other options." Rue raised her hands before her, a sphere of light as bright as the sun hovered above her palms.

"I suppose I will just have to let him go, then." Vaion lifted Corvus's hovering form up by his throat and slammed him back down into the ground with enough force to crack the hard earth beneath him. That was enough to push her off the edge. She raised the orb in her hand and hurled it toward Vaion. It exploded over his chest and face, liquid fire eating away at what was left of his clothes and melting the feathers that had sprouted over his skin.

"You bitch!" Vaion screamed as he burned, trying to scrape the fire from his body with little avail. Rue moved to where Corvus lay on the ground. Blood pooled under his head from the impact. Sabrien and

Ardeth broke free from Vaion's spell and immediately rushed over to her and Corvus.

"Stay with him I'll finish this," she commanded them, getting up again before the sight of Corvus lying unmoving and bleeding could break her. He was going to be fine. He had to be...

Rue charged toward Vaion again, launching another orb his way. This time, it exploded at his feet, the flames crawling up his body. His screams echoed through the chamber, reverberating off the walls and shaking them with the force of an earthquake. Clouds of dust and dirt swirled around them, and craggy, broken bits of rock rained from the ceiling.

Immediately, she looked back to Corvus and the other Veridae. Sabrien and Ardeth hovered over Corvus' still unresponsive form. The sight of him there, in their arms, only made the blaze in her chest burn brighter. Hotter. She wasn't finished with Vaion yet. The searing flames that had enveloped him had died down, leaving behind embers and the last bits of his melted clothing.

Before she could take another step toward him, Vaion raised his hands. The same black shadows from before began to seep through the rock below him and up into his palms. She had to act quickly before he could summon any more of his shadow soldiers. She was stronger now, but she could only fight so much on her own.

She tried to call another orb to her hands, but whatever power had been there was too weak to answer her call. The shadows must be blocking something out. She was going to have to fight dirty this time. Ardeth's bo staff lay on the ground beside her, and she knew this was the only chance she would have to beat him.

If she could at least break his concentration and stop the shadows from fully manifesting, maybe they would have a chance. With all her might, Rue cocked her arm back and launched the staff like a javelin as hard as she could in Vaion's direction.

The staff whistled through the air between them and landed solidly against his shoulder, sending his body forward and throwing him off guard. He stumbled, struggling to regain his balance. His swaying momentarily stopped the miasma from leaking into the cavern. This was her chance to turn the tide; it was now or never. Rue ran as fast as she could push herself — hoping the goddess inside her was also capable of helping her speed — and slammed her body into his.

Her elbow collided with his spine, sending him to the ground before he could fully right himself again. She landed on top of him, the sudden impact thrusting her forward before she could stop it. He kicked and thrashed beneath her, and in that moment, she had never been more grateful for the extra padding on her body. She pressed her palm hard into his back, feeling bones crack beneath, and used his spine to push herself up from the ground.

"That was the wrong choice," she snarled the words, quickly shoving her heel into the back of his neck, desperately trying to pin him before he could stand again. Vaion's hands slammed onto the ground, and the shadows returned. His entire body swallowed the dark tendrils that rose from the ground. A small group of the shadow soldiers slithered out from the cracks in the walls around them, moving closer at an alarming speed. She turned to see more from the other side of the cavern, making a mad dash toward Corvus and the others.

CHAPTER THIRTY-FOUR

SHE WAS TRAPPED. VAION had them pinned from either side and was forcing her into submission. He knew there was no way Solira would allow Corvus to fall and use it against her. Rue felt the goddess forcibly pull her foot away, releasing Vaion. She turned and ran to the other side of the pit, where both the others still hovered over Corvus' body. The shadow soldiers were converging on them, with sharp, spindly limbs creeping closer.

"Rue, hurry! He's not breathing!" Sabrien screamed, and the distress in his voice shot through her. She needed to do something, and she needed to do it now. There was no way she was going to close the gap and get to Corvus in time, and even if she could, what could she do?

Before Rue could decide on a course of action, it was done for her. That fire in her chest sparked once again, but this time alongside her anger, was pain. The pain of losing him again so soon after getting him back. Pain of history repeating itself. She wouldn't break again. She refused.

Intense heat spread from behind her ribs and immolated every part of her. Flames crawled up her throat, and she opened her mouth to scream, but no sound came out. Instead, her entire body was encased in a bright white light that blazed hotter than the sun, yet she remained unburned.

An explosion of light speared the shadow soldiers, their bodies twisting and writhing in the divine fire before crumbling into nothing more than ash and dust. From somewhere behind her, she could hear Vaion scream, but she didn't care. Let him scream, she thought. Let him feel the agony she'd felt.

Rue's breath came out in heavy bursts, adrenaline slowly fading from her body as the light began to dim. She blinked a few times, allowing her eyes to readjust to the darkness that had returned in the cavern.

Her heart cracked in her chest once she realized the screaming she had heard wasn't Vaion at all.

It was Sabrien.

He was on his knees with his head cradled in his hands. His mouth still hung open with anguish, but his screams had gone silent. Without thinking, she rushed over to him, sliding on her knees as she got closer.

"Sabrien? Sabrien, are you alright? What happened?" Rue pleaded with him, her hands shaking as she grasped his shoulders. Sabrien remained silent, but the pure agony and pain that rippled off of him was devastating.

Ardeth groaned beside her as he sat up, rubbing his eyes and temples, trying to regather himself.

"It seems Corvus is breathing again, but he's still out cold." Rue heard him say, but his voice was far away. Her eyes never left Sabrien, who had finally closed his mouth but still didn't speak.

"I—" She began, turning to Ardeth, "I don't know what happened. It was like something took over my body and then everything was white..." her voice trailed off and her head snapped back to Sabrien. He had been the one closest to her when the light explosion happened. With a light that bright...

"Sabrien, your eyes..." Rue reached for his hands, the tremor in her own worsened with the realization of what most likely had happened to him.

"I can't see anything, Rue," Sabrien finally gasped out, the pain in his voice so visceral it cut through her like a knife. She slowly pulled his hands away from his face as though if she were tender enough, she could reverse the damage she had done.

"Oh gods, Sabrien—" She started, but her voice was cut off as tears came to her eyes. She hadn't meant for this to happen. She only wanted to save them.

"Where is Vaion?" Ardeth spoke once more, pushing himself to stand and looking around the room. Rue's head snapped away from Sabrien as panic filled her.

"He's gone!?" she cried out, a mix of anxiety, fear, and rage coursing through her. "How did he get out? Sabrien said the way back out was sealed—"

Before she could finish, a small chunk of stone bounced off the top of her head. She looked up to the ceiling of the cavern to see where it fell from. A long crack twisted through the rock, warm amber light from the sunset outside filtered in exposing a hole just big enough for a person to get through.

"That bastard! He's gone and we still don't have the book," Ardeth growled out, slamming his fist into the dirt floor.

"I don't care about the book," Rue whispered. She knew she didn't really mean that, but at the current moment, Sabrien's ailment and the fact that Corvus was still unconscious took precedence over her emotions. Ardeth didn't say anything, though the irritated look on his face told her he would have really liked to.

"We have to get them out of here. But Corvus can't fly and Sabrien can't see." Her voice was barely a whisper, she was forcing herself to keep it together. She had to.

"Can you get help? Maybe Oliver or Jasper or someone?" Rue turned to Ardeth, thick trails of tear streaks covering her cheeks. She must have looked desperate because Ardeth's expression softened, replaced with one of pity.

"I will stay here with them, just...please, go get help." She begged him, not caring how pathetic she might have sounded.

Without another word, Ardeth crouched down before launching himself into the open crack. He stumbled in the air for a moment before righting himself again. Rue breathed a soft sigh of relief. She knew Ardeth also wasn't in any shape to fly, but he was the only hope they had of getting out.

Sabrien sat beside her, silent tears still streaming down his face. What could she say to him? Nothing. There was not a single word she could utter to make this right again. She knew the guilt would eat at her from this moment on. Hesitantly, she reached out, taking his hand in hers again, giving it as reassuring a squeeze as she could muster.

"Ardeth is going to get help. We are going to get out of here," she repeated quietly. Sabrien slipped his hand out of hers, giving her an almost imperceptible nod, and pulled his knees to his chest, leaning his forehead against them.

Rue bit her lip, trying desperately to keep her tears at bay. Deep inside, she hoped he wasn't upset with her. She did the only thing she could to keep them all from dying to Vaion's shadow soldiers, and in time, she hoped he would understand that.

Pulling her battered and bruised body across the dirt, Rue gently tugged Corvus' shoulders, laying his head in her lap, and began to stroke his hair.

"We're going to get you out of here, so hold on for me...please hold on." His face was so peaceful. His long lashes brushed against his scraped cheeks. She wanted nothing more than to lean down and press soft kisses to those lashes. She wanted nothing more than for him to open his eyes.

Neither of those things happened. Rue sat in the uncomfortable near silence of the cavern as they waited. Sabrien's sniffles and Corvus' soft, labored breaths the only sound echoing around her.

It felt like days that they sat there. Time mocked them, moving slower to draw out every second of their suffering. Sabrien had finally stopped crying and moved closer to Rue, leaning his head on her shoulder. Corvus still lay unconscious in her lap, his breaths becoming increasingly more sporadic, causing worry to flare in her chest again.

"Rue..." Sabrien croaked out, making her jump.

"Yes?" Her voice came out in a choked whisper. The anxiety of what he might say to her gnawed at her heart.

"I don't blame you. I need you to know that."

"Sabrien, I—" she started, but he put his hand up to silence her before she could continue.

"I know you did what you had to, and we are going to figure this out, but even in the silence, I can feel the energy radiating from you. I just want you to know that I don't blame you at all. If you hadn't done what you did...who knows if we would even be alive right now. My eyes are a small price to pay for our lives."

Rue swallowed hard, she knew if she opened her mouth to speak right now, the only thing that would come out would be a sob and she needed to keep it together, at least for Sabrien's sake.

"We are going to get out of here. Ardeth and Oliver will come back, and then we can regroup and kill that mother fucker."

The fury in Sabrien's voice was more than palpable. It was the fury of a man who now had a score to settle. This was more than just getting the book back, it was personal. For all of them. Rue let out a shaky exhale, trying her best to steady her emotions before speaking.

"I won't stop," she told him, with every ounce of conviction she had, "I will not stop until he's defeated and the book is safe. But for right now, we need to focus on getting everyone to safety and healing."

It wasn't what he wanted to hear — his silence said as much — but Rue knew that Sabrien was smart enough to know she was right. There was no way they were fighting another battle like this without taking the time to properly heal and formulate another plan first. Vaion was missing and without any sort of trace of where he might have gone. They were back to the beginning.

They sat together in a more comfortable shared silence now, waiting for their rescuers to return. The heavy atmosphere had faded at least minimally now that Sabrien told her he didn't fault her. It didn't stop the guilt burning in her chest, but it had at least reduced the flames to softly glowing embers.

Another hour had passed, or it could have been several. There was no way of truly knowing. The muted color of the sunset had died long ago, replaced with darkness again. But now, a soft orange light spilled through the crack in the ceiling. A swell of hope surged in Rue's chest.

The sun.

In a place that always rained, that had perpetually grey skies and seemed to smother any light that dared peek through the clouds, the sun had come out. It wasn't much but in her current predicament, even the smallest amount of hope was worth something.

"The sun is out..." Rue mused quietly, more to herself than anyone else.

A moment later, a shadow flashed over the crack. Rue's spine straightened as she craned her neck to see as far as she could. Had they finally returned? Or was it Vaion returning to finish the job while they were vulnerable?

Sabrien lifted his head, his sightless eyes wide open.

"They're here. I can sense the ravens."

Rue's grip tightened on Corvus' shoulder. They were finally going to get out of here. Before she could finish her thought, a loud crack that sounded almost like thunder echoed through the chamber. Her hands immediately went to her ears. What was happening?

Chancing a glance at the ceiling once more, she saw the hole that Ardeth had gone through was torn wide open, and Oliver's sweet face was peering down at them. She had never been happier to see him.

"Oliver!" She called, waving her arms.

"Hold on! We're coming down to get you all!" he shouted back before swinging his legs over the ledge and drifting down into the cavern.

Rue would never forget thinking that he looked like an angel, even with his dark raven wings. She pushed herself up from the floor, tripping over the torn hem of her dress, and launched herself into his arms, holding him as tight as she possibly could. There was no stopping the tears that flowed down her cheeks. Oliver's arms immediately encircled her, returning her embrace with equal fervor.

"I'm so glad you're alright. I didn't know what was going to happen when you didn't make it out." Rue could hear the hopelessness in his voice.

"We are alive, but..." She swallowed down the bile that rose at the back of her throat, "Sabrien and C-corvus... They..." She lost the words, dissolving into muted sniffles.

"Shh, it's okay. We don't have to talk about this right now. Let's just focus on getting out of here." Oliver consoled her, hands rubbing gently over her back. Rue couldn't hold it in anymore and broke into sobs. Even after all their careful planning, nothing had gone right, and now they were back at square one.

And it was all her fault.

Those words rang over and over in her head, drowning out every other thought and sound. She was still in a daze when Oliver slid one arm around her back and the other around the back of her knees, lifting her up and pulling her close to his chest. He was so warm and smelled like rain. Rue turned her head into him and closed her eyes. Relief began to wash over her, and her eyelids were like cement blocks, too heavy to keep open for a moment longer.

Oliver said something quietly, but in her addled state, Rue couldn't make it out. It didn't matter anyway. He bent his knees, launching them into the air, and for that moment, Rue felt weightless.

Rue didn't know how long she'd been asleep. She didn't know if she was in her own bed or back at the temple. Sitting up, still bleary-eyed and groggy, she looked around the room for something familiar, but it was still too dark to see anything.

"Hello?" She called out, voice cracking from disuse. Her throat was dry as desert sand. Slowly, she stood up from the bed, her legs nearly collapsing under her. How long had she been here? How long had it been since they escaped that cavern?

After a few moments her eyes began to adjust to the darkness around her. Vague shapes sharpened and became discernible. A tall pitcher of water and a glass sat on the small table next to the bed. She grabbed it and haphazardly dumped its contents into the glass, sending nearly half the contents sloshing out onto the floor. Greedily, she guzzled it down and refilled it another two times before she was satisfied.

"Hello?" She called again, louder now that her throat didn't feel like it was going to tear if she spoke any louder than a whisper. There was no answer. Panic crawled up her stomach. Was she here alone? Where had the others gone?

Before she could formulate more of her own paranoia-fueled answers, a door opened and light poured into the room, making her squint against the brightness. A tall figure stood in the doorway, rimmed in the too bright light, face obscured by the darkness.

"You're awake!" a familiar voice said.

"Jasper!" Rue jumped up and launched herself at him, the force of her hug tackling him to the floor. He'd made some noise of protest, but she didn't care.

"You're here. You're okay," Rue said over and over again, touching his face and ruffling his hair.

"You think you could be rid of me that easily?" Jasper grunted and tried to sit up, but Rue kept him there on the ground while she had her fill of him. It didn't take long for him to give up and let her have her way. He wrapped his arms around her middle and held her tightly. She inhaled the scent of pine and tobacco that always lingered on his clothing, the scent that was so uniquely Jasper.

Normally, she hated that smell, but after everything, she cherished it. Cherished the fact that her brother was here and unscathed.

Unscathed...

Calm vanished, replaced with the same sinking feeling of dread from before.

"Corvus...is he—?" She started, throat closing before she could get the rest of the question out.

Jasper's soft smile was replaced with a frown. Rue's heart sped into overdrive.

"Come on, I'll take you to him."

Rue had to lean on Jasper for stability for the short walk to one of the other rooms. Jasper pushed open the door, the hinges creaking loudly against the deathly quiet. She felt nauseous, her stomach turning with anxiety and expecting the worst.

"Corvus..."

He lay there, still as stone, with a thin, moth-eaten blanket pulled up over his chest. Eyes closed and chest rising and falling in short, labored breaths. Tears stung her eyes, blurring her vision once again.

"He hasn't woken up since we returned." Another voice said from somewhere behind the bed. She didn't look up, her eyes still trained on Corvus' face. How could he look so peaceful when she was falling apart?

Rue let go of Jasper and pushed her way over to the bed, sinking to her knees beside him. She pushed a single damp curl from his forehead, fingers stroking down the side of his jaw.

"Can I please have some time alone with him?" She asked without looking up. No one answered but the shuffle of their feet and subsequent creak and click of the door closing was answer enough. Rue sat there with him, silently tracing the strong features of his face. Even battered and bruised he was still the most beautiful man she'd ever seen.

"If you can hear me..." She started, her voice small and shaky with emotion, "I'm sorry. I'm so sorry, Corvus. I never meant for this to happen. I just wanted to help and instead I made everything worse. I got you hurt, and Sabrien—" she stopped. The thought of Sabrien and what had happened made her want to crumble all over again.

After a long, silent moment, she collected herself enough to speak again, "I need you to wake up. I need you. I can't do this without you. I don't even know how to do this without you." The dam she'd hastily built to contain her sadness had broken. She couldn't speak anymore. Her mouth opened in an agonized sob as she clutched the blanket over him.

Eventually, her tears slowed before subsiding completely. Her entire body felt heavy. Rue closed her eyes, resting her head on his chest, straining to hear the slow, barely there thump of his heartbeat under his ribs.

He would wake up.

He had to.

ACKNOWLEDGEMENTS

It's hard to believe that this story stemmed from a wacky idea I had on a random Thursday a few years ago and now, we're here. This book is absolutely a love letter to every piece of media I have ever loved — all the things that shaped me and inspired me to create in the first place.

However, I could not have done all of this without the incredible support I had behind me.

First and foremost, thank you to my wife, Sam. Thank you for listening to my endless whining and self doubt every step of the way through this process. Also thank you for being my acting developmental editor and spackling every plot hole I had. This story wouldn't be what it is without your help.

Thank you to my closest friends — Oli, Beca, Jayme, Lillianna, Amanda and Bri just to name a few. You were all so integral to getting me here and I cannot thank you enough for always hyping me up and believing in me even when I struggled to believed in myself.

Thank you to my Mom for always indulging my creative endeavors even when you didn't understand exactly what was going on.

And thank you to all of you who have made it this far and are still reading. You mean the world to me and the amount of thanks I can truly express through this tiny bit of text doesn't even come close to fully encompassing the love I have for you just for giving me a shot.

About the Author

C.M. Aragon (she/they) is a dark fantasy and horror author with a love of all things spooky. Obsessed with the macabre from a young age (Thanks in part to their mother allowing them to watch Army of Darkness in third grade) they always dreamed of writing stories that created rich atmosphere with a pinch of humor and a dash of romance. *The Call of Chaos* is their debut novel.

When she's not writing or dreaming up her next big idea she can usually be found playing games with her wife or snuggling their two cats.

You can find them on most platforms under the name Worldso-fAragon